"WE KILL YOU NOW. YOU DIE. . . ."

That was the rough translation of the message the aliens had just broadcast to the *Shenandoah*.

"CO, this is Special Sensors. We see multiple small two hundred kilogram targets approaching from the west. Estimate range three clicks."

"Guns, CO here. Fire two fish, concussion war heads! Detonate warshot in the center of the oncoming sonar target swarm."

"Guns here. Two tubes fired. Warshots on the way!"

Two underwater guided missiles sped outward toward the oncoming horde of Awesomes.

"CO, Special Sensors. Six Awesome targets are almost directly over us and diving fast toward us."

"Guns, put three fish under them. Fire now!"

"Three tubes fired. Hang on! The warshots will shake us up when they blow."

The shock of the three nearly simultaneous firings was like three quick hammer blows to the sub's hull.

"Captain, Special Sensors. We see four immobile Awesome targets floating over us. The warshots must have got them. But we can't account for the other two. I think they're on our outer hull!"

STARSEA INVADERS:

THIRD
ENCOUNTER

by

G. Harry Stine

A ROC BOOK

ROC
Published by the Penguin Group
Penguin Books USA Inc., 375 Hudson Street,
New York, New York 10014, U.S.A.
Penguin Books Ltd, 27 Wrights Lane,
London W8 5TZ, England
Penguin Books Australia Ltd, Ringwood,
Victoria, Australia
Penguin Books Canada Ltd, 10 Alcorn Avenue,
Toronto, Ontario, Canada M4V 3B2
Penguin Books (N.Z.) Ltd, 182-190 Wairau Road,
Auckland 10, New Zealand

Penguin Books Ltd, Registered Offices:
Harmondsworth, Middlesex, England

First published by Roc, an imprint of Dutton Signet,
a division of Penguin Books USA Inc.

First Printing, May, 1995
10 9 8 7 6 5 4 3 2 1

ROC REGISTERED TRADEMARK—MARCA REGISTRADA

Printed in the United States of America

TO:
Ginny and Dane Boles

He has honor if he holds himself to an ideal of conduct though it is inconvenient, unprofitable, or dangerous to do so.

—Walter Lippmann,
A Preface to Morals, 1929.

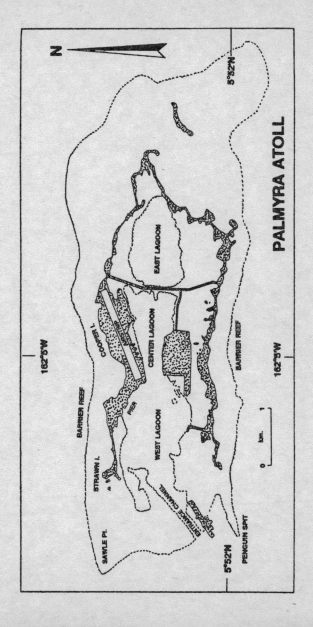

1

"Captain, this is the OOD!"

The female voice was like a distant call from a far-off world.

But it wasn't just another voice from afar. It was the call of duty.

If CAPT William M. Corry had not been the Commanding Officer of the SSCV-26 U.S.S. *Shenandoah*, he might have ignored it. But he couldn't. He was responsible for the lives and well-being of 750 men and women and the multibillion-dollar, 390-meter carrier submarine that was their home and their duty.

In spite of the fact that he was exhausted, his sleep had been restless because of disturbing dreams. At first, the voice seemed to be part of one of the dreams. But he quickly realized it wasn't, because he knew where he was, even while half asleep.

His eyes flicked open and he saw the familiar surroundings of his cabin in the dim night-light.

But he didn't respond verbally for a few seconds while he gathered his wits and controlled his breathing. He didn't want to stutter. He'd always suffered from that minor speech impediment, and he controlled it with an iron will except in extreme emotional circumstances. He believed that stuttering wasn't dignified or proper for the Commanding Officer of a major ship of the United States Navy. Too many lives depended on his capability to issue succinct, unambiguous, and clearly enunciated orders.

Instead, without looking, because he could have laid his hand on anything in his cabin, even in total darkness, Corry touched the answer pad on the ship's intercom over his rack. It sent the response signal that he was there.

Finally, he replied in careful tones, "This is the Captain speaking."

"Captain, this is the OOD. Lieutenant Brewer on deck. A secure coded SWC message has just been received for you from CINCPAC."

Before retiring to his cabin, Corry had left his usual message in the night order book: *In case of doubt, do not hesitate to call me.*

It wasn't doubt on LTJG Barbara Brewer's part that caused her to interrupt the Captain's sleep, however. She was doing her job and notifying her Commanding Officer immediately of the receipt of a message that had to be important.

It was important automatically if it arrived via the highly classified scalar wave communications system while the ship was running submerged three hundred meters beneath the South Pacific en route to Pearl Harbor.

"Thank you, Lieutenant Brewer," Corry told her. "Please have the yeoman deliver it to my cabin at once."

"Aye, aye, sir," Brewer replied, paused, then added, "I need to inform you, sir, that another coded SWC message was received immediately following the one for you. Its recipient is Commander Matilda Smith."

"Thank you. Carry on."

Now Corry was fully awake. The digital clock on the far bulkhead announced that the ship time was 0546. Three hours before, it had been set ahead to Hawaii time because the U.S.S. *Shenandoah* was returning northeastward to Pearl Harbor after a mission in the Solomon Sea.

The message meant that something had changed.

Corry's last order from VADM Richard H. Kane, CINCPAC, had told him to return ASAP to Pearl Harbor. The ship had been under way from Honiara, Guadalcanal, since sundown six hours before.

The Captain had gotten two hours' sleep.

To have a coded SWC message arrive from CINCPAC this quickly, followed immediately by another one to CDR Matilda Harriet Smith of Naval Intelligence who was also aboard ... well, it spelled a Big Problem Somewhere for the Commanding Officer of the carrier submarine.

Something had come unbonded at CINCPAC or CNO.

Or the balloon had gone up between China and her avowed, traditional enemies on the Asian continent. Things were not peaceful in the twenty-first century. Otherwise, the United States would not have needed a strong navy.

And Bill Corry might have been a commercial space pilot instead. Given the real world as it was, Corry had elected to maintain the family tradition of naval service, and especially naval aviation. Another William M. Corry had been Naval Aviator Number 23 in the last century. As long as there was a United States Navy in which to serve, he was doing what he had to do.

He instructed the cabin lights to come on as he rolled out of his two-meter-by-one-meter rack. The commanding officer of any ship, especially a submarine, never totally undresses to sleep; he can be called at any time. In thirty seconds, he'd pulled on a khaki shirt and trousers, slipped black shoes on his feet, and looped a black silk tie around his neck under his collar. He didn't have time to shave the stubble from his chin or even to run a comb through his thinning dark hair before the door annunciator buzzed.

It disturbed him that he didn't have time to present a shipshape appearance.

The crew didn't drag their feet. Corry commanded by respect, not by terror. Thus, when he gave even a small order such as he had, the crew snapped and popped. The yeoman was at his cabin door in forty-five seconds and gave him a small memory cube. He initialed the receipt and noted the time thereon.

He decided he wouldn't bother his Executive Officer, CDR Zeke Braxton, until he learned what the message was. No sense in disturbing the rest of his exhausted crew until he had the chance to evaluate the message. He knew it couldn't be minor. The SWC system was a high military secret of the United States. It allowed a deeply submerged submarine to communicate with others who had it. SWC wasn't used for frivolous purposes.

He retrieved his personal dedicated processor from the safe, turned it on. The computer screen queried him for his name and password, which he entered. Then he inserted the memory cube and entered the decode key phrase.

The screen flashed, *"System boot failure. Unexpected interrupt in protected mode."*

That was a false message in case someone managed to get around the basic arctic boot-up security locks. Corry therefore entered the proper secondary unlock key phrase.

While the little machine crunched the megabytes to decompress the message, decode it, and then decipher it utilizing the dictionary association program unique to that date, Corry suddenly realized how tired he really was.

"There are more tired commanders than there are tired commands," he reminded himself *sotto voce*.

The past several days hadn't been easy.

The world was again on the verge of a general war. China and India were threatening to break over their borders and take on Russia and Muslim League. As a diversion, both East World nations had sent submarines into the Solomon Sea. This was supposed to be viewed as a move to blockade the Pacific Rim sea-lane traffic between North America and Australia. That southern continent and the islands of New Zealand were historically a thorn in the side of any Asian power that had attempted military expansion on the Asian landmass itself.

Everyone except NSC, JCS, CNO, CINCPAC, and the crew of the U.S.S. *Shenandoah* was supposed to believe that the carrier submarine had been sent to the Solomon Sea on a power projection mission to head off the East World naval thrust.

But the United States Navy's most powerful and advanced capital ship was on another mission entirely.

On an earlier mission, the crew of the *Shenandoah* had discovered an unknown aquatic animal "fishing" for human beings off Makasar in Sulawesi. One of those animals had been captured dead; it wasn't terrestrial. The Chinese knew of this because the People's Navy had had a submarine at Makasar. The Chinese had videotapes and radar records of what had happened. Beijing had released some of the video, claiming the United States was field-testing a new weapon system to use against East World. Washington kept quiet.

But someone in Washington sent the U.S.S. *Shenandoah* on a second mission. The Chinese were watching the East Indies area carefully for additional extraterrestrial activity, hoping to capture artifacts and use the alien technology to get a leg up on the incredible high technology of the United States. So the boat's second mission was to the Solomon Islands, where, on the basis of what Corry and his people had learned at Makasar, alien aquatic activity was suspected.

The Captain of the U.S.S. *Shenandoah* had orders to reconnoiter and, if possible, capture alive one or more aquatic aliens. A special team of six experts, none of whom were submariners, had been covertly put aboard to help. At first, they were more trouble than they were worth, but they came through when the going got tough. In a bizarre operation, the crew of the *Shenandoah* had not only encountered these beasts again, but discovered *another* species that was unmistakably alien.

Now the carrier submarine was headed back to Pearl Harbor. On its hangar deck, tucked in among the aircraft of its three squadrons, was a saucer-shaped alien craft heavily guarded by a detachment of the ship's Marine batt. In an equally guarded sick bay were two live but wounded insectlike aliens. Yet another was stone cold dead in one of the frozen food lockers. The dead one was no problem, but the live ones were mean and nasty.

If VADM Richard Kane at CINCPAC hadn't known Corry since Naval Academy days, he might not have believed Corry's terse and objective mission report. But Kane's orders told Corry it was "show and tell" time. CINCPAC's orders were direct and to the point: Return ASAP to Pearl Harbor with the "artifact" and the "specimens," as the orders euphemistically referred to the *Shenandoah*'s catch.

And that's what the U.S.S. *Shenandoah* was doing at the moment.

The decoded, deciphered, decompressed, and dedigitized SWC message was worded with equal euphemism as it came up on the little screen:

To CO SSCV-26. This message is classified Cosmic Top Secret with INTEL and ORCON caveats and SCI compartmentation for which CO SSCV-26 is hereby cleared. Revise present destination. Make for Palmyra Island. Cruise in stealth condition. Arrive no sooner than 25 August. Stand by submerged off north coast of Palmyra Island for further orders. Mission control and jurisdiction have been assumed by OP-32. This order is in support of and modifies JCS Execute Order 07-032-47N. Transmitted 1400Z. Kane VADM CINCPAC.

OP-32 was the Office of Naval Intelligence.

Corry noted from the message transmission time that

Kane had probably been involved in an all-nighter with
CNO and God knew who else in Washington.

He tucked the message into his breast pocket and
granted himself five minutes to shave.

Then he had two things to do immediately.

"Captain on the bridge!" LTJG Barbara Brewer called
out as he entered the nerve center of the boat.

"Carry on, Lieutenant. You have the conn," Corry told
her. "Stand by for a change of course. Have the Navigator
lay in a course for Palmyra Island."

"Aye, aye, sir. I have the conn. Change course. Make for
Palmyra Island," Brewer responded in the redundant order
mode to ensure she had received the order and would com-
ply. She passed the order to LT Bruce Leighton, the Assistant Navigator who was on watch with her.

Leighton repeated it back to her, entered the information
into the navigation computer.

The navigation elements flashed on the positioning
screen:

Present position: South Pacific Ocean 7° 32′ 14″ S, 163°
22′ 40″ E.
Destination: Palmyra Island 5° 52′ N, 162° 5′ W.
Initial heading 070.
Distance 2,247.3 nm.
ETA at present speed 56h11m.

"Please display the routing," Corry told her.

"Aye, aye, sir!"

On another display screen, a Mercator projection of the
Pacific Ocean appeared. The curving line of the boat's
great-circle course overlaid the chart.

"Sir, I have a recommendation," Leighton ventured.

"Go ahead."

"The great-circle course takes us right through the Gil-
bert Islands. We'll have to come to shallower running
depth and navigate with masdet if we can't use sonar."

Corry saw that. He was pleased that the Assistant Navigator had, too. In stealth mode, he didn't want to go to active pinging. And at forty knots cruise speed in shallow
water, he didn't want to bet the boat on the accuracy of the
boat's new mass detector. "Mister Leighton, prepare a dogleg course that takes us south of the Gilberts and keeps us

in deep water. Display your recommended course, and let's look it over."

"Aye, aye, sir. Working."

The powerful navigational computer of the *Shenandoah* went to work at Leighton's beckoning. Within seconds, it had checked the charts, investigated depths, and calculated the shortest deepwater dogleg course. It then projected it on the chart screen.

Leighton was watching the computer digital readouts. "Sir, I recommend a heading of zero-seven-six true until crossing one-eight-zero longitude, then turn to a heading of zero-five-nine, direct Palmyra," Leighton said. "That will take us well clear of shallow waters and run us between Arorae and Naumea. It gives us the straightest deepwater shot. And it adds only eight-six nautical miles or a little more than two hours' cruise."

Corry nodded. His navigators were good, and so was their equipment. LCDR Natalie Chase ran a sharp shop. "Very well, let's do it, Mister Leighton. However, our new orders instruct us to arrive off the north coast of Palmyra no earlier than the twenty-fifth," Corry told him. "Ignoring the deep ocean currents between our present position and Palmyra, what speed must we make to meet that schedule?"

Corry knew. He'd done it in his head. He was a carrier submarine commander, but, in his gut, he was still a naval aviator. In spite of modern computers, he'd learned to do navigational problems in his head. In combat, the computer could be shot out or otherwise go tits-up. This had happened to him in his flying career. He was "dry and alive" because he'd learned to do navigation the hard way.

But he didn't wish to usurp the navigation officer's job. And at some future time, LT Bruce Leighton might not serve under a Commanding Officer who could do nav probs mentally.

Leighton knew that, too. But he hadn't told Captain Corry that his department chief, LCDR Natalie Chase, required that everyone in the Navigation Department know how to do the job the old way with printed charts and ancient instruments of the navigator's craft. Furthermore, he was unwilling to put his total trust in a computer that could be wrong (but never was). So he ran the problem in his head.

"Sir, the OOD should be requested to reduce speed to thirty-one knots," Leighton stated. He hadn't rung the underwater currents into his mental calculations. He would do that later and then issue minor midcourse corrections.

"Well done, Mister Leighton. Thank you," Corry complimented him. He then said to the OOD, "Lieutenant Brewer, come to a heading of zero-seven-six true, make thirty-one knots, and level the bubble at three-zero-zero meters."

"Aye, aye, sir! Come to zero-seven-six true, make thirty-one knots, level the bubble at three-zero-zero."

It used to be more difficult, Corry knew. But he was glad that it wasn't that way any longer. He had enough to worry about, and anything that would relieve the workload was welcome.

And he had a workload now because of Kane's SWC message.

2

Corry activated the intercom at his command console. "Commander Smith, this is the Captain."

No answer.

That told Corry that the Naval Intelligence officer wasn't in her cabin.

He called the main wardroom. The night steward reported that no one was there.

So Smith had to be in someone else's cabin.

Obviously, she wasn't as exhausted as he.

The U.S.S. *Shenandoah* was at Condition Three in submerged cruise mode with underway watches set. Corry had instructed his XO to open the Dolphin Club.

The Dolphin Club wasn't a social gathering place. It was jargon for a situation that maintained sanity in a mixed-gender Navy. In brief, when the Dolphin Club was open, it meant that the Commanding Officer had suspended Naval Regulation 2020 for personnel not standing watch or having other official duties. "Reg Twenty-twenty" was simple in concept: no physical contact of any sort was permitted between personnel except that required for official business. Monkey business wasn't considered official business. The Tailhook and Ragout scandals were in the past, but they'd had a major impact on the naval establishment. The Navy didn't bend Regulation 2020 for anyone. Naval personnel of both sexes and even with high rank had been bilged with dishonorables for "busting Twenty-twenty." This wasn't prevalent any longer because the court-martial decisions had been tested and confirmed at the highest judicial levels. As a result, naval personnel weren't about to mess up a good thing. Or at least as good a thing as they could get, which was far better than nothing at all.

If the CO didn't know where CDR Smith was, one person on the bridge did. "Lieutenant Brewer, did you cause

Commander Smith's SWC message to be hand-delivered to her?"

"Yes, sir!" Brewer snapped smartly.

"Did she sign for it?"

"Yes, sir."

"Do you know where she is?"

Pause. "The yeoman reported her location, sir." LTJG Barbara Brewer was acting quite properly, answering truthfully the questions put to her but maintaining discretion without being insubordinate.

Corry didn't probe deeper. He didn't have to. If personnel of the U.S.S. *Shenandoah* and guests were not expected to have some small measure of personal life, cabins would not have been provided. So Corry stood up. "I'll be in my quarters. Please ask Commander Smith to join me there as soon as she can do so."

"Aye, aye, sir!"

It took Smith twenty-two minutes to arrive. Corry was writing up his personal log covering the message receipt and subsequent change of course when Smith signaled at his door.

If she had been visiting the Dolphin Club, her appearance didn't betray it. Corry would never ask her, of course. It wouldn't be proper. Corry was a gentleman.

Matilda Harriet Smith was a tall, striking women. The way she wore her crisp tropical whites let the world know that she was indeed a New Millennium American woman who not only had full gender equality but demanded all the traffic would bear without being obnoxious.

She carried a small, robust shoulder bag.

She stood before Corry's little table desk. "Commander Smith reporting as requested, sir."

Corry indicated the chair on the other side of the table. "Please sit down, Commander. And close the door behind you. This is a private conversation that may involve classified material."

She swung the door closed and latched it without hesitation. This was official business now.

"I understand you received a coded SWC message within the last hour." Corry stated this with an interrogatory inflection as a pseudo-question.

She nodded. "Yes, sir, I did."

"So did I. I'll be posting it on the ship's bulletin board

within the hour. But because it affects you and your position in this ship, I want you to read the hard copy first." He unsealed his breast-pocket flap, withdrew the hard copy, unfolded it, and handed it to her.

She only glanced at it and quickly tried to hand it back. "I'm sorry, Captain, but I mustn't read this. I did read as far as the second sentence dealing with the classification level and caveats of the message. It means it's 'eyes only,' sir. It's a violation of United States Code, Titles Eighteen and Fifty, for me to read the message. I could spend the rest of my life in a naval prison if I read it."

"Perhaps ashore, this is true." Corry made no move to take the hard copy from her outstretched hand. She had made a sterling effort to integrate herself into the crew and adapt to submarine life. But Corry felt he had to remind her again that this wasn't the shore establishment. And he wanted to do it in an informal way. Both of her given names really didn't seem to fit her, so Corry invented one right then. "Smitty, we're not in the Pentagon. We're all together inside a composite submarine pressure hull three hundred meters below the surface of the world's largest ocean. We have an extraterrestrial artifact and two live extraterrestrial life forms aboard. We acquired the artifact and organisms because we defended ourselves against an attack in accordance with the rules of engagement. As a result, we may be the subject of an intense search by other extraterrestrials. I don't know the full extent of their weapons capabilities. Therefore, I *will not* withhold information of any sort from *anyone* in this ship. Doing so might mean that we don't make it back to Pearl. I can still give you a direct order and require that you carry it out. But I will only ask you to read this."

Smith thought about this for a moment. She was surprised by Corry's use of a nickname for her. In her naval career, she had been surrounded by the paranoia of intelligence and security procedures. She was learning that life in a carrier submarine was quite different from her day-to-day routine at OP-32. "Sir, I hope I never have to testify about this in a general court. Or in any court."

Corry said nothing in reply.

She read the message and handed the hard copy back. She made no comment.

"As I remarked when you came in, I know you also received an SWC message, Smitty," Corry recalled. "May I read it?"

Smith phrased her reply carefully, realizing that she was dealing with the most powerful person in her world at that moment. "With all due respect, no, sir. Not until I do so."

"You haven't read it yet?"

"No, sir. I have not."

"Commander, an SWC message in a submarine is categorized several levels above 'urgent,' " He tried not to reprimand her. "CINCPAC believed your message was important. After all, you are the de facto leader of the special team aboard this vessel. I realize that the past day or so has been extremely stressful and that you may not be accustomed to that level of stress. I realize that the Dolphin Club is open and . . ."

"Dammit, Captain, I haven't gotten around to the message because I was almost in . . . Never mind! That's my business, sir!" she snapped, her tone reeking with irritation at the world in general. Her safety valve had popped and she impulsively let off some of the steam that had been building up and hadn't been released. This was totally out of character for someone in Naval Intelligence who had risen to her rank. It was also quite inconsistent with the nononsense, almost flippant attitude she'd projected thus far. It took her a moment to regain control, then she went on, "Captain, I didn't get the opportunity to relax. Or to do anything. The message cube was delivered to me and I was going back to my own cabin to decipher it when the yeoman showed up again with your request to come here!"

Corry let the outburst pass. He understood what had caused it. He'd spent his life in the mixed-gender Navy. He knew that men and women were different, and he understood some of the differences. Because he was a man, he knew he'd never understand everything about women. Trying to figure them out and getting along with them was the most frustrating problem he'd ever tackled. But he'd done well enough over the years. So he suggested to her, "Smitty, why don't you go to your cabin and print out that message now?"

She reached down and picked up the shoulder bag she'd carried into the cabin. "Sir, I don't need to leave if you'll permit me to do it here." Opening the seam, she withdrew a small cipher machine.

"Proceed," Corry told her. "Do you want me to leave the room while you do it?"

She shook her head, her dark hair bobbing. Then she smiled. "Captain, if you can figure out how I get the message out of the cube with this secret decoder ring of mine, I'll ask Admiral McCarthy to co-opt you for OP-thirty-two!"

"You can always try. But I don't believe I'm intel material," Corry admitted. "Do you mind if I continue to draft my rough log while you go through your procedure?"

Smith was doing something with the keypad and trackball. A hard copy zipped out of a slot on top of the little device. "I'm afraid there won't be time, Captain," she remarked as she began to read the message that had been produced.

Her expression changed as she did so.

When she handed the message to Corry and he read it, he found out why.

The cruelest lies are so often told in silence. To CDR M. H. Smith aboard SSCV-26. This message is classified Cosmic Top Secret with INTEL and ORCON caveats and SCI compartmentation. (1) CAPT W. M. Corry CO SSCV-26 and members of SSCV-26 crew are hereby cleared to this level with access to caveats and compartmentation as necessary and to be determined by recipient. They will be debriefed by OP-32 personnel later. Transmit the contents of this specific message immediately to CO SSCV-26 for his coordination and request his cooperation. Members of the special team aboard are not cleared beyond their present level, if any, pending further OP-32 individual background investigations under way at this time. (2) Special artifact and life forms in SSCV-26 are under the jurisdiction of OP-32. As OP-32 senior officer in SSCV-26, you will take direct control of life forms, living and dead, and artifacts. Under no circumstances will personnel from any intel organization other than OP-32 be advised of existence of artifact and life forms in SSCV-26 without personal approval of the undersigned. Access to artifact and life forms to other than OP-32 and SSCV-26 personnel must be denied. Use of deadly physical force to ensure this is hereby authorized. Recipient should request that CO SSCV-26 establish proper safeguards using the SSCV-26 Marine contingent. (3) This order remains in force until personally changed or revoked by the undersigned. (4) Recipient and CO SSCV-26 are cautioned that other forces may be at work here and that the potential level of hazard is extremely high. (5) Upon arrival of undersigned at Palmyra Island, you are directed to report ASAP. Transmitted 1400Z. Signed McCarthy RADM CO OP-32. Tact is the intelligence of the heart.

Corry realized that it was indeed an intel message. The first and last sentences were aphorisms that amounted to an uncrackable code. They would confuse anyone who might intercept the message, and they served as positive identification of the sender.

Corry handed the hard copy back to her.

"I wish I knew what the hell was going on here, Captain," Smith said.

"Yes. That bothers me," Corry admitted. "You're intel. I expected you to know."

"Hah! Last to know and the first to go, sir! How are we going to carry out this order?"

"By using the personnel of the Marine batt."

"I mean, how are we going to keep the uncleared members of the special team away from the Mantids and the Corona?" Smith asked, referring to the alien creatures in sick bay and the disk-shaped flying machine on the hangar deck.

"I don't see that the order denies access to the special team members," Corry said. "They were put aboard to do the work they're involved in."

Smith shook her head. "They aren't members of the crew."

"They're members of a special team put aboard to assist in the conduct of an official mission under an Execute Order," Corry reminded her. "They already know as much as if not more than we do. Commander Zervas is the team's expert in exobiology. He's probably running an autopsy on the dead Mantid alien even as we speak. As for the enigmatic representative from Majestic Corporation, Allan Soucek seems to have an extensive background about these aliens already. Doctor Duval is an expert oceanographer. And Doctor Lulalilo can talk fluently with those Mantid aliens because she understands the Pidgin English they learned in the Solomons. Therefore, the team members are part of the crew for this mission, and I can't deny them access to what they already have seen."

Smith sighed. "I have to keep reminding myself that you are the captain of this ship and therefore 'the last of the absolute monarchs.'"

"And until you are in such a position, Commander, you have no concept of the awful weight of responsibility it entails." Corry sat back and thought for a moment.

Smith paused, then went on, "Captain, you may be disobeying Admiral McCarthy's order. You may have to answer for it."

Nodding, Corry reflected, "If reported, yes. And I shall answer because I am the senior responsible officer and the Captain of this vessel. However, I cannot disobey any order she issues unless it is a lawfully issued order that comes through my immediate superior, Admiral Kane."

Smith had grown to admire Corry since she'd come aboard the U.S.S. *Shenandoah*. But his remark presaged trouble, at least in her experience. So she warned, "Sir, being a sea lawyer could get you into a heap of trouble . . ."

"Noted, Commander. However, writing *and* giving an order is an art form that most blue-water line officers know how to do very well. The same isn't true in the shore establishment," Corry pointed out.

Smith paused to think about that. She decided that this man was no fool and probably knew a lot more about it than she did. And, at the moment, she really didn't know what to do about the message she'd received. Or the Captain's reaction to it. So she took the bit and asked, "May I ask what you intend to do now, sir?"

"Go to bed."

"Sir?"

"And I suggest you join me."

"Sir!"

Corry caught what he thought was a gaffe and responded at once. "I'm sorry, Smitty. I'm weary and I didn't think about my comment. I'm never allowed to visit the Dolphin Club because, as Commanding Officer, I'm always on duty."

Smith hadn't considered it a gaffe. She softened, and Corry was surprised to hear her say, "I'm truly sorry to hear that, sir. Even Commanding Officers need to . . . well, I'm surprised that anyone could think of sleep when alien vessels may be searching for us, as Admiral McCarthy's message implied. I wrongly anticipated that we would be on guard against a possible attack."

"Smitty, I am on guard. The boat is running deep, silent, and with passive sensors out. I therefore consider the boat to be secure at this time," Corry told her, and now the weariness crept into his voice. He struggled not to stutter. He recognized Matilda Smith's invitation, and he didn't comment to it. He could not accept it, Commanding Officer or not. He had once taken a marriage vow he considered to be as binding as his oath as a naval officer. So he told her, "My next move will be to discuss this with Commander Braxton after breakfast. I want you to sit in on the conversation. Then, I'll talk to the special team, again with you present. But right now, everyone is asleep or relaxing. I won't disturb them. This can wait until after breakfast."

"Sir, as you reminded me earlier, an SWC message is considered to be several levels above 'urgent.' "

"It was indeed urgent that you and I learn the contents of the messages, Smitty. I didn't mean to imply that an SWC message always requires instant compliance with the contents unless that is specified. I do not like to make quick decisions or take immediate action when I am tired and when my crew is exhausted."

He rose to his feet. "Thank you for coming, Smitty," he told her, deliberately and resolutely bringing the conversation to a close. He then used a common phrase signifying she should resume what she had been doing when he'd summoned her. He hoped she'd catch the hidden meaning. "Carry on."

"Yes, sir. And, by the way, thank you for the nickname you've given me. I like it."

In their fatigued condition, neither of them had caught the critical part of the message from the Chief of Naval Intelligence.

3

"Palmyra? That island is a pimple on the butt of the world!" Marine Major Bart Clinch growled, reacting to CAPT William Corry's announcement of the boat's new destination.

"Bart, why the hell can't you be a little bit poetic for a change?" CDR Teresa Ellison, the CAG, admonished him. "According to the natives, most Pacific islands are 'the navel of the Earth.'"

"Okay, then Palmyra Island is the armpit of the Earth," Clinch corrected himself in his gravely voice. "Hell, I've been there. I wish I hadn't. We used to conduct amphibious training operations there ten years ago. Nothing but coral and jungle. My Marine batt needs some liberty. We weren't in Honiara long enough. And Palmyra is a damned poor excuse for a South Sea island."

"It isn't an island," LCDR Natalie Chase, the Navigator, corrected him. "It's an atoll."

"So what's the difference?"

"The difference is," interrupted Doctor Barry W. Duval, the tall, skinny oceanographer of the special team, "that an atoll is technically a ringlike coral reef. If some portions of the reef are always above water at high tide, they qualify to be called islands, but they're part of the atoll."

"Palmyra has at least fourteen islands, not counting the one that was created by dredging the central lagoon during World War Two," Natalie pointed out. "Terri, you'll be happy to learn that it has a sixteen-hundred-meter airstrip."

"The Air Group doesn't need an airstrip," Terri replied quickly. "We've got the *Shanna*. An airstrip is an easy target for almost any smart weapon you want to toss at it. It can't move."

"Maybe Naval Intelligence needs that airstrip," CDR

Zeke Braxton remarked, looking at Harriet Smith for a reaction.

The officer from Naval Intelligence didn't react.

CAPT William Corry sat back and listened.

His people were upset that they weren't going home to Pearl Harbor and some well-deserved rest, recuperation, and recreation. The cruise hadn't been long, but it had been very intense. At this Papa briefing in the wardroom, Corry had given them the news that they were going to Palmyra instead. So he let them blow off a little steam to take the edge off their disappointment and to allay the onset of channel fever.

Corry also fostered such exchanges during Papa briefings when everyone was being brought up to speed on the latest hot skinny. He encouraged brainstorming. The officers of the U.S.S. *Shenandoah* were smart people and had a plethora of interests beyond submarine, air, and Marine operations. Life in a submarine was once described as "hours of boredom punctuated by moments of sheer terror." During those hours of boredom, people read and studied when they weren't involved with the boat's limited social life. They not only kept current in their professional knowledge but ranged afield. As a result, each person accumulated a unique personal database of information. Corry encouraged this. He wanted his people to have wide interests. As a result, the free exchange of information in a Papa briefing usually led to interesting new ways of doing things and produced atypical solutions.

This cruise certainly had been one that demanded atypical approaches to very dangerous situations. No one in the Silent Service, much less CNO or JCS, had ever anticipated that the crew of a carrier submarine might encounter ETs and UFOs.

Corry thought wryly to himself that he was probably the only submarine commander in history whose crew had torpedoed a flying saucer, to say nothing of boarding one and even taking it aboard as a prize.

Many ship captains were nothing more than supervisors or super systems managers. Few, even in the United States Navy, ever saw any action in an entire thirty-year career. Corry had now commanded a major capital warship in two engagements during which weapons had been fired with intent to destroy property and take lives. Combat command did indeed have a certain satisfaction associated with it, the knowledge that the power of death and destruction could be unleashed and yet controlled.

He decided it might have been interesting, after all, to be a privateer on the Spanish Main in spite of the primitive shipboard conditions of that period. Or to have served in the "wooden walls" of Nelson's fleet at Trafalgar or with Dewey in Manila Bay. And especially to have skippered a Taffy 3 escort carrier off Samar or a DD in Surigao Strait.

When Zeke didn't get a response from Smith, he asked her directly, "Smitty, do you know why we're being sent to Palmyra?"

She shook her head. "XO, I'm languishing at the same level of ignorance and confusion as you. I showed you my SWC message. It's just as vague as the one sent to the Captain."

"Isn't that unusual, Commander?" LTJG Ralph Strader, the boat's Intelligence Officer, knew something about Naval Intelligence, although his responsibility in the boat wasn't connected with OP-32.

"No, it's not," Smith admitted. "One of the principal policies of intelligence work is to give operatives and agents—that's me in this situation, even though I serve in Naval Intelligence—only enough information to get the job done. It's part of the principle of compartmentation. If someone were to board and seize the boat, I couldn't spill my guts because there's nothing there to spill. Right at the moment, I'm merely the custodian of a flying saucer you call a Corona ship, plus two live alien Mantids, a dead carcass, and some parts of a fourth alien that were scraped off the bulkheads."

"So who's going to take and board this boat?" LCDR Mark Walton, the First Lieutenant, wanted to know. "How the hell are they going to find us? The ocean is damned big, and we're running deep and stealthy."

"Mark, the Corona on the hangar deck found us submerged a hundred meters down in the Solomon Sea," LCDR Bob Lovette, Operations Officer, reminded his colleague.

"And we never identified the target lurking to the south of us," Chase added. "We lost masdet contact with it when we went into Iron Bottom Sound and Honiara. That IX could be another *Tuscarora* that's tracking us beyond sensor range." The crew had hung that appellation on targets that appeared to be large alien ships. [Author's note: See "U.S.S. *Tuscarora*" in Appendix III, Glossary.]

LT Charles Ames, the officer in charge of the new and highly classified WSS-1 mass detector, had been a quiet and seemingly introverted techie officer when he'd come aboard months ago. The close social atmosphere in the carrier submarine and the presence of ladies who were also technically sharp and qualified—he'd been terrified of women—had brought him out of his introversion. He knew he could speak with technical authority, because he had gained the respect of the others by his performance. And speak up he did. "I'll anticipate your question. No, we haven't detected any *Tuscarora* stalking us. I don't see anything out there except a bunch of islands, reefs, and underwater mountains. And those are exactly where they're supposed to be, according to the charts Commander Chase has shared with me."

"Is it possible that a *Tuscarora* could use those to hide among?" Lovette wanted to know.

Ames nodded. "Yes, sir, but I'll see it eventually. Goff, Brewer, and Strader have been working with me to adapt their noise rejection codes to masdet work. I'm getting to the point where I can pull a meaningful signal out of what seems to be white noise."

"The biggest problem," Sonar Officer LT Roger Goff put in, "is the enormous number of targets this creates. I think we've located every ship that's been sunk out there in the last hundred years or so."

"So we're looking for something that moves," LTJG Barbara Brewer added.

"We see a lot of moving targets on the surface and in the air. But their signatures pretty much match those of commercial surface ships and transpacific aircraft," Strader explained. "The computers have been programmed to reject those targets."

"And also programmed to alert us when they're on an intercept course," Ames said.

"Be careful," warned Allan Soucek. The thin-faced, sallow little man from the enigmatic Majestic Corporation, who seemed to know a lot about UFOs and extraterrestrials, had come aboard covertly with the "special team" at the beginning of the cruise. He was overbearing at first, because he seemed to be frightened beyond rationality by what he'd been assigned to do by his boss at Majestic Corporation, which turned out to be a supersecret UFO intelligence agency in Washington. Only after the crew had taken the Corona flying saucer and its treacherous, insectlike Mantid occupants had Corry and his people believed Soucek's wild stories about predatory aliens, earlier interstellar wars, and the surveillance of Earth by at least seventy interstellar species for centuries.

Had it not been for the fact that the U.S.S. *Shenandoah* and her crew had encountered a predatory underwater alien species fishing for human beings off Makasar, Corry and his Medical Officer, CDR Laura Raye Moore, would have considered Soucek insane and confined him under sedation and heavy guard in the sick bay.

Given the Makasar encounter, the discovery of more underwater aliens in the Solomon Islands, and two UFO attacks on the *Shenandoah* and a Chinese submarine off Guadalcanal, Corry now listened to him.

So when Soucek uttered those words of warning, he had the attention of everyone in the wardroom. And they wanted to hear more.

"We have a Mantid ship and its crew aboard," Soucek went on. "We know that the Mantids are aware of this, because they came looking for us in the Solomon Sea and attacked the Chinese boat instead. Granted that we drove them off. Frankly, I'm amazed at how well all of you handle and apply the technology of this ship. I wasn't aware of the progress of submarine technology; I've concentrated on tracking aerospace technology and missed what you people can do with this ship of yours. I believe we have a good chance to make it back to Pearl Harbor—or now to Palmyra—without being attacked. But we must be careful. We don't know all the tricks the Mantids might try."

"Mister Soucek, what do you know of Mantid weaponry?" Corry asked.

"Only what they've revealed over the last hundred or so years of encounters."

"Did you see anything new in the Solomons?"

"No."

"In your examination of the Corona, have you seen anything new?"

"No, and that surprises me," Soucek admitted. "I once

saw the Corona vehicle the Aerospace Force has kept in storage for decades. The one we have on the flight deck is almost identical. It's as though the Mantids have made no technological progress at all in a hundred years."

"Didn't you remark that the Mantids weren't a very bright species?" Smith reminded him.

Soucek nodded. "That I did. All data indicate they've 'borrowed,' bartered, or otherwise appropriated nearly all their technology. They're not space scientists. Or biotechnologists. We taught them how to synthesize the human endocrines and other tissues they need for their own medical purposes to combat the results of radiation damage suffered during a supernova in their stellar sector. However, they couldn't apply it. So they're still abducting and mutilating humans, now with the help of the underwater aliens you call the Awesomes." He paused, noted that the extremely pragmatic and realistic naval officers in the room were indeed listening carefully to him now, and went on, "The Mantid force beam weapon used against us and the Chinese submarine in the Solomons matches what was reported as long ago as 1949."

"Well, we can't match it, but we can sure as hell beat it," Terri Ellison pointed out. "And we can beat the Mantids. They don't check six. They don't watch minus-x. My chickens overwhelmed them with saturation attacks."

"And they don't know a damned thing about our firearms," Bart Clinch said. "When they grabbed the M-thirty-three carbines from two of my gun apes, they didn't know they had only high-tech clubs because the guns had no ammo in them."

"Neither did we," Laura Raye Moore reminded him. "And thanks for telling us. Or didn't you care that Doctor Lulalilo and I were scared to death when the Mantids captured us with those unloaded guns?"

"I didn't want to tell you," Clinch admitted. "Your actions might have caused those insects to go physical, and I didn't know how strong they might be. What are you bitching about, Doctor? We saved you."

The Medical Officer put her hand to the side of her head where one of the Mantids had clubbed her with an unloaded M33. "Not before one of those insects did go physical with his high-tech club. I would have taken it away if I'd known. When I feel better, Major, I invite you to go two falls out of three with me in the gym, and I'll show you how guile can overcome brawn. In the meantime, thanks for the headache. Don't worry; I'll figure out some way to reciprocate."

"I don't get any respect around here," Clinch groused. It wasn't a complaint. He didn't dislike Moore and vice versa. In fact, no one in the *Shenandoah* disliked anyone there; they were a team and worked out their differences privately, as Moore had implied. They were together in the big composite bottle under the sea, and they were there because they'd volunteered. The sea was their primary enemy. Their secondary enemy depended on their orders from CINCPAC and CNO. And the third enemy was boredom.

"Captain, the female Mantid called Merhad is complaining this morning about being locked up and guarded," said Dr. Evelyn Lulalilo, the special team's marine biologist, who could converse with the Mantids because they spoke Pidgin English. The Mantids had learned it in the Solomons to converse with the islanders.

"Let it complain!" Laura Raye Moore snapped. "Those big insects are vicious!"

"Merhad is female. Her companion, Drek, is male," Eve insisted.

"Doctor Lulalilo is right. We have examples of both Mantid sexes," Dr. Constantine Zervas, the special team member from Bethesda Naval Hospital, added.

"Male or female, I won't let them loose in my sick bay again," Moore stated firmly.

"How are they this morning, Doctor?" Corry asked.

"The female has a broken third leg. The male that was wounded in their hostage incident is conscious," the Medical Officer reported.

"I spent most of the night doing an autopsy on the dead third Mantid," Zervas put in. He looked as if he'd been up all night. However, his fatigue hadn't affected his haughty manner. "I've learned enough about Mantid anatomy to be able to tell Doctor Moore how to treat the wounded Mantid."

Laura Raye kept quiet. As far as she was concerned, Zervas had been as helpful as tits on a torpedo. She'd had to proceed to treat the wounded Mantid without his help,

because she couldn't wait "a few more minutes until I dis-
sect the alimentary tract a bit farther."

"Keep the Mantids under close security," Corry ordered.

"Captain, Merhad claims that such treatment is contrary
to some kind of law that all interstellar species follow,"
Eve pointed out. Corry believed she had far too much empathy for the treacherous Mantids. Her professional life
had involved unsuccessful attempts to communicate with
dolphins, and in the *Shenandoah* she had discovered a way
to communicate with a truly alien species.

"Doctor," Corry told her gently, "please tell your Mantid
that they are on our planet now and they'll follow our
rules. They attacked us and threatened your life along with
Doctor Moore's. They will both remain under Level One
security until we reach Palmyra and are told what to do
with them."

"Captain, something bothers me," LCDR Bob Lovette
put in. "It doesn't make sense to me from an operations
standpoint. I know that orders sometimes don't make sense
when they're received. But does anyone have a good idea
why we're going to Palmyra instead of Pearl?"

"Security isolation," Ralph Strader suggested.

"Isolated it certainly is!" Natalie Chase exclaimed.

"But security at Pearl is outstanding with the SSCV pens
now on Ford Island," Lovette observed.

"And when we show up there, everyone in Honolulu
will discover that the *Shanna* has returned from the Solomons with a broken Number Three periscope," Strader reminded everyone. "Given the international situation right
now, that could start some rumors."

"And if the Corona is taken off the boat there, we'll
have to put up screens for security. Everyone will know
something happened, especially if the Chinese behave as
they did after Makasar. They broadcast to the world their
videotape and radar data showing the *Tuscarora* we chased
together, and they claimed it was a secret American
weapon," Terri said. "You're right, Mister Strader. Security
is the issue. Smitty, I'll bet your intel people will unload
the Corona at Palmyra away from all eyes and fly it God
knows where."

"What kind of an airplane can carry that Corona? It's
damned big," Bart Clinch pointed out.

"Ten meters across? An Aerospace Force Condor will do

the job nicely," Soucek said, reaching into his extensive knowledge of aerospace matters.

"It won't be an Aerospace Force airplane," Smith corrected him.

"What do you mean? It's got to be the Aerospace Force. The Navy doesn't have any heavy airlifters," Terri said.

"You can bet your wings, Terri," Smith told her, "that Naval Intelligence hasn't let the Aerospace Force in on this yet. Not with my boss coming to Pearl Harbor and taking charge. I know Admiral McCarthy. She isn't going to let the Aerospace Force spooks get their hands on this Corona, not after the way they've hogged all the early UFO and other data to themselves. CINCPAC and CNO will drag their heels with the flyboys long enough to get the Corona and the Mantids safely tucked away somewhere in the ZI. The Admiral will even manage to keep it from the CIA until she's changed the locks on the doors."

Smith paused and looked around. It was apparent she'd interjected a new element into the equation: interservice rivalry. It had never occurred to the officers in the wardroom. Now the orders began to make some sense to them.

"Palmyra is a natural. The Navy owns it—actually, the Navy leases it from the Honolulu entrepreneur whose resort scheme failed many years ago. Who wants to spend two weeks in the jungle of an atoll without any decent beaches, only coral?" Smith went on, sharing her thoughts with them as if she wasn't an outsider but had become one of the *Shenandoah*'s people, as indeed she had in the past several weeks. "We weren't ordered to Johnston Atoll, in spite of its very secure facilities that were once used for nukes; the Aerospace Force owns it! Palmyra belongs to the Navy. It's isolated. It's still under the space defense umbrella of Hawaii, so we won't have to worry about orbital kinetic kill weapons coming in on us if we stay on the surface. And the Admiral has probably arranged for some clandestine contract airlift from one of our cover firms like T&G Airlift out of Yuma."

"Smitty, you're making sense. That's unusual for an intel spook," Terri quipped, then mused, "Yes. Of course. The Chinese or Indians won't dare come near Palmyra. It's only about eighteen hundred klicks from Pearl, well within the ASW umbrella of Frank Kendall's Ospreys from VS-thirty.

Not that we can't handle any East World sub threat that might develop, of course. . . ."

"So what's the plan, Captain?" Zeke asked.

"This was supposed to be a Papa briefing. All of you were supposed to tell me," Corry reminded them easily.

"Sir, there's no room for discussion of a plan," Lovette told him. "We follow orders, period. We cruise deep and fast in stealth. We look out for anything that might be a *Tuscarora* and, if attacked, we blow it out of the water or the air, wherever it is. No sweat; we did that before, we can do it again. We go to the north side of Palmyra Atoll and wait there submerged until we get further orders. End of plan."

"We don't know what's going on out there," Zeke added. "East World may be at war with some parts of the West World, or maybe not. The Chinese may be on the offensive against the Russian East or India may be going after Pakistan again. We don't know. They weren't two days ago, but a lot can happen in two days. And we don't know the enemy naval disposition. Our only prudent course of action is to do what we're told and what CINCPAC is expecting us to do. Admiral Kane may have his hands full of problems, so we'd better not make another problem for him by being where we're not supposed to be when he calls us. Frankly, I don't like this interservice rivalry that we may be embroiled in. We've got no control of that. So if we get new orders, we obey those. I agree with Commander Lovette. We do what's expected of us."

"Which we will do, of course," was Corry's comment. "But now all of you, including you members of the special team, know the situation and can act accordingly if something comes unbonded somewhere. I agree, XO; the interservice wars can be far more dangerous to one's career than armed conflict. We'll try to stay out of that and let the shore establishment handle it." He rose to his feet, and the other officers followed suit. "No change in the standing orders, XO. Steady as she goes. Carry on. Three potential adversaries are plenty to worry about—Aerospace Force, East World submarines, and the *Tuscaroras* that may be running free out there looking for us."

4

Other forces were indeed at work, and some of them had been for a very long time. CAPT William M. Corry and his colleagues in the U.S.S. *Shenandoah* had guessed correctly about some of them, but not all.

The major one was the "board of directors" of Majestic Corporation. Allan Soucek didn't know everything about the company he worked for. It was over a hundred years old, having been formed in 1947 by an Executive Order of then-President Harry S Truman. The Majestic 12 was originally a clandestine intelligence commission reporting only to the President of the United States and responsible for collecting, evaluating, and analyzing information about the "flying saucers" or "unidentified flying objects" that first gained widespread notoriety following World War II. It had become Majestic Corporation over the years as its membership of twelve highly placed people from the military, academia, and the government had come and gone, changing as years caused attrition among the original members.

The members of the Majestic 12 and the directors of Majestic Corporation were still highly placed in the military, academic, commercial, and government circles of the United States. But they weren't Americans. In fact, in the twenty-first century, no terrestrial human beings remained in the Majestic 12.

This didn't mean that the members of the Majestic 12 couldn't pass for terrestrials. They could and they did. But they had a different origin, a different culture, and a different philosophy from terrestrials.

Fortunately for the world, the twelve men were members of one of the seventy-one known extraterrestrial species that had a benign code of ethics. This did not prevent them from being ruthless when necessary.

As the U.S.S. *Shenandoah* continued its underwater jour-

ney across the Pacific to Palmyra, the Majestic 12 met
again in their clandestine offices high in an office building
near the White House in Washington. In spite of being a
Delaware corporation licensed to do business in the Dis-
trict of Columbia, paying corporate taxes like any other
firm, and filing regular annual reports to the D.C. Corporation Commission and the IRS, Majestic Corporation and
the Majestic 12 didn't officially exist. The Presidential Science Advisor was the only one in the White House who
knew of the firm. However, Dr. Jonathan Frip wasn't an
American; he was sitting in the meeting as a member of the
Majestic 12.

The Majestic 12 felt very secure. The official headquarters of Majestic Corporation was on the floor below the
one where the meeting was taking place. The meeting floor
could be reached only by a special elevator to which only
a limited number of keys and voice codes had been issued.
That elevator never opened its doors in the lobby of the
building, only in the parking garage beneath. The elevator
stopped only at the hidden floor. Other elevators went right
by it. No one knew the hidden floor was there except those
who had built the office tower decades before and were
now long dead.

The Majestic 12 and their meeting place therefore didn't
exist.

The meeting room was kept at a temperature of thirty-five
degrees Celsius so that the members of the Majestic 12
wouldn't feel cold.

"Naval Intelligence has diverted the *Shenandoah* to Pal-
myra," ADM Stephen Tyonek reported. "I intercepted an
SWC message from Dolores McCarthy, who's at
CINCPAC right now."

"I didn't think you could do that, Tyo," General Hoyt
Beva of the United States Aerospace Force Space Command said.

"You didn't hear it from me, Bev. You don't know that
I can. And you shouldn't. After all, you're Aerospace
Force and I'm Navy. We must keep up the sham."

"Naval Intelligence! No wonder I haven't heard anything!" General Hoyt Beva exclaimed. Then he admitted,
"Then maybe you can tell me where the *Shenandoah* is.
We've lost track of her. She changed course, and my very
covert surveillance network lost lock on her."

"I didn't think the Aerospace Force had the masdet yet, especially in satellites," observed General Danforth Chesmu of the Defense Mapping Agency.

"We don't," Beva explained. "I called Star Guard for help in this situation because of its sensitivity and criticality. Star Guard put one of their corvettes under the Pacific like they did off Makasar. Now it's lost the *Shenandoah,* too."

Lyle Muraco, CEO of a major aerospace corporation, burst forth with a curse in another language. "Bev, that was stupid! If we can't get this situation fixed before the Sector Inspector finds out how badly we've screwed up this assignment, we're *denot* food! Contacting Star Guard for help was risky!"

Beva nodded. "I know. I agree. I had to break comm silence to do it. I just hope that one of the Navy's SWC stations didn't pick up the message."

"We didn't," Tyonek assured him. "But we could have if we'd been looking for it." He paused, then added, "The *Shenandoah* went stealthy shortly after it changed course. We lost our beacon aboard. The National Reconnaissance Office lost track of her, too. But I had my experts make several computer runs and calculate a probable position based on the course she'd have to take to Palmyra and her best underwater cruise speed. I could find her if we wanted to."

"Human technology is getting very good," was the comment from Dr. Jonathan Frip. "They could break off this planet to the stars anytime now. They're not ready for it. And we're not ready for them."

"Yes. We underestimated them and didn't do anything about it. And that's why we could be in big trouble with the Sector Inspector if we don't do something about what appears to be laxity on our part," Newell Carew, the CEO of Majestic Corporation, pointed out.

"You should fire Soucek," Fergus Antol suggested.

"How can I? He's in the *Shenandoah.* If I could reach him and raise hell, he might cause trouble. And he knows about the Majestic Twelve," Carew explained.

"He's unmated. I mean, unmarried. When he gets back, get him off this planet. Reward him. Send him to Almara," Dr. Bourke Renap said.

"Not on my credit!"

"You don't think you could talk the Ministrator into doing it?"

"I do not. Soucek is my responsibility. I'll be a bit more careful about those you recommend in the future, Songan!"

"He was one of my most brilliant students, Carew."

"Too brilliant, if you ask me. I can only hope I scared the living *broll* out of him before I sent him off to the *Shenandoah*. I didn't have anyone else I could send."

"Some members of this species are becoming less and less frightened of the unknown," was the comment from Fergus Antol. "We can't use that ploy very much longer, if at all."

Dr. Jonathan Frip leaned back in his chair and put his long hands behind his head. "Let's quit complaining about the screwup," he said. "Time to get busy and fix it if we can. Fast. Before we have to report it. How do we get to the *Shenandoah*?"

"We can have the Star Guard ship intercept her," General Beva pointed out, "if we can find her."

"No," Dr. Armand Grust insisted. "That's direct interference. Fourth Canon of Metalaw. Possibly the Sixth as well." [author's note: See Appendix II, Metalaw Definitions and Canons.]

Beva sighed. "Very well, we don't. What can we do when she surfaces at Palmyra?"

"Very little. CINCPAC and Naval Intelligence will be all over it like a carpet," Tyonek reminded them.

Beva brightened and sat forward. "Not if I get the Aerospace Force involved. I can do it internally in the Pentagon. Aerospace Force will get nasty about it to the Navy. The Aerospace Force has had the monopoly on UFO and ET information for a long time. I can see to it that Aerospace Force raises a little fuss about Naval Intelligence trying to hold this recent beam ship and Sama capture to themselves. That will kick up some confusion in the E-ring. Maybe I can even get DIA involved."

"No, they're riddled with CIA agents. We've got to keep CIA out of it if we can. We don't have any deep penetration there," Frip reminded him.

"Look, let's not sit around here without some sort of purpose for this meeting. What's our objective? What's our plan? We can't go in and grab those stupid Samas and their ship. Grust, you pointed out that to do so might be a gross violation of the Canons of Metalaw and get us all in even deeper trouble," Carew said, reminding them of their basic operating ethical code. "I don't want to be the one who tests this in metacourt. And I don't want to get us shipped off to some planet on the edge of the galaxy to watch sentient grass grow and keep others from moving in to eat it."

"Who said anything about any of us doing anything?" Grust asked rhetorically, speaking as the chairman of the Majestic 12. "Overtly, that is. Why do you think all the effort has been expended over the years to put us in the positions we hold? We'll just act as triggers. We'll arrange it so the Americans screw it up themselves. And if they don't make a mess of it with their bureaucracy and turf battles, we can always stir the boiling pot with East World. We can manage to let the Chinese know that the *Shenandoah* has something."

"Ah, it could get nasty at Palmyra," Tyonek mused.

"The United States Navy could lose a carrier submarine and maybe a couple of admirals," Carew guessed.

"And we'd lose our beacon."

"Soucek? He's reached the end of his usefulness."

"We never throw away loyal supporters. We'll try to get him out and reward him."

"No, I was speaking of our beacon. He isn't American. He's one of us. And I don't want to take the responsibility for consigning him to termination. We could get away with allowing Soucek to apparently pull his own switch, but we can't abandon our beacon."

"Well, yes, there's that."

"So we'll just have to stay on top of this and try to be metalegal at least with our own."

"If we do it right, we can stay metalegal across the board. But we can't sit back and play a secondary role now."

"How can we play a stronger role without becoming known?"

"That, my colleagues, is what we're going to have to spend some time here figuring out. Don't think about going home tonight."

On Oahu, going home was still a workday away. And often the officers and staffers at CINCPAC didn't go home at night. Not when a major operation was taking place, and certainly not while CINCPAC was at the shore establishment counterpart of Condition Two.

"Richard, we've got two strikes against us even as we come to the plate," RADM Dolores McCarthy complained as she came into the office of CINCPAC.

VADM Richard H. Kane, CINCPAC, hadn't taken the time for breakfast. He was running on strong, hot coffee at the moment and had a mug of it in his hand. "Only two?" he wondered. "What's the problem, Dolores?"

"Number one, we're five hours behind Washington," the Chief of Naval Intelligence reminded him.

"So?"

"So they've got five hours up on us."

"Not when we pull all-nighters like we just did."

"Still, Aerospace Force Headquarters has gotten wind of what we're doing. That means spies in your organization, Richard." It wasn't an accusation as much as it was an observation and a warning.

"My organization?"

"I don't know where else the leak could be. Naval Intelligence is watertight."

Kane keyed his screen. "And we haven't twigged about what we're really doing. Look at the way the dispatches have been worded," he suggested.

She waved away the offer and told him, "I'm not accusing you, Richard."

"I know that. But if I've got leaks, I haven't got the time and manpower available to hunt them down. Your shop is better equipped for that than I am. Feel free to start looking," Kane told her, knowing that she didn't need his approval to do so. But the fact that he'd given it freely was a message to her confirming what he'd just said.

"We have," she admitted. "We can't find anything. But General Strasser at Aerospace Force Headquarters knew all about it. He was briefed within the hour by General Beva of Space Command."

"Okay, Admiral," Kane told her officiously, "that's beyond my purview. I can do nothing about that."

"I know you can't, but I need to brief you about what's going on," McCarthy explained. "I know where Beva got it. Steve Tyonek told him."

"National Recon Office? How the hell does he know?"

"We'll find out," the Chief of Naval Intelligence promised. "Apparently General Dan Chesmu of the Defense Mapping Agency knows, too, because he's involved in spreading the *Shenandoah* story around the Pentagon today."

"What the hell kind of a network is *that*?" Kane asked rhetorically. Both the National Reconnaissance Office and the Defense Mapping Agency were well out of the main line of command and communications, although both organizations were involved in surveillance and recon on a worldwide basis. USAF Space Command might have picked up some air-space movement of the *Tuscarora* UFOs reported by the *Shenandoah,* but the United States Navy hadn't offered to elaborate about the *Shenandoah*'s involvement with those targets.

"It's certainly off the main line," McCarthy admitted. "We're checking on the possibility it might be a new subrosa interservice network designed to subvert all the normal intelligence organizations." She sat down without being offered a chair, took out her pocket scratchpad, and turned it on. "I wanted to check with you on the other arrangements for Palmyra. It occurred to me that something may have leaked about that."

"I seriously doubt it," Kane told her earnestly. "No one has been given a rationale for the operation, and the elements involved don't know that they're part of a bigger picture. Some ships believe it's just another exercise, something that has to do with the East World situation."

Kane paused and sighed in weariness. "I want you to know, Dolores, that it hasn't been easy to pull together the Palmyra task force on the sneak. I've got the SeaBee batt cranked up for you and ready to depart. VR-thirty is ready with airlift. Three SSF attack boats—the *Morton,* the *Ramage,* and the *Dealey*—will be off the north side of Palmyra on schedule to serve as a submarine screen. For aerospace defense, I've moved the *Glenn,* the *Schirra,* and the *Conrad* into position to provide coverage."

"That may be overkill," McCarthy interrupted him.

"Eh?"

"Moving that many ships around is likely to cause someone to sit up and take notice," she explained. "Whether or not the elements know they're part of a larger operation, scuttlebutt gets around and someone can easily put the pieces of the puzzle together if enough exist. Maybe you ought to cut back."

Kane shook his head and replied vehemently, "Not a bet, Admiral! I won't put the *Shenandoah* at risk off Palmyra! Not with what Corry has aboard! I've got to have those attack boats positioned around Palmyra, because the Chinese may have figured out why Corry left Guadalcanal in such a hurry. Hell, the Chinese captain saw Corry's aircraft fight off that UFO. Tell me there are no Chinese spies in Honiara. Or Honolulu, for that matter."

"The surface ships have me concerned," she admitted. "Why put three of our best aerospace defense cruisers out there? Palmyra is under the Hawaiian space defense umbrella."

Kane got up and poured himself another cup of steaming coffee. As an old salt, he drank it pitch-black without sweetener or creamer, condiments that were strictly for shore establishment types. "Want some coffee?" he offered McCarthy.

"No thank you. The stuff you drink out here takes the lining off my mouth," she admitted. "I'm used to Pentagon coffee."

"My sympathies," Kane remarked and sat down. He went on, "Look at it this way: Some Aerospace Force scope dope at Hawaiian Space Defense sees something heading for Palmyra. He isn't going to scramble an interceptor on it or even beam it. He'll report it instead."

"Are you implying that the Aerospace Force would let a kinetic kill weapon take out a Navy ship just because it's Navy?"

He shook his head. "Not at all. Interservice rivalry has nothing to do with it. The scope dope probably won't get the word about our Palmyra operation, not even a 'no-action' order from Space Command. When he sees that orbital telephone pole heading toward Palmyra, he'll figure it's not a threat because he knows through official channels that there's nothing at Palmyra except some gooney birds. He'll decide the space rod has been mistargeted somehow. So he'll just report it through normal pink line channels and let someone else figure out what to do if another one comes along shortly. Or maybe Space Defense bumps things up to DEFCON Two just in case. However, that doesn't keep that rod from going clean through the hull of the *Shenandoah*. Sorry, Dolores, but I'm going to put my own space umbrella over Palmyra so I don't have to tell Space Defense what's going on there. And then they won't report it up the line to Beva and Strasser. That would just confirm what I hope is being received as a somewhat fantastic rumor back in Playland on the Potomac."

"Very well, then, since you're laying on that much defense, I want an additional masdet available," McCarthy told him. "The SSCV-thirty *Savannah* has just finished fitting-out trials with the WSS-one. She's getting ready to put to sea. Get her down here from Whidbey Island."

"Dolores, I don't even own that boat yet!" Kane complained.

"You will. I'll see to that." Rear Admiral Dolores T. McCarthy smiled. "I will take that cup of coffee after all, Richard—if you'll cut it about fifty percent with water. I should have thought of the operational aspects of this whole thing. But I didn't. It means I need that coffee to jump-start the brain this morning. You do indeed have a grasp of operations that I don't."

"My dear, that's because you've been intel for your whole career. Spies may get shot, but they rarely sink."

"Yes, I can't remember that we've ever had a computer terminal torpedoed. They go down, of course, but they usually do that on their own."

"Those electronic brains do have little minds of their own, don't they?" He got McCarthy her cup of coffee, suitably cut with hot water, then said, "Given the situation with the Aerospace Force, I expect a call from General Martin over at Hickam in an hour or so. She'll request to be included in the operation." Kane smiled. "It will be a pleasure to reply, 'What operation?' "

McCarthy smiled, too. "I'm having a bad influence on you, Richard. You're picking up the operational philosophy of a Naval Intelligence officer."

As if on signal, the telephone sounded.

It was General D. D. Martin, commander of the 5th Aerospace Force at Hickam AFB over on the other side of South East Loch. "Okay, Dick, what's the story?" Martin wanted to know straight off. "What's the big operation you're laying on?"

As if on cue, Kane replied innocently with a straight face, "What operation?"

"Palmyra," the Aerospace Force general fired back. "Hell, you can't cancel leaves for the crew of the *Glenn* and the *Conrad* without my people finding out. And you're provisioning the *Morton* less than a week after she returned from a three-month patrol. That's not SOP for you, Dick, unless something's hit the impeller. What do you know about the Chinese situation that I don't?"

The Chief of Naval Intelligence was out of videocamera view, so Martin didn't know she was there. McCarthy just smiled. Kane wanted to, but maintained a straight face. Martin had just revealed that USAF intelligence hadn't contacted him yet. She was working from local data inputs of her own.

Kane didn't want to alert him to the intel data stream. "You mean, you haven't gotten orders yet?"

"No. East World?"

"D.D., you know as much about that as I do."

"Yeah, it doesn't look good over there in Asia," Martin admitted, now thrown completely off the track. "But why Palmyra?"

"D.D., I was told to send stuff to Palmyra. I guess it was to keep it away from prying eyes around Pearl. And Palmyra is still under your space defense umbrella," Kane said, not telling her anything she didn't already know.

"They'll see it there."

"Probably. And so will you."

"Yeah. Hopefully, I'll know more about it than they do. So what the hell were your orders?"

"D.D., I wasn't told to share them. I suspect you'll be getting your own. If I were you, I'd wait and see what they tell you to do. Remember, it takes us longer to move capabilities around, so we usually get orders ahead of you."

"Yeah, yeah, okay, I guess we have to suffer for our Mach ten reaction time. Okay, we'll see what the hooter coughs up today. Then maybe we can coordinate where necessary to conserve forces. Damned budget cuts are drying me up," the USAF general complained.

"Well, we're hooked to the same spigot, D.D."

"Roger that! Okay, I'll keep a cool stool and a hot pot. And wait to see what happens."

"Nicely handled," Dolores McCarthy told him when the connection was cut.

"It wasn't easy," Kane admitted. "But she thought she

was one-up on me anyway when she called. She beat the hell out of me at golf last Sunday morning. So I don't owe her anything."

"And by the time she talks to the E-ring, those ships will be out of Pearl and on their way. And we'll drop off the face of the Earth ourselves."

Kane looked at her quizzically.

"Oh, the two of us are going, Richard. I've got to get you out of the loop here at Pearl. You're too accessible and you know too much. I don't want to burden you with having to cover up for days on end. It could backfire on you and hurt your career. So consider this an 'invitation,' Richard. I hope you can run CINCPAC from Palmyra for a few days."

5

A 390-meter SSCV is not a small vessel. Because it had about 300,000 cubic meters of internal volume, it was impossible for CAPT William M. Corry to carry out a walkaround inspection on a regular basis. Much of the *Shenandoah* was taken up with machinery, buoyancy tanks, compressed air reservoirs, aircraft fuel bunkers, the lower flight deck, and the hangar deck. However, she was such a big boat that three squadrons of aircraft and 750 people fit in her with far more room than in even the old surface aircraft carriers.

Corry suspected she had some compartments and volumes he hadn't seen, although he'd done his best to know the entire ship.

So a walkaround inspection wasn't a regular affair. Corry did it when he could. Often, it was a truncated walkaround taking him only to those parts of the boat he could reach in the time he had available.

But with the U.S.S. *Shenandoah* in submerged cruise mode en route to Palmyra Atoll, he had time. Corry asked CDR Zeke Braxton and SCPO Carl Armstrong to accompany him on a walkaround. The XO and the Chief of the Boat came to his cabin at 1300 hours.

"Looking for anything special today, Captain?" Armstrong wanted to know. As the top rate in the boat, he prided himself on knowing more than the Captain did about the ship, but he was also discreet enough not to say so. Corry would not have minded in any event. After years in the United States Navy, Corry knew that the petty officers really ran the show.

Corry shook his head. "No, not really. I want the crew to see that they still have a captain who's more than a disembodied voice on the PA system. And I haven't been around to some parts of the boat since we left Pearl," he admitted. Then he smiled and went on in a lighthearted tone, "Let's just say that I'd like to make sure that you and the XO haven't let part of it get away."

"It was all there last time I looked, Captain," Zeke responded in an equally blithe manner, taking his cue from Corry's facetious remark, "unless someone has decoupled the forward part of the boat and is feeding dummy signals into the bridge circuits and monitors."

"I don't suspect that, XO, but one does tend to fall into the fantasy that the whole world is nothing but the bridge and quarters," Corry pointed out. He rose to his feet. "And, Chief, this is a pop inspection, nothing formal. I don't intend to bilge anyone unless it's a major infraction. I'll make comments to you and the XO if I see anything."

"Aye, aye, sir," Armstrong replied, knowing that this was Corry's way of running things. A comment to the XO or the Chief of the Boat was equivalent to a direct order to get it fixed on the bounce. "May I suggest, sir, that we start at the stern and work forward?"

"Good idea. I haven't been in the engineering spaces since I talked to Stocker's crew at Makasar."

A submarine propulsion expert in the previous century would have had trouble believing the small size of the *Shenandoah*'s propulsion system. If the nuclear fission reactor had caused a revolution in submarine technology, the fusion generators of the SSCV-26 U.S.S. *Shenandoah* were yet another revolutionary step forward. Gone was the requirement for massive radiation shielding of the old fission reactors. The two Deseret Energy Corporation Type PF9N fusion generators were only a small part of the self-contained propulsion system. Furthermore, it was absolutely silent because the only moving part was water coursing through it. The system hydrolyzed seawater to purify it for propulsion and potability, then it extracted hydrogen from it for use in the fusion process. Convective-type pumps eliminated the need for moving parts. The steam generated by the system was forced through the two General Jet Corporation aquajets to provide silent propulsion.

Technically, the U.S.S. *Shenandoah* could cruise endlessly with no need for refueling, recoring a reactor, or replenishing the fusion generator catalysts. From an operational standpoint, however, the United States Navy liked to replace the fusion generator catalysts every five years "just in case" the catalysts might have gotten progressive poisoning. In any event, the boat could remain at sea longer than her crew, because her stores weren't internally renewable. Food supplies had to be replenished. In addition, equipment had to be replaced because it wore out or became in-op beyond the on-board repair capabilities to fix it.

"I have no problems, Captain," reported CDR Ray Stocker, the Engineer Officer.

"Do you ever have any?" Braxton asked.

Stocker nodded. "Sure, what engineering department doesn't? But we're redundant on everything, and I keep it working. If maintenance won't do it and something fails, I fix it. You'll hear about it only if it's going to be off-line long enough to affect the performance of the boat."

"Well, I know you can cruise on one fusion generator," Zeke pointed out.

"Hey, the big units are never the problem. It's the little stuff that craps out. But, yeah, if one of the generators went down, we could continue to cruise, but not at forty knots. Twenty-five maybe, and then only if I took some aux equipment off the bus." Stocker was a typical Navy specialist. He knew his equipment, he knew its technology, and he had a "fix it" approach to things: "Anything can be fixed. And if it isn't broken, I don't try to fix it. It lets me know soon enough when something is about to go tits-up."

"Have you had a chance to look at the Corona yet?" Zeke asked, referring to the saucer-shaped alien craft now sitting on the hangar deck.

Stocker nodded. "In spite of Ellison's techies, who try to keep it to themselves, my crew has been over it a few times in the last twenty-four hours."

"What makes it go?" Zeke asked.

Stocker shrugged. "I don't know. I'm in the same damned position as the Engineer Officer of the old *Nautilus* if he saw my shop. He wouldn't know how it worked unless I explained it to him. He'd have no trouble understanding it then. But it would take him a long time and a lot of busted equipment to figure it out for himself. One thing for certain: Those Mantids have figured out how to put ten pounds of crap in a one-pound bag."

"How so?" Corry asked.

"Their liquid fuel must be subnuclear, like some of Guns

Weaver's classified warheads. It doesn't burn at all. Yeah, I've tried to make it burn. The stuff comes apart somehow—I don't have that secret yet. When it does, it's got to release a hell of a lot of energy. The rest of the system looks like it's electromagnetohydrodynamic."

"That's easy for you to say," Zeke kidded him. "What's that?"

"When the fuel comes apart and releases energy, it apparently forms some sort of plasma," Stocker guessed. "Since a plasma has electric charge and some weird electromagnetic characteristics, it provides enough juice to run the Corona's electric space drive. But don't ask me how it works."

"Someone will figure it out, Commander," Chief Armstrong observed. "We've seen Coronas fly. We know they can do it. Some of the rates are already kicking ideas around in bull sessions."

"Well, hell, Chief, you know as well as I do that what's impossible to one generation of techies is commonplace to the next." Stocker reflected on the situation for a moment, then added, "I'd sure like to have that system in the *Shanna.* Hell, Captain, we could go anywhere! We'd have enough power to operate submerged as well as airborne."

"Jules Verne's flying submarines," Zeke recalled. "Just like the alien *Tuscaroras* we've encountered."

"Yeah. Pisses me off that we can't chase them once they leave the water."

"You weren't nearly as pissed off, sir, as some of the people in the Air Group," Armstrong told him.

"Yeah, but think how pissed off the Aerospace Force is going to be."

"They already are," Corry reminded all of them. "They've been chasing UFOs for more than a century without any intercepts."

"Well, we didn't shoot one down. We torpedoed one and the Air Group ran the other one off, sir," Armstrong recalled.

"Qualifies us to lash a broom to the periscope when we sail into Pearl," Stocker said.

"We'll do that . . . when we get there," Corry promised.

On the hangar deck, the Marine battalion was engaged in close order drill. Corry, Braxton, and Armstrong paused to watch.

"I can't figure out, sir," Zeke said to Corry, "why the Marines continue to do close order drill. As I recall, that's a holdover from a couple of centuries ago when military formations had to go from column to line and back again so they could fire volleys into an enemy who was also arrayed in line of ducks."

"XO, then why did all of us march in formation and do close order drill at the Naval Academy?" Corry asked him.

"So we'd learn to respond immediately to orders and perform as a team," Zeke responded. "It seemed to me that it had no other practical function."

"And during our plebe years, close order drill turned a mob of irresponsible, individualistic, egocentric, teenaged volunteers into an organized group of goal-oriented adults with a respect for constituted authority and the ability to respond immediately to orders," Corry reminded him.

"Well, Captain, with all due respect, it didn't work," Zeke pointed out. "None of us came through that as a piece of cannon fodder that responds blindly to orders."

Corry smiled. "Yes. I suspect you recall your company commander ordering the outfit to march off the end of the pier in full land combat gear . . ."

"Uh, yeah. We wouldn't do it."

"Did you catch hell?"

"Of course! Insubordination. Twenty demerits and twenty tours."

"And while you were sitting in detention or walking those tours, did you reflect on the fact that you were alive and able to sit or walk?"

"Yes, sir." Zeke paused for a moment, then went on, "If you ever gave me an order that I thought was irrational or wrong, I'd respectfully question it. And if I didn't like the answer I got, I'd refuse the order and stand for the court-martial. But I would never expect you to give such an order."

"I might. Would you?"

"I'd think very carefully before I gave it, sir." He turned to the Chief of the Boat. "What would you do, Chief?"

Without hesitation, Chief Armstrong replied, "Sir, not all orders are rational. If I ever got a strange one—and I have from time to time—I'd salute and maybe drag my feet a little and hope the officer would suddenly see the error or until the situation changed so the order was no longer valid."

"Both of you, think about that a little bit in the next day or so," Corry warned them. "We may find ourselves in such a situation at Palmyra."

Major Bart Clinch walked up to the trio. "Afternoon, Captain, XO, Chief. The batt was getting soft. Terri allowed us to use this end of the hangar deck for some drill."

"We were just discussing the need for close order drill, Bart, even though it has no utility on the battlefield any longer," Zeke told him.

"Damned well could, XO!" Clinch fired back. "Not all fights involve shooting. If my batt looks and moves and acts sharp, it may cause the Bad Guys to decide they won't shoot today. Sort of a Marine form of surfacing the boat in the harbor at dawn. Got to look like we're too powerful for the other side to take on and beat. It's all a matter of bluff, sir. Really it is."

"You ready for Palmyra, Major?" Corry asked suddenly.

Clinch replied without hesitation. "Captain, we're always ready, even if we don't know for what. We shall prevail. Semper fi, sir!"

Other parts of the hangar deck were crowded with the fifty-one aircraft—F/A-48 Sea Devils, P-10 Ospreys, and C-26 Sea Dragons—of the Air Group's three squadrons. CDR Terri Ellison kept a third of her aircraft fueled, armed, and ready for immediate launch. They were positioned near the lifts to the upper and lower flight decks, the F/A-48s configured for CAP and the P-10s for patrol. Another third was in standby, the F/A-48s positioned with various armament suites on deck nearby ready to be installed, depending upon the mission their pilots were called upon to carry out—CAP or surface attack. Two EP-10s were on standby for airborne surveillance and command/control while three C-26 Sea Dragons were ready for Marine airlift. The remaining one-third—minus the F/A-48 that had been shot down in the Solomon Sea—was either in standby or undergoing routine maintenance.

LT Willard L. Ireland, the Aircraft Maintenance Officer, saw the three and came over to them on an electric scooter. "Good afternoon, Captain! XO! Major! Can I take you somewhere or show you something?"

"Just a walkaround, Mister Ireland," the XO assured him.

"Everything copasetic here, sir. Except we're short a Sea Devil. Commander Bellinger's ship went in the drink—what was left of it after that Corona's force beam hit it. But he's back in the air. Or will be if we have to launch aircraft."

"How so?" Zeke asked.

"Commander Ellison gave him her double-coconuts bird, sir."

Corry nodded in silent approval. Terri Ellison was CAG and had her choice of aircraft to fly. Although she'd made her reputation as a highly aggressive P-10 Osprey pilot, she'd opted to fly the hot F/A-48 Sea Devil as the ship's CAG. For her to give it to the attack squadron commander who'd been shot down over the Solomon Sea was a gesture of concern for her Air Group and its people over and above her own flaming desire to fly hot and fast. She could, of course, fly any airplane in the Air Group at any time she chose. And sometimes she chose the docile C-26 Sea Dragon but flew it like a fighter/attack ship. Zeke knew she had a way with flying machines just as she did with men.

But it was a careful and cautious CDR Terri Ellison who drove another electric scooter up to them and stopped. She'd told Zeke that it was far more dangerous to drive around the hangar deck than to fly combat because the reaction times were shorter on the deck, there were more idiots there, and she didn't want to ding any of her aircraft. "Looking for the Corona, Captain?" she asked.

"Are you psychic, Terri?" Corry wondered.

"No, sir. I just know you pretty well, sir. You wouldn't make a walkaround inspection without wanting to see everything you could. You haven't seen the Corona yet, and I figure the walkaround might have been a good excuse to come up and look it over. If not you, then the XO for sure." Terri was always candid except when circumstances required that she be discreet and formal. This wasn't one of them. Her two superior officers and the top chief were in Air Country. "I'm headed for the Corona myself. You're all welcome to ride with me. Pax seats available on this run. Next bus may not be along for a while."

It was a long ride from where they were to the corner of the forward hangar deck where the silvery Corona sat, propped up by a hastily constructed pallet of wood.

It was disk-shaped, about ten meters across, and totally devoid of markings. It looked like a huge metal coffee cup atop two saucers glued together to make a lens-shaped main body. Seawater dripped to the hangar deck from a gash in its bottom, and a round hatch about a meter in diameter opened inward on the cup portion of the body. A stainless-steel boarding ladder normally used on an F/A-48 Sea Devil lay against the lip of the main body.

It didn't look alien at all. Corry had seen stranger flying machines in the aerospace periodicals.

An aviation machinist mate third stood on the deck next to the ladder and a large multidrawer tool case on wheels. Up on the saucer next to the hatch was an aviation electronics technician first.

A chief aviation machinist mate struck his head out of the hatch and told the technician there, "Thirteen-millimeter deep Ducros socket!"

The technician passed the word to the machinist mate on the deck, who selected a tool from the case and tossed it up. "Thirteen-mike-mike deep Ducros comin' atcha!" The technician caught it and passed it to the chief in the hatch.

It was then that the machinist mate on the deck saw the three officers and the Chief of the Boat. "Captain on the hangar deck!" she called and came to attention.

"As you were. Carry on," Corry told her.

The chief stuck his head out of the hatch far enough to see over the lip of the saucer, turned, and said something to someone inside the Corona.

"Pretty plain on the outside," Corry remarked, running his hand over the mirrorlike metal surface of the Corona's bottom hull. "What's inside?"

Chief Armstrong clambered up the ladder and spoke to the man in the hatch. "Rex, are you air types stripping this thing for spare parts already?"

Chief Rex Caliborn told him, "Mister Soucek and Lieutenant Peyton are inside. They're poking around opening inspection hatches."

That caused Terri to scramble up the ladder, saying as she did so, "Dammit, no one is going to take this thing apart unless it's done with thorough documentation!"

Corry followed her. Although the upper surface of the saucer was as mirror-smooth as the underbelly, it wasn't slippery. He could stand on it easily even though he wasn't wearing topsiders. "If we dismantle this thing, we're in trouble!" he muttered. But he knew Soucek might try to do it.

Chief Caliborn suddenly knew things had gone to worms. He respectfully stepped out of the hatch onto the upper surface. "Sir, why don't you go inside yourself and see what's going on?"

Terri hadn't waited for an invitation. She quickly slipped through the hatch. Corry followed.

He was immediately assaulted by the stench. "What's dead in here?" he asked no one in particular.

"Three Mantids, Captain," Allan Soucek replied from where he was standing next to an open inspection panel on one side of what appeared to be a circular control deck. "Doctor Moore's people had to scrape two of them off the walls. That's the smell."

"What are you up to, Mister Soucek?" Corry asked.

"Getting a close look at the current model of a Corona," the man from Majestic Corporation replied. "I've seen the old one at Wright-Pat. It's in a condition of advanced decay. This is a new one. And it's the first time I've seen some of the things I've only read about in old reports. And I'm learning that some of those old reports are either outdated or worthless."

"I don't want you to dismantle anything," Corry ordered.

"Oh, I'm not doing that, Captain," Soucek tried to assure him.

"What are you doing?"

"Looking at things they couldn't identify back in the last century."

"What do you mean? Explain!"

"Captain, the Aerospace Force captured and evaluated the original Corona ship before we had lasers, fiber optics, solid-state electronics, room-temperature superconductors, nonintrusive man-machine interfaces, N-fones . . . well, just a lot of stuff we take for granted today. But they kept the Wright-Pat Corona under such tight security that no one has had a chance to reevaluate any of it in light of current terrestrial technology. So that's what I'm looking for. And it's amazing!"

"What's amazing about it?" Terri asked, wrinkling her nose in distaste. The rotting smell was terrible. She was surprised that Soucek apparently wasn't bothered by it. She thought she knew why. He was so engrossed in the Corona's technology that he simply ignored everything else.

"I think if we had the Corona's drive technology, we could probably build one!"

6

"What do you think about Soucek's evaluation of this craft, Terri?" Corry asked her as they walked away from the Corona.

"Captain, I don't design them or build them. I fly them," she stated candidly. "If someone wants me to drive this flying saucer, I'll try it. It can't be that different from a Sea Devil."

"Yes," Corry remarked. He was still a current naval aviator. "They all have a stick and a rudder, don't they?"

"Yes, sir. I could figure out how to control it, even if it takes four hands and two feet. Or four feet and two hands. Or whatever," she went on.

"Well, don't start thinking about it, because I won't let you."

Terri looked askance at him. "Captain, I wouldn't even *think* of taking it a millimeter above the deck until I was confident I could get it back in one piece. After all, it's my pink bod strapped into it. And I didn't see an ejection seat. Besides, the Corona is too valuable to risk."

"That it is," Zeke echoed her sentiments.

"Captain," Chief Armstrong put in, "one of my ratings is aviation machinist mate. I've had to bend tin and make things work. With all due respect, sir, I'm not sure that Mister Soucek has been through that school. Just let me say, sir, that it's a hell of a long way between knowing how something works and *making* it work."

"So you're saying that Mister Soucek hasn't gotten his hands dirty," Zeke said.

Armstrong nodded. "Yes, sir. He may be getting his hands dirty for the first time in the Corona. Lieutenant Peyton and Chief Caliborn were handling the tools for him."

"Thank you for pointing that out, Chief," Corry told

him. He knew that Soucek was a captain in the Naval Reserve but wasn't a naval aviator. Up to that time, he hadn't known if Soucek possessed any technical abilities. Many people could rise to high rank without knowing which end of the screwdriver went in the slot. "Zeke, you might ask Smitty if she really wants Mister Soucek doing what he's doing. She may not know about it."

"She knows, Captain," Zeke assured him. "She told me after breakfast that it would keep Soucek busy and out from underfoot. However, she wanted a couple of experienced aviation maintenance people there with him at all times.'

"Smart lady."

"Yes, sir. She is. She knows a lot more than she lets on."

"Most intel people do, Zeke," Terri reminded him. She refrained from asking him how much Smith was learning about the XO; the two of them had been seen together a lot in the last day. Terri wasn't jealous . . . much. She liked being at the apex of the triangle consisting of herself, Zeke, and Bart Clinch. There was something heartwarming about having two men vie for her attentions.

The next stop was two decks down and forward, the sick bay.

"Captain in the sick bay!" CPO Nat Post called out as Corry came through the door with Zeke and Armstrong.

"Carry on," Corry told him automatically. "How are the aliens doing, Posty?"

"Doctor Moore can give you a report on that, sir," Post answered properly. Only a doctor could make a medical report to the Captain. "Do you want to see them, sir?"

"I've seen them once," Corry told him with a touch of distaste in his voice.

"Yes, sir. I agree. Once is enough. I'll tell the Medical Officer you're here. Anything special you need, sir?"

"This is just a walkaround, Chief," Zeke explained.

"Yes, sir."

Post didn't need to call the ship's doctor. Laura Raye Moore came through a door into the reception compartment. "Good afternoon, gentlemen! What can I do for you?"

"Just a walkthrough, Doctor," Corry said. "I presume everything is shipshape?"

"Yes, sir. I would have reported if it were otherwise."

"What's going on with the Mantids?"

"Doctor Zervas is continuing to autopsy the Mantid cadaver we recovered from the Corona," Moore told him. "I assigned Mister Molders to him because he needed help. The two live Mantids are in separate detention compartments under Marine guard."

"Do the guards have loaded weapons this time?" Zeke asked. While the boat was in the Solomon Sea, the two living Mantids had attempted to escape from sick bay and get back to the Corona. They'd surprised their two Marine guards and taken their M33 carbines. However, the Marines had been following standing orders not to carry loaded weapons inside a pressure hull. That mix-up between standing orders and operational orders allowed Bart Clinch to save Moore and Dr. Evelyn Lulalilo and return the Mantids to sick bay.

Moore's expression grew grim. "I don't know much about guns, XO. But I made sure the Marines show me that their weapons are loaded on each watch. That little episode was enough excitement for a while."

"Doctor, each Marine now carries a carbine with a full clip but no round in the chamber," Zeke explained. He'd worked out that compromise with Bart Clinch. Corry had signed off on it. The accidental discharge of an M33 carbine inside the U.S.S. *Shenandoah* probably wouldn't breach the pressure hull but might create a stress concentration that could lead to a failure. Normally, Marine guards or a ship's police detachment would carry billies or police batons. But the present circumstances were unusual. No one knew where to hit a Mantid to disable it. Thus, carrying a carbine with no round in the chamber eliminated the concern about an accidental discharge. If it came to shooting—as it had in the Solomon Sea—the Marines were ordered to use the low-muzzle-velocity setting of the M33's variable discharge mode. Experience had shown that a round fired at low-V wouldn't go all the way through a Mantid.

"How do you feel today, Doctor?" Corry asked her.

"Not bad, considering that Posty reported I suffered a mild concussion when the Mantid hit me with that carbine," Laura Raye replied. "By the way, Doctor Zervas was little if any help to me when I was both unconscious and recovering. He may be an expert biotechnician, but his practical medical capabilities haven't seen enough use over the years to keep him current on procedures, much less diagnosis."

It was unusual for one doctor to speak of another doctor in that manner, so Corry simply asked, "Really?" He was probing for additional information, but Moore didn't offer it. She'd stretched her ethics to the limit when she said what she had.

"I thought you should know, Captain," the Medical Officer said. "Mister Molders is far more qualified to step in if something should happen to me. Next down on the totem pole would be Chief Post. Doctor Zervas certainly knows as much as I do about alien anatomy, but I was the one who patched up the injured live ones we have aboard."

"Thank you, Doctor. I'll keep that in mind," Corry remarked.

"Would you like to look around, Captain?"

Corry nodded. "Yes, but only to see what Zervas is doing and how the live Mantids are being quartered."

Moore showed them where Doctor Constantine Zervas was performing the autopsy. The officer from Bethesda Naval Hospital had taken over one of the two operating rooms of Moore's sick bay. He briefly looked up to see Moore and the visiting officers through the large transparent window, then went back to work.

In the room with him were CDR Matilda Smith and Dr. Barry Duval.

"I can understand why Commander Smith is in there," Corry said, surprised at the number of people involved in the autopsy. "But why Doctor Duval? What's an oceanographer doing in an autopsy?"

"Doctor Zervas wanted a photographer," Moore explained. "I guess Duval doesn't have very much to do now that we've left the Solomons. Zervas talked him into running the cameras because Duval was familiar with such equipment." She paused, then added, "Makes a good photographer for this task, doesn't he? He's so tall he can look right over both Zervas and Smith."

"Why isn't Zervas wearing mask, gown, and gloves?" Corry asked. Molders, Smith, and Duval were.

Moore shrugged. "His decision, Captain."

"He's dealing with an alien organism. Isn't he afraid of picking up some sort of poison or disease?"

"He says he isn't. However, I asked the others to observe sterile protocols for their own protection," the Medical Officer explained.

"I'd think Zervas would be worried about contaminating the dead Mantid," Zeke said.

"He says it's nothing to worry about. He may be right. At Bethesda, he did a thorough analysis of the dead Awesome we brought back from Makasar. Chief Post and his lab team analyzed the tissues and fluids from the Mantids that were killed in the Corona, and he reports nothing unusual thus far."

"But you don't sound like you're convinced, Doctor," Corry observed.

"I'm not."

"Why?"

"Many years ago, I discovered I wasn't divine. Some doctors never do," Laura Raye Moore pointed out frankly. From the way she said it, no one had any doubt that Dr. Constantine Zervas was one of those who hadn't made the discovery yet. "I'm not infallible when it comes to knowing everything about a human being—and I am one. I've been studying that specific organism for decades, and I'm continually surprised at the results of about four billion years of evolution. Now I've had the chance to to a quick survey of two alien organisms—Awesomes and Mantids—with an unknown number of billions of years in the making. And I don't know anything about the conditions under which that evolution took place. I *do* know one thing about the Awesomes and Mantids: Their physiology is different."

"I thought you told me that your analysis of their DNA showed very little difference," Zeke remarked.

"Well, it looks like DNA is DNA, no matter where you find it. But we don't know all the answers there yet, either. It may just be the common corkscrew of life, or maybe just in our corner of the galaxy. Ask me in a couple of hundred years or so, XO."

"So you're telling us we may be in for some surprises?"

"XO, medicine and biotechnology are full of surprises. Can you stand there and tell me that the universe itself isn't?"

"I think we're looking at one aspect of that." Braxton indicated the dead Mantid being dissected in the closed room.

"I trust you're taking what you consider to be prudent measures to keep poisons and unknown diseases from spreading from the sick bay?" Corry asked almost rhetorically. He knew his Medical Officer would and that the sick bay operated with its own isolated environmental control system for just that reason. An epidemic in a submarine could be a disaster.

"Everything I know how to do," Moore admitted. "Complete washdown before leaving the autopsy room, for example. Makes Zervas unhappy. But when he's outside that room, he's on my turf and I make the rules. If he wants to work without gloves, cap, and gown, that's his prerogative. But my team gives him a going-over when he comes out. So he stays in there and works as long as he can at a stretch. He's sort of nonsocial anyway."

Zeke knew that this last would bother Laura Raye Moore a little bit, because she was indeed one of the most social officers in the boat. The XO had noticed that Moore and Zervas tended to treat one another with only expected professional protocol.

"Sounds like he's obsessed," Zeke observed.

"He is. He wants to become the world's expert on extraterrestrial life forms. Good luck to him. If Soucek is right and there are seventy-one different known alien species out there, Doctor Zervas will maybe be top gun on two of them. Otherwise, he'll never make it. But he has the testicular fortitude to try, at any rate, and I'll have to give him credit for that. I've got my hands full trying to learn enough about human beings."

"You were certainly fascinated by the Awesomes, Doctor," Zeke reminded her.

"I wouldn't be much of a doctor if I wasn't. I figured maybe I'd learn something I could apply to humans. But, XO, I never became obsessed with it."

"You're right. You didn't. Your job as Medical Officer comes first, and that's why you're here," Corry reminded her. "Keep up the sterility protocol, Doctor. Let me know if Zervas gives you any trouble with it."

"Oh, he won't, Captain. We came to our little agreement about that a few days ago when we first brought the Mantids to *my* sick bay. Or was it last month? Or yesterday? Time slips away when you've been unconscious with a concussion."

In another sick bay passageway, two armed Marine guards came to attention as the Captain and his party approached. Dr. Evelyn Lulalilo was seated in the passageway. She held a little hand transceiver and was apparently talking to the two Mantids, who were in individual compartments sealed by the transparent polycarbonate doors as strong as steel.

Eve Lulalilo looked up and smiled briefly. "Good afternoon, Captain."

"Are you improving your ability to talk with them?" Corry asked.

"Oh, yes! I'd forgotten a lot of Pidgin English, and they've taught me even more," the marine biologist replied. "Both Drek an Merhad learned a somewhat different dialect from the Solomon Islanders. They often talked at length with their victims before they ... processed them." This last was said with obvious distaste. Eve Lulalilo was extremely upset with the knowledge that the Mantids were on Earth to obtain human biochemicals and certain human tissues. They said they needed them because the radiation from a supernova explosion near their home world had caused irreparable damage to their germ plasm. Unfortunately, the Mantids weren't brilliant biochemists and couldn't synthesize those human biochemicals and tissues. They kept harvesting humans on Earth, usually removing gonadal and colonic tissues without killing their victims first. They had tried to explain to Eve that dead tissues weren't exactly the same, but they didn't know why.

If that particular aspect of the Mantids' behavior wasn't repulsive enough, their appearance certainly was. A Mantid was about two meters tall when it stood. It had three main body parts, like a giant insect—head, thorax, and main body. Although it was covered with some sort of clothlike taut tan spandex, its skin was a lustrous brown like a roach. It had two multijointed "arms" ending in "hands" with opposing digits. These sprouted from the thorax along with its four multijointed legs. Breathing apparently took place through an orifice in the upper thorax. The head had only two eyes with nictitating transparent eyelids.

It wasn't a pretty alien and couldn't possibly have been turned into a cute one for kiddy-viddy shows.

Corry considered both Mantids to be repulsive in appearance in addition to being unspeakable in the way they hunted and butchered humans.

And he wasn't about to give them quarter of any sort. He would deliver them to Naval Intelligence at Palmyra—he hoped. Then he looked forward to being rid of aliens for a while.

William M. Corry was as much of an explorer as most naval officers and certainly wanted to be part of the continuing naval tradition of exploration. But, as far as he was concerned, Naval Intelligence or not, playing around with extraterrestrials was something for the Aerospace Force, not for the United States Navy, an organization that had specific roles and missions regarding sea control. Fanatical interest in UFOs was not something that befit a serious Navy career officer. *He* knew that the UFOs were real and that extraterrestrials existed, and in a way he was proud of his role in the situation as it had evolved. However, he, his command, or the United States Navy might be open to censure and ridicule because of it. The conflict of belief between exploring the unknown—which this certainly was—and carrying out his duties as a naval officer was a situation he was having a little trouble resolving for himself at the moment.

But he didn't have to resolve that conflict immediately.

"Captain, they won't eat," Eve said, drawing his attention back to the present situation.

"They don't look like they're starving," Corry observed.

"But they haven't eaten anything we've put in there since we recaptured them on the hangar deck." Eve sounded distressed.

"How often do the Mantids eat?" Zeke asked.

"I don't know."

"Ask them," Corry suggested.

"I did. They said they eat whenever they feel like it."

"So they probably don't feel like eating," Zeke suggested.

"No, they say they're hungry. Here, let me ask them." Eve picked up the little transceiver that would convey her voice into both of the detention compartments. "Eufala Drek, warem nao somting fo kaikaim?"

The breathy, hissing voice of one of the Mantids came back, "Ya, tanggio. Mifla laek somting for kaikaim. Mifala an Merhad laek somting fo kaikaim destaem noa."

"Warem nao? Eufala an Merhad garem kaikaim. Eufala an Merhad no laekem kaikaim iutufala garem."

It sounded like English to Corry, and yet the inflections and pronunciations were strange. It was Pidgin English, the "bastard language" of the South Pacific and China, a combination of inflected English words and Melanesian grammar. Eve was good at speaking it. She had grown up in Hawaii, where it was still spoken a little on the smaller islands.

"Captain," she explained after a long exchange, "they want to eat together. It's part of their lifestyle. They also want to be isolated when they eat. Apparently, no Mantid eats publicly. They consider it as private as we consider going to the bathroom."

"Well, they certainly don't treat urinating or defecating as a private act," Laura Raye Moore put in. "They're like animals. They do it anywhere and in public."

"And we eat in public, which offends them," Eve said. "As for their hygienic behavior, we certainly haven't given them private toilet facilities, Doctor."

"Well, you're right about that. I can put them in a detention room that has a private bath," Moore decided.

"And I'd put them together. I believe Drek and Merhad are mates. I think that Mantid mates eat together. After all, how would we feel if we were captured by them and kept in separate cells? Especially if we were married?" Eve Lulalilo was a very caring, empathetic person, even when faced with a pair of hostile aliens.

"According to Allan Soucek, humans captured by Mantids are treated like you might treat a lab mouse," Moore corrected her.

"Yes, but the Mantids are intelligent beings, although they look like big insects. They should be treated better than mere laboratory animals. Shouldn't we do unto others as we would have them do unto us?" Eve paraphrased the Golden Rule. "Shouldn't we treat them well? Maybe no one has! Maybe they're reacting to the way humans have treated them!"

"Doctor Moore, you may place these two Mantids in the same detention compartment," Corry told his Medical Officer. He didn't want to make things difficult for Eve. After all, she was learning far more about the Mantids by talking with them than Zervas was by cutting up a dead one.

"They are to remain under guard. And if they wish privacy during meals, pull a screen down over that polycarbonate door. And, Doctor Lulalilo, you are *not* to go into the detention compartment with those Mantids. Is that understood?"

"Captain, I'm a scientist, and if I feel it necessary to go in there to improve communication with those Mantids, I'll do it," she told him petulantly.

Corry cared for Eve Lulalilo. She not only reminded him of his daughter but she had an unsophisticated outlook that was often refreshing, especially during this difficult cruise. He was responsible for her welfare just as much as for that of any official member of the crew. He had had experience raising children, one of whom was like Eve in appearance and, to some degree, free-living temperament. Unconsciously, he acted again like a father and repeated, "Doctor Lulalilo, the Marine guards will *prevent* you from going in there. And if I get a report that you've attempted it, I'll confine you to quarters until we get to Palmyra and you are no longer in this boat and my responsibility. I repeat: You will *not* go in the detention compartment with the Mantids. And I ask you again: Do you understand that order?"

"I understand it, Captain." But she sounded like she didn't want to. She might be a disciplined scientific thinker in her specialty of marine biology, but she was undisciplined otherwise.

"Chief," Corry told his COB, "please post a woman police petty officer here with the Marine guard detail. I don't want any harassment charges later."

"Aye, aye, sir!"

Eve decided not to press the matter further right then. But she wasn't going to give up. She'd decided she'd do almost anything and take almost any risk to satisfy her scientific curiosity. In the Mantids, she'd found a nonhuman species with whom she could communicate. That burning desire had been the driver of her career. As she'd told Corry, she hoped she could learn something from another species that would help humans be less violent.

As the walkaround group left sick bay, Zeke ventured to suggest, "Captain, I think we've got trouble there in spite of your orders and Laura Raye's insistence on sterile conditions for the autopsy."

"Zeke, we've got trouble with the whole special team,"

Corry told him again. "They have no blue-water experience, much less any knowledge of how to get along in a carrier submarine."

"And an unwillingness to follow orders," Zeke added.

"Some of them have learned, XO. The ones who haven't will continue to be troublesome. Dealing with them in a kind and fair manner consistent with the safety of everyone aboard hasn't been the easiest command task I've ever faced."

"Captain, speaking for the crew, which I do," Chief Armstrong put in, "your treatment of the special team has caused absolutely no heartburn among the crew. Some of them wish you were a bit more strict. But I think you've handled it very well, sir."

"Chief, I guess we're going to find out eventually."

7

"You look more concerned than when we started this walkaround, Captain," Zeke observed as they strode forward to the sensors compartments toward the bow.

It was a long walk, but Corry knew he needed the exercise. Several times, they encountered crew members jogging through the passageways. Maintaining personal fitness was difficult in a carrier submarine, where modern machinery did nearly all of the heavy work. The various gyms aboard were always busy. Corry didn't favor mandatory exercise. He left it up to his division officers to run the fitness programs for their specific groups, because the physical demands on the personnel of the Ship Division, the Air Group, and the Marine battalion were different. Bart did it the Marine way, of course, with formal drills and calisthenics. The people in the Air Group preferred martial arts, while Zeke, as head of the Ship Division as well as XO, had adopted Corry's philosophy: Keep yourself as fit as you can, because your physical condition will affect your performance; if your performance deteriorates and the Medical Officer believes it's the result of lack of personal fitness, you'll be serving elsewhere after the cruise is over.

"In a way I am, XO," Corry admitted. "We find ourselves in the sort of multithreat environment we've experienced ever since this whole extraterrestrial affair began off Makasar. All the war games and exercises we've been through in the simulators ashore trained us to handle only dual threats and, on rare occasions, triple threats."

"Captain, I used to work on sims," Chief Armstrong recalled. "Sims can handle only two simultaneous threats. Sure, the sim technology exists to present multiple threats. But the big problem is the programming. Developing realistic multithreat scenarios isn't easy. Getting them to run so they're believable takes real genius. Frankly, sir, some of the science fiction I read off-watch does a better job of it than the Software Sammys."

"Depends on the author," Corry pointed out. "Some of them can't even handle a single-threat plotline."

"Well, we aren't expected to find ourselves in such multithreat situations," Zeke said.

Corry didn't believe this. "No, XO, that's not it. We're not supposed to *get* ourselves into such situations in the first place. Unfortunately, it happens."

"Like right at the moment," Zeke added. "Here we are with an extraterrestrial craft aboard with unknown technology; some of that technology could be toxic or even explosive if not handled right, because we're dealing with a lot of stored energy there. We've got live and dead extraterrestrial entities aboard, and we don't know if they carry toxins or diseases. The third threat may or may not materialize: other Mantids hunting us down in order to rescue their comrades and aircraft. An allied threat may exist because of Soucek's contention that seventy-some other alien species exist and have visited Earth. Three threats, all of them serious or possibly serious."

"You forget yet another one, XO," Corry reminded him. "We only touched it in the Solomon Sea. We face a possible East World threat, primarily Chinese and Indian submarines; I think we can handle that, because we have superior sensor suites and can see them when they can't see us. In fact, the balloon could go up in Asia at any moment, and we could find ourselves involved in something more than a regional war when we surface."

"Well, sir, we haven't received an SWC message telling us of a change in that situation," Zeke reminded his commanding officer.

"If it happened in the last twenty-four hours, sir," Chief Armstrong ventured to guess, "it may be that we're small potatoes, so to speak. In other words, CINCPAC may be busy as hell. They may not have had time to get around to sending us an SWC message. Or maybe CINCPAC wants to leave us hidden as a hole card."

"Yeah, Chief, when we're on the surface we're spoiled because we're used to instant worldwide communications in a wired world," Zeke said.

"And there's yet another threat, Chief," Corry pointed

out. "And it may be the biggest one. Interservice rivalry always has been, even in the midst of the big general wars of the last century."

"From what Commander Smith tells me," Zeke put in, surprising no one that he had talked to the Naval Intelligence officer about this, probably in private, "Naval Intelligence is playing spook games with the Aerospace Force and even the CIA. We may be the critical piece in that chess game. And I don't know what to tell you to expect, Captain."

Corry sighed. "XO, I have to believe the Navy will protect its own, but that's beyond our control. The people in the Pentagon have the modern computerized version of the ultimate weapon."

"Sir?" Zeke queried.

"I allude to a photo or a piece of art I once saw on the cover of an old science fiction magazine," Corry explained. "It was called 'The Ultimate Weapon.' It showed a museum exhibit of weapons including the stone ax, the gladius, the crossbow, the personal firearm, and even a suitcase nuke. These were arranged in order of lethality. The final weapon in the display was an old-time file folder. . . ."

They walked through a door into a light lock that prevented the low-level passageway illumination from seeping into the sensors department. The police petty officer third sitting next to the inner door rose from his chair. "Good afternoon, Captain! Good afternoon, XO! Good afternoon, Chief!" He was being extra-cautious with the protocol.

"As you were, sailor," Corry told him easily.

"Glad to see you're maintaining security access procedures," Zeke added. Not everyone in the ship was cleared to enter the compartment with the still-secret WSS-1 mass detector, the masdet that could sense the presence of external objects because of their mass. Everyone in the boat knew the masdet was aboard, but no one really knew how it worked. This included Corry. But he really didn't need to know how the masdet functioned; he was only interested in its capabilities. Those were good enough that the masdet had made the difference off Makasar as well as in the Solomon Sea.

"Dane, relax," Chief Armstrong told him. "You passed

your tests. You'll make E-five okay. I've seen the paperwork."

"Thanks for telling me, Chief. The wife can always find a way to spend the extra pay." The petty officer checked a hand-held terminal. "All three of you are cleared for access, sirs. Shall I let Commander Lovette know you're here?"

"If you wish. This is just an informal walkaround, not a pop inspection, sailor," Zeke told him.

"Sir, anytime the Captain comes around, we treat it as an inspection and we're ready for it."

"I commend that attitude. Keep it up," Corry complimented him.

LTJG Barbara Brewer was the duty officer at the moment. She met them as they came through the inner door of the light lock. "Anything special you want to see, sirs?"

"No, Lieutenant Brewer, just a how-goes-it," Corry remarked.

"But you can keep us from bumping into things until our eyes adapt," Zeke said. The multicompartmented section of the boat devoted to the operation and monitoring of the various sensors—sonar, radar, lidar, and the masdet—had a very low light level to allow the sensor operators to see every small detail on their respective screens. Although computers looked for anomalies in signals and could actually pull a usable sensor signal out of what appeared to be white noise, the ultimate sensor was the human eye coupled to the brain behind it. Artificial intelligence—Zeke considered that to be an oxymoron—could do a lot, but it lacked the capability of judgment. And since AI was the servant of human beings trained and experienced to exercise judgment, its development hadn't been pushed far in that direction by the United States Navy. Admirals who had come up through sea command knew the inherent shortcomings of technology and preferred to rely on educated officers and well-trained rates. This caused some of the far-out techie types ashore to consider the United States Navy to be hopelessly antiquated. That was far from the truth, because the Navy had achieved a far better balance in the human-machine interface than any of the other services, including the Aerospace Force.

"Welcome to the realm of the night owls," Brewer commented, using the nickname the sensors people had given themselves.

"Or the country of the blind," Zeke added.

"Sir, you'd better hope we aren't," she responded. "If we're blind, so is the rest of the boat." She was right, of course. Without the sensor suites, Corry and the rest of the crew would have no data from outside the composite bulkheads in the ocean beyond.

Radar and lidar units weren't searching, because the boat was submerged, but they were operated in standby mode ready to work the instant the boat broached the surface. Thus, they were minimally manned but not functional.

Sonar was different. A full complement of operators was on duty. The *Shenandoah* wasn't pinging in active sonar mode, but sonar operators were listening to the sounds of the ocean around them. Corry could see the sonar tracks of skunks, unknown surface ships that were the merchantmen and cargo ships plying the ocean routes above. Most of the world's commerce still traveled by water, because it was most economical to operate on what was known as a "constant gravitational surface." Subsonic air and fractional orbital transportation were used only when transit times were a factor. A lot more commerce went through and above the atmosphere above the Pacific Ocean because of the distances involved.

Every sonar track had been identified by computer analysis on the basis of hull turbulence and propulsion signatures.

No submarines showed up on the master sonar display. This didn't cause Corry to stop worrying about it, however. Some submarines were very noisy. But many of the new Chinese boats were nearly as silent as the *Shenandoah*. They would have no sonar track because sonar couldn't hear them.

"Anything worrisome out there, Mister Goff?" Corry asked the Sonar Officer.

Goff looked up and took off his earphones. "No, sir. A lot of fish and dolphin sounds. A few whales. We're picking up some Chinese submarine activity back in the Solomon Islands area. Those were tracks we'd identified and were following even while we were in the Solomon Sea." He paused and then indicated an intermittent series of weak signals generally all around the boat. "We just began picking up some very weak signals out at the limit of our noise reduction capability. Could be some East World submarine sounds. Or maybe nothing more than whales flatulating."

"Keep an ear and an eye on those, please, Mister Goff."

"Aye, aye, sir! As always."

LTJG Ralph Strader, the Intelligence Officer, was in the masdet compartment with LT Charles Ames, the Special Sensor Officer.

"We're picking up some signals that appear to be surface ships departing the naval exercise area around Kwajalein, sir," Strader reported when Corry asked him for a how-goes-it report. "My best guess says they're Navy surface ships. Two of them."

"Captain, they appear to be heading back to Pearl or to Palmyra," Ames added. "We'll have a better-integrated plot in an hour or so. But I agree with Strader. I'd tag them friendlies, because no surface ships should be in the Kwajalein region unless they're ours."

"Anything else?" Zeke asked.

"Yes, sir. Looks like surface and submarine activity around Hawaii. Might be coming out of Pearl. Again, could be ours. Probably is," Ames told him.

"Do you see anything in the vicinity of Palmyra?" Corry wanted to know.

"Negatory, sir."

"Anything in the air?" Corry knew that Ames had worked out a means, using some of the software from Radar and Sonar, to spot mass targets above their air-water interface. The masdet was supposed to be able to do that. However, Ames was one smart techie. He'd seen some masdet signals in the Solomon area—they later turned out to be Corona and *Tuscarora* alien aircraft—and proceeded to make a lash-up that gave Corry an additional masdet capability of air detection.

"I can't see as far above the surface as I can under water, sir," Ames admitted. "The best answer I can give you is that I don't know."

"Sir, what's that smudgy target off the starboard bow?" Chief Armstrong asked, indicating a signal on the masdet display.

"Chief, I don't know. We're watching it. It isn't closing.

In fact, it doesn't look like it's moving at all. No threat yet."

"Maybe the *Tuscarora* again?" Zeke guessed.

"It doesn't have that 'feel,' sir. But the signal is too weak to make that call. I'm trying to get a better signal-to-noise ratio on it. Right now, I don't have the computer power to hack it."

"Lieutenant, would it help to access Holland?" Armstrong asked, referring to the boat's big master mainframe.

"Chief, I don't have the authority to make that patch."

"Charlie, you can get that authority at any time by asking the XO or me," Corry stated, addressing him familiarly by his first name in an attempt to break through Ames' introverted personality. He knew that Ames was primarily a techie and not a blue-water sailor. In fact, the *Shenandoah* was the first oceangoing ship Ames had ever served in. He was still reluctant to approach the Captain, primarily because he stood in awe of the ultimate authority of CAPT William M. Corry. "If you want it, ask."

"Now, sir?"

"Now, Charlie."

"Yes, sir. Uh, I'd like to patch into Holland, sir. I'll need—uh—a few thousand gigabytes, if that's not too much."

"Permission granted. Do it. Let me know the results. Charlie, we need to know what's out there and what may be waiting for us at Palmyra. We're counting on you."

"Yes, sir. I'll do my best, sir. I'll put it up on the bridge masdet displays. And I'll report to you verbally the instant I have something, sir."

Back on the bridge, which wasn't far from the sensors compartments, Corry and Zeke went through the usual protocol of the Commanding Officer arriving on the bridge and declining to take the conn from the OOD.

Corry slid into the captain's chair behind the main conn console, and Zeke did likewise beside him. Chief Armstrong took his own position and began making arrangements for the female police petty officer to be on duty with the Marines outside the Mantid detention quarters in sick bay.

"Back in the saddle again," Zeke quipped.

"Not really, XO. There is no need for me to assume the conn. The boat is running smoothly," Corry observed. "As you know, there are times when I just want to sit and watch."

"Thinking again, sir?"

"Yes. And to anticipate your next question, I'm trying to sort out all the options that might become available when we get to Palmyra."

"I don't see that it's going to be such a big thing, Captain."

"With the possibility of five conflicts facing us? Maybe two or three at a time?"

"The multiple threat scenario again."

"More than that. And it won't be war game in a sim. I wish I had more data."

Zeke smiled. "Captain, with all due respect, you taught me not to worry about making a decision when inadequate data existed and no clear decision path was available. I've been told I shouldn't make a decision under such circumstances. If a commander waits until more data come in, suddenly the decision usually becomes obvious."

Corry didn't answer for a moment. Then he said, "You may have something there, XO. Perhaps I've been fretting because of the unusual nature of this operation."

"It's been a difficult cruise, Captain."

"Yes. However, having inadequate data doesn't mean that one shouldn't think through some of the scenarios to reach either a stuck point or a possible decision point." He was aware of the tensions tearing at him. However, he considered that to be part of command.

He didn't have time to ruminate on it further. LCDR Mark Walton, the First Lieutenant, stepped up and addressed Corry. "Sir, I've got a problem."

"And it's something the XO can't solve, Mister Walton?"

"Yes, sir."

"Then you'd better tell me about it."

"Sir, I spoke with Commander Lovette, and it didn't do any good," Walton went on. He turned briefly and waved his hand around the bridge. "I wanted Mister Ames to clean up this clutter of cabling and display units that he created when he installed those extra masdet monitoring screens and displays back in the Solomon Sea at your order. Bob checked with Ames. Ames says he doesn't have time or the personnel to tidy up his installation right now."

"And . . . ?" Corry prodded him.

"Uh, Bob didn't want to countermand your order to Ames to install this lash-up in here in the first place."

"Is that it, Mister Walton?"

"Uh, yes, sir."

"And you want me to order Mister Ames to clean it up?"

"Yes, sir."

Corry thought about this for a moment, then told his First Lieutenant, "Mark, what problems are being caused by the masdet display lash-up?"

"Well, sir, we're afraid to touch the stuff. It's sort of strange, sir, and it hasn't got any hard copy documentation. So we don't know what we could do to it or what it could do to us. If we trip over some of the cabling, we might cause it to go tits-up."

When Walton paused, Corry asked, "Is that all?"

The Captain's response startled Walton. He hadn't been expecting it. "Well, it's only part of it, sir. It's made a mess of the bridge. We've got all we can do running this boat from here without a lot of extraneous gear screwing up the carefully designed human-machine interfaces."

Corry knew that Walton was an Academy man who was fussy about his appearance (as was Corry, but for different reasons). The First Lieutenant also ran a spit-and-polish department with everything in its place. Walton took his duties and responsibilities very seriously, almost to the point of obsession. He was a regulation officer. He ran by the book. As a result, he was ultradependable. This was a fine trait for the First Lieutenant of a boat as large and complex as the U.S.S. *Shenandoah*.

When Corry didn't respond, Walton continued his attempt to justify his position. "Captain, a lot of work went into designing this bridge for the best human factors performance possible. We've gotten used to it without all this junk in the way."

Corry could have told his First Lieutenant to take slack or even to stuff it. But that wasn't the way Corry led his people. Without a word, he looked at one of the screens in the desktop before him and began to enter commands into the keypad. When he found what he was looking for, he projected it on one of the big bridge screens. "Mister Walton, would you please look at what I've asked Holland to display?"

No one on the bridge could keep from seeing it.

Corry had accessed the ship's computer and called up an old photograph of the control room of the German U-boat U-505, still on display in Chicago. "Mister Walton," Corry told him, "the crew of that boat did their duty with that sort of control room to work in. They sank more than twenty-six thousand tons of shipping. The only computer they had in the boat was the torpedo data computer there on the left. It was a mechanical analog calculator. Now, I don't intend to allow anyone to turn this bridge into that sort of a mish-mash of controls, instruments, cables, and such. However, if those submariners could operate and fight a boat under those conditions, even given that they took more time to learn how to do it, do you think you could put up with Mister Ames' rat's nest for a few more days until we get to Pearl and can have it tidied up? After all, it does provide us with additional sensor data. And we never have enough of that in a submarine anyway."

Walton knew when he was being gracefully put down. "Sir, I was merely trying to shape up the bridge before someone called me down about it for being non-reg. We've sailed the boat this way for days. And we've fought the boat pretty well when we had to. So the Deck Department will carry on as before, sir." He paused. "Sir, I'm sorry I brought it up. It wasn't thoughtful of me to burden you with additional decisions at this time."

"I would have bilged you if you hadn't brought to my attention what you considered to be an incorrect situation, Mark. You might want to consider doing it privately the next time instead of on the bridge. There was no way I could respond except in front of other personnel here."

Walton knew that he'd done it wrong, and he also knew that Corry had apologized in an oblique way for doing what he'd had to do in front of others.

"Steady as she goes, everyone," Corry cautioned. "Another day and we'll find out what's really going on at Palmyra."

But that was not to be the case.

8

William Corry recalled that he always dreamed most vividly just before he awoke. And this was again proving to be the case. In his dream, he was again courting his wife, Cynthia, in Hawaii during his first tour after getting his wings at Pensacola. It was a vivid dream, but it didn't make much sense. Cynthia kept metamorphosing into his daughter, Judy, when she was a teen. Finally—and this was extremely disturbing to Corry even in his dream—Cynthia/Judy became Dr. Evelyn Lulalilo.

In his dream, he said to the apparition, "You're all the same! How can you be all the same? You're different people!"

And the reply was also disturbing: "To you, we're the same."

The combined dream character Cynthia/Judy/Eve was in trouble of some sort. They were threatened by something, and no one knew what it was. Corry frantically searched for some way to eliminate the threat using the U.S.S. *Shenandoah*. But the submarine was such a big boat that it couldn't be maneuvered to assault the threat.

Corry awoke in a sweat when the sleep alarm went off at 0600, ship time.

He was almost relieved to be awake.

Once he'd hit the deck and started to shave, he banished the dream from his mind. He had other, real problems to worry about. And a Commanding Officer *always* has something to worry about.

The intercom chimed. "Go ahead," he called out.

"Breakfast, sir," came the voice of the chief steward.

"Bring it in."

Corry didn't wear the blue submariner's poopie suit as the rest of the crew did. He donned khaki slacks and was pulling on his khaki shirt when the door annunciator signaled. "Come!" he called out almost automatically.

Dr. Evelyn Lulalilo walked in carrying a tray with two breakfast servings on it.

This caught Corry completely by surprise, and he almost lost his temper. But he got control of himself because, in private, he couldn't bring himself to reprimand her for what was obviously an act of friendship and a desire for companionship. "Eve, you should have told me you wanted to have breakfast with me."

"I thought you'd be pleased," she replied, setting the tray on the little table.

He quickly tucked in his shirttail and reached for his black necktie. "I am pleased, but I'd like a little more warning next time," he told her. "I don't like others to see me un-un-un-undressed." He was sufficiently flustered that he slipped into stuttering.

She looked at him as he clipped the necktie in place and secured it. "Captain, you certainly look dressed to me."

"I am now. Sixty seconds ago, I wasn't. And I'm barely presentable now."

"You are certainly a most proper gentleman, Captain William Corry," Eve said as she sat down. "You would never cause a lady embarrassment. And as a Commanding Officer, I think you're outstanding. But I believe you're too shy around your crew."

"Not shy, Eve. I'm an example. I don't want the crew to see their captain in anything but the proper uniform." He came over to the table and sat down opposite her. "Besides, I believe you're biased in your assessment of the Commanding Officer."

"Don't belittle yourself, Captain. And, incidentally, you are also a very good friend."

"Thank you. I think you should know that I could never be this familiar with any of my crew members, although Commander Braxton and I often share a meal together. Sometimes we have ship's business to talk about."

"Do you ever take a meal with someone for other than business purposes?"

"Commander Braxton and I do on occasion." He paused. "Eve, I think I've told you before, but let me remind you. Command is lonely. It has power and satisfaction, but it's lonely. I can treat you differently from members of the crew. Witness this breakfast together. But even then I must be careful. Rumors get started with far less information."

"No rumors about us are circulating."

"Perhaps you haven't heard them because you might be involved."

She shook her head. "I may be a scientist, Captain, but I don't live in a separate world. Incidentally, that's one reason I wanted to share breakfast with you. I know you're under a lot of pressure, and a brief respite often helps. However, I also wanted to apologize."

"Apologize? For what, Eve?" Corry knew what she meant, but he wanted her to do it her way. He wanted to give her the opportunity to clear her own conscience rather than have him dismiss the incident as trivial.

"For behaving as I did yesterday in sick bay," she told him. "Captain, I was educated as a scientist, and a scientist absolutely rebels against any restriction that will prevent the acquisition of information or the testing of a hypothesis."

"I have a son who decided to be a research psychobiologist. I know what you mean, Eve." His son, Lee, had always rebelled against limits. That had led the young man into the most dangerous and speculative of all the emerging sciences in the twenty-first century. Delving deep into epistemology and the workings of the mind had caused scientific endeavor to come full circle; those in the emerging sciences had again become natural philosophers. Bill Corry was proud that his son had chosen such a life path, but disappointed that the Navy Corrys would continue only through his daughter, Judy.

"Really? I didn't know that. Well, certainly the psychobiologists are pushing the limits of knowledge . . . and public acceptance of their procedures," Eve replied. Corry didn't interrupt her, nor did he look directly at her. When a person was frightened or embarrassed, he never looked directly at him or her. He had to let her talk it out for herself almost as if she were alone. Otherwise, Corry knew from experience, a person would lose self-respect, and that could be even more devastating than fear or humiliation. "Almost like the biotechnicians of the last century. And the physicists before them. At any rate, I'm sorry I behaved as I did. It was foolish of me, especially in a submarine with alien beings and technology aboard. I guess I should be more cautious, because I'm dealing with the unknown."

"Yes, I think you should, Eve. Never approach the unknown carelessly. Our remote ancestors learned that. Those who didn't are not our ancestors."

"Ah, yes, evolution in action. And I understand why your son went into psychobiology. He gets his philosophical bent from his father."

Corry shrugged. "That may be. I certainly couldn't teach him discipline."

"Yes, my own experience yesterday revealed that you are indeed a disciplinarian, Captain. You must have been a very good father."

"It's too early yet to tell. And I'm still a father."

"Yes, you are. I've heard that the crew has a song: 'The Captain Is the Father of His Crew,' I believe it's called."

"It's known as a 'lower deck ditty,' and it's not sung in the presence of the Commanding Officer, Eve. However, I once sang it when I was a junior officer. It has double meaning."

"Even with Regulation Twenty-twenty?"

"No, in spite of it." He noticed that she hadn't finished her breakfast. When he looked at her, he saw that her face was somewhat flushed. "Something wrong with the breakfast, Eve? Are you feeling well?"

"Just a little flush and a chill," she revealed. "I got cold last night in my stateroom. Commander Smith didn't come in at all, and I think the heat balance of the room was off as a result of one less body being there. I'm really not yet used to spending all my time in air conditioning."

Corry knew that women often had different thermostatic swings from men. Cynthia often complained about being either too hot or too cold. He often thought that women must have evolved on another planet, one that was warmer or colder, but certainly one with somewhat lower surface gravity. However, in this circumstance, he didn't want to assume it was only womanly whim. He took his napkin out of his lap and placed it unfolded on the table. "Eve, I want you to go see Doctor Moore in sick bay at once."

"Captain, this is no more unusual than an occasional bad menses," she tried to explain.

"I'm not sure about that. You've been in very close contact with the Mantids."

"Not after you had them put behind those transparent doors, Captain."

"As I said, you've been in close and almost constant contact with the Mantids for almost two days now. No one knows what pathogenic organisms they may carry that are benign to them and deadly to us."

Eve sighed. "Captain, if Soucek is right, the Mantids spent months, maybe years, with humans in the last century."

"And we don't know the full story of what happened. Did you ever think that the problem that arose in the Dulce lab might have been caused by Mantid-borne organisms?"

"No, because the humans in that lab were supposed to be top biotechnologists."

"Think back at the level of biotechnological knowledge in the middle of the last century."

"Uh, yes, we didn't know very much, did we?"

"I don't want you to apologize again to me for resisting an order," Corry told her, "although it led to a pleasant meal. I want you to go down to sick bay at once and tell Doctor Moore of your flush and chills."

Eve tried to smile. It was now obvious that she didn't feel well. "Is that an order, Captain?"

"Yes, Eve, that's an order. A fatherly order, if you will. But do it. Not only am I concerned about your welfare, but I can't take the chance of an unknown disease getting loose in this carrier submarine. That's one reason we have a Medical Officer and a fully staffed sick bay aboard. AIDS and the owl plague in the last century taught us that even terrestrial organisms can mutate into some very nasty forms."

Eve remained seated. So Corry prompted her: "Well?"

"In a minute. I just had another chill."

Corry rose to his feet. Eve tried to do likewise, got partway there, and suddenly collapsed. There wasn't a lot of room for her to fall freely to the floor because of the cramped dimensions of even the Captain's cabin. She knocked her chair sideways as she fell.

When Corry got to her, she was unconscious. As he lifted her in his arms to place her on the still-unmade bunk, he felt that she was hot. She had a raging fever.

"Intercom! Officer of the Deck! This is the Captain!" Corry called out, his first word activating the voice-command auto-transmit circuit of the intercom unit. It had been keyed to his voiceprint and that signal word.

"Officer of the Deck here! Lieutenant Kilmer on deck! Go ahead, sir."

"Medical orderly team with litter to the captain's cabin immediately! Alert the Medical Officer and the sick bay!"

Eve was still unconscious when the orderlies brought her into sick bay. Corry accompanied them, because he needed to report to Laura Raye Moore about the sudden onset of the fever.

He was surprised when the Medical Officer didn't greet them. Chief Pharmacist Mate Nat Post logged Eve in with the terse comment "Another one."

"What do mean, another one, Chief?" Corry asked.

"Allan Soucek," was Post's comment. "Just brought him from his stateroom. He's running a fever of forty-one degrees and losing fluid out both ends. He's also delirious. Doctor Moore is trying to stabilize him. What happened here, Captain?"

"Doctor Lulalilo mentioned she was having alternate chills and fever symptoms," Corry explained.

Post was checking Eve over on the litter that had been placed up on a gurney. "So this was a sudden onset, sir?"

"Apparently, although I don't know exactly how feverish she felt. She tried to stand up and come down here. When she did, she collapsed."

"Did she become unconscious as she fell, sir?"

"Apparently."

Post checked the oral fever thermometer and shook his head. "Forty-one degrees Celsius! But no vomiting or diarrhea yet?"

"No."

"We'll prepare for it." Chief Post looked up at him. "Captain, she's in good hands now. Doctor Moore will report the diagnosis and prognosis to you. Will you be in your cabin?"

"Either there or on the bridge, Chief."

Dr. Constantine Zervas suddenly appeared in the door to the compartment. "Chief, why hasn't anyone answered my calls for help?"

"I haven't heard any calls for help from you, Doctor. Did you have your intercom turned on in the autopsy compartment?" Post didn't look up from where he was continuing his exam of Eve.

"Never mind! Jump to, sailor! Doctor Duval just collapsed on me, and he's vomited all over my Mantid cadaver in the process!" Zervas snapped in an imperious tone. "God, it's going to take hours and hours to clean it up, and he may have completely ruined the cadaver for decent tissue sampling!" He paused. "Oh. Good morning, Captain!" he suddenly said when he noticed that Corry was there.

Post looked up momentarily and called out to his orderly team, "Edwards! Sapin! Get into the autopsy room and bring out Doctor Duval!"

"Chief, I don't want you to send them in there," Corry suddenly put in. "I don't want to tell you how to run the sick bay, but I don't want those two orderlies to be exposed to whatever organisms may be in there. They might be contanminated in the process."

"Captain, they won't be any more contaminated than all of us," Post reminded him. "You've been in contact with Doctor Lulalilo. So have the orderlies. So have I. If Duval has the same illness, it isn't going to expose them further. If it's contagious, sir, we're all in for the same thing!"

"Is there anything we can do to prevent catching it?" Corry asked, knowing that he probably wouldn't get an answer.

He did. "Probably the best bet is to take two aspirin and call me if you get it! Good morning, Captain!" Dr. Laura Raye Moore swept into the compartment, her white coat stained with vomit. Having dispensed with protocol by greeting the Captain, she thence ignored him and asked, "Same thing, Posty?"

"Looks like it, Doctor. But no vomiting or diarrhea— yet."

"Doctor, do we have an epidemic brewing here?" Corry asked his Medical Officer.

She didn't look up. "Three cases don't make an epidemic, Captain. But I was serious when I told you to take two aspirin and call me if you get it. I honestly don't know the answer to your question. I don't know what hit these people. I'll find out. In the meantime, the best advice I can give you is to take a dose of the best analgesic and antipyretic I know of. It won't hurt you and it might help you."

"I'm serious, too, Doctor," Corry replied testily. "I need to know soonest if it looks like the presence of the Mantids is the cause of what could be an epidemic. In a submarine running submerged a long way from port and a base hospital, this is not a trivial matter!"

"I know it, sir! I don't have an answer for you at the moment."

"When can I anticipate one?"

"Captain, first I must stabilize these patients. Then we'll run some tests and scans to see if we can identify what's going on. It may be common. We know of many forms of fever and chills, and we can treat nearly all of them. Once we identify it, then we can treat it in these people. And I can then advise you concerning steps that should be taken to reduce the spread, provided it is communicable. Right now, I don't know. I don't have any answers. I've got three people who may die if I don't get their fevers down. And right now, sir, you're in the way! I'll let you know as soon as I know something!"

CDR Laura Raye Moore was indeed under pressure at the moment, Corry decided as her sharp reply snapped him back to reality. He was in the way because he wasn't contributing to the treatment of Eve. "Please do, Doctor," he remarked gently. "Do you have any objections if I alert the crew to these symptoms and tell them to report to sick bay at once if they experience them?"

"Please do that, Captain. It may get crowded here. I hope it doesn't."

Corry left sick bay and made his way back to the bridge.

"Commander Smith, XO, we have a problem," he confided in CDR Matilda Harriet Smith and Zeke Braxton. Carefully, he explained to the Naval Intelligence officer and his Executive Officer what had taken place in the last hour.

Zeke agreed. "Yes, sir, we do indeed have a problem. And I think a timely announcement to the crew is definitely in order."

"Is that wise, Captain?" Smith wondered.

"Why do you think it might be unwise, Smitty?"

"Announcing it may cause some of your crew members to develop sympathetic responses."

"What do you mean?"

"Captain, some people are closet hypochondriacs," she

explained to him. "Whether or not they really have whatever disease the members of my special team picked up, they may think they're experiencing the symptoms."

"Are you a medical specialist, Commander?" Corry asked bluntly.

"No, sir, but I once ran into a similar situation when I wintered over at the South Pole." She didn't elaborate. Nor would she have done so if asked. It had been a very black program and it had had nothing to do with the present situation with the Mantids.

"If it's common in isolated situations such as ours, then Laura Raye is probably expecting that," Corry surmised, not willing to second-guess his Medical Officer, who had suggested he make the announcement throughout the boat. Then he thought about what the Naval Intelligence officer had just said. "Commander, do you find it significant that only members of the special team have come down with this affliction?"

"No, sir."

"Zeke, what do you think? You've been unusually quiet."

Braxton shook his head. "I don't find significance here yet. We're dealing with a very small statistical universe, Captain. But it is unusual the none of the people of the boat have reported it yet."

"Yes. Now, what difference is there between the special team members and the crew of the U. S. S. *Shenandoah*?"

Zeke stifled a chuckle because Smith was present. Instead, he replied seriously, "Sir, they aren't blue-water sailors."

"I mean from the medical point of view, XO."

"We've all had our immunizations just as you have, sir," Smith pointed out. "At least, everyone was supposed to have gotten them. I was in a hurry, so they shot me full of stuff at the base hospital at Pearl."

"I was thinking about any pathogenic organisms the members of the special team might have brought aboard with them," Corry pointed out.

"Captain, if that had been the case, it would have shown up by now," Smith insisted. She wasn't trying to fob off anything that her special team might have done. She was seriously concerned and was trying her best to contribute to this command conference. "We've been aboard about a week now."

"That isn't a very long incubation period, Smitty," Zeke replied. "On the other hand, as you pointed out, only special team members have come down with the fever. Which might mean that only one of them was vectoring it."

"If so, why haven't crew members come down with it?" Corry repeated.

Zeke shrugged and threw up his hands in frustration. "Captain, I've been trained to deal with a physical enemy—the sea and other people. Disease is an enemy I don't know how to fight at all. That's why we rely on Laura Raye. She's our expert in that area just as Mister Goff is our sonar expert and Mister Ames is our masdet expert. And as Mister Brookstone is our expert in underwater frog work. I have to count on them. I don't know the answers. I wish I did. I'd feel better about it."

"So would I, XO. So would I," Corry muttered.

"What do we do now?" Smith asked.

"Well, our training as submarine officers has included the ability to sit and wait until something develops so we can take action," Zeke said.

"And that's just what we're going to have to do," Corry said decisively. "XO, how many hours to Palmyra?"

Zeke keyed the navigation display to come up on their screens. "At present speed, twenty-two hours and a butt, sir."

Corry thought about this for a moment, weighing all the factors. Then he said firmly, "I want to get to Palmyra as quickly as possible. Do either of you have any problem with that? Comments?"

"Sir, we were ordered not to arrive at Palmyra before tomorrow morning," Zeke reminded him.

"That order was received before I had the possibility of a shipboard epidemic on my hands," Corry said. He turned to the attractive intel officer. "Commander Smith, as the Naval Intelligence representative aboard, do you concur with this? After all, your shop is in overall command of the entire operations at this point. Do you have any insight about CINCPAC's requesting a specific arrival time at Palmyra?"

She thought about this for a moment, then shook her head. Carefully, choosing her words, she replied, "No, sir.

It could be that CINCPAC needed time to make sure that a tight defensive umbrella was over Palmyra. Or it could be due to the fact that Admiral McCarthy needed to get all her ducks lined up. I feel fairly certain she's going to take some flak from Aerospace Force intel, and maybe even CIA. They'll want in on this, and I suspect Admiral McCarthy isn't about to let them. She can be pretty feisty, particularly in the face of the fact that Aerospace Force has kept Navy cut out of UFO matters for a long time. Now Navy has the hot material. She may be using that as a lever on Aerospace Force. And, in anticipation of your question, Captain, no, I don't know why."

"I keep overlooking the interservice-rivalry aspect of this," Zeke admitted.

"It's more than a rivalry, Zeke," Corry pointed out, calling upon his knowledge of naval history. "It's been just short of open conflict ever since the Aerospace Force took on the Navy over the strategic bomber versus the aircraft carrier back in 1949. The so-called Revolt of the Admirals had long-range repercussions we're still living with."

"And still affecting our intel operations, I might add," Smith revealed. "Captain, why would you want to arrive at Palmyra early?"

"This unknown illness could get out of hand very quickly," Corry reminded them. "We don't know anything about it yet. Therefore, getting to Palmyra early gives me the option of being able to surface there if I have to declare a medical emergency. Then Terri can start air evac to Pearl for the serious cases if it comes to that. Or I can call on additional air support from CINCPAC."

Zeke nodded in agreement. "Good option, sir. We'll be under Hawaii's space defense umbrella there."

"You asked for my input, Captain, so I'll tell you I'm happy with your plan," Smith said, also nodding. "You won't have to surface unless things really get out of hand. If you don't have a medical emergency, you can remain submerged and wait for further orders as we were told to do."

"If we're fortunate, Commander. If we're fortunate. This may be something that's somehow confined to the special team for some reason," Corry said, expressing his innermost hopes.

They were immediately dashed.

"Captain, this is sick bay. Lieutenant Molders reporting!" came the call over the intercom.

"Captain here. Go ahead, Mister Molders."

"Sir, the Medical Officer asked me to report to you that Lieutenant Paul Peyton, the Flight Deck Officer, has just been brought into sick bay with the same high fever and other symptoms as the other three people. The Medical Officer will report to you as soon as she has a moment to do so. We're pretty busy down here right now, sir."

9

"First, I've got news. And then I've got news," CDR Laura Raye Moore stated flatly as she warmed her hands around a mug of coffee. She looked tired. Her morning had been filled trying to help four people suffering with raging fevers. She looked around the wardroom where CAPT William M. Corry had called a working lunch for his division and department officers and CPOs. "Sorry, Captain, but I can't differentiate between good news and bad news right now. If you asked me, I'd have to report bad news and worse news, I guess."

"Then we'll take what we can get, Doctor," Corry replied philosophically. "Please give us a full report."

"I'll skip the gory medical details, Captain, and try to talk straight English," Laura Raye suggested. "I hope we can stanch the rumors."

"That was the purpose of my short report to the crew on the boat's PA," Corry said.

"Captain, that helped. But when you did it two hours ago, I didn't know very much. I still don't. The lack of hard data always creates rumors."

"We've done our best to kill the scuttlebutt, but we couldn't stomp it all," Zeke admitted. "Submariners have very fertile imaginations when it comes to an unknown disease possibly loose in the boat."

"We damned well ought to load those Mantids back into the Corona, put a line on it, have it overboard, and tow it to Palmyra!" Major Bart Clinch muttered.

"At forty-five knots? Maybe you've got a line that will hold, but I don't!" Mark Walton told him.

"I didn't realize the boat had gone to maximum cruise speed," Clinch admitted.

"Well, it has, Bart," Terri Ellison snapped. "I'd like to get the Corona out of my hangar deck, too. Especially if it's a twenty-first-century Typhoid Mary. But we worked pretty damned hard to get that flying saucer and its crew in the first place. Lost one of my Sea Devils and dinged a few others in the process. Giving it the deep six is too high a price to pay for squashing a little scuttlebutt."

"Very well, we're going to stop the scuttlebutt for certain right now," Corry insisted. "The boat is in no danger at the moment. I intend to maintain that situation. Let's go through this as we normally handle a situation report. Then we'll Papa brief on an overall strategy. After that, I want each of you to report our conclusions and plan to your subordinates. Doctor Moore, you have the floor. Give us the full story as you understand it right now."

"As I said, Captain, I don't know how to evaluate this fever. I'll know more as time goes by and I begin to see some trends," the Medical Officer of the U.S.S. *Shenandoah* began. Laura Raye Moore was a doctor whose primary interest was to keep the people in the U.S.S. *Shenandoah* in good health. She was different from Dr. Constantine Zervas of Bethesda Naval Hospital, who'd come aboard as a member of the special team. Laura Raye didn't believe she was an omnipotent deity. She likened herself to an electronics technician or a machinist's mate whose responsibility was the maintenance and repair of the human body.

She immediately filled in the background of the situation for those who might have heard only rumors. "Doctor Evelyn Lulalilo and Allan Soucek of the special alien investigation team were brought to sick bay about oh-seven-hundred today. They were running very high fevers of unknown origin. Forty-one Celsius oral is what is known as a hyperthermic FUO—fever of unknown origin. Another one to two degrees is lethal. At forty-two to forty-three degrees Celsius, the colloidal structure of our organic semiconductors begins to break down. Crystalline semiconductor materials stop semiconducting at high temperatures, and so do the jelly ones in our bodies. Mister Soucek's fever was apparently more advanced than Doctor Lulalilo's; he'd become incontinent. He'd lost all physical control and was unconscious. I saw Doctor Lulalilo at what might be an earlier stage of the fever; she'd only lost consciousness.

"However, the loss of consciousness of both Lulalilo and Soucek was a signal that the malady causing the fever was also beginning to affect the central nervous system. The first thing to do in such a situation is to initiate antipyrexis. So I started trying to get their body temperatures down with antipyrogens."

Laura Raye paused for a moment, then told Corry, "Captain, I wasn't trying to be facetious this morning when I told you to take two aspirin and call me if you got a fever. Aspirin is still one of the best antipyrogens we have. That was the first medication I gave to Soucek and Lulalilo. With Soucek, I had to go further. We initiated gastric lavage with cool saline. He needed the fluid and it would help bring down his deep body temperature.

"Then Doctor Barry Duval collapsed in the autopsy compartment." She paused, took a swallow of coffee, and went on, "I've got some interesting new data there. I'll discuss it in a minute. While we were struggling with those three people, Lieutenant Paul Peyton was brought in with the same symptoms but still conscious. We managed to keep him conscious and stabilize his temperature rise. We had a two-hour period there when no one else came in. That respite was a godsend. I'd almost dared to hope that those four were going to be the only ones.

"They weren't. At eleven hundred hours, Doctor Constantine Zervas had to stop his autopsy of the Mantid carcass and submit to treatment. Zervas was running a forty-point-five fever when he finally admitted to himself that he needed my help. Like most doctors, he's a lousy patient. A few minutes later, Chief Caliborn of the Air Group reported in with a rising fever. By that time, my team had developed a procedure that seemed to work: aspirin for the early symptoms, cool gastric saline lavage for the advanced, immediate bed rest, and intravenous injection of water and electrolytes."

She sighed and reported, "We've got six people confined to bed in sick bay. Three of them are in serious condition. The other three are in what I might term guarded condition.

"Anticipating your question, Captain: No, I don't know the cause of the fever. We did blood workups right away. White counts aren't elevated. Electrolyte balances are shot to hell because of dehydration. We find absolutely no gram-negative bacteremia. We may be seeing only a symptom. If so, high fevers with rapid onset are symptomatic of a lot of diseases. And, at the moment, I cannot pinpoint the cause of the fever. So I don't know what it is or how it's vectored. I don't even know if it's contagious."

"Could the Mantids be carrying it?" Corry asked.

Laura Raye shrugged and threw up her hands. "I don't know. That was my first thought, of course. However, many people in the boat have been in contact with the Mantids. They haven't reported a fever."

"Yet," Zeke added.

"Right. Yet. No one in sick bay has reported having the fever symptom. We've been in close contact with the Mantids, living and dead, ever since we picked them up in the Solomon Sea. One definite order should come out of this meeting, Captain: *Anyone* with the slightest fever should report *at once* to sick bay."

When the Medical Officer suggested that an order relating to health be given to the crew, Corry treated it as a must-do. "Consider it done, Doctor."

"I've been as close to the Mantids as anyone," CDR Matilda Harriet Smith put in. "I feel fine. No problems at all."

"That's just it," Laura Raye said. "I suspect the Mantids may be the carrier. But no pattern of contagion has surfaced. Some of us who have been in close and frequent contact with the Mantids show no symptoms at all. Then Mister Peyton and Chief Caliborn reported in with a fever. So that blows the simple hypothesis right out of the water."

She drained her coffee mug and set it firmly on the green-covered table before her. "So I'm back to basics. My lab team is checking for viral agents, but that takes time. We don't see anything thus far. We're also looking into the mechanisms of the immune system. The disease might affect those people whose immune systems are slightly less efficient."

Being a pilot and somewhat of a health nut as a result, Terri Ellison was following this discussion with great interest. A good combat pilot—and she was one—must wreak extreme physical strain on the human body and therefore gets to know it very well. Furthermore, Terri knew the right words. "Laura Raye, do you have any ideas of the etiology?"

"Some, but not enough," the Medical Officer replied frankly. "From what I know for certain right now, the causative agent appears to affect only the thermostasis mechanisms of the body. Therefore, it may be purely chemical in nature. Or it could be a pseudo-endocrine. How do I know this? It wasn't because of a leap of intuition, believe me. It came as a discovery I made this morning that's going to surprise the hell out of some people here."

She looked around and announced, "Doctor Barry Duval is not a human being."

She expected the stunned silence from the people in the wardroom. However, an unexpected response came impulsively from LCDR Natalie Chase, the Navigator. "That can't be! Barry is a fully functional man!" Then, realizing the implications of what she'd just said, she reddened.

"Oh, he's got all the necessary physical equipment, Natalie," Laura Raye agreed. "He can certainly pass as a human being. In fact, he's probably done so for a long time. An ordinary physical checkup probably wouldn't show anything unless the physician was looking for so-called second-order effects. Even his blood work would get through most labs. A CBC would show small anomalies. Phlebotomists would ignore the results. They'd figure that something probably went wrong with the automated equipment and write off the anomalies because they aren't that anomalous. What tipped me off that his blood was indeed different and not an anomaly of the analysis equipment was the degree of his fever and his body's response to it. That's what led me to consider some new possibilities as to the cause.

"At the risk of being pedantic, let me give you a quick course in biothermodynamics here. You should be aware of the principles involved or you may have trouble understanding how I got from Point A to Point B." She looked around the wardroom and asked, "Who knows the two critical temperatures for a human being?"

It was the Engineer Officer, CDR Ray Stocker, who spoke up. "Temperature conditions in the boat are my bailiwick, Doctor. So I can tell you that one of the critical temps is normal body temperature, thirty-seven Celsius. The other is twenty degrees Celsius, which is air comfort temperature. But temperature alone isn't important. I have to consider relative humidity, dew point, air movement, ion balance . . ."

"Well, you're correct from your viewpoint, Ray," the Medical Officer told him. "But those two critical engineering temperatures are determined by the real critical biological temperatures: five-point-six and thirty-one Celsius ambient."

"What I told you, Doctor, is true and correct from the engineering standpoint," Stocker insisted.

"Of course it is. As an engineer, you'll understand the reason I consider the other two temperatures to be more critical," Laura Raye told him without resentment. "Human beings lose the body heat of metabolism mostly by radiation. Twenty percent of that comes from the arms, hands, and fingers. Between five-point-six and thirty-one Celsius calm air temperature, regardless of the relative humidity, we maintain our thermal balance by radiation. Our circulatory system is the main heat-transfer system. Blood returns from our extremities through veins wrapped around the arteries. Venous blood is cooled by this body radiation and thus also cools the outflowing arterial blood."

"Sort of a biological heat exchanger," Stocker analogized, nodding his head.

"Right! That's exactly what it is! However, when the ambient temperature rises to above thirty-one, we can't radiate enough of our body heat quickly enough. So the venous blood returns to the heart through an emergency system, a vein network close to the surface of the skin. This increases our ability to radiate heat and also supplies water to our sweat glands. On the other end of the scale below five-point-six, the venous blood also shifts to this emergency system to warm our arms and hands. Because of the climate where our ancestors evolved, some of us have slightly different systems. An Inuit or Tibetan can withstand severe cold that would kill an African or Arab. And vice versa. Racial differences thus exist, and they were evolved as a result of climate. However, Duval is different from any of the normal racial human subtypes." She looked at the Navigator. "Natalie, Barry Duval was always warm, wasn't he?"

Natalie Chase rose above embarrassment. She decided she didn't need to apologize for visiting the Dolphin Club with anyone. The crew of the U.S.S. *Shenandoah* all wore the paired dolphins of the submariner's badge, and most of them had qualified for the hypothetical Three-Dolphin Rating as well. "Yes, but he said he was just one of those people who have a higher body temperature because he's tall and skinny."

"That's a good excuse and will fool nearly everyone," Laura Raye agreed. "Except me when I start looking for the causative agent of an unknown disease in a submerged carrier submarine. I began to suspect that something was different about Barry Duval when Mister Molders told me he had trouble finding a vein to take a blood sample. This isn't unusual, by the way. But when we needed to begin intravenous injection of fluids because gastric lavage wasn't working well enough to reduce his body temperature, Chief Post couldn't find a vein suitable for a drip. So I looked closer. I got Duval into my scan facility and started running NMR scans on him about two hours ago. I spotted the absence of a normal blood circulation system in Duval right away. This led me to make both thoracic and head scans. I will tell you right here and now that, internally, Duval is different."

The Medical Officer paused. "If I hadn't been looking at high resolution for hypothalamic differences—and they were present as well—I might have missed seeing what I thought at first were little malignancies or brain lesions. So I increased the resolution. What I saw were three tiny globules less than a millimeter in maximum size. They looked very much like the sort of implants now widely installed as cardiac pacemakers, cochlear prostheses, neurophonic receivers for nerve-deaf people, and neurological pain blocks."

"Are they like ordinary nanotechnology implants, Doctor?" Terri asked.

"If you mean, are they colloidal? No, they're crystalline in structure. That I did discover, because I was curious and I have that capability in my scanning equipment." Laura Raye often used her various scanning devices to perform nonintrusive biopsies that would identify the atomic elements, much like a mass spectrograph. "But they aren't ordinary. Most of the implants we use are based on gallium arsenide semiconductor technology. My scans reported that Duval's implants contain gallium and bismuth. Gallium bismide, to be exact."

"Damned fine semiconductor material, but also damned expensive, because it has to be made in the weightlessness of orbit," Lovette remarked. He had been promoted to head of the U.S.S. *Shenandoah*'s operations department because of his outstanding service as Communications Officer in the SSCV-7 U.S.S. *McCain.* He was an outstanding engineering line officer who had an intimate knowledge of modern semiconductor technology. "We don't use it in mass-production electronics, but we do have some in certain highly classified equipment I can't talk about even in this assembly."

Several officers in the wardroom—Corry, Zeke, Terri, Lovette, Walton, and Chase—knew what he meant. The SWC equipment couldn't exist without gallium bismide semiconductor technology.

"I'd like to see those modules. Maybe my experts could figure out what they are," Lovette said.

"Bob, I am *not* going to do neurosurgery on what appears to be a *third* alien species!" Moore told him forcefully. "I never got more than a nodding acquaintance with the anatomy of the Awesomes. Maybe Zervas knows what goes on inside a Mantid, but I doubt it. And I just discovered Duval this morning! Give me a break!"

"Okay, maybe we can work from your scan photos," the Operations Officer suggested.

Laura Raye shook her head. "Sorry, Bob. Legally and ethically, those images are part of Duval's medical records. I can't show them to you without Duval's permission—and he's in no condition to respond to the request at the moment."

"How about under orders from the Commanding Officer?"

"If and when such orders are given," the Medical Officer admitted. "However, Mister Lovette, I will have to include in my medical log that I believe obeying such an order is a breach of medical ethics."

A strained silence filled the wardroom. It was broken only by the sound of one of the red jackets refilling coffee mugs as he went around the table.

Finally, Corry spoke up and asked, "Doctor Moore, if it came to a choice between the welfare of the crew of this boat and the ethics of revealing medical information about an alien being of unknown capabilities whose covert presence among us is unknown, how would you make the call?" He had carefully and deliberately phrased his question. Corry was unafraid to give the order that Lovette requested. However, he wanted to make certain that Laura

Raye understood that the order wouldn't be given thoughtlessly.

The Medical Officer knew immediately what her Commanding Officer meant by his almost rhetorical question. No one had ever had to make a decision such as this with an alien being involved. Barry Duval had been friendly and helpful on the voyage thus far. His company was enjoyed by members of the crew. He was not-human but human at the same time. It was a tough call that Laura Raye Moore didn't want to make without support. Now she knew she had that support.

"Sir, I would still enter the matter in my medical log, but I would refrain from commenting upon the propriety of it from the ethical standpoint. Perhaps I was improper when I intimated that I would make a judgment call about it," she replied carefully. It was not a cop-out on her part nor a cave-in to her Commanding Officer. The relationship between a Commanding Officer and a Medical Officer is often unclear, especially in those nebulous areas where their authorities conflict.

Therefore, Corry didn't issue a direct order but phrased it in terms of a request—which had the same effect as a direct order, as everyone knew. However, when a leader deals with people, often substance must be reinforced by perception, but perception alone is inadequate.

"Doctor, I would like to have every technically cognizant person in the boat take a look at the data you have on Doctor Duval," Corry told her gently. "We need to find out what those nanotechnology modules are and whether they might be communications devices of some sort. Doctor Duval may be aboard for one of two reasons, or perhaps both. His task may be merely to provide covert communications and positioning information to others of his kind. If that's the case, I need to know about it so I can take measures to separate Duval from the information flow. However, he may be aboard the U.S.S. *Shenandoah* to sabotage the mission."

10

"Captain, this is the OOD!"

Corry looked up from where he was studying the chart of Palmyra Atoll. "Captain Corry here. GA, please," he called out to the wall-mounted intercom.

"Sir, this is Lieutenant Strader on deck. We are now approximately five hundred kilometers from Palmyra. Special Sensors reports several solid new targets. I think you and the XO should see this, sir."

"On my way! Call the XO."

"Aye, aye, sir."

"And please ask Commander Smith to come to the bridge," Corry added. He straightened his black necktie, patted his shirt pockets to make sure the flaps were closed, and stepped out of the captain's cabin into the passageway leading to the bridge.

He met Zeke Braxton coming out of the XO's cabin. CDR Matilda Harriet Smith was with him.

"Captain, this may look like . . ." Smith started to explain.

"Not to me," Corry replied and forgot about it. At this point, he didn't care, because he either had to trust his Number Two or find another one. Zeke had never even given the perception of busting Twenty-twenty. In any event, given that the boat was running submerged at high cruise speed five hundred kilometers from Palmyra, this was no time for Corry to reprimand his XO, even for the appearance of being improper. The boat had been at Condition Two since the working lunch a few hours ago. He had other matters on his mind.

"Captain, Commander Smith was filling me in on Admiral McCarthy and what she might be doing," Zeke explained.

"When we get time to scratch, please do the same for

me, Smitty," Corry told her. "Zeke, when we get to the bridge, call Terri and Bart. And I want all department heads on line."

"Aye, aye, sir." Zeke took two paces, then went on, "Captain, I think I know what might happen at Palmyra."

"New data, Number Two? Or just a sit-guess?"

"Speculation, sir, based on what Smitty has told me about the situation in Naval Intelligence."

When Zeke paused, Corry prompted him. "Well?"

"Sir, I believe Admiral McCarthy will put another special team aboard. CINCPAC will then send us to the ZI with the Mantids and Corona. I suspect our destination will be the old boomer base in Puget Sound," Zeke said as they walked slightly behind Corry down the passageway.

"No, Zeke," Smith objected. "That's too close to the East World action. My guess is we'll go to the other old boomer base at Bangor," the Naval Intelligence officer hypothesized.

"Through the Panama Canal? That's risky, Smitty!"

"No, around Cape Horn."

"The Horn is alive with Chilean and Argentine subs!"

"And this boat can run stealthy with its masdet," Smith pointed out. "You can do it. I saw you operate undetected in the Solomon Sea with Chinese and Australian submarines."

As they stepped onto the bridge, Corry told both of them, "We'll confront the post-Palmyra operation when we find out what it is. Right now, let's find out if there's an external threat. Mister Strader seems to think Special Sensors has detected something worth calling us to the bridge to see."

Actually, Corry's standing orders required any OOD to call him if and when solid sensor data was obtained on any possible external threat. As a result, some cautious OODs bothered him continually with a stream of insignificant contact reports. He considered that preferable to ignoring what might turn out to be a major one. He trusted the boat's Intelligence Officer, LTJG Ralph Strader, to exercise good judgment on such calls, however.

Corry got a quick glance at the jury-rigged masdet displays on the bridge. Targets were displayed that he hadn't seen when he'd passed through an hour ago. He decided that Strader was indeed exercising good judgment in this matter.

"Captain on the bridge!" Strader called out.

"Carry on, Mister Strader. You have the conn."

"Aye, aye, sir. I have the conn."

Corry took a seat at his action station and checked the status of critical systems. "So what have you got for us, Mister Strader?"

Using a laser pointer, Strader indicated targets on the main masdet and tactical displays as he spoke. "Sir, this target is Palmyra Atoll, distance now four-niner-three kilometers. Mister Ames has identified these green targets from their propulsion and hull sounds to be merchant ships following the regular sea-lanes; they have been tagged as innocents. We see three other surface ships converging to the vicinity of Palmyra here . . . and here . . . and here. One has come from Kwajalein. The other two appear to have sortied from Pearl."

"Identification?" Zeke asked.

"Not yet, sir. Mister Ames reports initial estimate of thirty-two thousand tons for each."

"Speed?"

"Approximately sixty-five knots, sir."

"Foil ships," Zeke guessed. Only hydrofoil ships could move that fast on the surface.

"Yes, sir. From their speed and displacement, I believe they may be laser cruisers, CLs, aerospace defense ships," the intel officer remarked.

"Watch them. See where they go," Corry ordered.

"Aye, aye, sir!"

"It would be a whole hell of a lot easier on the nerves if we had some foreknowledge of what's going on," Zeke grumbled.

"Naval Intelligence doesn't work that way, Zeke," Smith explained. "This is especially true when Admiral McCarthy is laying on a covert operation."

"Yes, you told me. But this looks like a damned big operation shaping up. Three laser cruisers! That's half of the Navy's surface aerospace defense capability in the eastern Pacific!"

"Number Two, I suspect that Admiral Kane wants direct control of space defense over Palmyra," Corry observed.

"My God, sir! Would the Aerospace Force stand by and

allow someone to toss an orbital KE weapon at us off Palmyra?" CDR Smith obviously didn't like or believe that the other service would abide an attack on a naval vessel. "As I told Zeke, deep differences exist between Naval Intelligence and our Aerospace Force counterpart, especially regarding UFOs. But allowing East World to shoot KE weapons at us would be bordering on treason!"

"Not treason at all, Smitty. Ordinary interservice rivalry," CDR Terri Ellison put in as she sat down at her command post on Corry's left.

Corry was glad he had an aggressive CAG in Terri Ellison. He had specifically requested that she be assigned to his boat as CAG when he'd assumed command. The Commanding Officer of the U.S.S. *Shenandoah* didn't reply to Terri's statement. He noted an edge in her voice. He knew that the stresses imposed on his people during this cruise had been high, and the voyage wasn't over yet. He'd been ordered by CINCPAC to take the boat to Palmyra for unknown reasons, and Naval Intelligence had added fuel to the fire in an independent message to Smith.

This was no time for channel fever; one fever in the boat was enough, although channel fever merely referred to the crew's attitude on the homeward stretch. He expected some short tempers and a few edgy reactions. This didn't indicate that the efficiency of his people had dropped, only that they were beginning to suffer from chronic fatigue and a lot of anxiety. He felt it himself, and he knew that neither he nor the people in his crew were superhuman.

The experience of nearly a generation of Blue and Gold crews on the old boomers, the SSBNs, had helped the Navy design tension and boredom relief facilities into its twenty-first-century submarines. But sometimes these weren't enough.

Now the presence of *two* alien species in the boat had raised the level of tension even higher. No one knew if the "Mantid fever" was contagious, and Laura Raye Moore hadn't announced a prognosis for the course of the disease yet.

It was not the kind of multiple-threat situation that led to the sort of calm, practiced, cool professionalism that some people expected submariners to exhibit.

"Smitty," Zeke said to the Naval Intelligence officer, "it's not that we blue-water types distrust the Army and the

Aerospace Farce. However, look at it our way and 'remember Pearl Harbor.' The Navy has never forgotten that."

"Oh, you mean when the Army's Opana mobile radar station on Kahuku Point spotted the first wave of Japanese carrier aircraft?" Smith responded. "They assumed that the targets were Army Flying Fortresses coming in from the mainland. Whether the additional warning time would have been significant to the outcome is a moot point."

"You're learning to think like a blue-water Navy type," Zeke admitted.

"What are you getting at, Zeke?" she wanted to know.

Terri Ellison answered instead. "Smitty, if the Aerospace Farce at Hickam sees a KE weapon heading for Palmyra, they may ignore it."

"Why would they do that?"

Zeke explained, "They may not have been told by CINCPAC that we're at Palmyra. So they'd believe that nothing of importance or value is at Palmyra. Therefore, they'd treat the bogey as a low-priority matter to be reported up the line but not threatening enough to fire upon."

"I see," Smith admitted. "Yes, the Palmyra operation is very covert. So I suspect CINCPAC doesn't want to take the risk that the Aerospace Force wouldn't act."

Zeke nodded. "It's general naval doctrine to proceed using a 'belt and suspenders' policy."

"What are suspenders?" Smith asked.

Before Zeke could answer her question—the primitive "shoulder harness" for trousers was seen only in the agricultural midwest these days—Major Bart Clinch thumped into his CIC position. "The Marine batt is ready, Captain. Semper fi!"

"Thank you, Major," Corry told him and proceeded to get back to the serious business at hand. "Now, Mister Strader, please continue with your presentation. I see numerous skunks out there plus three IX targets that may be CLs. What are the other targets?"

"Sir, these other two targets approaching Palmyra from the northeast appear to have come from the vicinity of Hawaii," Strader told them. "They are submerged. Displacement about twenty thousand tons. We have another similar submerged target heading toward Palmyra from the general direction of Howland Island. All of these submerged targets have emitted monopulse sonar signals at random intervals. Mister Ames, Mister Goff, and I believe they are Honor class attack boats."

"They could be Chinese Ming class attack boats," Smith interrupted. "They have nearly the same displacement."

"Yes, ma'am, but Mister Goff and I have analyzed the sonar monopulse. It looks like the signal from a BQQ-fifty-four multipurpose sonar operating in long-range monopulse mode."

"The Chinese have a similar monopulse sonar," Smith insisted.

"Yes, ma'am," Strader said deferentially. He knew she was a top-ranking Naval Intelligence officer. However, he was the boat's intel officer and believed he had a better knowledge of specific potential threats. "However, the Chinese monopulse waveform isn't the same. And Goff can tell the difference."

"What's the range to these submarine targets, Mister Strader?" Smith pressed him.

"Mister Ames estimates six hundred to eight hundred kilometers, Commander."

Smith gave a little snort. "Huh! How can your Sonar Officer know at that distance? Sonar pulse shapes get degraded pretty badly over ranges that long."

That statement didn't faze Strader. "Yes, ma'am, we know that. Mister Goff has some noise-reduction and pulse-distortion algorithms that can discriminate a dolphin's bleat out of the background noise at a thousand kilometers . . ."

"Dammit, why haven't we been told that at Naval Intelligence?"

"Commander," Clinch muttered, "remember the old truism: There's always someone who doesn't get the word!"

"Smitty, Op-thirty-two probably has been told," Terri pointed out.

"A lot of operational information gets buried because the shore types tend to pay more attention to the techie reports from the labs," Zeke added.

"And if the Air Desk in the Pentagon ever discovered all the unauthorized, unofficial, and nonregulation things my Air Group *really* does to the aircraft they give us, we'd probably be court-martialed for destruction of government property. As you've discovered in the last week or so,

Smitty, we're almost in our own little world in a carrier submarine."

The informal use of nicknames among officers of equal ranks and roughly the same responsibilities was new to Smith. She realized it was SOP in the tightly knit crew of the U.S.S. *Shenandoah*. Smith suddenly realized that she was now considered to be part of that crew.

The SWC message from RADM McCarthy had officially given CDR Matilda Harriet Smith authority over the alien beings and artifacts second only to that of CAPT Corry. However, now she realized she was also becoming more involved with the actual operational planning of the carrier submarine's mission.

She was smart enough to realize she didn't know what she was doing in a line command position, not having served at sea before. Her fellow officers, having accepted her, now were patiently trying to explain things to her. They had the luxury of time at the moment, however. When General Quarters was called, she perceived that she'd have to get out from underfoot. That's why Corry had assigned her a GQ post next to him on the bridge, because he wanted to make sure she knew exactly what was going on if Battle Stations was piped. Her unique perspective of OP-32 could be crucial to the action now that the boat was officially on a spook mission.

With her relative ignorance of masdet displays, Smith didn't understand what she was seeing. So she asked Strader, "What's that smudgy target off the starboard beam?"

"Canton Island, ma'am."

"But it's moving. Since when do islands move?"

Strader looked again. So did everyone else.

LT Marcela Zar, on duty as the navigation officer of the watch, suddenly observed, "That isn't where Canton is supposed to be."

"New target, Mister Strader?" Zeke wanted to know.

Strader shook his head. "No, sir. It's been there since I came on watch. I hadn't noticed it moving. Stand by, sir. Let me check with Mister Ames."

"Mister Strader, have Mister Ames take a look at that other target that just appeared in the vicinity of Palmyra," Corry snapped. "In fact, it looks like multiple small targets."

"We must be getting close enough to Palmyra now to pick up some low-mass targets," Strader guessed. "Special Sensors, OOD here."

"Special Sensors here. GA, Ralph. This is Charlie on the main masdet. And, yes, I see the new targets around Palmyra. And for some reason I'm just seeing motion of that IX off the starboard beam," came the reply from Ames.

"Any ID on any of them?"

"Just a wild-ass guess, Ralph."

"Special Sensors, be advised that the Captain and the division officers are on the bridge," Strader warned him.

This was followed by a few seconds of silence, then Ames replied, "Roger that, OOD! Negatory on the ID."

Corry slipped his N-fone communicator behind his right ear and toggled it. He could now "think" commands and remarks into the system without vocalizing them, and the N-fone would in turn impress on his auditory nerve the sound of others talking on the comm net. N-fone communication was about five times more rapid than vocalizing. People trained to use the N-fone didn't have to waste time converting their thoughts into sounds.

"Going to N-fone," he warned Zeke and the others, a signal that they, too, should activate their own units. "Smitty, turn on your N-fone. Terri, show her how to do it."

"I remember how, Captain," Smith responded.

Conn, reduce speed to forty knots, Corry snapped to the OOD.

Reduce speed to forty knots. Aye, aye, sir!

The cavitation speed of the *Shenandoah*'s hull was fifty-one knots. A few knots below that speed, random cavitation popped up here and there along her hull. This made her very noisy and extremely susceptible to passive sonar detection. At forty-five knots, her cruise speed since leaving the Solomons, a sudden change in sea temperature, salinity, or current turbulence could cause spot cavitation to take place. Corry's order reducing the boat's speed to forty knots put her well below cavitation speed and made her very quiet indeed. Privately, he said to Zeke and the other division officers, "Five knots won't make that much difference in our arrival time at Palmyra."

"We'll arrive forty-five minutes later than estimated," Zeke reported on the mental calculation he'd just made.

"That will put us off the north shore of the island at twenty-one hundred local."

"What about the people in sick bay, Captain? Would you be able to airlift them to Pearl, then?" Smith was concerned about the other members of her special team.

"We could hack it now if we surfaced," Terri reported. "We're within Sea Dragon range of Pearl."

Corry decided it was time to get an update from his Medical Officer. *Sick bay, this is the Captain. Is Doctor Moore available?*

CO, this is sick bay, Chief Post reporting. The Chief Pharmacist Mate was using verbose communication rather than the N-fone, and the response seemed incredibly slow, with pauses between words. *Doctor Moore is not available, sir. We just had three more fever cases show up.*

Three more?

Affirmative, sir. Lieutenant Ireland and two aviation machinist mates, both running forty-degree fevers.

"Damn!" Terri Ellison exploded verbally. "My maintenance officer and two of my rates!"

"Terri, did those three have any contact with the Mantids?" Zeke suddenly asked, an idea erupting in his mind.

"Let me check on another channel," she told him and went silent while she communicated on one of her dedicated Air Group comm channels.

"Captain, this could be contagious!" Smith told him anxiously. "Nine people have come down with this unknown fever now!"

"Smitty," Corry replied easily, trying not to allow his voice to show his concern, "at that point, it isn't the number that's important, but the rate of affliction. The overall number is still very small. And we may have a pattern emerging here."

"Captain," Terri put in, having gotten the information she needed by querying her Air Group people on a separate channel. "Mister Ireland and the two rates were involved in cleaning up the Mantid mess on the bulkheads and deck of the Corona vehicle."

"How many Air Group people were involved, Terri?"

"About two dozen, sir. They worked in shifts."

"Were Ireland and the two rates on the same shift?"

"No, sir."

"And none of the sick-bay people who helped them have come down with the fever yet," Zeke observed.

"It's a selective disease," Corry concluded. "Not everyone exposed to Mantids or Mantid remains gets it."

"It may be contagious human to human," Smith guessed.

"We don't know," Zeke told her.

Smith grew a bit frightened at this. It was stressful enough being in a huge underwater vessel with live aliens aboard and with unknown ships converging on Palmyra Atoll with them. The fever disease was an added stress item that Smith didn't really know how to handle. "Captain, we should surface and get the sick people on their way to Pearl."

Corry shook his head. "No, Commander, that I will not do at this point. It is not an emergency, although I admit that it's a concern. It's another threat in the equation."

Smith knew when to quit. She said no more, because she realized her comment had come from her personal fears.

Corry went on, "Terri, please have everyone in Air Group who had contact with the Mantids or Mantid organic material check with sick bay as soon as Laura Raye gets this current brushfire out and has some time. Maybe if she has a chance to examine people who haven't come down with the fever, she might be able to learn something."

Terri nodded. "Aye, aye, sir. When in total ignorance, do anything and be less ignorant."

"Precisely. In the meantime, however, I see other potential threats on the masdet displays," Corry went on slowly, almost thinking aloud. He often did this in the presence of his department chiefs. Basically, it was his way of letting them in on his thinking processes so they could comment or critique if they wished. "I can reasonably assume that the fast foil ships and the submarines are part of the Navy support force converging on Palmyra. However, I'll rate them as a low-priority threat until they're positively identified. What has me worried is the two unknown masdet targets—the big one off our starboard beam and the multiple small ones at Palmyra."

The Executive Officer of the U.S.S. *Shenandoah* was also studying the displays. With a bit of hesitation in his voice, Zeke finally remarked, "Captain, I can't back this up with any data. However, that starboard target sort of 'feels' like the big *Tuscarora* UFO we encountered in Makasar

Straits. It also feels like the unknown that was shadowing us in the Solomon Sea but never made a close approach."

"Yes," Corry replied simply. "I'm going to consider it as a *Tuscarora* target until we get a better signal from it."

Bart Clinch was no masdet target expert, but he did have some experience with underwater aliens that backed up what he added as he pointed at the multiple targets around Palmyra Atoll. "And those smaller targets could damned well be alien underwater sea monsters, the Awesomes. Hell, I fought them in Makasar Straits and missed getting another shot at them in the Solomons. But I'll never forget them. I think we've had a tendency to do that now that we've got their Mantid bosses aboard."

"So what are they doing at Palmyra?" Smith asked.

"Fishing," was the Marine major's curt reply.

"For what?"

"Maybe a carrier submarine. Maybe us," he told her.

"What can an Awesome do to a carrier submarine, Bart? Have you been taking stupid pills again?" That was almost a standard rhetorical question from Terri to Bart.

"I don't know, but I sure as hell don't want to assume that they can do nothing," Clinch replied. "Remember that the Navy once trained dolphins to place explosives below the waterline of ships. I don't know what kind of explosives the Mantids or Awesomes might have, but I'd sure as hell get more than a little antsy with a swarm of them around this boat. One thing for sure: They're not friendlies."

"Thanks for your insight, Bart. I hadn't considered that possibility," Corry admitted. "Until I know more, I'm just going to watch them very closely. But right now, whatever they're doing at Palmyra is anyone's guess. And if the Mantids have somehow learned our destination—maybe from our wired special team member, Doctor Duval—it's going to be an interesting situation at Palmyra."

11

When the watch changed at 1800 hours, Corry went to the bridge and slipped into his chair. Zeke was already there, sitting and quietly watching the displays. LCDR Mark Walton was OOD and carried out his duties without noticing the two men. Walton knew what his job was, and he did it quietly and efficiently. He was a comer; he wanted his own SS command someday.

Corry had the mess steward bring him supper, a tuna salad sandwich and cole slaw. Corry wasn't very hungry. The mission was coming up on a critical cusp point. He already had a lot of worries on his mind, but he had good people delegated to handle them. The toughest thing for a Commanding Officer like CAPT William M. Corry to do was to sit back and let his people do their jobs without having their elbows joggled.

The U. S. S. *Shenandoah* continued to cruise at forty knots just below a deep scattering layer at 180 meters. The telltales and displays on the bridge showed that it was being buffeted by deep ocean currents. Despite the mass of the carrier submarine, a few bumps could be felt through the deck.

"We're in the rip between the south equatorial and the counter current, Captain," Zeke observed. "It's surprising that it's so turbulent at this depth."

"Yes," Corry replied in his typical laconic manner. He thought into his N-fone, *Navigator, what is sunset time at Palmyra?*

Eighteen fifty-two, sir, LT Bruce Leighton replied.

Corry could see the navigation display, but he asked, *What is the present distance to Palmyra and our ETA off the north beach of Cooper Island?*

Range forty-nine kilometers, estimated time of arrival eighteen thirty-seven hours, sir.

The multiple targets around Palmyra Atoll were now much sharper on the masdet display. *Special Sensors, this is the Captain. Confirm the existence of multiple underwater targets off Sand Island and the entrance channel to the west lagoon of Palmyra Atoll.*

CO, this is Special Sensors. We confirm twenty-three small targets submerged within one kilometer of Sand Island and Penguin Spit. Targets are operating in shoal waters, sir.

"Captain," Zeke remarked verbally, "those masdet targets look a lot like the Awesome targets we saw in the Solomon Islands."

"Yes, XO, and the ones we tracked in Makasar Straights," Corry confirmed. Then he asked one of his typical questions: "What would you do about it, Zeke?"

Zeke came right back without hesitation. "I'd see if Charlie can get a match between the recorded data from Makasar and these Palmyra targets, Captain."

Corry nodded and directed his subvocalized thought into the N-fone: *Special Sensors, this is the Captain. Can you get an ID on those twenty-three targets? Do they look like anything you've tracked before with the masdet?*

Affirmative, sir! We have a nine-nines match with the signal strength, target mass, and target behavior of the targets tracked in the Solomons and off Sulawesi. I would tag those targets as Awesomes, sir, except for the twenty-third target that is south of Penguin Spit. It appears to mass twenty thousand tons and have a nine-five probability of matching the Awesomes' mother ship we saw in Makasar Straits. I can't get an exact signal from it, sir. It's trying to hide in the coral reef.

"Somehow, the Awesomes and their Mantid bosses in the mother ship learned we're coming," Zeke guessed.

"How?" Corry asked curtly.

"Probably Duval."

"We have no report on that from sick bay yet, Number Two."

"Sir, until additional data become available, I'd stick with that hypothesis."

Captain, Sonar here. As we get in closer to Palmyra, we're beginning to pick up the keening sound we heard off Makasar. The Awesomes may use that for communications. The signal is a combination of frequency modulation with pulse width modulation. Signals are in the range of ten-point-seven to fourteen-point-nine kilohertz, sir.

Any ranging sounds yet?

Negative on ranging sounds coming in our direction. They're ranging among themselves and into the coral reefs. But no ranging pulses strong enough to give them a return bounce at this range, sir.

"They aren't expecting us yet," Zeke concluded.

"I agree, XO. So I'm going to pause here, wait until sundown, and see if the Awesomes go back to their mother ship for the night."

"They did off Makasar."

"Yes. If they do home for the night, then we'll slip past them and go to the bottom off the north coast of Palmyra."

"And let them try to find us there! Captain, they very well could find us if Duval turns out to be some sort of locator beacon they've managed to smuggle aboard."

"Strader and Atwater are sweep-monitoring anything that could possibly get out of our hull, especially the SWC channels. If Duval is a beacon, we're likely to find out very quickly."

"If he turns out to be, I'd suggest having Laura Raye put him into deep anesthesia."

"We don't know if that will turn him off or not." Corry thought for a moment before he remarked, "Zeke, I'd hate to have to kill him to protect the boat. But I may have to."

Zeke caught the extreme reluctance of his Commanding Officer to even consider such a move. "I wouldn't like it, either. But it may be the only thing we can do if we get into the tight furball at Palmyra."

"It's my intention to prevent such a confrontation," Corry said quietly. *OOD, all engines stop. Come dead in the water. Do not reballast to maintain depth.*

Aye, aye, sir! All stop. Negative on reballasting. Maintaining silent running.

"We'll allow the sun to go down, Number Two. If the Awesomes knock it off for the night, we'll move to the north shore and go to the bottom. And there we shall wait." Corry's plan seemed prudent at that time. "We should receive an SWC message sometime tomorrow morning telling us what's next."

"Can we go to Condition Three once we're on the bottom, Captain?" Zeke asked with concern. "We've been in

Condition Two and four-on-four-off for over a day now. The crew could use the rest. It's the end of a long cruise."

Corry nodded. "Agreed, XO. Provided nothing happens to change things as we see them right now. CINCPAC and OP-thirty-two should be giving us a heads-up tomorrow on schedule." He paused, then added, "If not, and if Doctor Moore hasn't managed to do something about Mantid fever, I'm likely to ask Terri to airlift those people to Pearl late tomorrow. I don't want to jeopardize their lives."

"She hadn't made any additional headway when I talked with her an hour ago," Zeke reported. "But she hadn't started intensive search routines on medical histories. If anyone can find out what's going on, it's Laura Raye Moore."

If the Medical Officer of the U.S.S. *Shenandoah* could have heard the Executive Officer's expression of confidence in her abilities as a diagnostician, it certainly would have helped her at that moment.

In her private medical conference cabin, Dr. Laura Raye Moore was in a professional semi-confrontation with Chief Pharmacist Mate Nat Post. "Chief, doing a mix-and-match controlled merge-and-search with the medical records might indeed reveal a common factor," she told him. "But I don't have medical records on the special team."

The Chief Pharmacist Mate had an idea, but he couldn't pull medical records from the ship's computer without the authorization of the Medical Officer. "Doctor, perhaps an analysis of the records we have of the crew members suffering from Mantid fever will show some correlation somewhere. This might lead to the proper question to ask the other members of the special team when they become lucid again," Post insisted.

"God knows when that will be."

"It could be tonight, ma'am. The fevers have broken with Doctors Lulalilo and Zervas. Look at the monitors. A steady trend of a tenth of a degree per hour down from the peak."

"Two hours of data don't give me enough data points to make that sort of a prognosis, Chief," Laura Raye Moore told him flatly. "I don't like to bet with a human life."

"Doctor, I can't run the analysis of the records without your permission," Post admitted. "I'd like to get that permission. I'm willing to put in the time necessary to do the analysis. Then I'll present the result to you. If you think it's garbage, so be it. But I think everyone agrees that the Medical Department is up against the bulkhead. We have no idea of the etiology or prognosis of these fevers. The only common factor thus far has been contact with Mantid tissue."

"Then why haven't you and I contacted the fever, Chief?"

The Chief looked at her earnestly and tried to make the best pitch he could. "Doctor, if we could answer that single question, we might be a lot closer to knowing what to do. Since an analysis of medical records doesn't jeopardize the lives of the patients, I'd like to see what can be found. I'm not a doctor. I didn't make it to med school because of family finances. But I did make it up the ladder to a Chief Pharmacist Mate. On some smaller ships, I'd be the only medical person aboard and a de facto ship's doctor. In fact, I came to the *Shenandoah* from the *Gilmore* where I was just that."

Laura Rayne Moore was tired. She'd been hard at work all day. So had her Chief. They'd been dealing with life-and-death situations with nine people. And they had no basis on which to act. They were trying anything on an empirical basis, hoping it would work. So far, no one had died. But they weren't getting very much better very fast. And the two live Mantids were being difficult; they'd refused to eat human food even when they were given privacy in which to feed. So Chief Post's last comment almost pushed her to the edge. She asked him in a low voice, "Chief, are you challenging my authority?"

Post was tired, too. And he realized that he might have pushed too hard. So he shook his head and replied, "Certainly not, ma'am! You're the doctor! What I'm trying to say—and probably making a botch of it—is I've learned that people suffering from the same apparent disease have some common factor. In fact, I believe that's the basic paradigm behind diagnostic medicine in the first place. Therefore, I think we can find a common factor in the Mantid fever. And the first place to look is in the medical records, because it's the only database we have for this situation. I do have some background in medical diagnostics. And I'd like to run an analytic review of the available medical records to see if I can find a common thread."

Moore sighed. She knew she wasn't thinking straight, and this was a dangerous condition for a medical doctor to be in. She felt as if she were back in residency again. She desperately wanted to get an hour's sleep. She was too tired to battle her Chief over matters of privilege such as this. Like other naval officers, she knew that the chiefs and the rates really ran the United States Navy. In the past, she'd relied on Chief Post. She had always trusted him in the past, and he'd never given her any reason to belie that trust. Now he wanted to try something, and Moore realized that the only reason she was bucking him was her own fatigue. "All right, I don't see what harm that can do. And you seem to have a good grasp of what you want to try to do. Go do it. Just don't let it interfere with your other duties in sick bay."

"I won't, Doctor. But you'll have to unlock the files when I get to that part of the log-in."

Moore keyed the terminal in her desktop, then got up and told him, "Here, you're all logged in. Use my terminal. I'm going to catch a few minutes' sleep."

"Thank you, Doctor," Post replied as she walked out the door.

Ten minutes later, Post gave up in frustration. He punched up the Chief Staff Petty Officer on the intercom.

"Whoever the hell it is had better have one damned good excuse for bothering me!" came the growl from Chief Al Warren.

"Post here, and I've got two. The corks are still in them. They're in my locker at Pearl, and they're guaranteed to be at least twelve years old."

"That will do for a start. What's the hot skinny, Nat?"

"I'm trying to run some matching files programs with the med computer," Post explained. "I've run out of memory. Holland tells me it hasn't got any to spare because of some stuff the Special Sensors people are running to massage signals."

"So?"

"So you've got the overrides on Holland. That's your department. I need a few terabytes. Can you hack it for me?"

"Tell me again what you want."

Post did, explaining to him what he was trying to do.

"Forget the scotch. If you can nail that fever so we all don't get it, that's worth it. But I'll let you buy me a beer in the club at Pearl when we get there," the Chief Staff Petty Officer told him. "Are you interested in speed or capacity?"

"Capacity. I can let it crunch all night if I have to. I don't want to, but I'll live with it."

"Okay, it's about a fifteen-minute hack. Your program will run simultaneously with the Special Sensors one," Warren explained. "I'll fix it so Holland runs it in the interrupt breaks while the display scans overwrite."

"Just don't get Commander Lovette on my case, Al."

"He'll never know. Give me about three minutes to find the interleave program I wrote last week, and then I'll patch this kludge together for you."

"Al, you're a gentleman, a scholar, and a judge of fine bourbon."

"I thought it was scotch. And I'm not a gentleman; I'm a chief. Now lemme go back to sleep. Good luck. Bust this thing for us, will you? Last thing I want is to be flat with the creeping crud when we hit Pearl. The wife will have a fit if I'm not fit."

"I know what you mean, Al."

"How could you? Last I knew, you weren't married."

While Chief Post was working in the sick bay, Terri Ellison and LCDR Pat Bellinger, commander of VA-65, were at work in the cockpit of the alien Corona vehicle stored on the hangar deck.

"Terri, I think I could fly this heap," Bellinger decided as he studied the controls and instrument panel. The controls were somewhat different from those in his F/A-48 Sea Devils parked elsewhere in the hangar deck. "What is there to flying anything? Up, down, left, right, faster, and slower. Stick, rudder, and throttle."

He reached out and touched a pair of what appeared to be levers. "Throttles, maybe. And here is a touch pad for left and right. And this dingus here—hell, I can get my hand around both of them—this must be up and down. I think this machine translates rather than flies. You don't point it. You tell it what direction to go. I saw it fly, remember? It can move sideways like a helicopter. And it sure as hell couldn't be any more difficult to fly than those old helicopters!"

"Yeah, Bells, but this heap was designed to be flown by Mantids, and they have two hands and four feet. Or four hands and two feet, maybe. No one knows too much about them yet," Terri pointed out. Formality among the pilots of the Air Group was minimal, as between pilots anywhere. Insignia of rank merely told everyone how many airplanes you could command. The critical icon was the Navy's gold wings.

"Well, these controls can't be too much different from some of them in the air battle games my kids play on their simple gamer hardware," the attack squadron leader reminded her. "I haven't been home enough lately to hook up the full aircraft-style control auxiliary I bought for them. So they fly those games with trackballs and cursor keys. And they're damned good at it, too!"

"Did they whup your ass a couple of times, Bells?" Terri asked with a smile.

"Yeah. More than a couple. They had more practice with the limited control suite. My reflexes are tuned to the full Sea Devil system of stick and rudder," Bellinger admitted without remorse. "That's why I want to get the full control suite hooked up. Maybe I can beat them then. But that's why I think I could fly this thing, Terri. Control in six degrees of freedom is the same, no matter how many fingers, hands, and feet you've got!"

"You'd prang it, Bells. You don't know the reaction time programmed into whatever computers they've got hooked between the controls and the effectors," Terri told him.

"Can't be that much different from ours. Otherwise, we wouldn't have won that air fight in the Solomon Sea."

"During which you got shot down," she reminded him.

"Somebody had to catch it in the crotch before we could figure out how to whup their asses. The bastard slewed this thing and got me in the force beam. I wasn't expecting that," Bells said. "Look, we learned about the Mantids in that furball. Their reaction times may be a little slower than ours, but they sure as hell aren't faster."

"Okay, I saw that."

"And we found out that they either focus on a given task or are incapable of handling multitasks the way we are."

"They sure as hell didn't check six," Terri admitted.

"So we ran them off with saturation attacks even though they had a much superior air-to-air weapon in that force beam of theirs."

"I wish we could learn how that works. It might come in handy if we tangle assholes with those Mantids again."

"If we can get this ship back intact, the tech weenies may be able to figure it out," Bells told her. "In the meantime, I wouldn't want to mess with that. I just want to try flying it. I think a good human pilot can do it. Look at it this way: If the Mantids have to concentrate, it means that the controls and displays are designed to accommodate that. Therefore, no complex piloting operations are required for this thing. Kick the tires and light the fires. Put the throttle through the gate and it goes. And it reports what it's doing in very unambiguous terms. Hell, Terri, the Sea Devil does that!"

"So you think you can fly it?" Terri asked.

"Yeah, I can fly it."

Terri paused for several seconds before she told him, "I think I can, too."

Bellinger looked at her in surprise. "Why didn't you say so in the first place instead of letting me get it all hung out there?"

"Because I wanted to make sure I wasn't stroking my own ego," Terri admitted. "I think I can fly it. Hell, I can fly anything. And I have. And damned good at it, too! But with one of Uncle Sams aeroplanes, I have to go to ground school taught by factory reps and then pass a check ride with a company pilot or an IP. I don't think those insects down in sick bay will agree to check us out in this thing. So we're flying blind with it. I've got to admit that I've never done that with an aircraft before." She sat back and sighed. "None of us have. We can get away with bending an airplane during training if it's not pilot error. And we get to try again in another one. But we have only one of these. We can't bend it. Hell, we can't even put a ding in it."

"So?" Bellinger responded. "We're just going to have to be check pilots for each other."

"The blind leading the blind, Bells. Now I know how Orville and Wilbur felt at Kitty Hawk."

"Well, as I recall, they had a lot of glider time before they turned the props."

"Okay, Bells, if we surface off Palmyra and if I can talk the Captain into it, we'll haul this up to the upper flight deck and tether it so it won't lift more than a few centimeters."

"The Captain probably isn't going to let you do that, Terri," Bellinger warned her. "And Smith sure as hell won't let us risk this UFO."

"I'll get to Smith," Terri promised.

"How?"

"Through the XO," she promised. She looked around the interior of the Corona. "Damn!" she whispered. "I'd sure like to log some time in a flying saucer! Wouldn't it be great to have UFO time in your logbook?"

12

Nothing?

Nothing, Captain, was the N-fone reply from LT Ed Atwater. *No incoming traffic of any sort.*

CAPT William M. Corry shook his head. It was now 0730 the following morning. The U.S.S. *Shenandoah* had been sitting silently on the bottom 137 meters down off the north side of Palmyra Atoll since 2330 the previous night.

I'm expecting an SWC message from CINCPAC, Corry told his Communications Officer.

Yes, sir. I'm aware of that, sir. I'll let you know the moment the SWC machine begins to talk to me.

Please do so, Mister Atwater. Now, regarding Doctor Duval, have you detected anything?

No, sir. I haven't detected any sort of transmissions from Doctor Duval. And I've got my most sensitive detectors down there with him. They're the ones I use to check our own radiation stealth, sir.

Very well, Mister Atwater. Inform me the instant you hear from CINCPAC or detect radiation from Duval. CO out!

Corry rose from the chair at his command post on the bridge. "XO, I'll be in Special Sensors or Sonar," he told Zeke Braxton verbally. "You have the conn."

"Aye, aye, sir. I have the conn," Zeke repeated back. He knew that his Commanding Officer was tense and uneasy. Normally, Corry would remain on the bridge, watching the data as it streamed in and was projected on the displays. When Corry decided to visit a specific department whose activity was crucial at the moment, his officers and crew knew he was anxious. So Zeke remarked easily to him, "Captain, do you wish to remain at Condition Three?"

"Affirmative. I see nothing on the bridge displays that would press me to go to a higher level of alert, Number

Two. However, I want to have a look at the masdet and passive sonar data as close to the source as possible," Corry told his Executive Officer, rationalizing his actions. Zeke knew that, for normal operations, the bridge displays were clearly adequate. However, when he had the time available and the situation was tense, Corry preferred to be right over the big displays in the Special Sensors and Sonar/Lidar compartments. He felt that they often showed little nuances that somehow got scrubbed out of the data when it was displayed on the bridge repeaters.

If the Commanding Officer of the U.S.S. *Shenandoah* was approaching the stress-out point, this wasn't true of the officers and rates in the sonar shack. LT Roger Goff was almost relaxed. He replied to Corry's apprehension, "Captain, we know the location of every ship, whale, and dolphin within a hundred klicks of us. And except for the three submerged targets, we hear the surface masdet targets Mister Ames has spotted."

"Do you hear the Awesomes this morning?"

"Yes, sir. They woke up about sunrise, and we have their positions nailed dead nuts."

"Does your hydrophone data jibe with Charlie's masdet?"

"Affirmative, sir. The Awesomes are still on the west side of Palmyra Atoll. They haven't come around Saule Point and Strawn Island to the north of the atoll yet."

Corry was using his usual command policy of asking questions to elicit the maximum amount of information as well as to discover what his people really thought. "What do you suspect the Awesomes are doing here at Palmyra, Roger?"

Goff knew what Corry was up to, so he replied, "Captain, I think they're here because they're looking for us."

"Got any idea how they found out the boat was going to Palmyra instead of Pearl?"

Goff nodded. "Sir, I've heard that Doctor Duval is a walking, talking SWC beacon. Uh, is this true, sir?"

"I don't know, Mister Goff."

"Lieutenant Atwater told me he's detected nothing radiating from Duval," Goff ventured.

"He's reported that to me as well. But I haven't heard from the Medical Officer this morning. Doctor Duval is apparently still unconscious from the fever. Maybe he isn't transmitting now."

"If he does, Ed will spot it," Goff promised.

"I'm sure he will. In the meantime, Mister Goff, I'm not going to spend my time fretting about matters I can't control," Corry told his sonar officer. "We've got our hands full here at Palmyra. I must presume that the Awesomes are the underwater allies of the Mantids. I suspect they want their colleagues and the Corona back in their hands. I don't know how they got the information that we were headed toward Palmyra. But your sonar data plus Charlie's masdet targets tell me they were looking for us to come in from the southwest."

Goff grinned. "Yes, sir. I think you did an end run around them."

"Thank you, Mister Goff. I believe that's exactly what we did," Corry agreed. He studied the twelve-hundred-centimeter horizontal sonar display screen. He knew that Goff read science fiction, because they'd swapped several books between them. So he commented, "Everyone assumes that extraterrestrials are omnipotent and omniscient. On this cruise, we've learned they have shortcomings just as we do."

"Well, sir, omnipotent aliens were necessary for the plots. They provided suspense as well as convenient villains with super-technology. The heroes always had to beat them with human technology."

"Do you see something different here, Mister Goff?" Corry wondered. He did, but he wanted to make sure Roger Goff was thinking beyond the obvious.

"Yes, sir. We're using our technology to help us beat these Awesomes and Mantids. In many ways, our technology isn't as advanced as theirs. After all, they came from another planet somewhere, which means they have star drive technology of some sort. But it looks like we use what we have more effectively."

"Why do you think that might be so?" Corry persisted. Some officers quailed when Corry began his infamous "ask the next question" routine, because it often exposed serious weaknesses on the part of the questionee.

However, Goff appeared to respond to it as a challenge, much as Zeke did. "Sir, really powerful technology can make you feel godlike. But if you realize it has shortcomings, you tend to use it better. 'Powerful technology corrupts powerfully.' "

Corry chuckled. "Mister Goff, with that philosophy, I understand why you do so well with the sonar and the lidar."

"Sir, any equipment has its shortcomings. I like to figure out how to work around them. My daddy was an engineer. He taught me to make the best of what I had to work with."

The CO nodded. "That's classical engineering. Carry on, Roger."

LT Charles Ames had more targets on his master masdet display. He pointed them out to his Commanding Officer with commentary. "Sir, here are the three submarines. They're dead in the water at the moment about fifty klicks to the north and west of Palmyra. They haven't moved in the last three hours. They're ultrasilent, sir."

"Why do you think they're there, Charlie?"

Ames shrugged. "Maybe CINCPAC decided to protect an investment, sir."

Corry nodded. He liked the way his people conducted their thinking. "What else is out there?"

"The three surface ships have taken up similar positions a hundred klicks to the north, west, and south of Palmyra."

"Mister Goff believes they're space defense cruisers. What do you think?"

"I agree with him, sir. Their displacement appears to match that of the Astronaut class space defense cruisers. And I think they're out there for much the same reason as the attack subs, sir."

"Can any of them detect the presence of the Awesomes?"

"I don't know, sir. I'm not a sonar expert. I doubt it."

"Why?"

"Roger didn't hear the Awesomes at first. We thought the sounds were coming from indigenous marine life—dolphins, whales."

Corry pointed at a nearby target. "What's that?"

"Commander Chase says it's the sunken remains of the yacht *Sea Wind* that went down here about fifty years ago. It's shown on her chart. It's still a massive target, because yachts back then were made of Fiberglas. So it didn't rust out on the bottom."

"Where's the *Tuscarora?*" Corry wanted to know. "It wasn't displayed on the bridge screens."

"Sir, about two hours ago, it slowly slipped behind Washington Island over here to the southeast at a distance of two hundred and thirty klicks," Ames reported, indicating the signal generated by the mass of Washington Island.

Corry thought about this revelation for a moment, then told his masdet officer, "Charlie, I want you to notify me the instant the *Tuscarora* changes position."

"Yes, sir."

"And I want to know at once if you spot any additional *Tuscarora* targets."

"Yes, sir. That's SOP, sir."

Corry thought for a moment, then asked, "How about airborne targets? Have you spotted anything above the air-water interface?"

In the Solomon Sea, Ames had worked out a non-spec method of seeing airborne targets with the submerged masdet. That was a feature that the White Oak Naval Laboratories might have suspected but didn't claim as a feature of the WSS-1 special sensor. The masdet wasn't supposed to have that capability. Actually, it did. Ames had turned that newly perfected feature into an operational attribute.

"Yes, sir. I've been tracking commercial aircraft en route between Hawaii and the South Pacific," Ames announced with a touch of pride in his voice.

"That's new," Corry agreed. "Do you mind telling me how you did it?"

"Sir, I can't tell you how I tweaked the masdet. That's classified, and I haven't been told that you have a need to know. I'm sorry about that, sir. Orders," Ames said with some hesitation. He didn't like being in the position where orders and security regulations wouldn't permit him to discuss his equipment openly with his Commanding Officer. It was a definite shortcoming in his orders, and he intended to lodge a formal complaint about it when the boat returned to Pearl Harbor.

"Don't sweat it, Charlie," Corry told him easily. "I don't need to know how it works. I only need to know what it can do when you tell it to stand up and sing. You're very good with the masdet."

Ames felt a little better about it after that remark. "Well, sir, I didn't do it alone. Barbara and I put our heads together and refined that noise reduction code of hers." Ames didn't mention that he and LTJG Barbara Brewer had put more than that together. The man had been deathly afraid of women when he'd come aboard with the masdet several months ago. However, he'd found the ladies of the U.S.S. *Shenandoah* as comfortable to work with professionally as the scientists at White Oak, and this had helped him overcome his extreme shyness. Because of their close working relationship in the sensors area, Brewer had been the one to break the ice of reticence around Ames. To Ames, it had seemed natural in retrospect. But he had yet to learn about women.

Corry had suspected this. Ames' reference to the Radar/ Lidar Officer by her first name confirmed it for him.

"Excellent! Charlie, we're likely to get into a furball of unknown size and intensity here at Palmyra," Corry confided in him.

"Captain, I've got to admit that this is a little scary," Ames confessed. "The whole scenario smacks of a poorly written science fiction TV series."

Corry tried to put the man at ease. The Commanding Officer was concerned, too. But he didn't want his apprehension to be transmitted to the crew. "Well, Charlie, look at it the way I have to by considering each of the elements involved. We know the Awesomes are here, but they don't yet know that we are. They're probably accompanied by Mantids with whom they work. They probably want their companions and Corona back, as you pointed out. We've tangled with the Awesomes and the Mantids, and we prevailed both times. As for the *Tuscarora,* it has some sort of interest in this whole matter, but we don't know what it is, what's motivating its commander, and what its capabilities are. However, remember this: When we tangled with a *Tuscarora* the first time off Makasar, it ran. The second time, it acted like a game warden or coast guard cutter, and it looked us over very carefully without any aggressive moves. I don't believe we're in immediate danger, or we wouldn't be at Condition Three."

"Well, sir, CINCPAC has apparently laid on a heavy ASW and aerospace defense. Looks like they have some heartburn about it all."

"We don't know what they know or don't know," Corry admitted. "But also remember that this is now an intel operation. We're dealing with the spooks. With all your experience on this classified masdet program at White Oak, you certainly must know about security people."

"Yes, sir. They're paranoid. They suspect anything and everything."

"So you've just explained why CINCPAC has laid on the heavy protection," Corry told the worried officer. Ames was young and the *Shenandoah* was his first blue-water posting. "I haven't any idea how this is going to play itself out. But we can and will defend ourselves. We know we can do that against any weapons they've used against us thus far. Part of our ability to defend ourselves depends on you. You're in an absolutely crucial position here. Along with Lieutenant Brewer, Mister Goff, and Lieutenant Atwater, you're the eyes and ears of this boat."

"Yes, sir. We're all very much aware of that, sir." The quiet and seemingly introverted masdet officer had begun to come out of his shell since he'd come aboard several months ago. Corry often wondered if this was due to the close social interaction that took place in a carrier submarine or the result of having confronted and overcome a lot of fear in combat situations. Probably, he decided, it was a little bit of both. But Ames added more information by remarking, "Sir, this has been a lot different from working in a laboratory with only the possibility of the equipment failing a test. A lot of people in this boat are counting on me to help keep them alive. It, uh, makes a difference, sir."

Corry nodded. "That it does, Charlie. That it does."

This was a typical submariner's outlook. But there were other crucial departments in the U.S.S. *Shenandoah,* and one of them was sick bay.

"Posty, you look like death warmed over," was Dr. Laura Raye Moore's comment when Chief Pharmacist Mate Nat Post approached her in the receiving area.

He had a sheaf of hard copy printouts in his arms. "Doctor, I've spent the night with the computer, crunching data," he replied, indicating the hard copy with a nod of his head.

"You found something?"

"I think so," Post admitted. "Or I may be imagining things because of my condition."

"Good news or bad news?"

"I think you told the Captain once you had news and news. That's the way I feel about this." Post admitted. "I'm not going to make a judgment call. In the first place, I shouldn't. In the second place, I'm too damned pooped to be rational."

"What do you think you found?" the Medical Officer prompted him.

"I'll let you decide, Doctor." He went over to a gurney and spread out some of the hard copy sheets. "Doctor, I know where you got your last immunizations, but do you recall where?"

"Uh, San Diego, I think. When I came off leave and shipped out to this boat before the Makasar mission." Moore remembered only because the head of immunology there was a rather handsome three-striper she'd dated after getting her shots.

Post nodded. "Says so right here," he pointed out after he riffled through several sheets of hard copy and came to her name. "Same place I got mine. So did Lieutenant Molders."

Moore had gotten several hours of sound sleep and felt better. But she hadn't made her rounds yet, and she was worried about her patients' progress or lack of it during the night. "Get to the point, Chief!"

Post did. "Doctor, I've found a common factor among everyone who's come down with Mantid fever. They all got their shots at the dispensary at Barber's Point."

Moore checked carefully where Post had indicated the data on the printout.

She nodded. "Okay, I see that, Posty. The special team all got their immunizations there, too. They'd been flown in from the States, did an RON at the Barber's Point VOQ, and then were flown right out to the *Shenandoah*. But, what the hell, Commander Smith hasn't reported in with the FUO!"

Post riffled through the printouts and pointed. "She apparently goes on foreign assignments a lot, Doctor. I couldn't pull down her service records, of course. She's intel. But she was immunized at Bethesda a year ago."

"Then why did Zervas . . .?" Moore began.

"Because he probably never expected to leave Bethesda, Doctor," Post pointed out. "He shipped out on this cruise on an emergency basis, I expect. He got to Barber's Point and they discovered he hadn't had his shots. So he got 'em there."

"And, of course, all the Air Group people would . . ."

Post shook his head. "Not necessarily so, Doctor. Commander Peyton, Chief Caliborn, the two aviation machinist mates, and about twenty people in Air Group were also immunized at Barber's Point dispensary before the Makasar cruise. I have the list here. The rest of the crew got their shots at the submarine base dispensary on Ford Island."

Moore thought about this for a moment. "So why would the FUO hit only those who were recently immunized at Barber's Point?"

"They received immunizations from the same batch of vaccine," Post stated flatly.

"So? Was the vaccine no good?"

"No, Doctor, but it was different from the vaccine used at Ford Island and elsewhere. The reason it took me so long to do this data-crunching was my search for the common factor of the common factor," Post explained. "That wasn't so easy. Fortunately, the medical records always show the make and batch number of the vaccine used. All of the eight patients we have in sick bay at the moment were given ProColCor Type Seven from Batch Number Three-zero-seven mutliphasic tropical vaccine. Immunized against typhoid, all the other exanthems, the important aboviruses, the rickettsials, and a whole lot more." He paused.

"So? Continue to lead the blind, please," Laura Raye prompted him. "What's so special about that make and batch?"

"Doctor, remember when they came up with the synthetic vaccine for all those agents about five years ago? The stuff they created by genetic mutation and nano-mechanics?"

"Yes. Big breakthrough. The Navy Medical Service put in a large order for it right away because it stores better and longer. And it was a lot cheaper."

"Well, Doctor, the orders also went out to use up existing stocks of the old vaccine made using chicken eggs, the classical method," Post explained. "I was temporarily stationed at Barber's Point while I was waiting for the *Shenandoah* to be commissioned. I remember that the dispensary there had a ton of the old stuff."

"And you weren't shot full of it?"

"No, ma'am. I wasn't due until we got back from Makasar, and I got the synthetic stuff."

Moore began to nod as she thought about this. "Okay. Okay. Yeah. The symptoms of Mantid fever do resemble the onset of smallpox, yellow fever, typhoid ... If so, it should resemble the etiology and epidemiology of those diseases. And why didn't it show up in the blood work?"

"It may have, Doctor. We could have missed it because we weren't looking for something that straightforward. As for the etiology, the Mantids appear to be insectlike, right?"

She nodded. "They seem to have a definite anatomical similarity."

"But we haven't checked them for their symbiotes and parasites," the chief pharmacist mate pointed out.

Moore pondered that for a few seconds before she responded, "Yes, of course! Maybe they've got something similar to the infectious mites that live on such terrestrial insects as ticks."

Post nodded, although it was more of a shake of his head as if to clear his mind. He was bone-weary after an all-nighter. "Doctor, that's certainly a viable hypothesis. Let me get some sleep, then I'll check these live Mantids for their body organisms. I'll bet we're going to discover the FUO source there, maybe in the feces of their body mites."

"My God, if it's something like that, it's probably been carried throughout the boat in the air system!" Moore gasped. "If that's true, Posty, I sure hope you're correct in your wide-assed guess that Mantid fever will hit only those who've been immunized with the old vaccine."

"Doctor, we've got a lot of the new vaccine aboard."

"Enough to vaccinate everyone who didn't get the synthetic vaccine at Barber's Point?"

"Yes, ma'am. I keep a complete pharmacopoeia in this boat. It's your call, but maybe we ought to shoot them up with it *before* they become our patients."

"Provided it isn't too late, Posty."

"Well, Doctor, I've got a good stock of interferon, methisazone, and macrolies, too."

"Let's hope we don't have to use them. We'll check the blood work again. The fact that we missed on the first pass indicates some secondary causative and not the primary viral factor." Dr. Laura Raye Moore was excited now. She had a lead to work on. It had come from the professional dedication of her CPM and his ability to manipulate the technology. When she looked at him, she saw he was exhausted. "As for you, Chief, I believe you're suffering from acute fatigue. I can't have you out of action for very long. You're too important to the Medical Department. So this is an order: Hit the rack. I'll see you in a couple of hours. In the meantime, I'll do what I can based on your information. And, by the way, that was very good work, Posty!"

13

"No."

CDR Matilda Harriet Smith was curt and adamant.

On the other hand, CDR Zeke Braxton expected that answer.

"I rarely take no for an answer, Smitty," Zeke told her.

"I've noticed. And under those circumstances, I really didn't want you to. However, a lady and an officer must occasionally appear to have some propriety," Smith told him frankly. She enjoyed Zeke's company. Furthermore, she considered it a challenge to compete with CDR Terri Ellison for Zeke's attention. Thus far, she'd been reasonably successful. "But those times involved personal matters. This is a professional matter."

The cabin of the Executive Officer wasn't as large as the Captain's. However, the two of them hadn't minded the coziness. Until that moment, that is.

Zeke played it cool as usual. And he rarely lost his cool, even with his main rival, Major Bart Clinch. And certainly never with the ladies. Losing one's temper with a lady was certainly no way to garner cooperation of any sort. Zeke had learned long ago a woman responded to a direct order she disliked in the same manner as a cat: just barely. Personally or professionally, Zeke wanted full and enthusiastic response instead. And he usually got it.

So he cupped his hands around his coffee mug and looked at the steaming brew inside it for a moment. "Terri says she can fly the Corona," he said.

"She may be one shit-hot pilot, Zeke, but I have no authority to let her attempt to fly such a valuable artifact!"

"Were you ordered *not* to allow anyone to fly it?"

"No, but that's beside the point. I've gotten to know you submarine types now. You're used to working alone, your orders are usually very broad and loose, and you're expert sea lawyers."

"Smitty, the Silent Service learned long ago that forgiveness is easier to get than permission," Zeke admitted.

"Yes, you demonstrated that." She said it and meant it as a double entendre. Although this was just an early-morning coffee klatch with Zeke, CDR Matilda Harriet Smith had made certain she was more than just presentable. Ship's Stores had issued her a couple of blue poopie suits, but she rarely wore them. Other women crew members did because of comfort and ease of care. Some even had tailored versions. But Smith wore either khakis or tropical whites. They made her stand out. Because of the *way* she wore what was otherwise a commonplace uniform, she never lacked for social companionship at mess. What appearance did to break the ice was compounded by her feminine behavior that followed. Some of the ladies of the boat were jealous, but they knew she wasn't going to be aboard forever.

"And *that's* beside the point!" Zeke fired back and went on to explain what he really had meant. "Let me put it in a different context. Too many land sailors believe that everything is forbidden except that which is covered by orders or regulations. At three hundred meters depth in the middle of nowhere with an enemy trying to find us and kill us, we have to operate with the principle that everything is permitted except that which is expressly forbidden. Orders tell us what's expected of us. Rules of engagement tell us specifically what we cannot do."

"Zeke, let me give you a rule of engagement right now. I cannot allow Commander Ellison to attempt to fly the Corona!" Smith stated emphatically. "Period. End of discussion."

"I don't think it is," Zeke persisted. He didn't give up easy. In the first place, he hadn't had time to present the full argument. So he pushed on. "What are you saving the Corona for? A bunch of Patuxent test pilots whose job it is to bend prototype airplanes? They don't give a damn if they prang the ship as long as they can punch out and live to fly another one. On the other hand, Terri knows full well that her career is finished if she even dings the Corona."

"She put you up to this, didn't she?"

Zeke nodded. "Yes, of course. She asked me to ask you," he replied truthfully.

"What's the matter? Is she afraid to come to me directly?"

Zeke shook his head. "Not at all. But I'm the Executive Officer of this boat, and she's only the CAG," he explained. "Technically, she can't make an official request directly to you. It should come through me. And it has."

Smith wasn't very happy about this course of events. "She used her personal relationship with you, and you're using your personal relationship with me. That's not being professional!"

"It has nothing to do with being professional," Zeke countered at once and asked her in return, "Do you mean to tell me you don't use personal contacts to get the job done in your line of work, Smitty? Sure you do! Hell, we all do! We all prefer to work with people we know and trust! Tell me, do you trust Terri?"

"As an individual?"

"And as a pilot. With Terri, they're inseparable," Zeke pointed out. "Do you think she's a good enough pilot to fly the Corona and not prang it?"

"She's a good pilot. She has to be good to be where she is. But she isn't a test pilot."

"Smitty, if you were a pilot, you'd know that every pilot is a test pilot. Every cat shot, every ski-jump takeoff, and every trap is a test of the pilot and the aircraft. It doesn't cut it that the airplane worked the last time. Or that personal reactions and capabilities were sufficient the last time. *This time* could be different. Every flight is a test." He got up to get a fresh cup of coffee. "Warm it up, Smitty?"

"Yes. Thank you." She handed him her cup. "Dammit, you're not going to give up, are you?"

"Not easily."

Smith sighed. "I've got a lot to lose if something goes wrong. Tell me what I've got to gain if she flies it successfully."

"In the first place, how are we going to get it off this boat and into or onto something else?" Zeke asked as he returned to the little table and set a filled coffee mug before her.

"I imagine Admiral Kane will arrange to have a tender

at Palmyra," Smith speculated. She didn't really know. She hadn't thought about it. But she didn't admit that to Zeke. "The Corona can be lifted off the flight deck with a tender's crane and put on the tender."

"At sea?" Zeke asked rhetorically. He had visions of what could happen, and he tried to explain them to her. "Smitty, we'd have to wait for dead calm and no swells. We might find that in the lee of the atoll, depending on the weather and the sea state. Two ships heaving up and down riding the swells is *not* a situation in which delicate cargo is transferred!"

"Well, Palmyra has a harbor," she recalled, remembering the chart that Natalie Chase had pulled from the hard copy file and laid out for her on the bridge navigation table when she'd inquired about the atoll last night.

"*Harbor?* It's a lagoon that hasn't been dredged in about a hundred years!" Zeke had seen the charts, too. And he'd noted the pub dates on them. "No one knows how much bottom is available today. The printed charts indicate we'd have maybe ten to fifteen meters at low tide in some places, if the data is still valid. It probably isn't. Atolls are coral reefs that grow. The fact that Natalie has only printed charts with nothing in the computer database should tell you something about how current the hydrographic information is!"

"I understand that private yachts used to call at Palmyra."

"This is no yacht, Smitty. And that was because the Navy leased it."

"But it has a central lagoon!"

"And only one narrow entrance channel. We don't know how deep it is, either. If we put the boat in there, we may not be able to get it out in a hurry, especially if the Awesomes and the Mantids have some sort of welcoming party planned. The sonar and masdet data shows the Awesomes all around that end of the atoll. And their mother ship isn't very far away in the southwest shoals. Did you mention something about risk, Smitty? Please cut me some slack when it comes to seamanship and boat handling."

Smith knew that Zeke was lecturing her, and she didn't like it. She wasn't a blue-water sailor. That put her at a disadvantage, and she did her best to overcome it in other ways. "And *you* cut *me* some slack when it comes to intel work, Zeke!"

"I'm trying," he replied easily. "Smitty, I merely want to point out that it may be less risky to fly the Corona to another ship alongside using a bunny hop. Or fly it to the airstrip on Palmyra if Naval Intelligence has arranged airlift to get it out of there."

"You know the Navy doesn't have heavy airlift capability!" Smith was still angry and on edge. She was really worried about the possibility of Terri's crashing the Corona if flying was authorized. But she was running out of rationales in the face of reality. She hadn't thought too much about how to get the Corona off the boat. "And the Aerospace Force won't be involved. Judging from my orders and the fact that Admiral McCarthy didn't come out to Pearl just for leave, this affair has some very powerful interservice ramifications to it. McCarthy isn't about to let the Aerospace Force in on this. That's obvious!" She paused. "No, Zeke, no one is going to fly the Corona. It's going to stay in the hangar deck, probably for days to come. You're going to be ordered to keep the Corona on the hangar deck and head for Bangor. Or maybe Whidbey Island."

"Then why weren't we ordered to go direct to the ZI with the Corona? Why were we ordered to come to Palmyra and wait? And why did CINCPAC move ships all over the Pacific Ocean to provide sea and aerospace defense for Palmyra?" Zeke persisted.

"Maybe so OP-thirty-two could put some intel teams aboard. Maybe because the international situation has gotten touchy. Maybe because the Chinese are still upset about getting the short end of the stick at Makasar. Maybe so we can have three attack subs as an escort to the ZI," she guessed, and didn't like having to do it.

Zeke knew that. He fired back, "Maybe, maybe, maybe. But why Palmyra?"

"Why not?" she snapped, getting a bit irritated at this sort of interrogation. She'd been taught that intel types were the ones who were supposed to ask the questions. "McCarthy probably doesn't want us to sail into Pearl right under the snooping eyes of the Aerospace Force. So Palmyra is being used as a staging base. They may take my special team off and put another aboard! And I'm going to lose everything I've worked so hard for!"

She paused, realized that she was losing her cool, and tried to calm down. She'd also been taught not to lose her temper. That caused people to do rash things. Intelligence work wasn't based on rash actions. She took a sip of coffee, then admitted, "I don't know, Zeke. I just don't know. I do know what my orders from McCarthy say. I'm responsible for the Corona and the Mantids aboard. The security level and compartmentation tell me that it's sensitive to the highest possible level. McCarthy and probably CNO aren't letting any other intel outfit in on this. That's abundantly clear from the message."

"It's also abundantly clear that we face some dangers that McCarthy and CINCPAC aren't telling us about," Zeke recalled.

"They may not know. They may only suspect. But I know Admiral McCarthy pretty well, because I've worked with her for a long time," Smith said, then decided she could probably share a few Naval Intelligence operational bits with him. "She gave us the best heads-up warning she could. That's also typical of intel work, Zeke. Maybe all she knew at that time was that other forces were at work, but she didn't know what ones or what they were doing."

"Probably the Mantid-Awesome presence here. And the *Tuscarora* that's been shadowing us out at the edge of our sensor capability ever since we left Guadalcanal." Zeke didn't like those unknowns out there. Maybe Naval Intelligence believed it could fathom what those extraterrestrials were up to. But Zeke knew they were radically different from human beings. The Awesomes were underwater aliens who lived in an alien environment that Zeke also tried to operate in: the oceans. The Mantids—well, the Mantids were different beings entirely, and Zeke had no idea what their home world might be like.

"Look, Smitty," he went on, "this is a wild situation. We don't know what our own people are doing. We have no idea what the Mantids and Awesomes are planning. And we don't even know what that *Tuscarora* target is. Given all of this, Smitty, don't you think it might be a good idea if *someone* in this boat could fly the Corona if necessary?"

"Yes, but I've got to think about that for a while, Zeke. It's got a lot of ramifications. For example, Terri doesn't know how to fly a Corona any more than I do. So how would she go about *learning* to fly it?"

Zeke knew he was making progress. He had been convinced by Terri that it would be a good thing to be able to fly the Corona, and he was using some of the same arguments on Smith.

"Well, Terri won't just kick the tires and light the fires. She's a cautious pilot until she gets into a furball," Zeke explained carefully. Actually, he didn't know she'd approach it that way. However, he was a naval aviator and that's the way *he* would start. "So my guess is that she'd have the Corona lifted to the upper flight deck and given a partial load of fuel. Then it would be tethered so she could try liftoff, hovering, and landing. She can do a certain amount of stability investigation in tether. That's the way they learn how to fly VTOL aircraft. And how they test them at Patuxent, too."

"That means surfacing," Smith observed. She decided she'd talk to Terri about the matter. But she hadn't made up her mind yet. She always reserved that option. And that trait came from more than intelligence training.

"Yes. So we'll have to wait until we get further orders from CINCPAC. Until then, we sit here dead on the bottom and wait. And plan."

"Oh, there are other things to do, too. We can scheme. . . ."

Zeke grinned. He'd made his point about the Corona. As a naval aviator, he, too, wanted to see it fly with a human being at the controls. And if anyone could make that happen, Terri Ellison could.

Deep down inside, Zeke was still a pilot. He'd been required to keep his pilot's whimsy and rollicking approach to life somewhat subdued as the Executive Officer. His own logbook showed stick time in many aircraft. He thought it was a great idea that Terri might be able to log time in a flying saucer. He'd almost be willing to bend a few rules himself if he could get that entry in his logbook!

"Well, Smitty, we could sit here for weeks as long as the food holds out. Maybe we shouldn't be in such a rush to get further orders!"

She smiled back at him. "What would you call it? Bottom liberty?"

"I'm an officer and a gentleman by act of Congress, so I wouldn't put it in such gross terms."

CAPT William M. Corry really didn't like the idea of sitting on the bottom and waiting. The sooner he got rid of the Mantids, the Corona, and special team, and perhaps the feverish patients in sick bay, the happier he would be. He didn't relish sitting around with such valuable cargoes, and he was very concerned about the possibility of the spread of the fever among the rest of the crew. However, more than a day had gone by since Evelyn Lulalilo had come down with the fever in his cabin. No epidemic had spread through the ship. And he hadn't received a report from his Medical Officer yet indicating that anything critical was happening.

So he spent most of the morning in the sensor compartments, studying the masdet and passive sonar displays. He wanted to get a feeling for the situation. His ship was grounded in deep water off the atoll, and the bulk of the reef cut off his maneuvering room to the south. He contemplated potential courses of action should he be forced to move fast. His choices were limited only by whatever approached from true bearing 207 through 090. So far, no close-in targets had been spotted in that large sector. Except for the transpacific aircraft going overhead and the apparently random movements of the Awesomes around the southeast tip of the atoll, none of the targets showed any motion.

At 1100, he decided that something had come unbonded in CINCPAC's plans. No message had come in.

He didn't want to disobey the specific wording of his orders and surface to find out what was going on. After all, the boat was in no danger. It was lying silently on the bottom off the north side of Palmyra as ordered. Slightly more than three days had passed since they had left Guadalcanal. So he was where he was supposed to be when he was supposed to be there and doing what he was supposed to be doing.

He decided he would wait twenty-four hours. Terri would bitch and moan about having to fly in the simulators instead of doing the real thing. Major Bart Clinch would snivel about keeping his Marine batt on their toes by resorting to close order drill on the lower flight deck. But the

Ship Division would be happy to sit quietly on regular watches and take it easy. He could even use the respite.

But he wasn't going to get it.

He toggled his N-fone to the command channel as he left the sensors compartments and headed back to the bridge.

He hadn't gone ten meters before the message sounded inside his head: *Captain, this is the Medical Officer. If you're out and about, would you please come at once to the sick bay? Lulalilo and Duval have regained consciousness, and I've got problems with the Mantids again.*

14

"More news and news with no evaluation thereof?" Corry asked his Medical Officer as he greeted her in sick bay.

"Not precisely, Captain," Laura Raye Moore told him. She indicated with a nod of her head that she wanted to discuss matters with him in the privacy of her "office."

He followed her. She shut the door behind them and sat down at her desk, which doubled as a conference table.

"How do you feel today? Are you recovering from the effects of that head blow?" Corry asked with sincere curiosity.

"I'm all right," Laura Raye insisted. "I'm following the prescription I gave you. I take two aspirin and call myself occasionally to make sure I'm okay. I've been too busy to do anything else. In fact, we've all been busy in sick bay."

"I would suspect that, Doctor. How are the people you have here with Mantid fever?" He knew, but he asked anyway.

"They're going to be all right."

"Well, I'd classify that as good news."

Moore nodded. "So would I. And we *think* that *maybe* we've isolated the cause and identified the agent. I want to be sure that you realize this is a very preliminary assessment, Captain. We could be hit with the Big Surprise."

"We always face that possibility in anything we do, Doctor," Corry advised her. He looked around. "You normally ask me to chat with you in here when the discussion demands privacy and the outcome shouldn't be announced. Is there something about this Mantid fever that you wish to maintain in a confidential status?"

"No, but maybe some of the other things I have to report should be confidential. I'll get to them in due course, Captain. I try to be logical in presenting reports to you."

"From the simple to the complex. Of course."

"That's so you'll understand the biotechnical and medical facts." That was her normal way of handling her reporting. She and Corry knew that some Medical Officers tended to hide behind a facade of jargon because their Commanding Officers didn't care or really didn't want to know. Or because the Medical Officers felt less than qualified and wouldn't admit it. Neither Corry nor Moore fell into those categories.

"Very well, Doctor, please tell me what you've learned about Mantid fever. Is it contagious?"

"I wouldn't use that word to describe its epidemiology, Captain," Laura Raye told him frankly. "However, if you're asking if I think we're going to have an epidemic in the boat, the answer is no."

"Well, that's good news! I take it that you've got good reason to say that."

"I do. Except for the eight people present in sick bay and about twenty officers and rates in the Air Group, the rest of us in the boat are already immunized."

"Ah, so Mantid fever turns out to be something you already know about?" Corry asked.

"No, not really. I don't know what it is yet," the Medical Officer admitted honestly. "The immunizations we've gotten are protecting us for the moment."

"But apparently not all of us."

"I think I know why. I'll get to that in a moment," Moore promised. "My big concern is that it could be epidemic *outside the boat* if we're carriers. The disease itself may have been epidemic in the Solomon Islands. However, we don't know for sure. We never went ashore, and therefore I have no data on which to base such an assumption."

"Is the disease due to the presence of the Mantids?"

"In the boat, yes. Where Mantid fever came from and whether or not it's specific to the Mantids, I don't know. It could be a mutation of a terrestrial disease, and the Mantids could just be the carriers. Let me explain."

"Please do."

"Let me go back to the beginning of this." Moore folded her long, surgeon's hands on the table before her and recalled, "When Doctors Lulalilo, Zervas, and Duval came in with Mantid fever, I had blood work done as a standard procedure. The same with Mister Soucek, Mister Peyton, Chief Caliborn, and the two aviation machinist mates. At that time, neither my lab techs nor I spotted anything. It turned out we weren't looking for the right thing."

"That's fairly common, and not only in medicine," Corry told her.

She nodded. "Yes, I'm not omniscient. What happened was this: We suspected that the disease had been somehow vectored from the Mantids, alive and dead. But not everyone who'd been in contact with the Mantids was affected. I give Chief Post the credit for doing the impossible."

She explained what her Chief Pharmacist Mate had done in his all-night session with the computer.

"So the only people aboard who contacted Mantid fever are the ones who had their last immunizations with the old vaccine at Barber's Point?" Corry wanted to make sure he understood this.

"That's correct, Captain."

"Why?"

"I don't know, sir. I'm not an epidemiologist. I'll report the matter in detail to my medical colleagues at Pearl Harbor when we return."

"An honest answer."

"There is no other kind of answer that a doctor can or ever should give," Laura Raye remarked. "But I don't need to know why one vaccine works and the other doesn't in protecting the crew, which is my job. If I have time, I'll try to figure it out."

"Knowing you, you've already found a little time," Corry told her.

"Bill, you're getting to know me almost as well as I know you!" the Medical Officer told him with a smile. The relationship between a Commanding Officer and his Medical Officer always went beyond the bounds set by the regulations but never beyond the bounds of propriety. Laura Raye was the only officer aboard who could overrule the Captain. In fact, she could relieve him of duty under very specific circumstances.

"Of course I found a 'little time.' I'm one of the curious Medical Officers in the fleet. Someday, I may give up all this cruising around the world and settle down to some serious medical research based on what I've learned," she admitted.

"Well, you certainly have a ground-floor opportunity to get into exobiology, Laura Raye," Corry pointed out.

"However, I would accept your application for transfer only with great reluctance."

"You're not going to get rid of me that easily, Bill! I have a job to do here and we have a mission to complete. And maybe even more beyond that. Who knows?" She sighed. "In any event, yes, I've done some research beyond what Posty did last night. The Mantids, alive and dead, carry a parasite, a Mantid mite. I looked at the Mantid Zervas was dissecting, and Mister Molders and I found the organisms. They may be terrestrial in origin, but I can't say for sure. The mite waste becomes an aerosol. It carries an organism smaller than but similar to *Rickettsia burneti*. That's what causes Q fever. It may be a mutated version of *R. burneti*. However, the symptoms of Mantid fever are similar to those of Q fever, and we don't see much Q fever except in southeast Asia and Africa these days. But they're the pestholes of the earth anyway. If a disease ever existed, it can be found there. And most of our new diseases come from those parts of the world. Anyway, I don't mean to lecture you on medical matters. . . ."

"You're not. This is information I must know. Go on, Doctor."

"I had my lab techs look at the blood samples again and take new ones where necessary," the Medical Officer continued. "We didn't find *R. burneti*. However, we found something like it that we'd missed because it appears similar to some of the benign organisms in all of us. On the basis of that finding, I began treating Mantid fever as I would treat Q fever. Good old tetracycline knocks it down fast."

"What's this Q fever, Laura Raye? I haven't heard of it before."

"Q fever resembles influenza. It's nonlethal except in about one percent of the untreated population. It's worldwide, but we rarely see it in the United States because such a small percentage of the population comes in contact with farm animals these days. Mantid fever may be a variation of Q fever." The Medical Officer paused. "Frankly, Q fever isn't life-threatening and so it hasn't received much attention. It can be treated effectively with both tetracycline and chloramphenicol. So it's not a 'hot' disease whose study will ensure a research grant."

"Mantid fever could change that, Doctor," Corry pointed out.

Laura Raye Moore cocked her head to one side. A querulous expression came over her face. She thought about Corry's remark for a moment. "Not likely, Captain," she finally told him.

"Suppose your tetracycline therapy *doesn't* work here in the boat today?"

"It appears to be working already. Both Eve and Duval have normal body temperature, and their recent blood work shows the absence of *R. burneti.*"

"I'm glad to hear that. But we could be immune, as the Mantids appear to be. Yet the Mantids as well as the rest of us in the *Shenandoah* could turn out to be carriers of a new disease whose source is an extraterrestrial organism."

"I don't want to think about that."

"I believe we should. In fact, I must," Corry insisted. "I'm not a doctor, Laura Raye, but I do have a responsibility both to the crew and to others outside the boat."

Laura Raye sighed. "Captain, as your Medical Officer, my recommendation at this point would be to wait and see what course the Mantid fever takes. I think we've got it knocked. But I'm willing to withhold final judgment." She paused, then went on. "I don't have the facilities to run blood work on seven hundred and fifty people."

"When CINCPAC contacts me, should I inform them that we should be considered in quarantine until you have more information?"

Laura Raye shook her head. "No, don't suggest quarantine."

"I should report this."

She nodded in agreement. "Yes. I'll prepare a summary you can use, a preliminary report from your Medical Officer."

"Thank you. Please do that." Corry considered carefully what he wanted to say next, then spoke up, "I'm not trying to usurp your medical authority, Laura Raye. And I haven't taken out my do-it-yourself doctor kit. But I must tell you that the presence of Mantid fever in the boat causes me a great deal of concern. Perhaps because it's in the biotechnology area and not part of submarine operational knowhow. I intend to depend on you for information and recommendations as I always have. It's a threat, albeit one I'm not used to dealing with. I have to treat it that way."

"You'll have no problem from me, Captain," Laura Raye told him confidently. She was not yet concerned that Mantid fever might be pandemic or even epidemic. Her patients were responding well to treatment at the moment. She had the authority and the responsibility under Naval Regulations to go directly to the CINCPAC Deputy Commander, Medical Service, if necessary. Not that she intended to do so, of course. Such a move would be one of last resort. And she saw no reason then to consider it.

"Next matter," the Medical Officer said crisply. "Both Eve and Duval have responded enough this morning that they're asking to see visitors."

"Do you intend to permit that?"

She nodded. "Do you wish to overrule my decision?"

"No, Doctor. It's your sick bay. You can authorize visitation of your patients."

"Duval has asked to see Natalie Chase."

"I suspected he might."

"Natalie has mixed feelings about that, given what we discovered inside Duval's head. She would like you to be present."

"Natalie Chase is a fine officer, an expert Navigator, and an attractive woman. I have no desire to intrude on her off-duty life, because she's always acted with the utmost discretion in the past. Did she say why she wanted me there?"

"No, sir."

"I'll accommodate her wishes. Far be it from me to deny such a simple request from a trusted subordinate. I've suspected she was developing a serious relationship with Duval."

"Thank you. Captain, the revelation that Duval isn't human was a real shock to her."

"It was to all of us."

"She's a strong woman, but I think she needs a little fatherly support at the moment."

Corry thought again of the bit of raunchy doggerel called "The Captain Is the Father of His Crew" that he and his shipmates had sung at the Naval Academy. It dealt with the proclivities of a hypothetical Commanding Officer getting around the restrictions of Naval Regulation 2020. The song was many verses long and involved the Captain's relationships with every crew member. It was a joke, and the female midshipmen resented it at first (as they initially resented the label "midshipman"). They retaliated with a nautical version of "Schoolmarm Lil." Then both groups discovered an older ditty entitled "On the Good Ship Venus" that they sang together at parties where they didn't have to be ladies and gentlemen.

Corry now knew, as the result of years of service and the command of the SSCV-26, that the Captain did indeed have to serve as the father to his crew in a psychological if not a physical sense. Men and women who had chosen the life of submariners were often loners, orphans, products of broken families, or just people who needed and wanted the extended family environment of a ship's crew with its strong surrogate father commander.

He had never anticipated it from CDR Natalie Chase, however.

Corry wanted to speak with Duval in any event. However, he suddenly realized that he might learn more about Duval if he was present at Natalie's request.

"Whenever Natalie wants me, please call me," Corry told the Medical Officer.

"She's waiting in the pharmacy, Captain."

"Oh? Very well, let's go." Corry started to get up, believing that the conversation was finished.

Laura Raye held up her hand. "Captain, Eve also wants to see you. And I need to tell you something beforehand."

Corry resumed his seat and said nothing.

When Corry remained silent, the Medical Officer went on, "I may be compromising medical ethics here by doing this. However, I believe it's necessary that you know, both as the Commanding Officer and as someone who means a great deal to Eve Lulalilo."

"Eve and I have become good friends, Laura Raye," Corry admitted.

She nodded. "I know. But you've become much more than just a good friend to Eve. At least in Eve's eyes."

Corry didn't hesitate to tell his Medical Officer, "Yes, I'm aware of that. And I've told her that I can be nothing more than a good friend."

"I expected as much from you, Bill. Don't forget: I know you pretty well myself," Laura Raye told him in the most gentle and familiar manner she could. As the Medical

Officer, she was the only one in the boat who could call him by his given name, and she did that only in private. Corry himself had encouraged it, because he knew there could be no secrets or formality between him and the Medical Officer. Laura Raye Moore was very discreet and limited in exercising this privilege. "I'm aware of your family problem, and I applaud the way you've vowed to handle yourself in the face of something that has destroyed other men. Is Eve aware of it?"

"No. It's not her problem. I've simply told her that I love my wife and children very much and would never do anything to dishonor their trust. Laura Raye, Eve has been very willing, very enticing, and very frustrating! She reminds me of Cynthia when we were married, and she looks and acts very much like my daughter, Judy. That's been one of the biggest problems and distractions on this cruise. And I *must* be able to keep my mind on my duty and responsibility. Damm it, it hasn't been easy!" Corry shook his head. "And now you know the sort of hell I've been through. Eve knows where I stand. She knows that I cannot and will not cheat on Cynthia."

Laura Raye Moore sighed. "Then I have a real problem on my hands."

"If it's your problem, then it's also my problem. What has Eve told you?"

"Eve didn't tell me. She hasn't told anyone. But she's been flat in sick bay with a forty-one-degree fever. Last night, she was delirious. The fantasy world in her mind spilled forth," the Medical Officer reported. "Maybe I shouldn't let you know what came out in her delirium. Maybe I should have treated it with medical confidentiality. But on the other hand, I've never heard a woman— sane or delirious—who was so heartsick and heartbroken. Bill, her world has collapsed around her. I can treat her for Mantid fever. But she may never recover. In fact, she may die."

When Laura Raye Moore paused, Corry asked simply, "Why?"

"She's lost the will to live."

"Because of *me?*" Corry had trouble believing this. "She's a stronger person than that!"

"Not just because of you. Because her whole world has collapsed."

"I don't understand."

"Her world is built on wishful thinking. You and I may have trouble understanding that because ours isn't. She wants desperately to find a species that could teach us nasty human beings how to be kind and loving. She tried other terrestrial animals and failed. She hoped that the Awesomes or the Mantids would be the key, and she discovered that our Mantid guests are even nastier than we are. On top of that, Eve came from a broken family and finally found someone she could love but who could not because of circumstances return her love." She held up her hand as Corry started to react to that. "Bill, Eve may be a scientist, but she's also a romantic. And that's not your fault."

As the Commanding Officer of a major capital ship of the United States Navy and a proven leader of people, Corry was supposed to know how to handle personal situations of this sort. He felt somewhat helpless right then. But he called on his reserves of strength and asked his Medical Officer, "My fault or not, what can I do to help?"

The Medical Officer said two words: "Love her."

"I can't!"

"I think you can. Love is more than sex. Would you go to bed with your daughter? Of course not! You may secretly want to, because most parents have sensual feelings for their offspring of the opposite sex. But you love Judy. I know you do. And in different ways with different degrees of intensity, you love every person on this boat," she told him. "You treat them the way they would like to be treated. You're concerned with their well-being. They believe you think they're important to you and to themselves."

"That's friendship, Laura Raye."

"Bill, the line between love and friendship is very indistinct. In Eve's case, I repeat: Love her."

"D-d-d-d-difficult . . ." Corry couldn't control his stuttering.

"Well, we're making progress. A minute ago, you told me you couldn't."

"You have been helpful in that," Corry said very slowly and distinctly, controlling his breathing to control his stutter.

"We can get some more help if necessary."

"Oh?"

"The padre."

"Laura Raye, I don't think Eve is religious. And you know my own agnosticism. But if you think it will help to call on Tom Chapman's expertise . . ."

"He does have some expertise in these matters. I'm just a bedside psychologist. Have to be. The padre's full-time job is to handle human interrelations on a different level. You do it, too, on yet another level, and so do all the officers and chiefs."

"One of the problems of command is that I don't have all those people available to help me. I can only count on you. Which I do." Corry thought about this for a moment, then admitted, "I said it would be difficult. I've spent my life doing difficult jobs. And I've had to learn new things in the process. So I'd better get busy on this new one, Doctor. But first, we shouldn't keep the Navigator waiting."

15

"Thank you for agreeing to come with me, Captain," LCDR Natalie Chase told her Commanding Officer when they met in the sick bay pharmacy where she was waiting.

"I don't wish to intrude in your personal life, Natalie," Corry told her frankly.

"You're not, sir. I'm asking you to be present."

"At the risk of seeming to interfere, why do you want me there?"

"Because of what Laura Raye discovered about Barry," the Navigator replied. "We need to tell him that we know he's not human. And you need to hear his response, sir."

"The report of the Medical Officer seemed to surprise you," Corry recalled.

Without the slightest embarrassment, Natalie replied, "It did, sir. I hope my reaction was no surprise. Although I'm under the constraints of Regulation Twenty-twenty, Doctor Barry Duval is not. He's essentially a guest and passenger. However, I want to emphasize that I haven't taken advantage of that loophole in the reg, sir."

"I don't recall I implied you had."

"You didn't, sir. I just wanted to lay all the facts on the table at the start. I wouldn't want the ship to go into uncharted shoal waters without informing you or the OOD."

"It's my understanding that Duval asked to see you. Do you have any idea what he wants to talk to you about?"

"No, sir."

"I suspect," the Medical Officer interjected, "that he wants to see someone besides myself and my medical team. This is typical of most people who have been very ill. Furthermore, they usually want to talk to someone they feel close to. And from what I know, no one on the special team is close to him."

"No one on the special team is close to anyone else in

the group," Corry pointed out. "They were strangers before they came aboard, and most of them still are. Very well, Natalie, let's go. But if you wish to speak in private with Doctor Duval, please indicate that to me. I'll gladly leave." He had no desire to become involved in the private lives of any of his trusted officers if their behavior didn't affect their duties or jeopardize the ship.

It was hard to believe that Dr. Barry Duval wasn't a human being. He was tall and spare, but most human ectomorphs are. He was fair-skinned and certainly was no different in physical appearance from thousands of other people Chase and Corry had known in their lives. But beneath his skin, he wasn't human, according to Laura Raye Moore's examination of him while he was suffering from the Mantid fever. That morning, he looked normal but acted fatigued.

He greeted them simply: "Good morning." And he held out his hand to Natalie.

She took it and held it as she sat down alongside the bed. "Good morning, Barry. You're looking like your old self today."

"I'm a lot better than I was yesterday at this time," Duval admitted. "Now I'm just tired and a little cold, that's all."

Laura Raye Moore checked the thermostat on the compartment bulkhead. It was already set at twenty-five degrees Celsius. She put it up another degree. She knew that a recovering fever victim often felt cold during the recovery phase. "You're still running an oral temperature of thirty-eight degrees, but otherwise you seem normal," the Medical Officer told him.

"Well, I've always run a body temperature higher than anyone else, Doctor. This time, it went way higher. I haven't had a fever like that since I was a kid. Don't know where I picked up the bug. Natalie, I'm sorry I missed our lunch date because of it. I normally don't get sick when others do," he told her. He acted quite shy and reserved when he added, "I hope we can reschedule things."

"Maybe," Natalie said brusquely.

"Maybe? What's wrong?" Duval looked like a hurt little boy.

"You tell me, Barry." Natalie cut directly to the core of

her concern. "According to Doctor Moore here, you're not human. Did you know that?"

That statement didn't seem to faze him. "I'm a little different," he admitted. "That's because I was raised by aliens. My father—I always called him that—said he was an alien. I don't talk much about it, because people don't believe me. They think I'm crazy. But I'm human."

"Commander Chase has told me that you're human in many respects. I can confirm that this is true from a cursory visual inspection made at the start of my physical exam yesterday. However, beyond external appearance, my physical examination shows you may be humanoid but you're not human," the Medical Officer put in. "You're human in appearance. You have an ectomorphic physiology. Your body temperature runs higher than normal."

Duval didn't appear to be intimidated by that. "Many people have high normal body temperatures, Doctor."

"True, but none of them have a different circulatory system. You do."

"I do?"

"I discovered that yesterday during the admission workup," Moore announced. "It became critical when I was afraid your fever would lead to dehydration and require me to use intravenous supplements. I had a lot of trouble finding a suitable vein for the drip. I was very lucky—or perhaps you were—that a preliminary emergency IV of sodium bicarbonate and isotonic saline didn't kill you. When I got your blood work back from the lab ..." The Medical Officer paused for a moment, then went on, "No, let me put that another way: I got the report from the lab. To begin with, they couldn't type your blood. It didn't fall within the four major blood groups. The red blood cells checked out as Type O, but your serum reacted like Type AB. Your blood was acidotic, potassium was high, ammonia was high, the globulin makeup was all over the place ... everything was different, and very little of it made sense. A human being with that blood situation would be dead. Or would die shortly thereafter. Fortunately, you showed no sign of dying right then. However, it was a damn good thing you didn't need a transfusion, Doctor Duval. I have nothing in my blood bank that would have worked without a lot of laboratory modification, and

I'm not sure I would have had the luxury of time to do the mods."

"My parents told me I had a rare blood type," Duval admitted. "That's why they took me to special doctors when I got sick in childhood. But I rarely got sick."

Laura Raye Moore sighed. "I wish I had another hundred like you, Doctor Duval. Then I might be able to develop some standards for your alien species. Even your medical records would help. But the only medical information available is your immunization record from the Barber's Point Naval Air Station dispensary. When was the last time you had a physical exam?" Moore asked him.

"I never have."

"You've *never* had a physical exam?"

"I never needed one."

"How can a person go through life in the twenty-first century without being required to stand for a physical exam?" Natalie wondered. "Didn't you have to be immunized to get into school?"

"My parents always took care of the documentation, Natalie."

"Had you been immunized before Barber's Point?" Moore asked.

"No."

"Did the shots bother you?"

"A little. Felt sort of queasy during the airplane flight from Hawaii to the ship. Sort of chalked that up to airsickness. It was a pretty rough flight."

Moore thought she saw a pattern here emerging from Duval's answers. But she was looking at it strictly from the biological viewpoint. "God, I wish I had the facilities in sick bay to do all the genetic and DNA work here! Or even to attack some of the advanced metabolic and hemotologic aspects of this! It could very well be that the immunizations you received at Barber's Point made you susceptible to the Mantid mite aerosols. You could have triggered something in the vector that activated the disease. Epidemiology isn't my specialty. I'm just a naval pill pusher."

Duval seemed to be growing increasingly uncomfortable over the insistent interrogation. He seemed a bit confused. However, he'd reacted in a totally innocent way to the questions from Laura Raye. Corry could detect no hesitation on Duval's part in answering them. Nor did he sense any attempt by Duval to hide or cover up anything. He decided that Duval was either an innocent participant who was indeed a very humanoid extraterrestrial or a very highly trained agent.

"I'd help you if I knew what to do, Doctor," Duval told her with obvious sincerity in spite of his strained expression.

Corry spoke up, concerned about Duval's discomfort at the questioning. "The first thing you could do, Doctor Duval, is to tell us what you're doing here."

"Excuse me?"

"What are you *really* doing in this boat?"

"Why, I'm here because the Presidential Science Advisor told me an experienced oceanographer was needed, someone who had all the latest data and was also an expert in underwater volcanism," Duval replied in a candid and outspoken manner.

"He's all of those things, Captain," Natalie added in confirmation.

"I'm sure he is. Doctor Duval, what is the function of the nanotechnology modules that Doctor Moore discovered at three places in your head?" Corry asked, cutting directly to the major question his mind.

"I don't know. I didn't know they were still there. I'd forgotten about them."

"Why? When were they put there? Who put them there?"

"I told you, Captain, that I was raised by extraterrestrials. I don't remember much about it. Doctors implanted those many years ago. I was only a child. When I asked about it, I was told that they would help me think better and stay healthy."

"What doctors implanted them? At what medical facility?" Corry persisted.

"I don't remember. I think it was done at the same place my alien parents took me for medical treatment years ago. Captain, all this was a long time ago. Twenty to twenty-five years, maybe. I was pretty young. My memories then weren't as good as they are now."

"What do you mean by that, Doctor?"

"By what, Captain?"

"About your memories?"

"Oh, when I was real young, I didn't remember things

very well. I have no trouble remembering everything now. Maybe those nanotechnology modules have something to do with that." Duval acted as if he was having trouble at this point. Abruptly, he switched the subject. "Natalie, I needed to talk to you because I'm really worried. This probably doesn't have anything to do with the fever I've just suffered, but it could. However, I think it has more to do with the way we . . . did what we did." It was as though he didn't know the right words to use.

"Tell me," Natalie said.

"I can usually . . . know what people are thinking," Duval admitted. "That made it a lot easier for me in school and at the university. Oh, I knew my subject. But in my orals, I also knew the questions they'd ask. This . . . talent has always made it easier for me to get along with other people, and I want you to know that I've always tried to use it wisely and without hurting people."

"Are you trying to tell me that you can read my mind?" Natalie suddenly put in.

"I could—once. You were . . . so different from other women I've known. I admired what you thought and the way you did it. And that you wouldn't demand anything of me except my closeness and companionship. You were— are—someone special." Duval looked around, but he didn't seem embarrassed that Corry and Moore were also there at the bedside as he was telling Natalie this.

Natalie remained silent, even realizing that if Duval was indeed a telepath, it wouldn't make any difference whether she said anything or not.

When she didn't respond, Duval went on, hesitating occasionally. Corry realized Duval, whatever he was, was not embarrassed, only that, lacking certain social graces, he had difficulty expressing himself. "After leaving Guadalcanal when the ship went to cruise conditions and we . . . grew closer . . . I woke up afterward and discovered that *I didn't know what you were thinking!* You were just—there, period. Nothing more. And then I discovered I didn't know what anyone else was thinking, either. It was as if a switch had been turned off."

Natalie asked him, "Barry, that was your first time with a woman, wasn't it?"

He nodded.

"I thought so. I'm not being critical." She shook her

head sadly. "I'm sorry. I thought I'd turned you on. I guess I turned you off instead."

"Oh, I'm not complaining, Natalie! It's just ... strange, that's all. I'm living in a different world. It's a silent world. I learned over the years to tune out what I didn't want to listen to. Now I can't 'hear' anything, if that's the word to use, and it probably isn't."

Corry motioned to his Medical Officer by a nod of his head. "Doctor, may I speak with you privately, please?"

"Certainly. Natalie, stay as long as you wish."

"I have the duty at twelve hundred hours, Laura Raye. But, thank you. And thank you, Captain."

"We all learned something, didn't we?" was Corry's response as he got up.

In the passageway outside and well out of earshot of anyone, Corry told Moore, "It makes sense now."

"What makes sense, Captain?"

"Well, I think it makes sense. As much sense as this whole cruise has made. And the one before that. Laura Raye, I never thought I'd actually be living some of the science fiction stories I've read."

"It's probably a good thing you read them, Captain. They helped prepare you for this. I don't read science fiction. I've got to admit that if I didn't have a professional persona to fall back on, this would be a nightmare," Laura Raye admitted.

"Doctor, tell me if I'm wrong in my guesses here," Corry asked her. "Doctor Barry Duval must have suddenly experienced the effects of a lot of hormones released in his body by sexual activity, ones that had only been there to date as part of his natural development. Do you think that maybe those hormones turned off those nanotechnology modules in his head?"

She nodded. "It looks that way."

"Could other hormones be used to turn those nanotechnology modules on again? Or will they naturally come back on line as his hormonal balance returns to normal?"

Laura Raye Moore threw up her hands in exasperation. "Captain, I'm no endrocrinologist! I'm a naval surgeon whose full and total experience has been as a ship's doctor. I know a little about a lot of things but not enough about any, except as it comes to maintaining the health of a crew that was selected on the basis of good health in the first place. I don't know anything about the hormonal balance of extraterrestrials! Even ones that could pass as humans for thirty-odd years as Duval has!" She paused, got control of herself, then asked, "Do you think Duval has been put aboard as a telepathic transmitter?"

"I do, and I'm also convinced he doesn't realize it. I don't know anything about telepathy, but he apparently had some sort of telepathic talent. I don't know how the aliens—whichever of the seventy-some species Soucek claims have been here—detect and monitor this. But I think I know why all our sensitive radiation detectors in the boat found nothing."

"We don't know how to detect telepathy, if that's what it is."

"Correct. I don't know who's behind Duval or who placed him here. I'm not so sure it matters now. We're on the bottom north of Palmyra Atoll. Other boats are available to help if we break stealth and call them; I suspect they know we're here, even if they can't detect us. The Awesomes and their probable Mantid bosses are waiting for us off the southwest side of the Atoll; they don't know we're here. And the *Tuscarora* is sitting behind Washington Island; maybe they know where we are, and maybe they don't; maybe they're the game wardens we ran into off Makasar, and maybe they're not."

Corry paused in his verbal reassessment of the situation now that a new factor had been introduced. "The reason I asked if you could turn on Duval's talent, maybe with other hormones, is to see if we get a response from either the Awesome-Mantid force or the *Tuscarora.*"

"As I told you, I don't know, Captain." She paused, then added, "And I'm reluctant to try. I'm dealing with a new organism here, one that appears to be human but isn't. I might be able to identify Duval's hormones, and maybe I can't. And I refuse to experiment with him. He's not a lab animal. Neither are the two Mantids we have in detention here in sick bay." She didn't have to remark that she would refuse a direct order to do so. Corry knew that.

Corry was in an extremely stressful situation. He momentarily relaxed his iron hold on his speech impediment. "V-v-v-very well, Doctor. My only option is to continue to sit and wait. CINCPAC is late arriving, but at least we're on time." He paused. "Something must have changed. I wish CINCPAC would let me know what it is."

"They just have!" CDR Matilda Harriet Smith turned a corner and came down the passageway toward them. She held a memory cube in her hand. She appeared to be upset. "Captain, this coded message has just come in for you. I've received a separate one. Our arrangement is that we decode them together." Then she abruptly changed the subject, and Corry discovered why she seemed to be disturbed. "I'm glad I found you. The OOD told me you were in sick bay interrogating Duval. With all due respects, sir, why wasn't I part of the interrogation team?"

"Because, Commander, my Medical Officer invited me down. Doctor Lulalilo wanted to see me. In addition, Commander Chase asked me to be present when she met with Doctor Duval. Our discussion also involved medical matters that Doctor Moore wished to discuss with me. You were not neglected or disregarded, Commander. It was not an interrogation."

"Anytime anyone wants to meet with members of the special team, especially ones who have been stricken with Mantid fever, I should be extended the courtesy of an invitation to be present," Smith insisted. Her ego had been bruised. She obviously believed that her turf had been stepped upon with hobnailed boots.

Corry sighed. "Commander," he told her firmly but politely, "Naval Intelligence may be in charge of the operation. However, as you agreed, I'm the Commanding Officer of this ship. You have been given the privilege of serving in a high staff position second only to the XO. I will not argue this protocol with you."

He held up his hand to stem what was obviously going to be a respectful but heated reply from her. "Let's go at once to my cabin. I want Zeke to be present. And, Doctor Moore, will you please come along as well?"

Corry knew that this turn of events meant that he wouldn't be able to visit Eve right away. On the basis of what Laura Raye had told him, he felt he needed to do so at once. However, his responsibilities came first, even if it meant apparently neglecting someone he cared about who had lost the will to live.

16

By the time Zeke Braxton and Laura Raye Moore showed up at the Captain's cabin, CAPT William M. Corry and CDR Matilda Harriet Smith had run the SWC messages through their respective deciphering processors and were looking at hard copy printouts.

Corry was perplexed as he read the message from VADM Richard Kane at CINCPAC:

> To CO SSCV-26. This message is classified Cosmic Top Secret with INTEL and ORCON caveats and SCI compartmentation. On arrival tomorrow, 25 August, remain submerged one kilometer due north of northeast end of airstrip on Cooper Island until your special sensor detects the presence of the tender AS-88 *Wayne Rash* within one kilometer of your position, accompanied by CL-7 *Schirra* for aerospace defense. You are then requested to surface and, weather permitting, come alongside AS-88. Prepare to trap three C-26 Sea Dragons with undersigned, Chief of Naval Intelligence, and staff. Additional C-26 Sea Dragons will be landing on Palmyra airstrip with additional CINCPAC staff. SSF-17 *Morton* will stand by 5 kilometers west of your position for additional ASW defense. Be prepared for air defense of Palmyra Atoll and denial of landing to other aircraft. Additional details when we meet. This order is in support of and modifies JCS Execute Order 07-032-47N. Transmitted 2230Z. Kane VADM CINCPAC.

"This doesn't make sense, Smitty," Corry said to the Naval Intelligence officer as he passed the hard copy to her. "What does your message say?"

She shook her head. "I don't see anything wrong with mine, Captain. Very straightforward. Here, read it." She handed her message to him.

A historian is a prophet in reverse. To CDR M. H. Smith aboard SSCV-26. This message is classified Cosmic Top Secret with INTEL and ORCON caveats and SCI compartmentation. Undersigned arriving with CINCPAC via C-26 Sea Dragon tomorrow, 25 August. Please be prepared to provide a complete mission briefing with hands-on inspection of artifact and organisms. Be advised that other forces are at work in vicinity with intentions that may not be benign. With CINCPAC assistance, OP-32 will defend your acquisitions. Transmitted 2226Z. Signed McCarthy RADM CO OP-32. Tyranny is always better organized than freedom.

Corry read it and shook his head. "Either these messages got delayed twenty-four hours or they are in error. We were here and waiting yesterday, which was twenty-five August." He looked up at the digital clock display that was part of his wall intercom. It told him that the date was 25 August.

Braxton thought about this for a moment, then suddenly realized what had happened. "Uh, Captain," Zeke ventured to say, "we got caught by a major goof, the same one that caught Phineas Fogg."

"What does a Jules Verne novel have to do with this, Zeke?"

"As you recall, sir, Fogg went around the world in eighty days eastbound. He believed he'd lost his wager with the gentlemen of the Reform Club because he was detained and got back to London a day late according to his count," Zeke explained. This was embarrassing to him, too, because he knew he should have caught the mistake. "Both Phileas Fogg and the U.S.S. *Shenandoah* crossed the International Date Line going east. We lost a day. The ship's master clock wasn't reset."

"But that's a simple computer program!" Corry objected. "It's supposed to reset itself when the INS tells it the boat has crossed the date line!"

"Yes, sir, but the Navigator disabled it because it made it easier to run the navigation going back and forth across one-eighty longitude the way we've been doing lately," Zeke explained.

"And Commander Chase didn't reset the calendar portion of the clock when she shifted us to Hawaii time on leaving the Solomons. It's actually twenty-four August," Corry muttered. For the first time in her naval career, Natalie Chase had screwed up. As a result of the conversation with Duval and Chase in sick bay that morning, he knew why.

"So we got here a day ahead of time," Corry went on. He sighed. "Well, no harm done. Just a little more wear and tear on Engineering for pushing us at forty knots instead of thirty." He studied the messages again, then added, "So CINCPAC and Naval Intelligence won't be here until later today. That gives us a little more time to get our own house in order."

"I *may* have the Mantid fever problem solved by then," Laura Raye Moore put in. "At least to the point where we don't have nine people in sick bay. If Soucek, Zervas, and Duval continue to respond well, Smitty, I can release your team back to you tonight."

"Except for Duval," Corry warned her. "We don't know what he's transmitting with those nanotechnology modules in his head."

"He doesn't know, either, Captain."

"I'm not yet totally convinced of that. Doctor, please explain to Zeke and Smitty what you discovered today."

"Yes, Doctor, I'd like to know what went on in sick bay when one of my special team members was interrogated," Smith insisted.

"No problem, Smitty," Moore told her easily. "My standard sick bay video monitors caught it all. Captain, because the monitor videotape of our conversation with Duval this morning is confidential medical data, I need an order from you to show it to Commanders Smith and Braxton. That might be easier than trying to give a separate briefing, and Smitty can see and hear for herself."

Corry waved his hand. "Please do it, Doctor. However, I presume that Natalie is still with Duval. So it isn't necessary to give us the instant replay of the conversation between Doctor Duval and Commander Chase after we left. Big Brother I'm not."

Moore looked up at the wall clock. The forenoon watch was about over. "No, Natalie left sick bay with me. She has the duty in ten minutes." She paused, then remarked. "Captain, I certainly hope you can find a few minutes to visit Eve and the others—"

"I'll do my best, Doctor." Corry wasn't dodging difficult duty. He wanted to see Eve. But he was forced to operate on a strict set of priorities right then. The ship and the crew came before an individual.

Moore had the video signal from her sick bay monitor piped into Corry's cabin, and they all reviewed what had taken place in Duval's compartment shortly before.

"Duval is certainly noncommittal about it all. It's hard to tell whether he's lying or not," Smith remarked as the videotape ended.

"He's not lying, Smitty. He actually believes he's human and was only raised by extraterrestrials," Moore told the Naval Intelligence officer.

"How do you know?"

"Laura Raye's handy-dandy little lie detector was plugged in and working," the Medical Officer revealed. "I monitor the vital signs of all sick bay occupants. Duval was still being monitored during the conversation. If he's lying, he's got better control over his heart rate, blood pressure, and breathing than a human being. That I doubt, because when I did a quick check before coming up here, I saw the glitch in his response when Natalie confronted him with his alien nature. And I saw the usual sort of variations I see when people are talking to or about someone they care for. No, Barry Duval might be an alien, but he believes he's human and he's exhibiting human responses."

"What about this telepathy thing?" Smith asked. "Could he somehow be transmitting thought waves or something, a kind of radiation we can't detect?"

"He might have been, but he admitted that his telepathic talents had somehow been turned off after he began his relationship with Natalie," Moore pointed out. "That's got him bothered, ladies and gentlemen. I believe if he somehow gets it back, he'll let me know about it. Or he'll tell Natalie for sure. But, Doctor Duval's objections notwithstanding, we've got two alien species on board right now."

"That we know about," Zeke added.

Moore nodded.

"What about the Mantids?" Corry asked her. "You mentioned earlier that you were having trouble with them."

The Medical Officer sighed, then carefully considered how she was going to say what she had to tell them. Finally, she remarked, "The live Mantids I've detained in sick bay don't want to eat. They say our food tastes spoiled. I don't speak Pidgin English as well as Eve, but I got the sense of what the Mantids were trying to tell me about the food. They consider what we eat to be carrion—tissue from dead animals and plants. They say they kill their food just before they eat it, or they eat it while the animal is still alive. And ... they like 'long pig,' which is a slang term for human flesh."

Corry simply told her, "Tell the Mantids they'll have to make do with what we feed them. Calories are calories. If the Mantids want to play like spiders and suck their victims dry, we don't run that kind of a restaurant here. They won't starve if they'll eat what we give them. As I used to tell my children, when they get hungry enough, they'll eat what's put before them."

Everyone in the cabin fell silent. Corry looked around, then went on, "Very well, we have an additional day of time. We're going to continue to sit on the bottom here and watch for the *Rash* and the *Schirra* to show up. We're not going to move or make a sound until then. We're going to continue to watch the Awesomes and look out for that *Tuscarora*. But we're going to be ready for CINCPAC and Naval Intelligence when they show up."

He looked at Zeke. "Number Two, when we surface tomorrow, I want Terri to put a heavy CAP over us and the other two ships. And I want the Marine batt to be ready to go ashore to provide additional security for the CINCPAC staff that will be landing and setting up shop on Cooper Island."

"So you want to change the operational readiness level, Captain?" Zeke wanted to know.

"No, Number Two, let's stay at Condition Three for now. No one and nothing knows we're here."

Corry was wrong about that, and he discovered it almost at once.

"CO, this is the OOD!" barked the wall intercom speaker.

Corry recognized the voice of LCDR Mark Walton. "CO here! GA!" he called out.

"Sir, ten Awesomes spotted on masdet and by passive sonar heading eastbound toward us! They just cleared Sawle Point," Walton snapped. "Now we see another ten targets behind them! Awesomes from their passive sonar sounds. First ten running shallow, second ten running just above the bottom. Now we're getting enough data to integrate their paths. They appear to be operating in a search pattern heading toward our present location!"

Corry didn't hesitate. Somehow, the Awesomes must have discovered that the U.S.S. *Shenandoah* was already submerged off the north shore of the atoll.

"OOD, this is the Captain! Battle Stations! I say again, sound Battle Stations! Underwater Special Team report armed to the water locks! CO and XO on our way to the bridge!"

Corry was on his feet and headed toward the door. Zeke was right behind him. Smith remained seated. It was obvious that the call to GQ surprised her. She looked confused.

Glancing over his shoulder at the Naval Intelligence officer as he reached the door, Corry told her, "Follow me, Commander! Your battle station is on the bridge alongside me! Shake a leg!" There wasn't time for him to stutter, although he'd almost lost control at that moment.

Slipping into his seat at the command console on the bridge, Corry told Walton, *Going to N-fone. Commander, I have the ship.*

Roger, sir. You have the conn.

Corry looked at the masdet and sonar displays. *Where are the Awesomes?*

Most of them are at about a kilometer range to the west and closing, LCDR Bob Lovette announced from the operations console.

Any reading on intent?

Negative, sir.

Arm tubes with concussion warshots. Stand by to launch fish.

Aye, aye, sir. Arming missile tubes with concussion warshots. Guns Weaver reports ready to launch.

Captain, the boat is at General Quarters, Zeke announced. Corry had been so engrossed with gaining situational awareness that he hadn't noticed that Terri and Bart had assumed their posts on the command gallery of the bridge.

Thank you, XO.

CO, Deck here. Special Underwater Team is in water locks. They are pressurizing for exit at our present depth of one-hundred-two meters. They are armed with spearguns, sir, Walton reported.

Captain, I can have a Marine platoon ready to scuba in five minutes, Bart Clinch put in.

Mister Brookstone and his people are trained to go outside the hull in deep submergence, Major. However, you might have one of your platoons get ready and stand by. You should be aware that I'm not going to put anyone out in the water with the Awesomes until we learn what they're up to, Corry remarked. He checked the masdet displays again. *Where is the Awesome's mother ship, Mister Lovette?*

Masdet reports the Awesome mother ship has moved in defilade northward from Penguin Spit. It is now located approximately one klick north of the entrance channel to the West Lagoon, sir. The Operations Officer paused because he was getting input on another N-fone channel, then went on, *Sir, Sonar is reading audio communications of some sort apparently between the mother ship and the Awesomes. I'm not sure that the sounds are communications, sir, but they come close to matching what we heard and presumed to be communications off Guadalcanal.*

"We need to get a closer look at that Awesome mother ship," Harriet Smith put in verbally. She was wearing an N-fone set to receive-only mode because she hadn't had the training necessary to use the transmit mode; that required keeping one's stream-of-consciousness thoughts below the level of intensity required for N-fone transmission lest the comm channels become saturated. "We don't have any data on it."

Zeke turned to her and replied, "How can you say that, Smitty? We have the masdet, sonar, and video records of the one we chased in Makasar Straits, plus the other one that came up to us and looked us over."

"Which one was an Awesome mother ship?" she fired back.

"Probably both."

She shook her head. "That isn't what your data showed. The one that looked you over was a 'game warden' ship, according to your evaluations. It drove off the Awesomes. The other one defended the Awesomes and attacked the Chinese submarine. If there are more than seventy alien species, doesn't it stand to reason there would be more than one *Tuscarora*-type ship? How can we be sure that this Awesome mother ship is the same as the one you chased into the air in Makasar Straits?"

"We can't," Corry put in, trying to focus on the rapidly developing situation. "If we have time to explore the matter, we will. Right now, we may be coming under attack."

"With what, Captain?" Smith wanted to know. "Barehanded Awesomes against your outer hull?"

"I don't know what weapons they might be carrying," Corry muttered.

"The Awesomes do have grasping handlike appendages and stereoscopic close-focusing eyes," Zeke reminded her. "They can handle tools and weapons. In fact, the one I killed was carrying some sort of handgun."

"If the intel briefing I got was thorough—and Admiral McCarthy insists that her subordinates be given full and complete briefings before going into the field—handguns aren't going to be a threat against your pressure hull."

"Smitty, with all due respect to OP-thirty-two, we don't know what the Awesomes might have in terms of weapons," Zeke told her. "We didn't know about the force beam the Corona shot at us."

"I did."

"But you didn't tell *us!*"

"I wasn't sitting in this seat next to the Captain when that happened."

"Captain, where we're sitting right now, you've got some of your most effective weapons in useless mode. Surface and let the Air Group have a go at that Awesome mother ship!" Terri put in.

Corry simply held up his hand for silence. He didn't need an argument between his XO and the lady from Naval Intelligence, not at this point. Smith had brought up an interesting point: They didn't know anything about the Awesome mother ship lurking on the west side of the atoll. Perhaps the Awesomes in the water were merely scouts sent out to find the U.S.S. *Shenandoah* so that the mother ship could move in with some sort of underwater force beam to breach the carrier submarine's composite hull.

"Terri, I am *not* going to surface! I'm not sure the Awesomes know exactly where we are," Corry told her. He didn't mind having to throw cold water over Terri Ellison's aggressive suggestions. He'd selected her as his CAG because, like Bart, she was a tiger. He needed tigers in the Air Group and the Marine batt, but he needed and had different personalities to run the ship itself.

CO, Special Sensors here! came the direct call from Ames, bypassing Lovette because of the urgency of the information. *The Awesomes on the bottom have apparently located the wreck of the* Sea Wind *to the west of us. I'll try to enhance their masdet images on the bridge repeater. They're converging rapidly on the wreck.*

Corry saw that. He also saw that the ten Awesomes near the surface had all done a one-eighty and headed westward again. *Thank you, Mister Ames. I see them.*

Whatever the Awesomes were doing around the wreck of the *Sea Wind,* they did it fast and quickly dispersed, heading westward with their companions.

CO, Special Sensors here. A Corona-type target has appeared a thousand meters above the surface about a thousand meters to the west of us. It is descending to land on the water over the wreck of the Sea Wind.

XO, have Guns target three fish with concussion warshots on that Corona. Stand by to shoot.

Aye, air, sir. We know how to handle that situation. They had done so in the Solomon Sea by simultaneous attacks with three underwater missiles against a floating Corona and used concussion warheads to split its underhull and disable its occupants. They had that Corona and its Mantid occupants aboard now.

And I want Guns to keep tracking those Awesomes now running westward. They haven't done anything yet but look menacing. There could be some other motive on their part. So I'm going to wait and see what happens. But I want to be ready to shoot concussion warshots into them.

Aye, aye, sir. Zeke knew his Commanding Officer. Corry wasn't prone to aggressive action unless necessary. He would attack first only if it appeared that the ship was in danger. Otherwise, Corry preferred to let the potential adversary make the first move.

CO, this is Communications. I am receiving an incoming message on the SWC. LT Ed Atwater's voice sounded both surprised and confused. The reason for that became evident as he went on, *Sir, it's in the clear, but it's garbled to beat hell! And it's on the limited-use naval command channel normally utilized by CINCPAC. But it isn't CINCPAC calling.*

Mister Atwater, record it and make a hard copy for the log. In the meantime, squirt it to me on my visual monitor.

Aye, aye, sir, if you don't mind getting it raw. Whoever is sending it doesn't fully understand NASCIC codes.

I'll take that into account, Mister Ames, Corry told him.

The left screen in front of Corry cleared and went to black, and a message slowly began to take form character by character and line by line.

MELICUN SUB MEREN SANENDOHA EE UMI BIM SIP TOP U UN WAWA# KAM FASTEM TOP# IUMI LAK BIM SIP IU TAK# IUMI LAK OLKETA SAMA IUFALA GAREM# NO DU NAO AN KAM FASTEM IUMI KILIM FINIS#

"It doesn't make sense!" Smith exclaimed as she watched the letters dance across the screen.

CAPT William M Corry thought it did. When he sounded it in his head, it vaguely resembled Pidgin English. He had heard it as a small child. He'd been born on Oahu, where Pidgin had once been spoken widely. It was rarely used in the twenty-first century because of the ubiquitous English language, the speech of world trade, commerce, tourism, diplomacy, and military/naval affairs. If Dr. Eve Lulalilo hadn't discovered that the Mantids spoke Pidgin, he probably would not have recognized it.

"It's butchered Pidgin English sent by someone who doesn't know how to write it but is trying," Corry guessed. "Let's see if we can sound it out phonetically and make some sort of sense of it."

It took several minutes. Finally, between Corry, Smith, and Braxton, they came to the conclusion that the message said this:

"American submarine Shenandoah, this is beam ship on top of you on water, period. Come to the surface fast, period. We like [or want] beam ship you took, period. We like [or want] all sama [meaning not known, probably refers to real name of Mantids] you have, period. If you do not do it now and come to the surface fast, we will kill you."

"Well, Captain?" Smith asked.

"We're at General Quarters. We're ready for anything we know can be used against us," Corry told her. "I'm not going to cave in to a message like that. If they want their Mantid or Sama colleagues back, they certainly will think twice about doing any serious damage to us. Therefore, I think they're bluffing. Let's find out."

17

CAPT William M. Corry didn't have to wait very long to find out.

The noise could be easily heard through the thick composite hull of the U.S.S. *Shenandoah*. The screech sounded like fingernails being dragged over glass. It put everyone's teeth on edge. Fortunately for the sanity of the crew, the sound lasted only a few seconds.

"What the hell . . .?" Zeke erupted, shaking his head.

Sonar reporting! We're off-line here until we get the overload breakers reset!

Special Sensors here! Captain, the wreck of the Sea Wind *is disappearing quickly from our masdet screens! We detect only a dispersing cloud of debris!*

"Molecular bond disruptor," CDR Matilda Harriet Smith remarked.

"What the hell is that?" Zeke wanted to know.

"Very classified. You're not cleared. No need to know."

"Commander," Corry told her sharply, "the safety and security of this ship and the crew—and perhaps your life—may be at stake here. If you know something that affects our safety, classification be damned! I have a definite need to know!"

After a moment's hesitation, Smith told him, "I don't know all the details myself."

"Then tell me what you do know!"

"Naval Intelligence has reports of some Army anti-armor work going on at Aberdeen and White Sands," Smith explained. "You're aware, I'm sure, of how ultrasonic vibrations will break the weak bonds between molecules?"

"Ultrasonic cleaning has been used for a long time, Commander."

"Army Ordnance is working on a system that will use

specific frequencies and combinations of frequencies that
will, at a high enough intensity, actually disrupt molecular
bonds," Smith told them. "I don't know how. But that
sound was similar to the recordings I've heard."

"And the demolition of the *Sea Wind* wreckage tends to
reinforce that guess," Terri Ellison added.

"My God, that would take a humping powerful trans-
ducer!" Zeke exclaimed.

"Well, White Oak has some sonar transducers that come
close," Smith admitted, but said no more.

*CO, this is Communications! Another garbled SWC mes-
sage for you, transmitted in the clear!*

Pipe it up to my bridge display, Mister Atwater!

Aye, aye, sir!

This message made about as much sense as the first one
until it was sounded out phonetically.

IUFALA PLIS KAM UP FASTEM NAO# IUMI SHO IUFALA NAMBATEN
IUMI DUIM# KILLEM FINIS NAO# IUFALA DAI FINIS#

"You please come up fast now. We show you worst we
do to you. We kill you now. You die," Corry translated
slowly.

*CO, this is Special Sensors! We see multiple small two-
hundred-kilogram targets approaching again from the
west. Estimated twenty targets, each probably an Awesome.
Estimated range three klicks.*

*CO, Sonar is back up! We confirm Special Sensors' tar-
gets. These targets are using active Awesome sonar and
communications.*

*Guns, CO here. Fire two fish, concussion warheads!
Detonate warshot in the center of the oncoming sonar target swarm.* Corry quickly passed the order to CWO
Weaver, bypassing Lovette because of the urgency of the
situation.

*Guns here. Two tubes fired. Warshots on the way! Sonar,
guard your ears!*

That's SOP, Guns!

Two underwater guided missiles sped outward toward the
oncoming horde of Awesomes.

*CO, Special Sensors! Six Awesome targets have departed
the Corona vehicle on the surface above the* Sea Wind!
They are almost directly over us and diving fast toward us!

Guns, put three fish under that Corona! Fire now!

Three tubes fired! Hang on! This is close in. The warshots will shake us up when they blow.

"They must have learned saturation attacks from me," Terri observed, frustrated that she couldn't do anything about what was happening.

"Either they learn fast or this is a more aggressive Corona crew," Zeke added.

The two warshots placed into the oncoming Awesomes were heard when they detonated.

But the shock of the three nearly simultaneous firings of the missile warheads nearly over the *Shenandoah* and under the Corona did indeed shake up the 58,700-ton carrier submarine. It was like three quick hammer blows to the hull.

Mister Walton, damage? Corry quickly asked.

None reported, Captain!

Captain, Special Sensors! We see four immobile Awesome targets floating over us. The warshots must have got them. And the oncoming Awesomes have either scattered or have gone immobile in the water.

Good shooting, Guns! Terri put in.

But we can't account for the other two Awesomes diving on us. I think they're on our outer hull! I can't discriminate any mass out there, and I can't see them if they're almost on us.

Launch Underwater Special Team now! Corry ordered.

Special Sensors here! I now see two Awesome targets proceeding away from us westbound!

The screeching sound that had been heard before was much louder this time. The whole carrier submarine resounded with the noise. It was short, sharp, and at about 125 decibels on the bridge.

Most people got their hands over their ears in time to stop most of the sound. But it also shook each of them briefly and violently. It caused a wave of nausea to go through Corry.

All hands, this is the Captain! Corry managed to say. He felt it imperative that he broadcast on the comm net at once. *That may have come from some sort of a mine placed on or near the boat by one of the Awesomes. I'm told it might have used a molecular bond disruptor warhead. We just saw a similar one reduce a nearby bottom wreck to a cloud of debris. XO, damage control reports, please, as quickly as possible. And belay the deployment of the Underwater Special Team.*

Almost immediately, the report came in from Ray Stocker in Engineering. *XO, this is Engineering! Damage control report. The outer and inner hulls have been broached at Station one-five-seven, level seven. That's a buoyancy tank with integral compressed air storage. It was flooded, but the mine punched through. It's lost its air.*

It must be a damned big hole, Zeke remarked. *Any estimate on size?*

XO, it appears to be at least ten meters in diameter.

Zeke whistled, but that didn't get into the N-fone circuitry. The amount of energy required to blow a hole ten meters in diameter through a composite hull designed to withstand the static pressure of a six-hundred-meter depth dismayed him.

But it was apparent by the Engineer Officer's rapid-fire delivery on the N-fone net that the man was even more deeply impressed by something else. *It's more than the size, XO. Whatever that charge was, it also punched a hole in depth. We show indication of water entry through longitudinal bulkheads perhaps twenty to twenty-five meters across the hull. Sick bay will have to undergo emergency evacuation immediately before we have to close the watertight doors on them.*

Zeke reacted immediately, *Sick bay, XO here! Get out of there! You've got water!*

Yes, we have water! Everywhere! Gushing in! Like the casualty trainer at New London! was the immediate and somewhat harried reply from Laura Raye Moore. *I'm going to lose the sick bay to flooding in a minute or less. All our patients are ambulatory at this time, so we're evacuating. But I may not be able to get the Mantids out.*

Their colleagues attacked the boat knowing they were here, Zeke reminded her and everyone listening on the N-fone comm net. *They expended them. Try to save them if you can, but don't feel guilty if you can't.*

Engineering here! Benedetti has a damage control team down there working the casualty already, Stocker reported. *We may be able to save those bugs, but we may need some help from the medical people.*

If the Mantids can't be saved, don't risk humans trying to do it! That's a direct order, Doctor! Corry insisted. He didn't want to consign the two Mantids to drowning, but he wouldn't put his crew at risk trying to do the impossible. He could justify to himself the death of the Mantids and he would have real difficulty justifying killing people in an effort to save them. After all, the Mantids in the Corona ship above them had attacked knowing they were aboard.

He had to let Zeke and the damage control parties handle the casualty. The external threat was still there, and he had to pay attention to it. *Special Sensors, CO here. What's the status of the overhead Corona target?*

CO, this is Special Sensors. We've apparently knocked out the Corona on the surface.

Sonar, do you confirm?

This is Sonar. We confirm that active pinging from the surface Corona has ceased. We detect no movement of that target.

Report status of the Awesome horde to the west.

Sonar reports some Awesomes sounding and communicating. However, it is much reduced.

Special Sensors, what are the western Awesome targets doing?

They're either running or floating, sir. The ones that got away are rounding Sawle Point in one hell of a hurry right now.

Something's gone wrong with the masdet displays you installed on the bridge, Corry told his Special Sensors Officer. *The targets have gotten very blurred. How many Awesomes survived our fish attack?*

I, uh, don't know, sir.

What happened, Charlie? Corry asked, noting that the technical officer's composure had obviously been rattled. So had that of many others in the boat.

Wait one, please, sir. We've got problems here, sir. After a pause, Ames went on, *Sir, I hate to report this, but that screech—the mine or whatever it was—well, it knocked some of my gear out of action or out of calibration. I can't see the Awesome mother ship now. Last plotted position was one klick south of Sawle Point moving north. I may be able to see if it comes out from behind the coral reef mass.*

No one was expecting the second intense screech that reverberated throughout the U.S.S. *Shenandoah.*

The intensity and combination of frequencies of this one

caused Corry to become sick to his stomach. His ears rang and he lost his balance, but he had enough control to vomit on the deck instead of his console.

A second Awesome mine, Captain, Zeke reported. He had taken over damage control command on the bridge. The Executive Officer was shaken but was one of the few people on the bridge who hadn't been so severely affected that they had lost whatever was in their stomachs. *Stocker reports ... Wait one, sir. ... Stocker reports the second mine was under the boat, station one-forty-six, level eleven, very close to where the boat rests on the bottom mud. ... Stand by, sir. I'm getting damage control party reports. ... Captain, Engineering damage control party reports the hull is broached in a second place. The force of the disruption was apparently nearly vertical. Looks like a hole punched upward through the boat almost to the hangar deck!*

Corry's first thought was for the safety of the boat. *Mister Walton, will the flooding from the two hull breaches prevent us from surfacing?*

Yes, sir! If we wait too long, we'll take on too much water to be able to blow all tanks and gain positive buoyancy. We have possibly less than five minutes, sir!

Corry had unambiguous orders to remain submerged until he'd detected the tender *Rash* and the space defense ship *Schirra* over him, but that wouldn't occur until tomorrow morning. In surfacing, he would lay the boat open to possible space attack or, worse, air attack from other Mantid forces that might be airborne. He didn't know if any additional Mantid craft were overhead right then because the masdet had been damaged.

But he had to surface the boat to prevent possible sinking. And, if necessary, he would move the *Shenandoah* into shoal waters off the north side of the atoll where he could beach her to prevent her from sinking. Even on the surface, she was a formidable weapon with her Air Group, Marine batt, and deck guns.

But because he was a submariner and used to operating alone, he'd momentarily forgotten that help was close by.

CO, this is Communications. SWC message for you on that has just come in on the TBS channel, Atwater announced. *I'm putting it up on your screen now.*

That meant the message had come in the clear and on the

limited-range TBS channel. Atwater was correct in piping it up to Corry's screen at once.

CO CL-7 *Schirra* to CO SSCV-26 *Shenandoah*. Underwater sounds from direction of Palmyra Atoll indicate conflict situation. CL-7 *Schirra* can immediately proceed at flank speed to Palmyra, arrival in 57 minutes. Please advise. Signed CL-7 *Schirra* CAPT Thorne CO.

Corry looked at it while Smith viewed the screen over his shoulder. "I think we could use the help, Captain," she muttered. She really didn't fully understand the problem with the *Shenandoah* at the moment, but she knew it was leaking and might not be able to operate as it had in the past.

Smith was learning, Corry decided. There was no longer any taint of "keep it quiet because this is an intel matter." So he merely nodded and replied via N-fone, *Mister Atwater, please send the following TBS signal to Captain Thorne. Quote: We have been attacked with unknown weapons. Our hull has been broached in two places. We are taking water. Your assistance gladly accepted. We are surfacing off north beach of atoll and will probably beach to prevent sinking. Please forward this message to CINCPAC and say that full report forthcoming from me once casualties have been alleviated. Please notify other task force vessels to proceed to Palmyra Atoll at flank speed as timetable has been advanced by the attack. Get it off right away, Ed. And stand by to set up a satellite link to CINCPAC—wherever he happens to be at the moment— once we're on the surface.*

Aye, aye, sir!

"You're not thinking of surfacing, are you, Captain?" Smith asked, and then wished she hadn't.

Corry shot a quick glance at her. Momentarily, he lapsed and told her, "D-d-do you want to surface? Or to stay here on the bottom, perhaps permanently?"

Without further hesitation, he gave the order, *Blow tanks! Come off the bottom! Once clear of the bottom, come to best climb speed. Surface! Surface! Surface!*

Aye, aye, sir! Blow tanks. Once clear of bottom, all ahead to best climb speed. Surface! Surface! Surface! came the immediate reply from Mark Walton.

Corry intended to use forward speed to gain additional hull lift and thus come to the surface faster than would be possible by only blowing the tanks. But he got an immediate call from Zeke: *Captain, Engineer Officer reports flooding of one fusion reactor. We have only half power available.*

Duct steam from the single reactor to all available thrusters, Number Two. Get us off the bottom here fast before we're forced to stay here!

Aye, aye, sir!

Captain, this is the First Lieutenant. Sir, we can steer to surface directly under the damaged Corona on the surface and pick it up on the upper flight deck. That would give us two of them, sir!

Corry already had one Mantid Corona ship tucked away on the flight deck. However, given the opportunity to snare another one, he decided he'd better be a little bit greedy. A second one might come in handy later on.

"Smitty, I'm going to take it," Corry told the Naval Intelligence officer at his side. "It isn't often that opportunity knocks twice."

"By all means, Captain! It could give us some real bargaining power with the Aerospace Force if they started to get nasty!"

"I was also thinking of its value in possible negotiations with the Mantids at some future time," he said. "They were apparently so anxious to get the first Corona back that they were willing to sacrifice two of their own."

"We don't know the extent to which they value individual lives, Captain," Smith pointed out to him. "Many nations here on Earth would have done the same thing, especially those where life is cheap."

Corry nodded and told his deck officer, *Mister Walton, arrange to surface beneath the disabled Corona ship and recover it on our upper flight deck.*

Aye, aye, sir!

Corry turned to Bart Clinch. "Well, Bart, why are you sitting there? Here I've just given you the chance to board a Corona for a second time, and this time without getting your feet wet!"

Clinch was on his feet. "Yes, sir! On my way, sir!"

"Captain, that's going to foul the upper flight deck!" Terri complained.

"So use the lower flight deck and that portion of the upper that's free, Terri," Corry told her. "And I want a CAP over us at once. Stand by as well to launch all aircraft and possibly land them on the atoll's airstrip. We might find ourselves in a beaching position where we couldn't launch aircraft, and I'm not going to leave us wide open to the skies! We may have other Coronas around, and your Tigers may have to go at them."

"Aye, aye, sir! Can I do this from PRIFLY?"

"Better check and make sure PRIFLY isn't in the flooded portion." He turned to Zeke and unconsciously continued in the verbose mode, "Number Two, what's the damage status now?"

Zeke came back via N-fone although he'd heard the Captain directly. *Captain, we've got a pair of ten-meter holes in this boat. Both will be below the waterline when we're surfaced.*

Very well, Number Two, we'll pick up the Corona, and then we'll beach the boat. That was a decision CAPT William M. Corry didn't want to make. Deliberately putting the ship aground meant that he'd lost freedom of maneuverability. The U.S.S. *Shenandoah* would become a land airfield, provided he was able to beach it in a way that kept the decks level enough for flight operations. If not, the Air Group could operate from the atoll if some way could be figured out to refuel the aircraft from the ship's supply. *But once we get her aground, we can send down Brookstone's team along with repair teams in scuba. We can patch those holes. At any rate, once beached, we won't have to worry about going to the bottom. We can repair the boat and save her. If we can't, there's a repair ship on the way and due tomorrow.*

He paused, then added, *We've taken a couple of bad hits from an unknown weapon. But I want everyone to know that I intend to sail this ship into Pearl Harbor again under her own power!*

But he could not conceive of the possibility that a 51,000-ton aircraft carrier submarine, one of the most expensive of all naval vessels ever built, could even remotely be considered an expendable pawn in a larger game.

Nor could he conceive of the possibility that he might not sail the U.S.S. *Shenandoah* into Pearl Harbor again.

18

Sonar, this is the CO! Go to active pinging! Tag the Corona vehicle above us on the surface as Corona Two. I want the best sonar data you can give me on Corona Two! Corry shot the order to LT Roger Goff. He knew it was redundant. Goff always gave him the best data available. So did everyone else. He was breaking stealth by ordering active sonar, but at this point it didn't make any difference. The Mantids and Awesomes knew where the *Shenandoah* was located.

Aye, aye, sir! Going to active pinging! We have active sonar returns from Corona Two! The steersman might find lidar helpful as we close ... if the water is reasonably clear.

Radar/Lidar here, sir! We'll give it our best shot. I have no idea of the water transparency at the moment, LTJG Barbara Brewer added.

Special Sensors, CO! Any new data on the Awesome mother ship?

Negatory, sir! We've had to pull some of the gear off the line down here to recalibrate it. I've got only very rough mass detection capability at the moment.

How soon before you're operational again? This was important to Corry. The masdet had become an important sensor for the boat. He discovered that he'd gotten used to depending on it. Now he felt blind with only sonar.

Fifteen minutes, sir, if no one joggles my elbow here.

Corry got the signal. In his own techie way, Ames had just told his boss to get off his back. He wasn't as diplomatic about it as the line officers in the boat. Corry didn't react. He had other things on his mind, and Ames was too important to bilge for a minor infraction of protocol incurred in the heat of action.

Captain, this is the Deck. We are now at ten meters, up-

per flight deck reference. The retractable sail and dodger bridge are clear of the surface. The dodger bridge can be manned if necessary. We have periscope capability, reported LT Mark Walton.

Level the bubble! Up the periscope! Periscope view on my screen! Let's see if we can conn the boat under the Corona Two, Corry snapped. Much as he might have wanted to conn the ship visually under the Corona Two as he'd done with the original Corona, now Corona One, he knew his place was on the bridge itself at the moment. Too much was happening. The periscope display came alive on one of his screens as the videocamera came on line, but the periscope head hadn't come out of the sail yet. So he asked Braxton, *XO, damage report, please.*

Captain, we're still taking water. Watertight doors closed and sealed. Pressurizing the air head in the watertight compartments and reducing depth have slowed the incoming water. Stocker is also running pumps. So we've delayed the critical time before we get into buoyancy trouble. Provided, of course, we don't get any more leaks. And provided the hull integrity holds.

Zeke didn't need to launch into an explanation of that. Two large holes had been punched into the composite hull of the U.S.S. *Shenandoah.* No one at this point knew the condition of those holes. Normally, a composite submarine hull was designed and laid down with "rip stop" construction. Composite materials were extremely strong, but they behaved differently in the failure mode from ordinary crystalline metal alloys, which failed along stress cracks. Composites failed catastrophically. Special construction techniques had been developed over the years to prevent the catastrophic disassembly of overstressed composites, and the hull was supposed to withstand such punishment. The materials had performed well in laboratory tests. But this was an extreme case in the field with a composite structure much larger than a laboratory sample.

Earlier in the century, one of the first SSFs with a composite hull, the U.S.S. *Rainbow,* had collided with the old U.S.S. *Jackson,* an old SSBN. The *Jackson* had been fabricated of titanium alloys; the damage didn't destroy the hull and the boat got home. The *Rainbow* apparently went to the bottom with all hands, because the hull had delaminated and then disassembled. Except for laboratory test analyses, data were sparse and no one wanted to volunteer to make a field test with a full-scale submarine because of the U.S.S. *Rainbow* disaster.

However, it now appeared that the U.S.S. *Shenandoah* was going to be the field test.

If the hull did disassemble, the boat was in reasonably shallow offshore water. The catastrophe would occur almost without warning, but the chances of most of the crew getting out alive were better than if the boat had been in deeper water.

Corry also knew—as did all others aboard—that any submarine is a boat that is always on the ragged edge of sinking. Its buoyancy is extremely marginal. Otherwise, it would be too difficult to flood it to negative buoyancy and submerge. Or to surface it again, for that matter. Any breach of a submarine's hull is a serious matter. A breach easily tolerated by a surface ship could be a disaster to a submarine. Thus, the two ten-meter holes in her hull were indeed serious. On top of that, the Mantid weapon had punched deep into the bowels of the ship, taking out layers of watertight integrity. Fortunately, the boat was not running deep, or the hull might have collapsed. A broached submarine hull always means a greatly reduced crush depth.

Roger, XO. We're moving in to pick up another Corona. Corry turned his attention to the periscope screen.

The periscope head cleared the surface as he looked. The bright green of the water suddenly gave way to blue-white nothingness.

He could barely make out the sea-sky interface.

It was raining heavily.

And the U.S.S. *Shenandoah* was rolling and pitching in the heavy storm sea. It was very unusual to feel the deck moving under him. The carrier submarine was usually as solid as a rock when submerged.

Mister Lovette, erect the satellite antenna and get me a weather picture, Corry snapped. He checked the sonar display. The Corona Two should be resting on the water about five hundred meters ahead and slightly off the starboard bow. He should be able to see it. *Periscope view dead ahead!*

Metsat photo in thirty seconds, Lovette replied.

Periscope view is now dead ahead, wide angle on the view, Walton responded.

"There it is!" Smith exclaimed, pointing at Corry's screen. "It looks like a duplicate of the one we have on the hangar deck."

The Corona Two was hard to see in the rain, because its silvery, mirrorlike surface reflected the sky and the sea.

Manipulating the joystick, Corry swung the periscope to put its cross hairs on the Corona Two and commanded tele-view. The Corona Two jumped in size on the screen as the periscope camera lens zoomed in on it.

All ahead, five knots. Come right zero-seven degrees on the helm, Corry ordered.

In less than thirty seconds, the forward flight deck slid in under the floating Corona Two.

Corry wasted no time. *Come to full surface!*

Full surface!

Black Bart, when the flight deck is above water, you are clear to take the Corona Two. Shoot if necessary. I've had it with sneaky Mantids! Corry told his Marine batt commander. He was sorry he'd said it, and inwardly he knew better. He'd studied the principles of metalaw at the Naval Postgraduate School during his last posting there. He'd taken the course because the Navy believed that its high-ranking officers should have some knowledge of this budding new field of interpersonal relationships. Metalaw was indeed useful in dealing with people from other cultures on Earth, but Corry had never guessed he'd find himself applying it to extraterrestrials.

On the other hand, he didn't apologize to himself. Metalaw was grounded on the principle "Do unto others as they would have you do unto them." He didn't yet know how the Mantids behaved toward one another, so he didn't know how to behave toward them according to this principle of metalaw. He did know that the Mantids appeared to be very distasteful beings. However, he now knew that the Mantids considered taste in the victual manner, and that humans weren't distasteful to them. In fact, the Mantids liked to eat humans . . . alive if possible.

He didn't feel bad about ordering them shot if necessary. He only hoped that the two they'd captured in the Solomon Islands were still alive. If they were, he wouldn't need to be as careful with the ones in this second Corona ship.

Yessir, and this time I know how to get into the damned thing! Bart replied.

CAG, this is CO! Corry called to Terri. *Get your flight deck crews to dog down the Corona Two. The deck is heaving. I don't want it to slide overboard!*

Wilco, Captain! I'm glad we trained for this. We normally don't operate on the flight deck in this sort of sea! And the deck isn't the only thing that's heaving at the moment. Some of my crews don't have their sea legs! But we'll lash it down, sir!

Corry knew she'd see to it and report only when completed or if she got into trouble. So he turned to Braxton and asked him in verbose mode, "Zeke, did the personnel of the Medical Department get out of sick bay?"

"Yes, sir! They've set up a temporary sick bay in one of the Air Group's squadron rooms, thanks to Terri." Braxton then anticipated Corry's next question. "Yes, Captain, they brought everyone out of sick bay without difficulty."

"How about the Mantids? Did Benedetti's damage control party get them out of there, too?"

"Not yet, Captain," Zeke admitted. "The detention compartment flooded before the damage control party could get the door open. They didn't have the lock code. Laura Raye was out of there by that time."

"Did we lose the Mantids?"

Zeke shrugged. "I don't know, sir. Benedetti reports that some air was trapped in the compartment when the watertight doors closed off that section. The damage control team is in sick bay now working in scuba gear. They should have our two Mantids out of there in a few minutes. They don't know if the Mantids have drowned or not."

"Have Doctor Zervas stand by if he's recovered sufficiently from the fever."

"He is, Captain. He doesn't want to lose them, either!"

"No, I suspect not!"

CO, Black Bart here! We're inside the Corona Two. No live Mantids in this one. All four were splattered this time.

Black Bart, this is CO. Thank you. Stand by. The flight deck crews are going to dog the Corona Two to the deck.

They're already doing it, Captain!

Corry directed his attention toward his First Lieutenant. *Mister Walton, work from sonar data and the charts Commander Chase shows you. Move inshore. I want to beach*

*the ship in about thirteen to fourteen meters of water, just
a little more than our normal draft. Think you can find us
a level place to do it?*

*I'll try, Captain. It would be nice if we could find a bar
to go aground on.*

*Navigator, what's the north side of Palmyra Atoll like?
Any beaches?* Corry asked Chase.

Sir, the charts and the data are old, Natalie told him
honestly. *The bottom drops off very rapidly beyond the
reef. I wish I could see something through the periscope,
but it's raining too hard out there. Sonar soundings are
telling me something, but they don't match what I see on
the charts!*

Then she added a personal observation that should not
have gotten through into the N-fone net. However, the frustration of Natalie Chase at that moment overwhelmed her
rigid naval training. *Damn! I've spent my career trying to
keep boats from accidentally going aground, and now I've
got to deliberately beach one! Damn!*

Corry let it pass as he had Ames' protocol oversight.
The highly disciplined and trained crew were being pushed
to their limits right then. But they were performing brilliantly.

He turned to Smith. "Commander, go to the temporary
sick bay and talk to the Medical Officer. See if Doctor
Duval is in any condition to come up here. We need his expertise! Find him and bring him to the bridge!"

"But he's an alien! You'd trust him?" Smith wondered.

"Yes. He could very well go to the bottom with the rest
of us. And he doesn't believe he's an alien," Corry told her.

"Do you *really* believe that, Captain?"

"Yes, Commander, I do. Get him up here if he's able to
come. We'll hold position on the surface in the shallowest
water we can find in case we can't remain afloat. However,
the quicker you get back here with him, the less chance we
have of ending up in really deep water. I dislike having to
give you a direct order, but under the circumstances ...
Move, Commander!"

CDR Matilda Harriet Smith knew when an order was indeed an order, an instruction not to be argued with, something that she was expected to obey at once and on the
bounce. She moved.

"I know the way. Back in five minutes or less, Captain."
And she was gone.

*CO, this is Communications! I have CINCPAC on a sat
link for you!*

*Thank you, Mister Atwater. I'll take it on the verbose
handset here,* Corry told him. He wanted verbose conversation with Admiral Dick Kane. He wanted the nuances of
stress and emotion to come through, because this was far
from a dispassionate situation. He reached out and picked
the handset off the rest on his console. "Corry here!"

"Bill, Kane on this end! We've heard some unusual signals on passive sonar as well as garbled stuff on SWC. And
I've gotten a report secondhand from you through Thorne
on the *Schirra.* What's going on there? Report!"

"Admiral, we're on the surface about a thousand meters
off the reef on the north side of Cooper Island," Corry told
him.

"You were supposed to remain submerged in stealth until we got the whole task force there tomorrow morning!"

"It didn't work out that way, Admiral. I was lying on the
bottom off the north side of the atoll and was attacked by
a swarm of Awesomes being directed from a Corona-type
vehicle on the surface above me. The Awesomes managed
to place two mines against my hull," Corry reported, lapsing into standard navalese in which the Commanding Officer speaks in the first person for the entire command.
"Those contact mines used a new type of explosive I'll tell
you about when you get here. The mines blew two large
holes in my hull and punched almost all the way through
the interior of the boat. I am proceeding through the reef to
shallow water, where I intend to beach the boat to prevent
her from sinking. If I can do that, I won't sink before the
task force gets here." In his haste, Corry forgot to mention
that they had another Corona.

Kane was silent for a moment, then advised, "Thorne is
on his way with the *Schirra,* Bill. He can provide you with
close-in air and space defense. The *Morton* under LaCroix
is also being moved in to provide you with additional
ASW. The tender *Rash* will be there shortly after midnight
if Tropical Storm Fife doesn't get any stronger."

"I'm on the surface here, and I haven't had a chance to
look at the metsat data, but it's raining heavily," Corry reported. "The boat is also taking a pounding from the

waves. I've got to get her inshore and beached before I overstress a hull that already has two big holes in it. But I'll stay afloat until you get here. Where are you now?"

"Still in Pearl. Not nominally scheduled to depart until oh-three-hundred tomorrow by Sea Dragon. Arrival about dawn. Will you be in condition to trap us?"

"I don't know. If we can get inshore of the reef, perhaps. However, figure on landing on the Palmyra airstrip. I may have to evac my Air Group to that airstrip shortly. I don't want to take the chance of losing my aircraft or having them pinned down on a disabled boat."

"Can you remain afloat outside the reef in open water until the tender gets there?"

"Admiral, I won't take the chance. With a broached hull, a tropical storm in the area, and the possibility of the Awesomes coming back to finish me off, my first priority is the welfare of my crew, then the safety and integrity of my boat, and finally mounting a counterattack against the Awesomes and their mother ship, if they're still around. And in these seas, Admiral, I won't be able to come alongside and tie up to the tender in any event."

"Bill, if it looks like you're going to lose the boat, get your people off her first. But I know you won't lose the boat except under extenuating circumstances. So don't worry about the board of inquiry if you have to abandon ship. I won't try to tell you what to do. Run your show, and we'll be there as quickly as we can get a Sea Dragon off the ground here. We've just pushed the schedule up by twelve hours."

"Well, good luck to you, Admiral. I may be floundering on the surface here, but I don't envy you a flight to Palmyra under these weather conditions. Be careful, sir."

"I'll be sure to fly low and slow," CINCPAC assured Corry. The Admiral was also a naval aviator. It might have been a lighthearted remark between fellow airmen, but Kane's voice also had a tone of concern.

CO, Sonar reporting! I have an active sonar contact, bearing three-zero-one true, range five-three klicks, closing speed five-niner knots. The return has a nine-nines probability of being that of the CL-7 Schirra. The target is engaged in active pinging, frequency and wave shape consistent with a BQQ-five-four multipurpose sonar, sir.

"Admiral, Thorne is about fifty klicks out and coming in

fast. I'll use all the help I can get. But I'll keep the boat afloat until—"

CO, this is Special Sensors! The masdet is operational, sir. I have a massive airborne target now located stationary on a bearing of two-three-two true. No range data because I have no mass reference. But it could be over the last reported position of the Awesome mother ship.

CO, this is Sonar! We are now receiving passive sonar signals refracted around Strawn Point, sir. Sounds like both explosions and mine screeches.

"Admiral, it looks like I've got another furball brewing here," Corry told his boss. "I'm logging off because I'm frankly going to be too busy to talk to you. Call me when you get here."

19

CDR Matilda Harriet Smith came back to the bridge with Dr. Barry Duval.

The tall, skinny oceanographer was pale. Seeing him again in the familiar surroundings of the bridge, CAPT William M. Corry had trouble realizing that Duval was an extraterrestrial. He didn't doubt the findings of his Medical Officer in that regard.

However, Corry asked him, "Do you feel up to giving us a hand here on the bridge, Doctor Duval?"

Duval nodded. "I'm a little shaky. Other than that I'm about as well as can be expected after a bout like that." He hesitated for a moment, then said uncertainly, "I'm surprised you'd allow me on the bridge again."

"Why is that, Doctor?"

"Well, you think I'm an alien somehow in league with those who torpedoed the ship," Duval told him frankly.

"I don't know that you're an agent of the Mantids, Doctor," Corry replied. "As for your origin, that's a moot point now. The boat has been damaged and is in danger of sinking. If it goes down, your life is at stake along with ours. I need your help, Doctor, because this is an equal-opportunity emergency."

Corry's response surprised Duval. "What can I do, Captain?"

"I must get the boat inshore and beach it."

Corry's manner of speaking slowly and deliberately in order to control his stuttering under stress was a trait that Duval didn't understand. He interrupted the Commanding Officer, something that no one in the crew would think of doing, because Duval believed Corry had finished speaking because of the pause at the end of his sentence. "That's a drastic measure," was Duval's observation. As he'd remarked earlier, he'd spent a lot of time sailing off New England. Beaching a boat to save it was almost a last resort.

Corry overlooked the breach of protocol because he wasn't dealing with a sailor and because of the urgency of the situation. "Yes, but we have suffered drastic damage," Corry admitted. "Doctor, I need your knowledge of coral atolls. Our charts are several years old, and I know that coral atolls grow and change. With the ship damaged, I can't take any more chances than I absolutely must at this point. I need to find the best place to get through the Palmyra Atoll's coral reef and then locate a shallow but level bottom inside the reef where I can ground the ship."

"I see," Duval said thoughtfully. Then he went on in carefully measured tones, "Most coral atolls are built on the foundation of a dormant underwater volcano that is within twenty meters of the surface. Coral polyps need sunlight, and there isn't enough of that at depths greater than twenty meters. When the coral finally builds to a certain point, its weight tends to slowly sink the island. Then the barrier reef marks the original extent of the volcanic neck."

"Doctor, I don't need a Woods Hole course on atoll formation," Corry interrupted him. Academic scientists had a pedantic urge to deliver fifty-minute lectures. "We're in the margin of a tropical storm, as you might detect by the motion of the deck . . ."

"Yes, I'd noticed that we're pitching and rolling now. Very unusual."

"My damaged hull is taking a beating. I must try to get into calmer waters inside the barrier reef and ground this boat as soon as I can."

"Is there any natural channel through the barrier reef into the central lagoon?"

Corry brought up a chart of Palmyra Island on one of the bridge screens and pointed to it. "Yes, but it's on the west side of the atoll. I don't know if it's deep enough, and a Mantid mother ship is off its entrance."

"Oh . . . uh, yes. . . . Well, I don't expect the Mantids would let us into the lagoon even if it was deep enough. At least, not on the basis of what they've tried to do to this ship thus far."

"I wouldn't want to go into the central lagoon in any event, Doctor. No sea room there, and probably too shallow. So I want to beach off the north side of the atoll. Please sit down with Commander Chase," Corry told him. "Help her find the best pass through the barrier reef here on the north side. Then help her locate a suitable place inside the barrier for me to beach this boat."

"I can do that," Duval stated. Without another word, he went over to the Navigator's consoles and took a seat next to Natalie.

Corry turned his attention to the masdet display. He noticed that the large airborne target on the same bearing as the last reported position of the Mantid mother ship was still showing on the screen. It hadn't moved, but it was dithering in azimuth. *Special Sensors, this is the CO. What's happening to the target that's on the same bearing as the Mantid mother ship?*

It's definitely airborne, sir. It could be a very large object. I won't know until I can get some reference comparison data. The motion you see could be caused by the object's being buffeted by winds.

Mister Walton, what's the surface wind? Corry asked his First Lieutenant.

Sir, on the upper flight deck we have a Force Five breeze out of the southeast. Sea state is Hotel Two, sir.

Corry decided that the unknown target was being buffeted by the winds. On a hunch, Corry told his masdet officer, *Charlie, assume that the unknown airborne target is a Tuscarora vehicle in terms of size and mass. What can you tell me about it when those guesses are plugged into your magic machine?*

Uh, it will be only a guess, sir. Wait one, please, sir.

I'll go with a guess, Charlie.

If that's the case, sir, and if the target is fifty thousand tons and four hundred meters long like the one we saw in Makasar Straits, it would now be hovering about three hundred meters over the last position of the Mantid mother ship. Ames paused for a moment, then went on with additional data: *Range four-point-eight kilometers, bearing two-three-four true. But that's a guess, Captain.*

Your guess is received and duly noted, Mister Ames. Well done! Tag that target as the Tuscarora and let me know if it changes position.

Aye, aye, sir!

CO, this is Communications. SWC message for you, sir.

Put it on my screen, Mister Atwater.

The words began to march across the twenty-five-centimeter communications display screen before him.

CO CL-7 *Schirra* to CO SSCV-26 *Shenandoah*. Sea state precludes operation in hydrofoil mode. Forced to transition to HIW mode and 15 knots in heavy sea and Force 7 gale with heavy rain. My position is 41 kilometers north of Palmyra Atoll. Will be there when I can get there unless you are in emergency situation and need help soonest. Please advise. CL-7 *Schirra* CAPT Thorne CO.

Corry cleared the screen and told his Communications Officer, *Mister Atwater, please send the following reply via SWC to Captain Thorne. Message is: Thank you. We are still afloat. Situation serious but no emergency yet. Don't break your ship getting here. I doubt that anyone will mount an attack from orbit unless they've got excellent satellite imagery that will penetrate this storm to the surface. Conditions here are Force Five breeze out of the southeast, sea state Hotel Two. Presence of atoll quiets the storm on the lee side. Put my name on that and transmit it.*

Aye, aye, sir!

Corry turned to his XO and addressed him verbally: "Zeke, what *is* our present condition?"

"Sir, we're still taking some water but the volume has decreased," Braxton reported. "The hangar deck is secure and not flooded. We've lost one fusion reactor and half our steaming capability. All aux power and functions are nominal. We can maintain thirteen meters draft without danger of creating a negative metacentric height, sir. But we won't be very stable at that draft."

"Can we operate aircraft?"

"Not safely in these weather conditions, sir," Zeke told him, relaying to him the information that had poured in through him as the XO who was in charge of the internal boat capabilities in this semi-emergency severe-damage situation. "But in an emergency Terri could launch Sea Devils against any idiot who might be foolish enough to try to mount an attack in this weather! She'd have to trap them on the atoll, however."

Corry checked the upper flight deck videocam. The Corona Two was lashed down on the forward lift.

Commander Smith asked, "What's the situation with the Corona Two?"

"It's secure on the upper flight deck, Commander," Zeke told her formally.

"Can we get it down into the hangar deck?" The Naval Intelligence officer wanted to know.

"It would be risky in these seas to try to lower it on the lift to the hangar deck," Zeke told her. "This boat isn't meant to be very seaworthy on the surface in heavy weather. When it gets this bad, we're usually a hundred or more meters down, riding it out without a bump."

Corry added to his XO's explanation. "I agree with your evaluation of high risk to put it on the hangar deck, Zeke. Smitty, we've got to leave Corona Two where it is until things quiet down a little bit. Zeke, do you have any preliminary damage report on it?"

"Terri had her aviation rates go aboard, the people who powered down the Corona One. They've saved it. No damage reported. We didn't bust its bottom with our warshots this time. Terri reports it could lift if powered up again."

"And she'd like to do that, wouldn't she?" Corry put in, anticipating what his CAG might have in mind.

Braxton hesitated momentarily before he replied, "Uh, yes, sir. She's mentioned that to me, sir."

"Let's keep that as an option against whatever happens in the immediate future, Zeke," Corry told him, surprising him with that response. "Now that we have two Coronas, I'm not so worried about bending one of them if we don't lose someone in the process."

Smith also surprised him by saying, "I agree with that, Captain."

"Shall I tell Terri that, sir?" Zeke asked.

"No, XO, let's not get her hopes up," Corry told him confidentially, then turned back to the beaching problem. "XO, according to what you've just told me, we've got a little more time now to get this boat into quieter water. Tell Stocker and Benedetti to keep up the good work."

He went back to the N-fone channel. *Navigator, have you and Duval figured out where we can beach the boat?*

Sir, Navigator here. We're working on it. Right now, we're on the lee side of the atoll. The storm has lowered the water level by perhaps a meter or so. And the tide is out. The reef is above water all along the north side of the island, according to both sonar and masdet. The visibility isn't good enough in this rain squall to get any reliable lidar data above water, even at infra red frequencies.

Can you estimate the tidal effect? How much clearance between the reef and the surface will we have if we wait for high tide?

Sir, even if the storm passes, my tidal estimates indicate we'll have only about eleven meters clear. Less if the storm persists.

What's our likely bottom inside the reef, Natalie?

I estimate fourteen meters at high tide, sir.

Corry nodded. If he beached in fourteen meters, that would allow the upper flight deck to remain clear and useful. Thirteen meters would be better and twelve would be ideal, permitting him to use both flight decks. However, in this situation, he could work with the upper flight deck. So he'd take what he could get.

When is high tide, Natalie?

Twenty-three thirty-five local, and it's a spring tide. We'll have a full moon up there tonight ... somewhere above these clouds.

Corry checked the clock. That was more than eight hours away. He didn't know if he'd have the luxury of the wait in the boat's present condition. It was indeed taking a beating in the heavy sea.

He couldn't get the U.S.S. *Shenandoah* through the barrier reef. And in her present condition, he wasn't going to try ramming her through.

But the U.S.S. *Shenandoah* was a twenty-first-century warship. She carried explosives and warheads.

Perhaps he could blast a break in the barrier reef.

His first thought was to do it surgically. "XO, get Mister Brookstone up here. I want to see if he can put his team in the water, place some explosive on that reef, and blast a channel through for us."

"Why didn't I think of that?" Zeke said to no one in particular.

But Smith picked it up. "Because you're not the Captain," she pointed out quietly to him. She was rapidly gaining more respect for the man who commanded the world's largest vessel with such quiet competence and leadership.

LT Richard S. Brookstone reported to the bridge a few minutes later. He was a large, heavy-boned man who would probably someday grow so that others would respectfully refer to him as "stout." He listened carefully to what Corry said.

"Can you go into the water with a team and place enough explosives in that barrier reef to blast a channel for us, Mister Brookstone?" Corry wanted to know after he'd given the man a quick briefing on the situation.

"We'd need a channel about forty to fifty meters wide and about twenty meters deep," Brookstone mused as he looked at Natalie's charts. "We need to get in and over the barrier reef to position charges in it and on the atoll side. It will require a lot of explosives, Captain."

"Can you carry enough?"

"Oh, sure, sir! We can just make several trips carrying a manageable amount each time. It may take several hours, that's all," the Underwater Special Team officer explained. "Captain, may I get a look at the reef through the periscope? I need to get a feel for it. I haven't blasted coral since training days, and as I remember it's very tenacious stuff. Some of it is strong as hell."

Corry moved his chair to one side and offered Brookstone the periscope joystick. "Have a look, Mister Brookstone. You won't see very much. It's raining to beat hell, and we've got sea state Hotel Two."

Brookstone looked, then shook his head. "Captain, I would really hesitate to put my teams in the water under these conditions, sir. The waves are breaking on the barrier reef. It's not a real healthy environment for diving. I might lose some people. They could easily get dashed against the coral."

He paused, then added, "However, sir, if this is an emergency, we'll do it. I just wanted to advise you that putting divers out there to place explosives could be deadly, given the sea state."

Corry decided he didn't really want to put divers on the reef under the current conditions. The effort could end in failure to blow a channel as well as the death of several people. He decided the risks were too high.

Every Commanding Officer is reluctant to order people into deadly situations. However, if it had to be done, Corry was capable of giving that order. And he knew that Brookstone and his divers would go if ordered. "Thank you for your candid evaluation, Mister Brookstone. I agree with your assessment. Have you any idea how we might get explosive placed on that reef?"

Brookstone nodded, somewhat relieved at the Captain's decision. "Yes, sir. You've asked me to do it using human explosive carriers. Why not use some of the smart missiles we've got aboard? They'll do the same thing without worrying about being killed because they're expendable anyway."

Zeke looked up at that. "Guns Weaver has fourteen fish left, Captain. And we can supplement that with fire from the zip guns if need be."

Corry looked at his Special Underwater Team officer and told him, "Thank you, Mister Brookstone. You pointed out the obvious, something that had eluded me under the pressure of the situation. Stand by the water locks, because we may need your team for some hull inspection once we beach the boat inside the barrier reef."

"Yes, sir! We're ready to do that, sir."

"XO, Gunnery Officer to load four fish with maximum anti-ship warshots. command steering and terminal guidance. Guns will get the chance to pilot them in," Corry snapped. He got to his feet and went over to the Navigator's consoles. Verbally, he asked his Navigator and Duval, "Pick a spot to blast a channel. Where is the best place to do it? Where is the narrowest or thinnest portion of the reef?"

"Captain, I don't know . . ." Duval began.

"We have to decide. We haven't got time to study it to death. This is not a lecture room or laboratory, Doctor!" Corry didn't raise his voice, but it now had an edge on it. "This boat could sink before you studied it to your satisfaction, and I haven't got time for such pedantic thoroughness. This is the real world, and it's full of death and destruction. We have to operate in it with far less than wall-to-wall data. Get used to it! So where do we have the best chance of blasting a hole through that reef?"

Duval just shook his head. He seemed to grow agitated. Corry had never seen him behave that way before. It was a few seconds before he replied, but then he exploded. "Damn it, Captain, you're asking me to make a decision regarding the life and death of this ship and everyone in it! I just told you I don't have enough data to make that decision!" It was the first time Duval had ever responded in anger. He was wrong, of course. Corry hadn't asked him to make a life-and-death decision. But Duval, under pressure, had mistakenly understood it that way.

Although Corry was taken aback at this outburst, he realized he was dealing with a civilian. So he overlooked Duval's behavior and asked his Navigator, "Natalie?"

He didn't have to say anything more than that to her. She *was* used to making critical decisions, often on the spur of the moment with what she might consider insufficient data. "Sir, the distance between the reef and Cooper Island is less right here north of the airstrip. That might mean less subsidence of the island foundation in that area and less coral growth. I'm not an expert, sir, but I'd suggest trying to blast through right about there!" And she stabbed her finger at a portion of the chart.

Duval was really angry now. Chase was preempting his turf, his area of expertise. "What the hell do you know about it?" he yelled angrily and got to his feet. He started to storm off the bridge, took three steps, stopped, and looked back. Then he seemed to gain control of himself, and his composure returned. He walked back to the Navigator's console and sat down.

"I'm sorry," he apologized to both Corry and Natalie in a quiet and controlled voice. His anger had disappeared. He was almost meek. "Something strange happened just then. I lost complete control of my emotions again. But then I suddenly got my talent back! Captain, now I understand what you meant, because I know what you're thinking." He paused, then almost pleaded, "Please don't start treating me as a freak because of my talent. I've never told anyone about it before. This is all new to me. I'm going to have to get used to being around people who know that I know what they know."

Figuring out how to handle a telepath on the bridge of a possibly sinking carrier submarine was a task that the Commanding Officer didn't want to even think about right then. Corry decided he'd handle it later, if he could. Other matters had higher priority. Only later did he learn the real significance of Duval's reacquisition of his special talent to what happened next.

20

Guns, what's the best type of warhead to use against a coral reef? CAPT William M. Corry asked his gunnery officer via N-fone.

The reply from the Chief Warrant Officer was querulous: *Sir? What do you want the warhead to do, sir?*

Guns, I need to blast a channel through the coral barrier reef between us and the island, Corry explained. *I've got to get the boat into sheltered waters and beach her.*

Weaver responded quickly, *Sir, how thick is the reef?*

Corry called through the silent bridge to Dr. Barry Duval at the Navigator's console. "Duval ..." he started to say.

"I don't know the thickness of that reef," Duval replied.

Corry had momentarily forgotten he was dealing with a telepath. "Give me an estimate, Doctor."

"Their vertical profile falls off rather sharply on the ocean side. The inner slope can be very gentle ..."

It was Corry's turn to interrupt the oceanographer, "How thick is that reef, Doctor?"

"Best guess is maybe fifteen to twenty meters."

"I'll go with that." Corry would have to go with it. It was the only figure he had. He passed Duval's estimate along to CWO Weaver.

Sir, to be absolutely positive of doing the job right the first time, I'd use a Mark One-oh-one variable-yield nuke.

How far off shore would we have to be to use it?

Five kilometers would give us a good safety margin, sir. Ten klicks would be even better, given the weakened condition of the pressure hull. At a range of less than about five klicks on the surface, the One-oh-one would have a dual kill capability: the reef and the boat, sir.

Corry shook his head. *I can't back off that far. Can we launch one closer than that? If we can't use a nuke, then what do you suggest, Guns?*

I'd recommend the Mark Ninety anti-ship warhead, sir. Will that do the job?

It may take several, sir.

How many do you have, Guns?

Fourteen, sir.

Get a half-dozen warshots ready. Report when ready to launch.

Aye, aye, sir! Give me ninety seconds to change out the warheads!

Corry looked up from the displays ranging around his command position to check who was on the bridge. He was very surprised to see a very pale Dr. Eve Lulalilo and a shaky Allan Soucek sitting in the gallery behind him. Both of them were installing their receive-only N-fones behind their right ears.

"What are you two doing here?" Corry asked.

"These are our battle stations, Captain," Soucek replied.

"Well, yes, but you're recovering from illness. Sick bay is where you . . ."

"The fever has abated, Captain," Eve reported, but her voice was thin. "I feel all right. In fact, I feel better being up here than lying on a litter on a hard wardroom table. It was a little scary getting out of sick bay when it flooded. We had to walk out. If I can walk, I shouldn't be taking up space in sick bay. My fever is gone."

"Mister Soucek, how about you? Are you up to being here?" Corry asked.

"Yes, sir. I might be needed here," Soucek replied, breathing hard. "I understand we were attacked by the Awesomes."

"Yes. They used some sort of special ultrasonic explosive to put two holes in our hull," Corry told him.

Soucek nodded. "Ultrasonic disruptors. I knew what they were when I heard them. I've heard recordings of that sound before. It's been reported in connection with some close encounters where aircraft and cars have been pulverized. Did it come from a Corona?"

"No. Awesomes placed the charges against our hull as mines. We did manage to bag another Corona as that was going on." Corry pointed at the screen showing the forward upper flight deck.

"That one looks like it's in excellent condition, Captain!"

"However, its Mantid occupants are not. The four Mantids aboard are dead. Did the damage control party get our two Mantids out of sick bay?"

Soucek shook his head. "I think they did, Captain. But I don't know if they were alive when they were gotten out. They weren't conscious when they were brought into the temporary sick bay. Doctor Zervas and Laura Raye are working on them now."

"I hope Zervas can save them," Eve remarked.

"So do I," Corry added.

CO, Gunnery here! Ready to launch fish with anti-ship warshots!

Stand by to launch, Guns!

CO, this is Sonar. We have some dolphins out there along the reef, sir, Roger Goff reported.

Are you sure they're not Awesomes?

Yes, sir! I know the difference between dolphin and Awesome sounds.

Well, they're in the wrong place at the wrong time. Sorry about that. Guns, put one fish into the reef, delayed fuze. We'll see what happens, Corry decided.

Aye, aye, sir! Ready to launch fish.

Sonar, this is the CO. Stand by for warshot detonation.

"Captain, you can't do that!" Eve called out. "The dolphins out there are riding out the storm in the lee of the atoll. The explosions will kill them!"

"Eve, I have no choice! We must get the boat inside the reef before this storm causes more damage to the hull." The deck was rolling and pitching beneath him. He knew she could feel that, too. It was an unusual phenomenon in a submarine.

"But, Captain, you'll be killing sentient creatures!" she objected. The real world had intruded on her again.

"It's either kill some dolphins or risk the lives of all aboard. Do you have an alternative, Doctor? If so, speak up! Otherwise, I have to do what I must do!"

Eve didn't answer, but he could see tears in her eyes.

Guns, this is the CO! Fire tube!

Tube One fired! Any place in particular you want the fish to hit the reef, sir?

Head on, due south of us.

That's where it's going, sir. Fifteen seconds to warshot activation.

Corry felt the detonation through the padding of his chair. It sounded as if someone had hit the hull with a big hammer. On the periscope screen, he saw a column of water rise from the reef where the warhead had exploded. The column of water disappeared into the mist of the heavy rain.

Sonar, CO here! What's the result?

Guns nicked the reef, sir, Goff replied. *Still a lot of debris in the water there. Give it a few seconds to clear. . . . Okay, I can get a better return now. Have Guns give it about three more warshots. Dive the fish deeper before impact next time. And the dolphin sounds have stopped, sir. The warshot either killed them or knocked them unconscious.*

Very well. Guns, stand by to put additional fish in on the same target area. Set for deeper detonation. Fire one at a time so we can see the results after each shot. I don't want to waste fish. Corry didn't know where or how he might have to use the underwater missiles against Awesomes or their mother ship in the immediate future. So he didn't want to let Guns Weaver bang away at the reef in an overkill mode.

Gunnery is ready with the next fish.

Fire tube!

Warshot away! . . . Running deeper this time. . . . Coming up on detonation. . . . Impact! . . . Detonation!

Four shots were required before Goff and Ames reported that the gap blown in the reef might be large enough to get the U.S.S. *Shenandoah* through it.

It will be tight, Captain, Goff reported. *We should go through very slowly with a lot of sounding.*

Mister Ames, what do you think?

Captain, I know you're willing to live with guesstimates, but I can't even give you a good guesstimate at this point, the masdet officer told him honestly. *There's a lot of mass out there in that reef, and the explosions shook up some of my calibrated equipment.*

Corry pondered the situation for a full minute. If the sea state weren't so miserable and dangerous, he'd put Brookstone's underwater team out to have a look and even to help him conn the boat through the gap in the reef. But he didn't want to risk killing them.

Finally, he asked his Executive Officer, "Zeke, what's

the minimum draft that we can ballast to in our present condition?"

"Right now, sir, with the condition of the hull and pumping like hell, we could blow to perhaps twelve meters."

"Suppose we blow the keel tanks, too?"

"Uh, Captain, that could put us in a very unstable condition. We might capsize," Zeke told him.

"Given that, XO, how shallow could we run?"

"Eleven meters," Captain."

Before Corry had the chance to run that information into the mental equation he was building in his head, another call came.

CO, this is Communications. SWC message for you from the CL-seven.

Corry really didn't have time right then to stop to read it, so he said, *Summarize it for me, Mister Atwater.*

Sir, Captain Thorne has heard our warshot explosions and has expressed concern.

Reply that we are blasting a channel through the reef, Mister Atwater. Tell him what we're doing.

Aye, aye, sir.

Corry decided to put one more fish into the hole and see if that might improve the clearance. *Guns, load and fire one more fish. Program it deeper and see if we can't blast more out of the bottom of the breach.*

Aye, aye, sir! Loaded! Ready to fire!

Fire tube!

Tube fired! Number five on its way!

When things had settled down after the fifth warhead had gone off, Goff reported, *Sir, I think we might have thirteen meters depth in the hole now.*

Corry had to make a command decision based on what he knew at that moment. He didn't like to do that. He felt he didn't have enough data to make a solid, well-reasoned decision. But he was faced with the imperative fact that he had to get the boat into calm waters as soon as possible, preferably before something else went wrong. He really didn't know the full story about the hull. Two big holes in the composite material could have seriously compromised the hull strength. Furthermore, the continual pounding of the heavy seas of the tropical storm wouldn't make it better.

He turned to Zeke. "Number Two, what do you think?"

He wasn't trying to spread the responsibility. Corry wanted input from his Executive Officer. Maybe Zeke had seen something or come to some conclusion that would help the Commanding Officer make the proper decision.

"Sir, I wouldn't be honest if I told you I wasn't worried about our hull integrity," Braxton replied. "This boat really wasn't designed to ride out a storm on the surface. When the weather gets bad, we dive. Maybe a DD or CL can take it, because their hulls are designed to withstand the beating a ship takes on the surface. But our hull was designed primarily to keep the sea out. It's essentially a vacuum bottle—one atmosphere inside and hundreds on the outside pushing in. It has indeed sustained damage, and its overall strength may have been lessened by those two ten-meter holes. Even a surface ship faces the possibility of having its back broken in a heavy sea. It might happen to us under a lot more benign conditions."

"What would you do now, Zeke?"

"Dive if I could, sir."

"I can't dive even if I had room to do so. If the hull is weakened to the point where the waves might break its back, it might also implode even at thirty meters. I say again: What would you do, Zeke?"

Zeke thought about it for a moment. He realized that he didn't have a lot of time to come up with another answer. So he gave the only answer that he could. "Sir, I'd take the boat through the reef. It might get stuck, or it might get bent, but it isn't going to sink if it's aground on the reef. The worst that could happen is that we'll all get a little wet until the *Schirra* or the *Rash* get here. But I sure wouldn't take the chance of sticking around out here in this sea state and having the boat go down with all hands. I don't known how long an inflatable life raft would stay afloat in this weather."

Zeke had supplied him with the basic rationale for trying to get through the reef. Faced with the many unknowns that might cause the boat to sink versus what could happen if he tried to make safe harbor, Corry made his decision to proceed with the data he had.

Very well! We're going through dead slow and sounding. Chief Thomas, go up on the dodger bridge and call out any difficulties you see from there. Help me conn the ship through.

Aye, aye, Captain! On my way.

Sonar, I want both display soundings and verbal call-outs. Give me all periscope views forward.

Roger from Sonar.

Mister Walton, come to minimum draft condition. All ahead slow.

Aye, aye, sir! Come to minimum draft. All ahead slow into the gap.

It was indeed an operation that involved what military and naval people of all services called a "high pucker factor."

Heading one-eight-zero. Speed five knots. Range, bow to reef, is nine-zero-zero meters, Walton called out.

Depth under the bow is five-seven meters, came the call from Goff in Sonar.

Dodger bridge here! Come zero-five degrees to port. Slack speed to three knots. We're closing faster than the five knots you want, Captain! reported Thomas from his external lookout position.

Corry didn't repeat the order from the Chief Boatswain's Mate. He didn't have to. *Coming zero-five degrees to port. Slowing to three knots.*

CO, Navigator! came the N-fone message from Natalie Chase. *We appear to have tidal flow situation through the reef gap, sir. The tide is rising and we'll have a spring tide in a few hours. So water is now flowing inward through the reef gap.*

Sonar, can you give me a speed referenced to the bottom? Corry snapped.

Doppler sonar shows eight knots and increasing, sir.

Mister Walton, what is our speed referenced to the water?

We have slowed to three knots, sir.

All thrusters stop! Corry ordered. *We'll let the tidal flow carry us in. Be prepared for reverse thrust if we need to slow.*

All thrusters stop! Ready for reverse thrust on all thrusters. We have approximately forty-eight percent thrust available, sir.

All steam to the aft thrusters and stand by.

Aye, aye, sir, all steam to the aft thrusters. Standing by.

CO, this is Chief Thomas! Slow it down, Captain! We're

coming in too fast to maneuver quickly. And we need to come three degrees to starboard immediately.

Coming three degrees starboard.

Sonar here! Sixteen meters under the bow and reducing rapidly. Come starboard a degree or so. We've got an estimated ten meters on the port and twenty meters on the starboard side. Reef reference speed now ten knots and increasing.

All thrusters back slow. Give me five knots reverse water speed. Corry wanted to slow the ship as it snaked its way through the narrow gap its missiles had blasted in the reef.

Five meters under the bow and decreasing rapidly!

Blow all tanks! I repeat, blow all tanks! That includes keel tanks!

Blowing all tanks including keel tanks! Sir, I must advise you that such an action gives us a potential neutral metacentric height, Walton advised his Captain.

Thank you, Mister Walton. Your warning is duly noted. Stand by to flood keel tanks as quickly as we can once we get through or start to roll over.

Sonar reporting! Reef reference speed now twelve knots and increasing. Depth under the bow is four meters and decreasing.

We're in the slot! came the call from Chief Thomas.

Captain, the presence of the boat in the reef gap is acting like a partial cork, Goff reported quickly.

Walton added urgently, *We're being pulled to port by restricted tidal flow!*

All thrusters back full! Corry snapped. No one had ever maneuvered a boat as large as the U.S.S. *Shenandoah* in such a restricted channel with such a massive tidal flow.

All thrusters back full!

How much thrust can I count on, Mark?

We have forty-eight percent of maximum thrust, Captain. It's not enough to kill our inward momentum now against this tidal flow.

CO, Thomas here! Come to starboard! Come to starboard now!

The Sonar Officer called in, *Depth under the bow, less than a meter! Sir, we're moving sideways in the gap!*

All back emergency!

All back emergency!

Depth reading under the bow is now increasing to three meters! Looks like the bow is through the gap!

Full right rudder!

Sir, that will swing the stern! The only way through is straight ahead full!

Mark, can you get any steering by differential thrusters?

Negatory, sir! That would swing the stern, too. The boat would rotate around its center of gravity, and God knows where that is right now with all the water we've taken. We'd need translational thrusters in order to . . .

Something seemed to hit the U.S.S. *Shenandoah* hard on the port side. The jolt jerked everyone on the bridge. The sound was transmitted through the boat's structure. It was a grinding, tearing sound.

Corry knew what had happened. So did everyone on the bridge. But the discipline of the crew was tight. There were no shouts, no screams, only the rustle of purposeful activity as people did what they had to do based on the training of endless drills.

"Captain, we're aground!" Zeke advised Corry.

"Where?"

"Port side, station one-seven-three, level nine and below," Zeke said, repeating the preliminary report from Ray Stocker and his damage control teams. "The tidal flow is trying to carry us through, but the hull seems to be lodged firmly on the coral."

"Any hull damage?"

"Yes, sir! The coral caught the aft edge of the bottom hole and continued to tear aft! The force of the tidal flow continues to force the boat forward!"

Mister Walton, full emergency aft thrust!

We are at full emergency aft thrust, Captain! But we've got less than fifty percent of maximum available because Engineering has lost one reactor.

The tearing sounds continued to reverberate through the boat's structure.

Can we hold position, Mister Walton?

No, sir, we cannot. The tidal flow is continuing to carry us inshore, and the hull is being torn down the port side by the coral.

"Captain, heavy flooding on the port side aft, sir," Zeke reported.

Flood all keel tanks now! Put us on the bottom right here, Mister Walton!

"Well, Captain, we got as far as the reef. If we're on the bottom here, we can't sink," Zeke pointed out.

"Yes, Number Two, but the tides and the waves could tear us apart in a matter of minutes." Corry knew what was happening. And he suddenly gave the order he hoped he'd never have to give: "Stand by to abandon ship!"

21

CAPT William M. Corry knew it was there. His Special
Sensors Officer had identified it with the mass detector of
the U.S.S. *Shenandoah*. It was hovering one hundred meters above the water about five kilometers southwest of
where the carrier submarine was now in serious trouble. In
the intensity of the moment, Corry had forgotten all about
it.

The crew of the U.S.S. *Shenandoah* had tagged it the
U.S.S. *Tuscarora*, the mythical United States Navy ship
that was the modern equivalent of the *Flying Dutchman*.

But the Dimuzi crew and passengers of the *Tuscarora*
knew it as the Amalgamate Corvette *Abiel*.

Its bridge didn't look very much different from that of
the terrestrial carrier submarine. And it was run basically
with the same organization of duties, responsibilities, and
accountabilities. A ship is a ship.

The Communications Officer, *Lurel* Hamon Niyen, reported to the Commanding Officer, *Torli* Valrah Resik,
"*Nalt*, I am receiving basic Level One telepathic broadcast
of emotions from the beacon in the *Shenandoah* once
again. The signal is ... disturbing, to put it mildly. Fear ...
even terror. ... I'm catching some native-language phrases
I don't understand because I don't think in that language.
But I do know one thing for certain: For some reason, the
Shenandoah is in difficulty."

"I knew it!" snapped *Torli* Resik. "I knew it when I
heard them! The Dagdas *did* emplace those disruptor lim-
pet mines against the hull of the *Shenandoah*! Three disruptors would be enough to disable even this ship if they
went off inside the shield! It's a miracle they're still
afloat!"

"If you hadn't elected to lurk so far away, we could have

gotten here in time to keep them from setting off those last two disruptors," Newell Carew told him.

"I'm still the *Torli* of this vessel, Carew, and it was my call to remain at a suitable distance because of your report of their new masdet capabilities. I can't treat those masdet-equipped submarines as I could when all I had to worry about was sonar stealth," Resik shot back. "We got here as quickly as I could."

"*Torli*, the *Shenandoah* is now transmitting emergency distress signals and messages on seven different frequencies," the Communications Officer broke in. The receipt of any distress call was an emergency, Priority Number One matter for the Communications Officer to pass along to the Commanding Officer. Niyen named the frequencies, the Dimuzi frequency nomenclature being different from but translatable into terrestrial kilohertz and megahertz.

That suddenly changed the whole situation. *Torli* Valrah Resik turned to his passenger, Newell Carew, and explained carefully, prefacing his remark with the Dimuzi honorific of respect, "*Nalt*, you're the project officer for this mission. In assisting you to carry out the mission, I was under your direction. However, I must now resume overall command and break off your operation against the Samas and Dagdas. A vehicle filled with intelligent beings is in distress and transmitting a request for help."

"Well, I don't expect that the Samas are now capable of going anywhere while you assist the *Shenandoah*. It looks like we've pretty well beaten them down," Carew observed.

"They're not going to interfere with the *Shenandoah* any longer, that's for certain! They've recovered all their Dagdas. However, their factory ship still has the capability to lift off and head for their home world," the Commanding Officer explained. "Without me hovering over them, there's nothing to stop them from doing that. I'm the only warden ship or cutter in this star system right now."

"That may be enough to justify a claim that we've carried out the intent of our mission," was the advice from *Lurel* Wilne Zalucas, the Metalaw Officer. Technically, his duties were to advise the Commanding Officer regarding the metalegal aspects of operations. He could not overrule the *Torli*. However, Resik paid attention to the metalawyer's advice because Zalucas reported directly to the Amalgamate's Office of Metalegal Counsel. "We stopped the Samas' fishing activity as we were ordered to do, but we won't be able to apprehend the responsible Samas."

"Well, when we finish helping the *Shenandoah,* we can chase the Samas' factory ship right back to its home world," Resik reminded him.

Zalucas shook his head. "The Amalgamate has no authority to land on their home world to extradite them after the fact, even if the Sama authorities would permit that ... which they probably won't."

Carew was generally unhappy about the whole state of affairs. Sector Inspector Bisanabi had detached Carew from his assignment as President and CEO of Majestic Corporation. Basically, Carew's new task was to get out in the Pacific Ocean with the *Abiel* and straighten up the mess the Majestic 12 had created by inattention to what human beings were doing with submarine technology. Over the years, he and his colleagues—the Majestic 12—had become lax in carrying out the agreement the Dimuzis had made with the Americans of Earth back in the last century. One of the great trading species of this part of the galaxy, the Dimuzis had promised to keep the predatory Samas— known to the crew of the U.S.S. *Shenandoah* as the Mantids—under control and off the planet. This had been in exchange for the American authorities' giving up the remains of one crashed Sama starship and keeping the existence of extraterrestrials a secret. Although the Americans could not have duplicated the Dimuzi and Sama starship technology then, the Dimuzis simply wanted to deny the Earth humans access to that technology as long as possible. The Earth humans might make good trading partners when they grew up and changed their operational paradigm to embrace metalaw. Until they did, the Dimuzis considered them to be too predatory.

It had been easy for the Dimuzis to carry out their part of the agreement. Because it quickly became obvious to them that the American government couldn't keep a secret for more than a few years, the Dimuzis simply took over the American government group responsible for monitoring the Dimuzi police actions. They'd done the job so well that the Dimuzi agents who had been assigned to Earth had either "gone native" or grown complacent over the decades.

They were paying the price now. The Samas had returned and were covertly slaughtering humans again.

Carew turned to the ship's Metalaw Officer, *Lurel* Wilne Zalucas. "What are the options?"

"We have none," the metalawyer told him frankly. "The *Shenandoah* was attacked by the Dagdas under orders from the Samas. The Samas are in direct violation of the Second Canon. And probably the Fourth Canon as well. That was the Sector Inspector's justification for ordering us in the *Abiel* to deal with the situation by force if necessary. We've done the best we could with the Samas, but *Torli* Resik must now respond to the *Shenandoah*'s distress call."

"We don't have to respond to every distress call from every Earth vessel!" Carew objected.

"If we don't assist the humans who were attacked by the Samas as a result of our actions or lack thereof, and if we don't respond to a distress call that arose from that situation, we could be held in violation of the Fourth Canon ourselves," the Metalaw Officer pointed out.

Carew turned to another Dimuzi, a humanoid like himself who was a skinny ectomorph by human standards. The home world of Nun was a much warmer place than Earth, and what human anthropologists knew as Allen's Rule also held true there. The Dimuzis were tall and skinny because this helped them maintain their body temperature on a warm world. "I'm reluctant to engage in direct interference here without a reading from you, *nalt.*"

Ministrator Adri Hakan was enjoying this sojourn to Earth. It had given him an excuse to get out of his office on Nun, where ministering the interaction problems of this corner of the galaxy usually required difficult metalegal decisions. However, he was quickly discovering that he would have to make equally difficult decisions here, and with far less time and information available. "You have already interfered. Majestic Twelve put a Dimuzi beacon telepath aboard the submarine. Now you know he's still there. Are you going to expend him, Carew? After all, he doesn't know he's a Dimuzi and he doesn't know that Zalucas is reading him, albeit now only on the primitive emotional level. Something happened to him in the *Shenandoah* that has destroyed most of his latency. What the Majestic

Twelve did with Duval could be considered a violation of the Canons, by the way, because it put him in jeopardy of his mental health without his consent and knowledge. This could get very messy in metacourt. You've played loose and free with many of the Canons."

"Ministrator, I follow the Canons as best I can," Carew objected. "They aren't easy to follow or to interpret."

"That's why we have metalawyers," the Ministrator reminded him. "And the Majestic Twelve has had no metalawyers in the group for the last fifty or so Earth years."

"That's not my fault, Ministrator. Complain to Personnel about assignments. I have."

"*Nalt,* the *Shenandoah* is about to be torn up by the storm seas and sink!" the Communications Officer interrupted them. "As of this instant, I've got to deliberately block Duval's transmissions. I can't withstand the emotion-laden messages of fear and panic I'm getting! The empathy I've developed for Duval has been strong, so his emotional distress could put me out of action for days! In fact, it may have already done so!"

"Protect yourself, Hamon," Resik told him. "Your well-being is top priority."

Ministrator Hakan evaluated this and said, "My fellow Dimuzis, we can't let the *Shenandoah* sink. We can't stand by and allow some of the crew to die. Metalaw notwithstanding, it would be contrary to our own scruples. There's a matter of basic ethics involved here. Without those, metalaw itself has no foundation."

"I agree wholeheartedly with the Ministrator," the ship's Metalaw Officer added and then began to rationalize the situation. "I can justify to the Office of Metalegal Counsel that we had to blow away a few Samas and Dagdas on this mission. They resisted arrest. And they're barely stellarized anyway and have never really fully embraced the Canons of Metalaw. We should never have let them off their planet in the first place. But our liberal-minded colleagues felt sorry for them because of the supernova explosion that disrupted their biological processes." He didn't like the way some metalawyers tended to twist the Canons in the name of "fairness." He believed that the Canons were the essential means of living together in reasonable harmony in a universe full of strange, violent, and rapacious beings and cultures. To him, the Canons were continually evolving and were more than intellectual abstractions. The definitions underlying metalaw being as slippery as they were, he didn't consider any entity as an "intelligent being" unless it was willing to do its best to embrace the Canons.

He went on, "As for the Dagdas, they willingly went to work for the Samas, knowing the possible consequences. On the other hand, these humans did nothing to warrant what's happening to them because of our failures. And, Ministrator, I'm willing to defend our actions in this regard in any court of metalaw!"

The Ministrator looked around. "What do we do? Consensus reading, please. The Metalaw Officer has agreed we must rescue. *Torli,* I know you do. How about you, Carew?"

Carew thought about this for a moment. "Well, the distress call takes priority—even from a species not yet part of the Amalgamate. It would not have been necessary if we had kept the Dagdas away from the *Shenandoah.* So we'll have to break off, even if it means allowing the Samas to get away instead of apprehending them to appear in metacourt for what they've done here on Earth. I don't like that."

"Don't worry. The Samas will probably go home for a few years until they get brave enough and run out of human-derived biochemicals," Resik observed. "Then I'll have to come back and do this all over again. That's why they pay me the big *rasniks.*"

Carew nodded. "So be it. Ministrator, you wanted a consensus here, and we've got it. I'll need it, too, as part of my justification when I make my report to the Sector Inspector." He took a deep breath and steeled himself to make the decision. "*Torli* Resik, break off the operation against the Samas and do what you can to help the *Shenandoah.*"

"*Hoy, nalt!*" Resik snapped in affirmative reply and took charge, snapping out orders to both the Dimuzi bridge crew and the voice recognition circuitry of the robotics. "Stand down from Battle Stations and come to Rescue Mode, Condition Two! Hold present altitude! Turbulence stabilizers full power! Force projectors stand by! Go over the atoll and position the *Abiel* directly over the *Shenandoah*! Shield at full for defense! Stand by beamers in case I have

to fire a shot across someone's bow! Other naval submarines, surface ships, and aircraft are heading this way, so
we have little time to act."

There weren't as many crew members on the bridge of
the *Abiel* as there were in the *Shenandoah.* Automatics had
taken over most of the work of controlling the starship. But
humanoids still sat in overall control of the robotics. The
Control Officer replied in the Dimuzi version of the affirmative, *"Hoy, nalt!* Holding present altitude, coming to a position over the target. Shields are at full. Beams standing
by. Projectors ready!"

The silvery, fishlike, four-hundred-meter craft moved silently through the stormy skies above Palmyra Atoll toward where the U.S.S. *Shenandoah* lay grounded and
leaking on the barrier reef.

"What are your intentions, *Torli*?" Carew wanted to
know.

"I'm going to grab it off the reef with tractors and move
it into the western lagoon next to the pier," the Commanding Officer explained. "It will be safe from the seas in that
lagoon. And I can put it on a shallow bottom so it won't
sink."

"Resik, do you know that a Rivers class carrier submarine masses almost as much as the *Abiel*?" Carew pointed
out. "How can you lift it?"

"I'll manage," Resik said easily. "Look, my drive can
accelerate this ship at multiples of even the high gravitational constant of this world. I could actually lift off with
the *Shenandoah* and take it home at hyper-photic. And if I
can't lift it with my drive because of some gravito-inertial
problem this deep in a gravity well, I can use force projectors to push against the atoll. Don't worry. I'll lift the
whole *Shenandoah,* shipped water and all. Easy! Piece of
korik!"

"In this wind?"

"Certainly! I can anchor to the atoll if I have to. It
doesn't blow around in a storm. It's anchored in turn to the
planet. Carew, if I can't do something you want, I'll tell
you that. Otherwise, I know this ship and I know my crew.
And they know what they're doing," the Commanding Officer of the alien starship said with confidence. He was a
professional, and in this regard he closely resembled
military-naval commanders of other species.

Then Resik smiled. "You know, Commanding Officers rarely get to work a starship down in such planetary meteorological conditions. I'm learning a lot on this mission! I think I'll write this up for the *Proceedings*." He didn't have to add that publication of such a radical paper would be a stake in the ground, making him the expert in near-planet operations where meteorological factors were predominant. It might even mean a promotion, or even a new assignment to someplace that wasn't at what he considered to be the end of the Known Universe.

"I'd suggest getting into communication with their commander before surprising him," Carew pointed out. "Humans scare pretty easily when faced with the unknown."

"What do you suggest, Carew? How would we do it? Niyen, can we use your talents through Duval on the *Shenandoah*?"

"*Sym,* Duval is a transmitter that isn't working very well at the moment, anyway. And we don't have a receiver on that ship," the Communications Officer reminded him.

"Niyen, you've been monitoring their distress frequencies. They must be guarding them now for replies. So talk to them that way," Carew told the Communications Officer.

"I guess I could haywire something together out of the stuff I have in the slop locker," Niyen said, nodding. "I think I put some old radio transmitters in there with the drums, signal flags, and blinker. But even if I get it cooking, I don't speak human language."

The Commanding Officer of the Amalgamate Corvette *Abiel* didn't hesitate. "None of us do except you, Carew. So I'm giving you an emergency assignment: communicating with the *Shenandoah*," he told the former CEO of Majestic Corporation. Now that Carew's role as project director was moot because of the rescue effort, this would get Carew out from underfoot as a de facto passenger and all-around bureaucratic nuisance on the bridge. Resik didn't have time now to report to and argue with a civilian. To emphasize his order, he added with relish, "Make it so!"

"No problem. I expected I'd have to do it," Carew replied without rancor. "Now that we've decided to save them, I can do some negotiating."

"How so?"

"They've got a Sama beam ship aboard," Carew explained. "At the same time, they took the four Samas of the beam ship crew you were monitoring in the Solomon Sea when it happened."

"Ah, so that's what happened!" Resik exclaimed. "I didn't know. It happened fast, and other terrestrial submarines were in the area. I caught *silibu* from the Sector Inspector for nosing around the *Shenandoah* and the Chinese submarine in Makasar Straits when I busted up that Sama factory there. I thought the new data on the American carrier submarine would be valuable. But, oh, no! I got reamed for revealing the *Abiel* to two separate vessels and their crews! So I deliberately stayed clear of the Solomon Sea encounter."

"In retrospect, *Torli*—and I'm not criticizing the Sector Inspector here—he critiqued you a bit too severely," the Ministrator remarked.

"Well, he certainly made me a little shy." He straightened up. "Well, I don't have to be shy here! I've got a legit distress call, and the protocol of my required response to it is quite clear. Let's get to work. Then maybe we can go home!"

"Not before I try to get the Sama beam ship and its crew back from the *Shenandoah*," Carew reminded him. "Don't worry. Let's save them first, then ask for the Sama ship and crew later in gratuitous payment for the job."

"Right! Anything worth doing is worth doing as part of a deal," the Commanding Officer of the corvette agreed. "That's why we Dimuzis have prospered. And that's why I have a job as a corvette commander responsible for enforcing agreements when they start to go sour. So, it's a living!"

Then he remarked to his Metalaw Officer, "Zalucas, I'd appreciate it if you'd get me a hot cup of *mika*. I need the boost because this operation is going to have a high *imala* factor."

22

In the U.S.S. *Shenandoah*, the situation was similar. But Corry and the other officers didn't have time for a cup of anything.

"Captain, let me get the two Coronas off the ship with the aircraft evac!" CDR Terri Ellison confronted him. Standard procedure in an abandon ship action was to launch as many aircraft of the Air Group as possible. Not only were the aircraft valuable if they were capable of being launched, but they would be useful in picking members of the crew out of the water and off their inflatable life rafts.

Even with the heavy seas breaking over the *Shenandoah*, her two flight decks were well above water and taking only the heaviest of the waves. The conditions weren't ideal for launching aircraft, but Terri's pilots were anxious to do it rather than get their feet wet. As for Terri, she was bound and determined to get as many of her chickens off the boat and onto the Palmyra airstrip as possible.

"Terri, I can't let you risk either Corona by trying to fly for the first time in a Force Six wind!" CDR Matilda Harriet Smith objected.

"Would you rather they got broken up and went down with the boat, Smitty?" Terri asked rhetorically. "Look. I know I can fly the Coronas! And as for the weather, the wind is decreasing. It's down to Force Five. The sea state has gone to Lima Three. The latest satellite image shows the storm is passing off to the west of us. I'm not going to lose those valuable artifacts!"

"We'll lift them off the ship."

"How? With what?"

"With a crane when the tender gets here."

"The boat could break up before that happens."

"If the storm is abating, what's the problem?"

"The seas may not abate for hours.

"I'm not going to argue further with you! Don't do it!"

"Try to stop me!"

"Commander Ellison," Smith countered, addressing the CAG by her rank and last name, "I can stop you. I'll give you a direct order."

"Give all the orders you wish, Commander Smith! I obey only the orders of the Commanding Officer!" Terri replied with equal vehemence.

"You're looking at a court-martial, Commander!" Smith threatened.

That was a mistake. No one threatened Terri Ellison unless he or she was immediately prepared to fight. Terri wasn't afraid of a court-martial. She was only afraid that she would lose something that she and her Air Group had fought for and had lost a Sea Devil for in the process. "Your prerogative, Commander. Provided we survive this ... and the court of inquiry that will follow the loss of an aircraft carrier submarine with the additional loss of valuable alien artifacts and organisms. And maybe the loss of many lives in the bargain."

Smith didn't reply directly to Terri. She saw she was getting nowhere with an equally headstrong woman. So she faced Corry at his console and said, "Captain Corry, as the officer in charge of the artifacts, I request that you issue a direct order ..."

Corry had sat quietly and watched the confrontation between the two. He decided that Rudyard Kipling had been right about the female of the species. He didn't want to find himself between two women going tooth and nail at one another, although he had no question in his mind about who would win. He had other concerns on his mind right then, and a battle between Ellison and Smith distracted him from those concerns. In a vexed tone of voice, he simply said, "Ladies, we haven't time to fight about this now. Smitty, those Coronas are technically the property of Naval Intelligence, and you are the representative of OP-thirty-two in this boat. As the Commanding Officer, I'm responsible for the care and preservation of the Coronas and the Mantids in this boat until Naval Intelligence can physically assume those responsibilities. Do you agree with my assessment?"

Smith grudgingly replied, "Not really, sir, but what

choice do I have? With all due respect, sir, I will tell you that I don't want you to risk the Coronas by allowing one of your officers to fly either of them."

"Evaluating the physical risk to the Coronas is my job, Commander, and I will not relinquish it. If the boat goes down—as it now threatens to do—we will lose the Coronas unless they are gotten off the boat. Do you agree, Commander Smith?"

"If the boat does indeed sink, I agree, sir."

"I must operate with the possibility that the boat will indeed sink, Commander Smith. Our abandon ship drill requires that all aircraft of the Air Group be flown off if possible. Commander Ellison is carrying out her duties delegated to her by me, and that will include getting the Coronas off the boat before it sinks."

"But, Captain ... !"

"I gave the order to prepare to abandon ship, Commander Smith. You should take whatever measures necessary to go over the side, because this is real, not a Postgraduate School or New London exercise that can be debated! Commander Ellison, treat the Coronas temporarily as part of your Air Group. Get them off the ship!"

"Yes, sir!" Without a word to Smith, Terri jumped to her feet and dashed out the door, heading at full speed for the flight decks and the Corona lashed down on the forward lift.

CO, this is Communications. Captain Thorne of the U.S.S. Schirra *is on the TBS and wishes to speak with you.*

I'll take it on my N-fone channel Victor, Mister Atwater. Corry removed the instrument from behind his right ear, made a quick adjustment, and slipped it back into place. *Corry here. Go ahead.*

Bill, this is Steve Thorne. I received your Mayday. The sea state is getting better, and I'm only about forty klicks north of you. So I'm going to hydrofoils now. I'll be there in a few minutes. Can you hang on? What's your status?

Dick, I'm hung on the north barrier reef just off Cooper Island, Corry reported. *I'm aground on the reef. I probably won't sink, but I may be broken up by the seas. I can't take that chance, so I called a standby to abandon ship and sent a Mayday. But I haven't gone over the side yet. I'll be flying off my Air Group immediately. I'll hold on here until I get information that my hull is breaking up.*

Okay, we're coming. Did CINCPAC get the word? Admiral Kane left Barber's Point a little over an hour ago.

I don't know if CINCPAC received my Mayday, Look, Dick, I'm glad you're coming, but I've got my hands full here right at the moment. Let me know when you sight the atoll.

I'll do that. Thorne out.

Corry turned to Zeke to get the latest damage report. But before he cold speak, LT Charles Ames called in: *Captain, Special Sensors here. The* Tuscarora *is heading directly toward us, closing rate fifteen knots, range now four klicks.*

Radar, CO! Are you tracking anything coming in from the southwest?

Negatory on radar. But I do have passive lidar track in the infrared and active lidar in ultraviolet.

Special Sensors and Radar, stay on that target. Stand by to feed data to gunnery. Guns, this is the CO! Are my zip guns working on deck?

Affirmative, Captain. They're all working.

A large target is approaching from the southwest. Pick up coordinates from Special Sensors, Radar, and Lidar. Go visual when you can. All zip guns to standby condition. Mount up all available air defense missiles, use laser guidance, and prepare to launch against that target. Track it and stand by, but do not—I repeat, do not—fire without a specific order from me to do so!

Aye, aye, sir.

CO, Radar! The Tuscarora *just came out of stealth! It's a big radar target, sir. It's blooming all over the screens.*

Captain, this is Chief Thomas on the dodger bridge. Sir, the rain has let up and the wind speed has decreased. I have a visual on that target to the southwest. It's flashing something like strobe lights, sir. And, goddammit, it's the biggest thing I've seen, even bigger than what we saw in the sky off Makasar! But I think it's the kind we saw in the water there.

Corry thought he knew what it was and what it was about to do. He was only partly right. *Keep an eye on it, Chief. I don't think it's hostile.*

"I agree with you, sir," Zeke said from his position next to him on the bridge. Anticipating what Corry would ask, he added, "Otherwise, why would it approach us, proceed to break radar stealth, and aid visual location with flashing lights?"

"Yes. It may be the same vessel that looked us over in Makasar Straits, Zeke, or a similar one. We decided then it was a game warden's ship, because it acted that way. And it wasn't hostile then. Well, let's see if my hunch is correct." Corry swiveled a periscope around with a joystick, located the flashing lights, and zoomed in on the target.

It did indeed look like the *Tuscarora* that had approached the *Shenandoah* on the surface in Makasar Straits. It even had the same shape and the silvery color. There, the two vessels had looked one another over with no aggressive intent or actions being displayed by either. The *Shenandoah,* then as now, was armed and capable of defending itself. Corry suspected that the same was true of the *Tuscarora.*

However, Corry felt confident he was right, confident enough that he commanded, *All hands, this is the Captain speaking. The* Tuscarora *is headed toward us in the sky. Don't panic! Hold your fire!*

But someone did panic. Fortunately, she was on the bridge and not in control of any weapons. "Captain, you've got to shoot! It could sink us!" CDR Smith said breathlessly. She was scared. That had caused her to be a little irrational. Corry recognized that. She was a Naval Intelligence officer, not a blue-water sailor. Her panic had caused her do something no submariner would *ever* do: try to give an order to the Commanding Officer. Corry ignored it. And he ignored her. He knew his crew would hold fire. At this critical moment, that was important.

And he knew he was right when LT Atwater suddenly interrupted: *CO, this is Communications. Message for you, sir. Someone named Newell Carew from the corvette* ABL *wants to talk to you on the UHF emergency freak. But CINCPAC didn't report any corvette inbound as part of the task force.*

"Newell Carew! He's my boss at Majestic Corporation!" Allan Soucek exclaimed. "What is he doing here?"

We'll find out, Mister Soucek, Corry told him through Soucek's receive-only N-fone. Many things suddenly started to come together in Corry's mind. He didn't have time to discuss them with Zeke and Soucek at the moment. A *big* target with unknown intentions was bearing down on them, and someone who was probably aboard it wanted to talk to him. He had everything to lose by not talking to this Newell Carew and a lot to gain—such as a United States Navy carrier submarine and her crew. *Mister Atwater, put him on the verbose speaker phone at my bridge position.*

He activated the speakerphone on his console. "This is Captain William Corry of the U.S.S. *Shenandoah*. Mister Carew, Allan Soucek is here with me. He's told me who you are. What are you doing in this vicinity and why do you wish to speak with me? We are in a distress situation at the moment, and I don't have time to engage in a social chat, sir."

"Captain Corry, I also know who you are. My regards to Allan Soucek, and my apologies to him for putting him in a situation that almost got out of control," said Carew's voice from the speakerphone. "And I know your current situation, Captain Corry. I'm aboard the Amalgamate Corvette *Abiel* approaching you airborne from the southwest at a range of approximately three kilometers. Our intentions are peaceful and we wish to help you."

"Be careful, Captain," Soucek warned. "Needless to say, I don't trust my former employer." That statement surprised Corry. He'd talk to Soucek about it later.

"I'm sorry that Allan feels that way, truly sorry. I'm partly to blame," Carew admitted. "As for trust, all I can say is that we are serious in our offer to help you. We owe it to you."

"That's good. We'll talk about that when we have a few moments available. Now, Mister Carew, if your ship maintains peaceful actions, I'll have no need to activate my defenses. And although I may be in trouble, I am not defenseless at the moment. However, I have transmitted a distress signal, and I can indeed use some help. What do you have in mind?"

"I don't want you to panic and open fire on us, either. We are not defenseless, and the commanding officer of the *Abiel* would regret having to respond to an aggressive attack. That's why I'm talking with you," Carew replied, using a tone of voice that was conciliatory and yet firm. Corry sensed that Carew had had a lot of experience dealing with human beings and negotiating differences. Alien or human, anyone who worked in the nation's capital and managed to survive the experience would indeed know how to negotiate and deal. Given the cosmopolitan nature of the town, even an alien could also easily pass as one who lived and worked there. "This is indeed a vessel from another world, but we have principles and ethics similar to yours. One of these is a requirement to offer help in a distress situation. As I said, this we wish to do in response to your distress message."

"Trust him, Captain, but cut the cards," Soucek advised.

"And as I asked you, Mister Carew, what do you have in mind?" Corry repeated.

If Carew heard Soucek's remark, he ignored it. He replied, "With your permission, Captain, the commanding officer will use various equipment in the *Abiel* to pick you off the reef and lift you into the western lagoon next to the pier. Then he will put you gently on the bottom of the lagoon at a place of your choosing. The lagoon offers a protected anchorage against the tropical storms that are prevalent here this time of year."

"*Pick me up?* Mister Carew, do you know the displacement of this boat?" Corry replied with surprise and skepticism.

"I do. You are a United States Navy Rivers class carrier submarine. Displacement fifty-one thousand tons standard, fifty-eight thousand seven hundred tons submerged."

"And you can lift that?"

"Yes."

"How?"

"Never mind. You don't have the technology yet. You have the scientific background but haven't discovered how to apply it. Call it magic if it makes you feel better. We can do it."

"Something like the reverse of the force beam the Corona uses?"

"Corona? Oh, you mean the beam ship that attacked you. Yes, something like that. Perhaps we can talk about that once you're in safe harbor."

"Perhaps. However, in the meantime, Mister Carew, be advised that my hull is damaged from mines placed on it by underwater alien creatures. I have not fully assessed the damage yet. Furthermore, this boat was not designed to be lifted out of the water. Add those two factors together, and lifting this boat could break her back!"

"We can lift you without further harm and put you where you'll be safe until the other naval vessels arrive."

Corry turned and looked at his Executive Officer. "Well, XO, what do you think?"

Zeke had been worrying the damage control situation, and he knew it wasn't good. He'd heard what Carew had said on the speakerphone. He had a perplexed look on his face. "Captain, in our present situation, we probably shouldn't question a *deus ex machina* coming down from the sky to save us. I don't think anything else could except a floating drydock! But something would have to lift us off the reef before the drydock would do any good. Take the gift from the gods, sir."

"Your Executive Officer is right in one respect. Your ancestors many centuries ago did indeed consider us to be gods in machines from the sky. I know you've progressed a bit beyond that," was the observation from Carew over the speakerphone. "We're over you now, Captain. We're ready to help. But we need and require your permission and cooperation. We can't act unilaterally."

Corry made up his mind. If super-technological "magic" would save his ship at this point, he was willing to give it a chance, because he didn't have any other choice.

He knew he'd probably have one hell of a time explaining this one to CINCPAC. An account of another ship lifting the U.S. Navy's largest seagoing vessel out of the water, taking it overland through the air, and depositing it in a safe harbor was likely to seem a very tall sea story. Nevertheless he replied, "Please inform your captain that I will gratefully accept your assistance, Mister Carew. May we document the operation?"

"I won't prevent that. You'll need the documentation to CYA. Why am I not concerned about what you might do with it? Because Mister Soucek knows I'm well aware of how things are done in Washington. We'll not interfere with your photographing or other data recording, because I know how it's going to be treated inside the Beltway."

"By your Majestic Corporation putting the lid on it, Carew?"

"Oh, no! Of course not! We won't have to do a thing, even if all the documentation is released publicly!"

Corry knew he was right. He could almost see the headline in the tabloid news media: "STARSHIP RESCUES SUBMA-

RINE! Photos and story on Page 2." The stories alongside it
would probably feature the three-headed calf from some
obscure town in Iowa, the latest psychic revelations about
the forthcoming end of the world as we know it, and the
discovery of the Face in the Andromeda Nebula ("Are Aliens Trying to Contact Us from Another Galaxy?").

Trying to explain all of this to CINCPAC might be awk-
ward. So Corry decided he'd do it as he'd done it before.
He wouldn't even try to explain it. He would just report it
as dispassionately as possible. He hoped Kane was having
a good flight from Hawaii to Palmyra and would thus land
on Palmyra in a good mood.

But Corry really didn't worry too much about what he'd
tell an old shipmate and fellow graduate of the Naval
Academy in private. Kane had accepted an equally bizarre
story from Corry after the boat had returned from Makasar.
Kane would be more interested in the fact that Corry had
done whatever he could to save the boat, even accepting an
impossible-beyond-belief source of help.

So Corry didn't waffle. "Then please proceed, Mister
Carew. Can we help you? What do you want us to do?"

"Just hang on, Captain Corry. Just hang on."

23

"And, Captain Corry, please stay on your speakerphone there," Carew went on. "We must maintain constant communication. It also helps *Torli* Resik to know you're doing such things as blowing tanks to reduce the mass of the boat."

"If you'll put your Commanding Officer on the phone, Mister Carew, we'll operate on a one-on-one basis," Corry pointed out.

"Not quite, Captain. Our people—aliens, in your eyes—are called Dimuzi. You don't speak the Dimuzi language and he doesn't speak English," Carew reminded him. "I'm serving as the translator here. So stand by. We're over you at an altitude of about a hundred meters. We'll prepare for lift. But we won't commence lifting until you get your photo aircraft clear. I don't want to take the chance of damaging them with our tractor beam."

"Under the circumstances. Mister Carew, I'll do whatever I can to assist your rescue activity."

Corry immediately called Terri. *CAG, this is the CO. Did you hear that exchange with Carew in the* Tuscarora?

Affirmative, sir. Atwater had it on the command net.

Launch a Sea Dragon—anything—immediately. Have one or two of our best cameramen aboard. I want documentation of whatever is going to happen, Corry told her.

Yes, sir. So do I, sir! I've never seen a carrier submarine fly before. Keep track of the time, Captain. I'll countersign your Form One so it will be an official logbook entry.

I really hadn't thought about that. Corry was still tense and anxious but nowhere near as much as a minute ago. *However, you won't like my next order. Strike below the Corona Two on the forward lift. I say again, strike below the Corona Two on the forward lift. Stick it safely on the hangar deck.*

Sir! Duke and I were getting ready to fly it off to the island!

Not now. The people in the Tuscarora *are going to want it back. And they don't know we have two of them! So which one do you want to give up? The one with holes in it, or the one we just bagged?*

Given the choice, I'd rather keep the second one. It didn't get partially flooded with seawater. And I know what seawater can do to flying machinery! Very well, Captain. Roger your last. We're striking the Corona below. Tell the Tuscarora *people that we need to clear our flight deck.* She paused for a moment, then added, *CO, we're launching the Sea Dragon and a four-aircraft CAP of Sea Devils in about thirty seconds.*

Corry turned to Zeke. "Belay the abandon ship order, Number Two. let's see what happens here."

"Aye, aye sir! Belay the abandon ship order."

Mister Walton, blow all tanks but flood keel tanks. I want to lighten the Tuscarora's *load as much as possible. But I also want to retain positive stability when we're put back in the water.*

Aye, aye, sir. Blow all tanks! Flood keel tanks!

CO, CAG here. Aircraft are airborne. We got off two Sea Dragons with photogs. I always call for redundancy, and this time my people really came through! Both Sea Dragons were ready. Can I put up another CAP flight?

Put them on the deck and on the cats, Terri. Be ready to go, but do not launch.

Aye, aye sir. That was one of the few times that Terri Ellison replied with that nautical phrase.

"Mister Carew, this is Captain Corry," he reported verbally on the speakerphone to the *Abiel*. "Our aircraft have been launched and are clear. You may commence whatever you're going to commence."

"Very well, Captain Corry. Stand by for lift. . . . We're lifting!"

The hull of the U.S.S. *Shenandoah* creaked, then began to groan. Corry heard the sound of rushing water telegraphed through the hull. Then the deck trembled slightly under him.

CO, Special Sensors! Captain, I've lost calibration! I show an infinite mass directly above us and nothing below us!

Record it, Mister Ames. Record everything!

CO, Walton here! The reactor coolant pumps are sucking air! Commander Stocker has shut down the remaining reactor and switched us to emergency backup power. He's continuing to run post-shutdown reactor cooling using ballast water.

Thank you, Mister Walton. That procedure was SOP, but the First Lieutenant was required to report it.

Captain, this is Chief Thomas on the dodger bridge. Sir, I'm submitting my request for retirement in a few hours. I've seen everything now! Or maybe I'm hallucinating and it's time for me to leave the Navy. The whole damn boat is airborne, sir! We're out of the water and about a hundred meters over the reef!

Corry could see that in the periscope views. *Hang on, Chief. We're going to take a little cross-country bunny hop here.*

Captain, this is Tikki in Photo One! was the message from LCDR Ginny Geiger, CO of VC-50 and command pilot of the C-26 Sea Dragon with the photographers aboard. *I'm sorry to break comm protocol, but I don't believe what I see, either! Stand by for the video signal so you can see it, too. The whole* Shenandoah *is out of the water and rising to a couple of hundred meters! It's right under the* Tuscarora. *And it has absolutely no visible means of support, sir! Now the* Tuscarora *and our boat are starting to move southwest!*

CO, Communications. I have a video signal from Photo One coming on line. Uh, I don't believe this!

That phrase seemed to be echoed by everyone in the boat. Atwater put the video up on every available screen so everyone in the U.S.S. *Shenandoah* could see the incredible thing that was happening to their aircraft carrier submarine.

The video view from Tikki's C-26 Sea Dragon flying alongside slowed the *Tuscarora* over the *Shenandoah*. Together, the two of them were flying over the tops of the palm trees and palmettos of Cooper Island.

This was confirmed by other independent channels of video from the periscopes as well as the flight deck surveillance cameras.

No one would ever forget the sight of a fifty-thousand-ton, 390-meter submarine and an equally large and massive starship doing what seemed impossible but apparently was commonplace because the Commanding Officer of the *Abiel* had highly advanced technology available to him.

Water was not only draining off the hull of the U.S.S. *Shenandoah* but was pouring out of two gaping gashes now visible on her lower port side about halfway along the hull.

When Corry saw the extent of the damage caused by the disruptor mines planted by the Awesomes, he silently thanked the naval architects and engineers for designing into the hull far more redundancy than required by naval specifications.

It was indeed a magical sight.

Then all hell seemed to break loose at once.

CO, this is Radar! I have incoming targets! I have a surface target that appears to be the Schirra *approximately five kilometers off the north side of the atoll. This target is also in visual range, because we're getting ruby-red lidar returns from it and it is also painting us!* LTJG Barbara Brewer continued, *Second target is an incoming flight of four aircraft, bearing zero-one-seven true, altitude three thousand descending, leader squawking four-triple-zero.*

Corry immediately knew what both targets were. He glanced at Zeke, and a knowing look passed between the two men.

The radar transponder identification code was that normally used for CINCPAC.

"Zeke, you have the ship," Corry told him. "I'm going to have my hands full with Carew, Thorne, and CINCPAC."

"Yes, sir. I have the ship. Any specific place you want the boat landed in the lagoon?"

"Your call, Zeke. I've got to make sure that Carew and his people don't get spooked by the inbound ship and aircraft. And I have to make sure that neither of the inbound targets is spooked by what they're seeing. Above all, I don't want the *Abiel* to drop us!"

It was a drop of a couple of hundred meters for the U.S.S. *Shenandoah,* and it would be a quick end to the boat and the people in her if the *Abiel* turned loose and decided to leave.

The U.S.S. *Schirra* was a laser-armed aerospace defense hydrofoil cruiser. It carried an outstanding phased array radar and a multi-megawatt narrow-beam optically directed excimer laser. The role of laser cruisers in the United States Navy was not only distant air defense for surface convoys but also defense for amphibious operations. They also provided defense of underway replenishment activities against orbitally launched kinetic kill weapons. Corry didn't know if CAPT Steve Thorne would spook and fire at the apparition over Palmyra, but he knew he had to do two things very quickly.

The other target was a flight of four C-26 Sea Dragons carrying CINCPAC and his staff. Corry honestly didn't know what to expect from them or what to do about it.

He decided first things first. "Carew, Corry here. I'm going to contact the Captain of the U.S. Navy cruiser that just appeared north of the atoll. He is Captain Steve Thorne. I know him, and I will instruct him not to shoot. I will leave you connected so you may hear this."

"I know. I see it, too. It's a laser cruiser. We have our shield ready and he can't harm us. And I doubt that he'll hit you by mistake if he fires. His equipment is accurate enough to take out an orbital KE weapon at a hundred kilometers. Please don't forget, Captain, that at Majestic Corporation I hold a security clearance several levels higher than yours," Carew replied easily. But there was a note of concern in his voice as he asked, "What are the incoming aircraft? Who's in them? Admiral Kane and his staff, perhaps?"

"I don't know, Mister Carew, but I'll have our Combat Air Patrol check it out with an intercept. Stand by, please." Corry remained in verbose mode and called his Communications Officer. He still used his N-fone, but he didn't want to reveal that he had it. Apparently, Carew didn't know about it in spite of his apparently extensive knowledge of the United States Navy. That wasn't unusual. The N-fone had been around for a long time, and most people either ignored it or took it for granted. "Mister Atwater, get me a link to Captain Thorne in the *Schirra* and put it on verbose at my CIC position here. CAG, have the CAP intercept and check out those incoming aircraft."

"Roger from Communications," Atwater's voice came through the speakerphone. Corry had quietly punched up his command net to the verbose mode.

"Commanding Officer of the *Schirra,* this is the Commanding Officer of the *Shenandoah,*" Corry opened the channel. "Are you reading me?"

"Thorne here! Bill, what the hell is happening? I see something that looks like your boat, but it's under a similar-sized vessel and proceeding away from me across Palmyra!" CAPT Steven Thorne's voice came back. "Is this a mirage? Are you being abducted or something?"

"No, Steve, we've just been rescued. I haven't got time to give you any more of an explanation than that at the moment. However, the boat and the crew are now in good condition," Corry reassured him. "Do not shoot! I say again: Do not shoot! The vessel located above me is friendly! And if you do happen to shoot, it's likely to drop me and shoot back. I don't want to be dropped. And I don't think you'd survive if it shot at you. It's got some pretty high-tech stuff!"

"Yeah, I guess it does! Is it Chinese?"

"No, thank God! I hope the Chinese haven't spotted us here at Palmyra yet. They probably will as this tropical storm abates and they start getting high-quality surveillance data." Corry paused a moment, then suggested, "Steve, we're all right here. So why don't you direct your attention to orbit? We're going to be vulnerable to beat hell here at Palmyra. By the way, were you sent here by CINCPAC to provide aerospace defense?"

"Affirmative! Okay, if you want, we'll concentrate on space defense," Thorne replied. "But be advised that my laser is cocked and ready to fire at that vehicle over you. I can slew from orbital coverage to anti-aircraft mode pretty damned fast, as you know."

It was Carew who replied. "Yes, Captain Thorne, I know you can. This is Newell Carew, the translator on the *Abiel*, which is lifting the *Shenandoah* to the western lagoon at the moment. I know what sort of weapon you've got: an excimer laser. I, too, would rather you concentrated on orbital coverage. I assure you that we in the *Abiel* will not harm the *Shenandoah*. We responded to Captain Corry's distress signal as we are both required to do. We'll be finished here shortly."

"Very well. I'll stand by a couple of klicks off the north side of the atoll. Bill, holler if you need me!"

"Believe me, Steve, I will! But at the moment, things are looking a whole lot better than they did a few minutes ago. Stand by this freak if you want to hear what's going on. And if it will make you feel better," Corry told his colleague.

"I'll do that, Bill!"

CO, this is Communications. The incoming flight of Sea Dragons has established communications with me, Atwater reported. *They are fuel-short and a bit upset. I'd better let you talk to Admiral Kane, because he wants to talk to you, too.*

Put him on verbose, Mister Atwater. I want Carew and Captain Thorne to be able to monitor the aircraft frequencies, too. At this point, several hundred meters in the air, Corry didn't want to upset anyone, especially the aliens in the *Abiel* who had such powerful technology available. Communications was key. Carew and the *Abiel* had been open with him thus far—at least, as far as they were willing to go, Corry believed. There was no reason for Corry to cut Carew out of the loop at this point.

In addition, if Carew had had access to naval information at Majestic Corporation, as had been implied, Corry wanted to stay in the open with Carew.

As it turned out, not everyone felt that way.

Aye, aye, sir! I have a big patch field here. Go ahead, Captain.

Corry did it verbose. "This is Captain William Corry, U.S.S. *Shenandoah*. I have Captain Thorne of the U.S.S. *Schirra* and Mister Newell Carew of the Amalgamate Corvette *Abiel* on the net with me. Go ahead, please."

"This is Admiral Kane," the familiar voice of CINCPAC replied. "Captain Corry, what is going on there? You were given an order to remain submerged until we arrived. Why have you surfaced?" Kane's use of Corry's title of rank and last name told Corry two things. First of all, Kane was upset. Secondly, the Admiral had suddenly become aware that others were patched in.

"Admiral, I'm not only surfaced, I'm airborne at the moment," Corry told him.

"*What?* Explain!"

"I arrived yesterday because of confusion of orders, sir. I therefore remained submerged as ordered. However, I came under attack by the underwater aliens we tagged the Awesomes. They placed two mines against me and broached my hull. I was forced to surface and attempt to reach sheltered waters. However, I was taking water and could not clear the barrier reef even after I had blown a large gap in it. I told the crew to stand by to abandon ship and transmitted a Mayday call ..." Corry explained in an abbreviated, curt fashion. He knew that Kane would expect a full and detailed report later, but that the Admiral wanted to be literally briefed with a brief report right then.

"We received that! Are you still in distress?"

"No, sir, we are not. The Amalgamate Corvette *Abiel* responded at once to the Mayday call and offered to help," Corry explained. "The *Abiel* has lifted us clear of the water and is transporting us to the western lagoon. We should be landing there shortly."

A long pause followed. Then Kane came back, "Bill, are you all right?"

"Certainly, sir!"

"What's this about being lifted off the reef and transported over the atoll into the western lagoon?"

"That is exactly what is happening at the moment, Admiral. Are you in visual contact yet?"

"Negatory! We're about five klicks out."

"Well, that explains it, then! Captain Thorne, you have a visual on the *Shenandoah* at the moment," Corry said, calling in help. "Will you confirm the situation as you see it?"

"Certainly! Admiral, this is Captain Steve Thorne, U.S.S. *Schirra*. I'm hove to three klicks off the north side of the atoll. I have the *Shenandoah* in sight. It has been lifted out of the water by the *Abiel* and is being carried over the atoll at the moment. Sir, I know it sounds impossible, but I'm watching it from my bridge! And our photogs are taping it!"

Another pregnant pause followed. Then Kane came back on. "We now have a visual! I didn't know what it was when we first saw it a moment ago while you were talking, Bill. I don't believe this!"

"I'm the one being lifted, Admiral, and I don't believe it, either!"

"Okay, I've got a photog on it now myself. What the hell is that thing over you?"

"It's the Amalgamate Corvette *Abiel,* Admiral," Correy repeated.

"What the hell is an Amalgamate Corvette?"

"This is Newell Carew, the translator in the *Abiel,* Admiral. This corvette is a small starship of the Space Navy of the interstellar organization known as the Amalgamate."

"And I'm Admiral 'Bull' Halsey!" Kane shot back.

Corry knew the man was scared by what he'd found over Palmyra. Corry had been one of his plebes at the Naval Academy and knew Kane well. What followed was, Corry knew, typical bravado from a rational person who has suddenly encountered the irrational. "Amalgamate, my ass! You're either Chinese or you're one of those cannibal dolphins Corry found off Makasar. I intend to find out! Carew, tell your Captain to put my submarine back in the water! Then land and be prepared to show me your papers! Palmyra Atoll is under the jurisdiction of the United States Navy, and you have thus entered the territorial waters of the United States of America! As the highest-ranking American officer present, I have every right under international law to inspect your ship and your papers! If you resist, I have a laser cruiser standing by . . ."

"We have no intention of resisting, Admiral Kane," Carew told him in an easy but frank tone. "And we're not the aquatic extraterrestrials you're now aware of. We're as humanoid as you are and perhaps a bit less aggressive because we're stellarized and you aren't. Once we've rescued the *Shenandoah,* I shall be pleased to meet with you on Palmyra. We have business to conduct with you."

"Business?"

"Yes. The *Shenandoah* contains artifacts and organisms that do not belong to you or the United States. It is our mission to recover them."

Zeke nudged Corry and passed him a scrawled note: "Over western lagoon now. Have them lower us next to the pier. Charts say dredged to ten meters there for cruise ships."

Corry nodded. "Mister Carew, if you would please lower us to the water just off the pier below us, that will put us in very good shape. Thank you for your help, sir!"

"You're welcome, Captain Corry. For the benefit of your superior officer, let me say that we would have done it regardless of what you have aboard. Like you, our rules require us to render aid and succor to ships in distress." Carew paused, then added, "I've been around humans long enough in Washington to realize that you're relieved that we didn't drop you. Well, sir, we wouldn't have done that, either. Vicious we are not. We kill only when necessary."

Corry hoped it wouldn't become necessary, but he had to get to Kane right away and let him know in detail what had happened.

24

The landing of the U.S.S. *Shenandoah* on the bottom of the western lagoon was so gentle that Corry didn't know it had occurred.

Ship is on the bottom! Lagoon depth is eleven meters, LCDR Mark Walton reported.

CO, this is Tikki in Photo One. The lagoon waters parted under the Shenandoah *as it was lowered. Once it touched bottom, the waters came back around it.*

Thank, you, Photo One. I saw it but had other matters to attend to as it was happening.

CO, this is Special Sensors. We are operational again. Reporting acquisition of a target airborne and accelerating vertically off the southwest side of the atoll. It appears from its signal characteristics to be the Mantid-Awesome mother ship.

Radar has it, too. Big target! We confirm the radar signature similar to the Tuscarora *we chased off Makasar.*

Chief Thomas here from the dodger bridge. Captain, in between rainsqualls, I see something rising vertically in the southwest.

"Mister Carew, I believe your quarry is getting away," Corry reported to the translator on the *Abiel*. "Do you want the *Schirra* to shoot it down?"

"No, thank you, Captain. We anticipated that. It was part of the loss we elected to accept when we came to your aid."

"And it also jacks up the ante for us when you talk with us about reimbursing you for the rescue, doesn't it?" Corry didn't know if this was the case or not, but he wanted to say it and thus be on record. Although he could understand the CO of the *Abiel* breaking off his assigned mission to come to the aid of the *Shenandoah*—Corry would have done it himself if breaking off would not jeopardize the boat and if no state of war was in effect—he wasn't quite ready to believe that these aliens might have done it solely out of the goodness of their hearts. It was obvious to him that they wanted the Corona and the Mantids back. Carew had said it wasn't a condition of the rescue. However, in Corry's mind, it certainly rigged any potential deal in their favor.

"As I told you, Captain, we do not require reimbursement for the rescue. However, we do need to talk." Carew paused, and Corry heard strange sounds in the speakerphone. They sounded like words, but it was a language he didn't understand. Apparently, the *Abiel's* captain was speaking to Carew. The translator finally went on, "Captain Corry, we have lowered you to the water in the western lagoon. We will retire off the southwest side of the atoll over the entrance to the channel. You need to get CINCPAC aboard, and then we'll talk."

"I can't speak for CINCPAC, Mister Carew, but I will strongly recommend that Admiral Kane speak with you."

"This is Admiral Kane. I've been patched into this channel through the *Shenandoah.* Just what kind of a deal are you looking for, Mister Carew?"

"One thing at a time, Admiral Kane. Talks are best done in a non-stress environment. We must recuperate from our own stress environment. Captain Corry should do likewise. And you've had a long flight through poor weather to get here. I'm glad the weather is improving. Carew and the *Abiel* going off-line and out. However, we will monitor this frequency. Call us when you're ready to discuss things."

"Admiral, this is Corry. Continue your inbound flight. I'll get things prepared for you. My CAG will provide you with an escort."

"Give us your positioning coordinates or turn on your landing system, Bill. This is marginal weather, and we may have to trap under instrument conditions," Kane replied. Then he admitted, "I flew this Dragon on the way down, but I'm turning it over to its nominal aircraft commander. I'm not current enough to attempt a trap under these conditions."

"Stand by, Admiral. Please let me check out the situation. We were damaged during the alien encounter, and I need to make certain that everything is copasetic. I'll be back to you in a moment, sir." Corry then toggled off that open frequency and went to his command net. *CAG, this is the CO.*

CAG here, Terri Ellison responded at once.

Launch an escort flight for CINCPAC incoming, squawking zero-four-zero-zero. Prepare to trap them.

CO, we may not be able to handle four additional Sea Dragons. My forward lift is still fouled belowdecks with Corona Two. And we're running on emergency power, which cuts deeply into our ability to trap and deck-handle aircraft.

"Zeke, what's the power situation?" Corry asked his XO.

"Captain, the Engineer Officer reports that the reactor coolant loops are again filling with seawater. It will take him about thirty minutes to purge the coolant system of air that got sucked in when we went airborne. Then he can commence the restart on the unflooded reactor. He expects to have half power available in an hour." Zeke was passing along the damage control information he was coordinating as XO, looking inward into the boat while Corry looked outward.

Braxton paused as he listened to the silent report coming in from Engineering on his own N-fone channel, then went on, "The flooding of the second reactor compartment abated when the water drained out. Damage control teams have sealed it now. Stocker says he'll have to do an inside-out major inspection of the second reactor and its systems. Getting the second reactor back on line may require an estimated three days to one week, depending on how much water damage occurred."

Corry thought about this for a moment, then observed, "That means we can't really handle CINCPAC's aircraft."

"Not four of them, sir. CAG is having trouble getting her chickens up and off, and she hasn't even had to begin trapping for fuel yet. She won't tell you that, sir, but I know it's happening."

"She'd damned well better tell me!" Corry snapped. Terri tried to act in a self-sufficient way, and most of the Air Group people behaved the same. As a naval aviator himself, Corry knew that the "zoomers" often fell into the trap of believing that an SSCV existed only for them. Then he remembered that he'd given Zeke the conn. "Or you," he added.

"She will, Captain. She just doesn't feel she's in any trouble serious enough to affect the operation of the boat."

"Well, she is in trouble if I can't trap Admiral Kane and his party," Corry pointed out. "We'll have to put them on the airstrip. In fact, we may want to move some of Terri's aircraft to the strip to gain some flexibility."

"Terri's aircraft will have to leave the boat in any event, Captain. We are not in seaworthy condition. We can't leave this lagoon with our hull in its present condition. Major repairs will be required, and they may take months. We'll certainly need that tender," Zeke said.

"What is the hull situation, Zeke?"

"Captain, we're again taking water through the breaches in the hull," Zeke told him. It was apparent that he wasn't a happy officer. "However, while the boat was airborne, the teams managed to close some watertight doors that had not closed previously. Thus, they have reduced by nearly sixty-five percent the volume of the boat that was previously flooded."

"Tell the damage control teams, 'Well done!' " Corry said. The U.S.S. *Shenandoah* was now in reasonably safe condition. However, it wasn't going anywhere else.

Corry now faced the task of handling the incoming VIP flight. *CAG, this is the CO. From what I see here, Terri, you may have some trouble handling the extra four Sea Dragons on the flight decks. I suggest you vector them for a landing on the airstrip. You can then shuttle the Admiral and his staff to the boat. I'll pass the word to Admiral Kane.*

Thank you, sir. Better you than me! I agree it's inadvisable to trap the VIP flight on the boat. We're in a power-short situation at the moment. Our landing aids are down or minimal. And I've got aircraft about to evac the boat for the island. As a result, I've just gotten a quick report on the condition of the airstrip, and apparently it's weed city. I'm about to hop over there and have a look. I'll also be on hand to render what honors I can to the Admiral and his party.

Take some side boys and a contingent of Bart's Marines with you.

Yes, sir, I'd planned to do that. Some for show and some for blow. Last I heard, Palmyra was uninhabited. But I want Marine security around my landed aircraft. We have an alien vessel sitting in our backyard, and I don't know where that Mantid mother ship went. Maybe I trust the Abiel *aliens, and maybe I don't. But I don't trust the Mantids; they may come back for a little revenge. Besides, it will give Bart's gun apes something to do instead of looking at bulkheads and drilling three times a day.*

Carry on, Terri, Corry told her, knowing that he could count on her and on Bart Clinch. Having such trusted subordinates made his job a lot easier, and he needed it made easier right then.

"Admiral Kane, this is Captain Corry," he called formally. "Sir, because of the condition of the boat at this time, I respectfully request that you land your flight of four on the Cooper Island airstrip. My CAG will be there to welcome you with such honors as I'm able to provide at this point. In addition, a Marine security detachment is being deployed to the airstrip. We'll shuttle you to the boat in one of our Sea Dragons."

Kane's voice came back with a note of concern. "Bill, you're still in serious trouble, aren't you?"

"Not as serious as we were an hour ago, Admiral. We are no longer threatened by alien attackers, going to the bottom, or being torn apart on the reef. But we have limited power on board at the moment."

"Admiral McCarthy and I will accede to your request . . ."

"Oh, my God, my boss is with him!" Smith breathed.

"Relax, Smitty! You look fine," Zeke assured her.

Kane's voice went on, " . . . and I fully understand that the task of saving your ship precludes your presence in welcoming us. In fact, Bill, relax the protocols. We've got too much to do and too much at stake here."

"You and Admiral McCarthy will be piped aboard the *Shenandoah,* sir!" Corry insisted. "The Navy may have changed over the years, but we should never be so preoccupied that we forget tradition."

"Ah, yes, tradition. As I recall, Winston Churchill once had something to say about tradition when he was Britain's First Sea Lord—something to the effect that the only real naval traditions were grog, sodomy, and the lash. But that was another navy. Bill, we'll see what your situation is before I move my flag to your ship, because you're not afloat at this time. See you shortly. Kane out."

Chief of the Boat! Corry called on N-fone. *Stand by to man the side for Admiral Kane and Admiral McCarthy.*

Aye, aye, sir!

"Captain, as a matter of curiosity, and as a member of the Naval Reserve, do you really intend to render honors with the boat in this condition and the aliens looking on?" Allan Soucek hadn't said anything for a while. He'd been carefully observing and listening from his General Quarters post above and behind the Captain in the next-up gallery.

Corry didn't know what Soucek had in mind or what role he was going to play from now on. But he answered the man proudly, "Mister Soucek, it is precisely *because* the aliens are probably looking on that I intend to render honors! I want them to understand something the Mantids apparently did not and do not: that we maintain our composures as gentle people even under stress, that our traditions are just as complex as theirs probably are, and that we adhere to our traditions and protocols in spite of hell. Remember that we Americans have developed the image of being the reluctant warriors, never the conquerors but always the peacekeepers who are ready and willing to fight if necessary. And image is important here! I think we're being evaluated."

"Yes, sir, I think we are, too," Soucek admitted. "I can tell you that Newell Carew is a very smart and observant person—if that's a term that can be used for someone who now appears to be an extraterrestrial. He's seen one image of America in our nation's capital. I know he's seeing a different image here. I know I am, and I thought I understood the United States Navy. Now I know that I did not. But I'm learning fast."

Corry asked the critical question that had been lingering in the back of his mind: "What role do you see for yourself in what's likely to happen, Mister Soucek?" Soucek had been a problem for him, but Soucek had been a frightened man, a person whose basic beliefs and deeply held convictions had been nearly demolished in the past few weeks. Furthermore, Soucek had been forced by circumstances to consider his own personal death. Few people can stand to think about this. Often, it scares people so badly that they become zealously religious. But Soucek seemed to have made it through.

Corry had learned to confront his own death many years

ago, and it had not been an easy lesson. He knew that Soucek had gone through the same drill since he'd come aboard and that it had changed him. Corry was trying to find out what the changed man was like and how he might behave in the future. Soucek appeared to have lost some of the exceedingly defensive attitude that had caused him to challenge Corry's authority and even attempt to usurp it.

"Captain, I'm still legally an employee of Majestic Corporation, and the firm has a contract with the United States government—specifically, with the Executive Office of the White House through the Presidential Science Advisor—to handle relations with extraterrestrial species," Soucek pointed out. "Now I know that the firm is directed and managed covertly by extraterrestrials."

"Do you know if the President knows anything about the real nature of Majestic Corporation?" Smith asked. "We certainly didn't!"

"I don't believe anyone knows except the Majestic Twelve, the directors of Majestic Corporation," Soucek admitted.

"That's what I thought!" Smith said.

"So what do you think your role is from this point?" Corry pressed.

"I'm not really sure. It keeps evolving. Perhaps it continues to be what it has been: the person with the data, the intermediary, the negotiator, and the translator. I hope it is. Frankly, we've been on the short and slimy end of the slippery shaft with the whole extraterrestrial gaggle for a hundred years or so. I don't like that. If I get the chance, I'm going to see what can be done about it."

"Soucek, what chance do we have against the sort of technology we've seen today, know-how that saved our lives?" Smith wanted to know.

"Commander Smith, remember what Captain Corry said about image and perceptions," Soucek reminded her. "If someone is going to be perceived as godlike, a few miracles must be demonstrated to impress the rabble. The Dimuzis just pulled off a good one! On the other hand, I can think of a few scientific facts that would have allowed us to do the same thing if we'd asked the right questions of the universe and used some of the principles we already applied to the mass detector."

Soucek paused, and Corry didn't interrupt. Then the man

from Majestic Corporation went on, "I believe we're nearly to their level of technology. Furthermore, we handle technology far better than the Mantids, who only borrow it. One thing for certain—we're better organized and are better managers. And we communicate very well, although we often don't listen to one another."

Corry decided that the man had indeed overcome most of his problems. Soucek had never talked like this before. However, Corry had to point out, "Technological aptitude alone usually doesn't count. Extraterrestrials are often conceived in science fiction as not letting us into the Galactic Federation or whatever because we're still children on the social level and are ignorant of proper conduct under metalaw."

"Ah, yes, you read science fiction, don't you, Captain?"

"Mister Soucek, I'll read anything I can get my hands on, and so will any submariner," Corry told him. "I happen to like good, hard science fiction, because it's taught me to keep an open mind." After a pause, he added, "Frankly, I would have been in a very difficult position during this cruise—as well as the last one—if I hadn't."

"I can see that," Soucek admitted. "As for our development of social maturity, I think perhaps we're getting there. On the other hand, when I was an adolescent, I remember thinking that I knew what being an adult was all about. And I really didn't know anything! As for social development, I'm inclined to believe that the Dimuzis probably operate under something like the metalaw you mention. We may be in an excellent position to talk with them on a nearly level playing field."

Corry didn't reply at once. Finally, he said, "I was hoping you'd say that. However, you should keep something in mind, Allan. You're going to become a secondary player here very quickly. So am I. One Captain does not equal two admirals. I'll do my best to work with Dick Kane. I've know him since my Naval Academy days. He's honest and fair. I'll try to position you as you just described yourself. On the other hand, I don't know Admiral McCarthy. To me, she's the unknown on our side of the equation."

"Well, I know her," Smith put in. "She's a devious person who is extremely cognizant of the politics involved. But she's also honest and fair. It looks like I'm going to be in the same position as the Captain when it comes to deferring to admirals. But Admiral McCarthy will ask me for guidance based on my experiences during this cruise. And I certainly intend to recommend that she listen to the expertise of others in the boat. Fortunately, we have a lot of expertise in this boat right now."

"Commander, did you expect Admiral McCarthy to come to Palmyra?" Soucek asked.

She shook her head. "No. Quite honestly, I believed that I would be given full authority to handle everything for Naval Intelligence. I was ready to try it, although I was somewhat overwhelmed by the leadership and management abilities I discovered in this boat. So in a way I'm glad my Admiral is here!"

Corry had not anticipated that this sort of meeting of the minds would occur at this place at this time. However, since it had occurred, he wasn't going to postpone it or attempt to adjourn it. Until Kane and McCarthy arrived—he estimated that would take thirty minutes—he had little of an urgent nature that required his attention. His quick glance around the bridge told him that his crew was taking care of shipboard matters under the watchful eye of Zeke Braxton. Zeke, on the other hand, was trying to listen to this rump Papa briefing with one side of his mind while taking care of the boat with the other. Corry knew Zeke could do it. He'd trained his XO well.

He would have to go topside and welcome the admirals aboard shortly. So he said, "CINCPAC will have brought along his staff, because the Admiral can't do everything all by himself. But his staff knows nothing more about all this than he does. Smitty, what sort of staff does Admiral McCarthy travel with?"

"I don't know, Captain. When I've met her outside of Washington, she's always been alone. I think she depends on modern communications with her staff in Washington."

"I hope that's the case. If so, we're going to become the admirals' de facto staff regarding this extraterrestrial situation," Corry explained. "All of us have had enough management training and leadership experience to know that a helpful subordinate can exert a lot of influence, often actually directing the course of the matter. So that's what we're going to become: the helpful and knowledgeable subordinates who see to it that things get done the way we want them. Now, we've got fifteen minutes to decide what we want to get done."

He looked at the people in the gallery, those who had come aboard as the special team.

Not all of them were there.

Duval, he knew, was at the navigation consoles. He could see him.

Zervas was undoubtedly with the Medical Officer.

"Where's Eve? She was here a few minutes ago," Corry said.

Soucek told him, "After your conversation with Newell Carew, she got up and left."

"Did she say why?"

"She muttered something about not being needed if the Dimuzis were only another violent species," Soucek said.

Corry knew he should have found some time to talk to her. But he didn't have the time. The fate of hundreds, if not millions, of people seemed to be in his hands, and the fate of only one would just have to wait a few hours. He hoped that Eve was strong enough to last. And that she would understand.

"I'm sorry about that, because she is indeed needed. I'll send a yeoman to find her. In the meantime, we have work to do and not very much time to do it!"

25

"Boatswain, pipe the side!" came the curt order from the Officer of the Deck, LCDR Mark Walton.

The eight side boys—four men and four women—in dress whites came to attention and the salute. So did the Marine guard in full dress uniform. The Chief Boatswain's Mate, CPO Thomas, flipped the silver pipe to his lips, and the screech of a boatswain's pipe echoed across the flight deck. Thomas knew how to pipe. He was one of the old boatswain's mates who, like CAPT Corry, didn't believe that a recorded pipe sounded quite the same.

The sky was still full of ragged clouds, but it looked like a Category Eight sunset was going to occur over the palms and palmettos of Palmyra Atoll. However, the flight deck was still wet from the rain, and the humidity was oppressive. Terri's landing of the C-26 Sea Dragon had blown some of the water off the flight deck. But everything was wet and clammy.

Although the U.S.S. *Shenandoah* was aground in the western lagoon of Palmyra Atoll with two huge holes in her hull, Corry insisted that the proper flags be flown—the ensign from the flagstaff and the union jack from the jack. The commissioning pennant hung limply from the peak over the retractable dodger bridge and conning tower. These flag customs had fallen out of favor in the last century with the boomer and attack subs, but the U.S.S. *Shenandoah* actually had a flat upper deck and the staffs that allowed these flags to be flown. Furthermore, Corry wanted the occupants of the *Abiel* to see that the United States Navy had traditions that included the rendering of honors.

The visitors debouched from the aft ramp of the Sea Dragon. VADM Richard Kane, CINCPAC, was first, followed by RADM Dolores McCarthy.

Kane wasn't surprised that boarding honors were rendered, but it caught McCarthy by surprise. She didn't normally visit ships. Although she knew the protocol, it had
been a long time since she'd used it.

"I request permission to come aboard, sir!" Kane said to
Walton after he'd saluted the ensign and the OOD.

"Granted, sir!" Walton replied, returning the salute.

McCarthy did the same, although she hesitated. She
wasn't sure whether to salute the ensign or the OOD first.

When the two admirals had cleared the side boys, Corry
stepped up and saluted. "Welcome aboard, Admiral Kane.
Welcome aboard, Admiral McCarthy."

Kane returned Corry's salute and turned to McCarthy,
"Admiral, may I present Captain William Corry. I don't believe you've met him."

"I haven't, but I've heard good things about him. How
do you do, Captain?" After returning his salute, she extended her hand.

It was all very stiff, ritualistic, and traditional. However,
at Kane's request, full honors for a visiting admiral had not
been laid on because of the situation and the condition of
the boat.

The formal protocol completed, Kane looked around and
indicated the dim silvery shape of the *Abiel* off the entrance channel to the southwest. "I hope we haven't
spooked those aliens with all our aircraft and ships."

The CL-7 U.S.S. *Schirra* was off the north side of the atoll, and the submarine tender AS-88 U.S.S. *Rash* had just
appeared through the humid haze from the northeast.

"Admiral, they know a lot about us already," Corry advised him. "They won't get antsy. They want something
from us. I laid on boarding honors for you so they
wouldn't think we were a bunch of barbarian pirates. It
also shows we're not buttoned down and afraid they might
attack. If they want to talk peacefully, I wanted them to
know we have protocols, that we'll insist on some structure
to the discussion. I expect they already know this, but I
wanted to make sure."

"What do you mean, Bill?"

"Admiral, at least one of the people aboard the *Abiel*
lives and operates inside the Beltway. He's been among us
for years as the head of a think tank, Majestic Corporation."

"Newell Carew is here?" McCarthy said.

"Do you know him, Dolores?" Kane asked her.

"I not only know him, I know about him. But I didn't know he was an alien." The Chief of Naval Intelligence probably had a fat dossier on him, Corry decided.

"What is your pleasure, Admiral?" Corry wanted to know. "Do you wish to inspect the boat?"

McCarthy immediately said, "I want to see the aliens you have aboard."

"The aliens—we call them Mantids—were trapped when the sick bay was flooded. I don't know whether or not they drowned; I don't know if they can drown. My Medical Officer and Doctor Zervas from Bethesda are trying to resuscitate them now."

"How does it look? Can they be saved?" McCarthy probed.

"Admiral, I don't know."

"Certainly you've been kept advised."

"Ma'am, I don't joggle my Medical Officer's elbow when she's handling an emergency."

"Then I'd like to see the alien vessel."

"Which one, Admiral?"

"*Which one?* Do you have more than one?" McCarthy was astounded to learn this.

"Yes, ma'am. We took one in the Solomon Sea. I reported that to Admiral Kane. We just took another one off the north side of Palmyra a few hours ago after we'd been mined." Corry paused, then added, "It seemed a shame to leave it foundering when we could pick it up so easily on the flight deck as we were trying to make the reef."

McCarthy turned to Kane. "Dick, you were right about this man and the *Shenandoah.*"

Corry went on, "I know you're anxious to see what the Navy has managed to get, Admiral. But it's likely to be confusing unless we bring you up to the same level of confusion that we enjoy. My officers have prepared a briefing in the wardroom. It's more comfortable there. And, Admiral McCarthy, you'll have a chance to see your subordinate Commander Smith. And to meet the members of the special team and my department heads who can be spared from emergency duties at the moment."

Admiral Kane wasn't wearing a necktie, but he ran his hand around under his open shirt collar. Like most naval officers, he liked the tropics and was used to the climate. But he was sweating profusely. "Let's go below! I was on Palmyra years ago, and it hasn't changed. This place is so damned tropical that even composite materials rot!"

As introductions were being performed in the wardroom, Corry asked Zeke, "Where's Eve?"

"She's in quarters, Captain. She claims she's indisposed," Braxton reported. "She's either suffering from the consequences of Mantid fever or she's just lost it, sir."

Corry wanted to be compassionate, but he was also the Commanding Officer. "Zeke, send the Chaplain to get her. If she's ill, have Chapman escort her to the temporary sick bay. Otherwise, tell her that she's got a job to do and people are expecting her to do it. We can't afford or abide temperament. She's our Mantid translator. I'll give her thirty minutes to unload on the Padre. But I expect her to be here, and so does Commander Smith."

The two admirals sat quietly through the briefing, during which Corry, Terri, Stocker, Walton, and Braxton covered the situation from their viewpoints. Harriet Smith presented the situation from the Naval Intelligence standpoint. Allan Soucek remained quiet. Corry could see that he was ready to speak if called upon, but apparently he didn't want to duplicate what Smith said.

But Corry directed his attention mostly to Admiral Dolores McCarthy. He didn't know her. Kane was an old Academy shipmate, and Corry knew the man. But this enigmatic woman from Naval Intelligence was a puzzle. Occasionally, McCarthy asked a specific question to clarify something that was said. But otherwise, she remained silent during the briefing.

Dr. Eve Lulalilo came in with LT Thomas Chapman, the ship's Chaplain, about thirty minutes after the meeting began. Corry tried to make eye contact with her, but she wouldn't look at him.

Finally, Corry announced, "Admiral Kane, Admiral McCarthy, there you have it."

"It's a miracle your boat didn't go to the bottom," Kane remarked.

"With all due respect, sir, it wasn't a miracle," Corry replied. "It's good damage control."

"I was thinking about the actions of the *Abiel*."

"That was just technology we don't yet understand, sir."

Kane directed a question at Zeke. "Mister Braxton, do you have an estimate of how long it will take to make the boat seaworthy again?"

"Sir, I estimate it will require several weeks of work alongside the tender to patch the hull well enough to allow us to cruise at minimum depth back to Pearl," Zeke reported. "We really need to be dry-docked. If we can't patch up enough to make it back to Pearl, we'll request an ARD."

"It will take some work to get a floating dry dock down here from Pearl," Kane mused. "But if that's what it takes, it's easier and cheaper than a new SSCV. I'll have my staff check it out."

The Commander-in-Chief of Pacific naval forces then turned to Corry and asked, "Captain, why did you show up at Palmyra a day early?"

Without hesitation except to control his breathing to prevent stuttering, Corry replied at once, "It was my error, sir."

"No, Captain, I can't let you take the blame!" Natalie Chase put in quickly. "I forgot to set the calendar clock back a day to account for crossing the International Date Line eastbound. It was the stupidest thing a navigator could do! I knew better. I have no excuse. I was tired and I got ... distracted."

"Yes, you've told me," Corry admitted easily. "Admiral Kane, I have given my Navigator a verbal reprimand as well as a 'well done.' "

"A commendation? What for? Why did you do that?"

"We got here a day early, but we were undetected. I know now the reason we were undetected: My Navigator unknowingly had turned off the locator beacon placed aboard the boat by the Dimuzi," Corry explained. "The locator beacon was a humanized Dimuzi with a latent telepathic talent and implanted nanotechnology transmitters."

"Captain, I'm human," Duval interrupted. "I may be a latent telepath, but I'm not an alien. I was raised by parents who were aliens. But I have no knowledge that I was transmitting anything to the aliens in the *Abiel*! I knew nothing about the implants! You *must* believe me!"

"I do, and if you're a telepath you know it," Corry told him honestly. "You didn't serve as a beacon knowingly. But the Medical Officer reports that you are definitely not

Homo sapiens. That makes no difference to me. You're an intelligent person. Therefore, I don't care what your background is any more than I pay attention to the racial or religious backgrounds of any member of my crew."

"Thank you, sir. I keep forgetting that you know about my telepathic talent and I don't have to cover up now."

Admiral Dolores McCarthy broke in at this point. She looked straight at Duval and said in a skeptical tone, "Doctor Duval, if you're an alien, you're the most human alien I've seen."

"Have you seen many, Admiral?" Duval fired back candidly.

This caught McCarthy off guard. "As a matter of fact, I don't think I have. But I've often had doubts about some of the agents and other intelligence operatives I've had to deal with. However, if you're a telepath, what am I thinking right now?"

"You're skeptical about me, yet worried because you've studied all the available Aerospace Force reports about extraterrestrials and realize it's all not just a bunch of paper reports. It's reality. And you're not sure this is all real. Mostly, you're a little bit frightened and trying very hard not to show that you are," Duval told her frankly in his usual manner of politeness but irreverence for rank.

McCarthy shook her head. "Damn! I can't even keep my thoughts private any longer! Duval, you're a threat to Naval Intelligence!"

"I am?"

"I'm going to have to hire you."

"I'm just an oceanographer."

"You can continue to be an oceanographer, but I sure as hell don't want you working for anyone else but me! Unless we can turn you off permanently. What turned you off earlier?"

She was also unprepared for the answer, which came forth from Duval in a straightforward way. "I grew fond of Natalie Chase while we were working together on navigation problems in the Solomon Sea. When she was off-duty, we had sex." Duval smiled. "Wonderful! My first time! I guess the telepathic intensity was so high that I overloaded and blew my fuses. That's probably an inept simile, because I turned on again earlier today when I became angry.

But I'd sure like to find out if I'd blow my fuses again. It was worth it!"

Natalie Chase didn't even blush. But she wasn't the blushing type in any event. "I would, too. On a permanent basis if things could ever be worked out."

McCarthy turned to Corry. "Captain, don't you enforce Regulation Twenty-twenty in your command?"

"Admiral, I opened the Dolphin Club once we left Honiara and started home to Pearl. It's within my prerogatives to do that, and it's supported by operational precedents," Corry told her, gently reminding her that the Captain of a vessel was still its master, regulations notwithstanding.

McCarthy sighed. She caught Corry's implied reminder. She'd never commanded a ship. "Commander Chase, things could be 'worked out,' as you put it. Tell me, if Doctor Duval accepts my offer, would you accept a transfer to Naval Intelligence?"

"Admiral, I'm a navigator and a mathematician."

"I'll find work for you in those areas, too."

"Admiral, please let me talk to Captain Corry," Chase replied, thus politely putting off her decision. She wouldn't accept without Corry's approval, although in any case he had the right under the regulations to approve or disapprove. Maybe she could convince him that LT Bruce Leighton was qualified to replace her once the U.S.S. *Shenandoah* was capable of being navigated again.

"Welcome aboard, Natalie," Smitty told her.

"Very well, Captain, if Doctor Duval wasn't operational, how did the Awesomes find you?" Kane wanted to know. He was going to have to report on this to CNO, and he was trying to ask the sort of questions ADM George Street was sure to ask.

"Their Mantid colleagues intercepted your SWC message to me telling me what ships were inbound and your planned arrival. That message stated our location." Corry wasn't blaming his boss, just stating a truth.

"They've got SWC?"

Corry nodded. "They communicated with us using it."

"Another classified system compromised!" Kane muttered.

"Look at it another way, Dick. We now know they have it," the Chief of Naval Intelligence pointed out. "It just means we'll have to use more satellite lasercom, and that means we'll have to increase our orbital capabilities in that regard. I'd better try to get that in the budget supplemental before Congress marks up the appropriations bill in a few weeks." She made a note on her pocket computer.

CDR Laura Raye Moore came into the wardroom and went over to Corry. The Medical Officer didn't look very happy. And she showed her fatigue. She whispered something to him.

"Tell them," Corry replied and said to the admirals, "This is Commander Moore, my Medical Officer."

Laura Raye looked at both flag officers and said sadly, "I've got good news and I've got bad news. The good news is: I saved Merhad, the female Mantid. Bad news: Doctor Zervas and I could not resuscitate the male Mantid, Drek."

"Dreck? That's a German scatological word!" Kane objected.

"That was the name he asked us to use, Admiral," Eve Lulalilo said, speaking up for the first time. She showed no emotion over Moore's announcement of the Mantid's death. "Laura Raye, I should go and talk to Merhad."

Moore shook her head. "She's in no condition to talk to you, Eve. I've got her on life support. And I'm not so sure my lash-up is going to work. Mister Molders is on constant watch, monitoring vital signs. It would be a lot easier if I knew what I was doing, but extraterrestrial medicine is sort of a new field."

McCarthy was apparently upset that she'd lost a live Mantid. She was counting on having live ones as possible bargaining chips down the line. "Why were they allowed to drown, Commander?"

"They weren't, Admiral," Laura Raye replied. "Chalk it up to 'friendly action' on the part of their colleagues who attacked the boat. When the Awesomes mined us, the sick bay was flooded. Lieutenant Benedetti, the Damage Control Officer, personally led the rescue party to get the Mantids out before they drowned. He was too late, and he almost drowned himself."

"What have you done with the dead one?" McCarthy wanted to know.

"I don't know the Mantid death rites, so I've ordered Drek's body to be frozen."

"Keep Doctor Zervas away from it!" Harriet Smith suddenly said. "The man is knife-happy! He'll want to butcher it!"

Laura Raye looked at her knowingly. "Smitty, I've refused to allow Doctor Zervas to autopsy it. He already has a Mantid for that purpose. I figure one alien is all he ought to get." She sighed, then went on, "I'm sorry to report that we failed. But we did learn a great deal more about Mantid physiology. I'll answer any questions as best I can."

"Doctor, although I'm not responsible for the negotiating team," Corry told her, "I will certainly recommend that you be present. I hope you can arrange your responsibilities accordingly. Carew is certainly going to want to know what happened to the Mantids who were flying the Coronas."

"Well, we've got six, plus the remains of two more," Admiral McCarthy recalled. "I certainly wouldn't recommend that we give both Coronas back to them. They don't know we have two of them. If we have to give them one Corona and four dead Mantids, that still leaves us with one Corona, two dead Mantids, remains of yet another, and a live Mantid."

"We can't keep the live Mantid if the Dimuzis want her back," Kane suddenly announced.

"*What?*" Admiral McCarthy exploded. "Of course we can! That creature is absolutely invaluable to the security of the United States! It's a national treasure!"

"Geneva Convention of 1949," CINCPAC explained. "As well as the Geneva Conventions of 1864, 1906, and 1929 concerning the treatment of wounded and prisoners."

"But no war was declared by the Mantids!"

"Admiral McCarthy, when the Corona attacked us, we were coming to the rescue of a Chinese submarine that it had attacked," Corry reminded her. "Granted there was no declaration of war by the Mantids. But they attacked. Off Palmyra, they gave us warning that they intended to attack. I'm not a lawyer, but I've had to study the rules of war. And I've also taken the new course in metalaw at the Naval Postgraduate School. Admiral, this situation is a legal mess!"

"Yes, that metalaw course was a good one. It opened my eyes to a lot of things," Kane agreed, then told the other admiral, "Dolores, the legal status of this situation is indeed murky. I have my legal staffer along. And Captain Corry has a legal officer aboard. I believe we can call on them for guidance. Or we can call the Judge Advocate General."

"We're not calling anyone until Naval Intelligence has this whole thing well in hand! And legality be damned! I don't want to lose this valuable intelligence material!" McCarthy tried to explain.

"The Chinese aren't going to get it, no matter what we do," Kane told her.

"Chinese, hell! I'm worried about the Aerospace Force! They're bound to know what's going on here! I discovered that General Hoyt Beva is a member of the Majestic Twelve!"

"So that's how D. D. Martin got the word at Hickam!" Kane said, nodding in understanding.

"And why should we talk with the aliens, anyway?" McCarthy wondered.

"Newell Carew told me he wants to meet with us," Corry reminded all of them.

Kane thought about this for a moment, and no one in the wardroom wanted to break the silence. Finally, the Admiral said, "What have we got to lose by doing it? There he sits in the *Abiel* right over the entrance to the lagoon. He wants something. We think we know what it is, but we don't know for certain. Let's find out. We'll meet with him. Now, who's our team?"

Allan Soucek spoke up, "Sir, Newell Carew is, in our lights, a civilian. So am I. I volunteer to lead the team."

"You? Why?" Kane had in mind that he would, being senior officer present.

"I think I can do the best job. One: I know Carew and he knows me. Two: I'm cognizant of the extraterrestrials and their history here on Earth, just as Carew is well grounded on human background," Soucek explained forcefully. "Three: I've read the infamous San Andrés agreement we concluded with the Dimuzis in the last century, the one where we gave them a lot of our Mantid material in exchange for their promise to keep the Mantids out of here. I believe I'm the only one here who's read and studied it. I don't want us to get into an agreement like *that* again! If we agree on anything, the new agreement must replace the old one and be a lot more equitable."

Corry was surprised. Soucek was coming on strong, as Corry knew he could. But this time he was making sense and not challenging authority. He was smooth, polished, and convincing. Some of his Washington political skills—and no one can survive in the nation's capital very long without developing those—were now coming forth. Corry saw that Soucek had risen above his fears, terror, and insecurity. He began to see the man for what was really there, and the Commanding Officer of the U.S.S. *Shenandoah* had ample experience doing that. So he found himself telling Kane, "Admiral, I think Mister Soucek wold be an excellent chief negotiator."

"Why should I trust you to do this, Mister Soucek?" Kane asked him bluntly. "A few weeks ago, you were working for Majestic Corporation, which is run by aliens!"

"And I still am. But maybe Majestic Corporation can become the neutral ground here. And now that we know about Majestic Corporation's board of directors, that can be changed. That must be part of the new agreement!"

"Again, why should you be trusted?" It was Admiral McCarthy who spoke this time.

"Admiral, Mister Soucek is a Captain in the Naval Reserve," Smitty reminded her boss. "I've seen his record. He came in through NROTC before he joined Majestic. Furthermore, he has a high-level security clearance, and Naval Intelligence double-checks all high-level DISCO and DIA clearances. I used to do that for you."

"I withdraw my question," McCarthy acceded. "However, Mister Soucek, you would have to be responsible to me."

"I have no problem with that," Soucek told her simply.

"And I want to be on the negotiating team."

"Again, no problem, Admiral. I would expect that," Soucek told her frankly. "I would also ask Admiral Kane to be on the team, along with Captain Corry, his legal officer, Doctor Moore, Commander Smith, Doctor Duval, and the CINCPAC legal staffer."

"You've got the job, Mister Soucek." Kane was used to making decisions about people. He felt that Soucek certainly had the edge when it came to knowledge of extraterrestrials. And he also knew that he could replace Soucek if Soucek couldn't hack it.

"Thank you, sir. Now, when can we meet with Carew?"

Soucek asked, taking charge. When Soucek did this, Corry immediately saw him shift into command mode.

"As soon as possible," was Kane's answer. "Where?"

"On Palmyra, of course. The closest we can come to having neutral territory, although the atoll belongs to the United States. Better than giving either side the benefit of meeting in one of the ships."

Braxton sighed with relief and said quietly to Smitty, "Good! I won't have to worry about the level of honors to be rendered to an extraterrestrial coming aboard!"

26

The weather was already unbearably hot and humid at 0900 the next morning as the delegation from the United States Navy stood on the cracked, weedy runway of the Palmyra Atoll airstrip and waited for the Dimuzi delegation to arrive.

The dodger bridge sail of the beached and disabled U.S.S. *Shenandoah* could barely be seen through the thick jungle growth. Beyond the dim treetops of Sand Island, the silvery shape of the A.C. *Abiel* hung silently motionless in the hazy air. The cranes, masts, and upper superstructure of the submarine tender U.S.S. *Rash* could be seen riding the swells just beyond the channel to the western lagoon near the *Abiel*. Kane had agreed to delay the entrance of the tender into the lagoon to come alongside the carrier submarine, not at Dimuzi request but to prevent the Dimuzis from clouding any issues by claiming that anything had been transferred to the tender.

The Air Group aircraft were now positioned, parked and quiet, on the airstrip. The pilots of the Sea Devils were standing by, trying to keep cool and comfortable, but the aircrews of the P-10s and C-26s were back in the *Shenandoah*. The airstrip was full of airplanes except for a hundred meters on the southwest approach end.

Major Bart Clinch, Battalion Sergeant Major McIvers, and Companies Alpha and Bravo of the Marine batt were on the island, armed and on guard. However, in their ghilly nets and tropical gear, they were invisible in the jungle nearby. Charlie Company was deployed visibly near the Air Group aircraft parked on the airstrip.

An object separated from the *Abiel*. No one on the island saw where on the *Abiel* it had come from. Video documentation from the *Shenandoah* and *Rash* would reveal that later. It grew in size quickly. Less than fifteen seconds later, it had skimmed the trees and water to come over the southwest end of the airstrip left clear for Dimuzi use.

The *Abiel*'s aircraft was a silent, bulbous, featureless, egg-shaped craft. However, as it came to hover, landing legs popped out of its bottom side.

"I don't know how it flies, but it's got a hydraulic system," VADM Richard Kane remarked.

"Probably electrical, Admiral," Commander Harriet Smith remarked. "The Coronas use superconducting electromechanical systems, no hydraulics."

"Hydraulics weigh less," Kane observed.

"And I guess it's possible that the Dimuzis don't have superconductors and the Mantids do," she conceded.

"That is probably not the case," Allan Soucek put in. "According to the archives, the Mantids aren't technological geniuses. They've stolen most of their technology." He was sorry now he'd put on a suit and tie. The naval officers and Duval were in khakis, poopie suits, or casual whites. Corry was the only other person who wore a tie. But Soucek believed he had to look the part of the Navy's chief negotiator, because he would be dealing with Carew, who had *always* worn a coat and tie to the office in Washington. As a result, Soucek was sweating profusely and growing more uncomfortable by the minute. He was glad that they would meet in the shade of a C-26 wing at a table where large quantities of water and fruit juice had been provided.

Four tall, skinny humanoids were lowered from the belly of the Dimuzi craft. They apparently rode some sort of force beam, because no ramp or stairs deployed from the craft. Soucek saw that Carew was dressed as he normally would be in Washington. The other Dimuzis, one man and two women, wore clothing that appeared to be uniforms and covered their entire bodies except their heads and hands.

The introductions on that hot, steamy atoll airstrip took a long time, because Carew had to translate English into a language that sounded to Corry like Farsi.

The negotiators on both sides showed an interesting mix.

For the United States Navy, it was Allan Soucek; VADM Kane; RADM McCarthy; CAPT Corry; CDR Laura Raye Moore; CDR Harriet Smith; Duval; the boat's legal officer, LT Darlene Kerr; and CINCPAC's legal staffer, CDR Roberta Apel.

For the Dimuzis, it was Newell Carew; *Torli* Resik, who commanded the *Abiel;* Sector Ministrator Hakan; and metalawyer *Lurel* Zalucas.

Something struck Corry as more than interesting. The Ministrator and the metalawyer were female, thus making the Dimuzi contingent equally male-female. The Navy's group had more women than men with the two women lawyers, Kerr and Apel.

It also struck him that the Dimuzis appeared to be very comfortable in the humid heat. Laura Raye Moore noticed this too and understood the reason.

"We've prepared a comfortable place to meet over in the shade where it's cooler," Soucek said once introductions were complete.

"We're quite comfortable, thank you," Newell Carew replied in unaccented English with a slight East Coast bite to it. "This climate is something like that we enjoy on Nun, our home world. But we can see you aren't comfortable. So let's go over to the table in the shade."

No circular tables could be found in the U.S.S. *Shenandoah*. Therefore, four mess tables had been arranged in a rectangle. The four Dimuzis sat down on one side.

The Navy group had done a little planning. Corry opened the discussion as decided by telling Carew, "We wish to express our profound thanks and gratitude for your gracious help saving the U.S.S. *Shenandoah* yesterday."

"It was nothing that we would not do for any intelligent beings in trouble and broadcasting a distress signal," Newell Carew replied after translating into Dimuzi language and then receiving *Torli* Resik's reply. This became the operating procedure for the conference. Although English had become almost the universal language on Earth, Corry had attended international conferences and meetings where other people insisted out of pride in speaking their native tongues and waiting for translation.

Resik went on, Carew translating, "Captain Corry, it's part of our tradition as it is of yours. It's done instantly upon request. In war, it's also done when an enemy asks for quarter and help. And always it's done with no thought of repayment of restitution."

"Our laws require it, too," Darlene Kerr explained.

CDR Roberta Apel, Kane's legal staffer, put in, "We're

beginning the process of coding some of our laws against a common background of what we call metalaw."

When Carew translated this, the faces of the other three Dimuzis lit up in smiles. "That's interesting," the former CEO of Majestic Corporation remarked. "In all my years in Washington, I never learned of that. Of course, I wasn't involved in the legal side of things there. I had more than I could do keeping abreast of politics. And politics has nothing whatsoever to do with law, of course."

"Except that politicians are usually lawyers who not only make the laws but also enforce and interpret them," Soucek observed.

The Commanding Officer of the *Abiel* laughed when Carew translated that. The fact that this alien species could laugh impressed Corry and the others. And when Resik replied, Corry knew the Dimuzis also had a sense of humor. "Frankly, most of us have the same problem you do! Here I sit today surrounded by two lawyers, only one of them a member of my crew and the other one a Ministrator who can tell me where to go! Once we thought it would be a good idea to kill all our lawyers. Then we discovered we probably couldn't live together without specialists whose job is really to resolve personal conflicts!"

Ministrator Hakin didn't think Resik's comment was humorous and didn't laugh. But she replied, "I'm not ashamed of being a lawyer and politician. We keep most Dimuzis from killing most other Dimuzis most of the time. I wish we were as successful in keeping species from killing other species. It's a real bother when a trading partner from another species somehow falls afoul of yet a third. We're basically traders, and it's impossible to do that without contract law, tort law, insurance law, and criminal law, for example. We earn our keep."

"Well, another species attacked us. In fact, we discovered that the Mantids came back bringing the Awesomes to help them," Soucek said, bringing the meeting back to the agenda. "Back in 1979, we made an agreement with the Dimuzis concerning this. I'm an employee of Majestic Corporation, which was originally established to monitor this. It seems to have failed. I've given nearly twenty years of my life to the corporation, so I'm upset about that, Carew."

"So that's what you call them. Off-world, they're known as Samas and Dagdas. However, the failure of the Majestic board of directors is the reason I'm here," Carew admitted. "I've been assigned to straighten out the mess."

"I would hope we can straighten them out, Carew! The Majestic Twelve—the board of directors I've worked for— have certainly botched the job!" Soucek snapped at him. It was apparent that Soucek had little love for Carew and, now that Carew was really no longer his boss, intended to dig in his heels as chief Navy negotiator. "When you briefed me before I left for Hawaii, you told me that some members of the board were Dimuzis. Later I learned from Commander Smith that all board members are Dimuzis. You took over a human organization whose job it was to monitor Dimuzi adherence to the San Andrés agreement. You turned it into a cushy posting for getting your ticket punched to move on to higher jobs. Okay, you were re-placed, Carew. What about the others? What happened af-ter I left for Hawaii?"

"The others will be withdrawn to Nun as it becomes possible to do so," Ministrator Hakan explained through Carew, wanting to take some of the heat off an already dis-tressed individual who had tried and failed to do his job, partly because the Ministrator herself hadn't been paying enough attention (and was also threatened with reassign-ment). "The scientists, academicians, and industrialists will be moved out in ways that seem normal to your culture. The military members will be eased out on regular retire-ment. Their replacements . . ."

"Their replacements will be Earth humans," Soucek in-sisted. "And they will be replaced soon. Carew, I haven't left Majestic Corporation, and you can't fire me now. So I'm going to see to it that Majestic Corporation is run properly as an intermediary between humans and Dimuzis!"

"And Majestic Corporation is going to operate differ-ently," Admiral McCarthy interrupted him. "Majestic Cor-poration was supposed to assist the then Air Force. Not only did Majestic Corporation screw up, but the Aerospace Force forgot and went blazing off into the wild black yon-der doing their own thing. This time, Majestic Corporation is going to be under a new contract to Naval Intelligence. As a result, Mister Carew, tell your team that we want a new agreement!"

This blunt statement from McCarthy led to spirited discussion in Dimuzi. The Navy team just sat there, sweating profusely. Laura Raye warned them to drink up and preserve fluid balance. They took this opportunity to do that. Duval wasn't bothered by the oppressive heat, but Corry and Moore knew why. Duval would eventually admit to himself that he was a Dimuzi. But Moore had cautioned everyone to let Duval do this for himself.

Finally, Carew translated a statement from the Ministrator, "We Dimuzis are basically traders. If you want a new agreement, we'll work it out on a value-received basis. What do you want?"

"Control of our own destiny," Soucek snapped. "Stay out of our backyard! And quit trying to keep us from the stars!"

"You'll get there on your own eventually," Carew replied.

"We'd rather get there on our own, and we will," Soucek replied. "If you give us the technology, we're no better than the Samas. And it might come with strings attached, caveats that would keep us from using it until you think we're culturally ready to join your Amalgamate, whatever that is."

"You're an adolescent species . . ."

"Perhaps, but we're not children any longer!"

"Most adolescents believe they should be treated as adults," *Lurel* Niyen put in. "I agree that you're rapidly getting there. You now recognize that you're going to have to live by rules of conduct and action that govern the relationships between all intelligent beings, not just yourselves. But you're still fighting among yourselves. Maybe you should try applying metalaw to yourselves first. Then you might convince some of the seventy-one extraterrestrial species that you can do it with them, too."

"The Samas don't seem to be doing very well at following it," Laura Raye Moore put in. "Nor do the Awesomes, the things you call Dagdas. We were no threat to them. They were killing and butchering humans, using barbaric procedures. And *they* attacked *us*! Both species did! I was there. I tried to help them. I spent hours treating the Samas we rescued after we counterattacked them. What did they do? They tried to kill me! In fact, one of them hit me hard enough to give me a concussion. As for you Dimuzis, you seem to be decent folks. Doctor Duval was a model patient, and he's well liked by many of us. And we seem to be getting along with you."

Soucek picked up the discussion topic again. "You know what *we* want. What do *you* want?"

The reply was instantaneous: "The Sama vehicle and its crew you captured in the Solomon Sea."

"I thought so," Soucek said. He paused, then asked what Corry would consider an Embarrassing Question: "Why should we give all this to you?"

"It doesn't belong to you," Ministrator Hakan said.

"Under our rules of war, it does. It's a war prize," CDR Roberta Apel told her.

"The Samas are not at war with you," the Ministrator countered.

"They act like it," LCDR Darlene Kerr put in. "They instigated one unprovoked attack. We could excuse that. Perhaps they thought they were protecting themselves while they were in the process of sinking a Chinese submarine."

"They warned you about the second attack off Palmyra."

"And that was a declaration of hostile action. War, in other words," Kerr explained.

Smitty decided she'd better speak up at this point. When women, and especially lawyers, began arguing with one another, it was time for a diplomat to step in. She knew Corry was a diplomat, and she'd learned a lot from watching him. But Corry's manner was to allow adversaries to slug it out verbally. She believed the argument about metalaw and the rules of war wasn't productive at the moment, so she said, "Mister Carew, we can't give you everything you want."

"Oh? Why not?"

"Only one Sama is still alive," Laura Raye explained. "And she may not live very long." She explained what had happened to the two aliens when the boat had been mined.

"We're sorry to hear that. We regret we didn't get here in time to stop the Sama-Dagda attack on you," Resik said through Carew. "Your boat is very stealthy, and we'd somehow lost our beacon once you left Honiara. We didn't know where you were until we got the communication messages and heard the mines."

"I'll accept your apology, Captain," Kane told the *Torli* of the *Abiel*. "But it is going to cost us to fix the damage."

Resik shook his head. "I can't help you. Your hull material is primitive. I don't have the capability to repair it."

"Well, tell us exactly what did it. That may help us figure out the best repair procedure."

"I can't reveal the workings of a weapon to you! That's against *my* regulations!"

"Captain, we have similar security rules," Corry put in easily in a nonchalant fashion. "However, you won't be revealing anything we don't already know. That mine was a straightforward sonic bond disruptor, perhaps subnuclear because of the intensity of its energy release. But knowing exactly how it disrupted the bonds of a composite material might help us to reestablish some of those bonds."

McCarthy looked at Corry in surprise. Was this some other covert program Naval Intelligence didn't know about? Smitty almost broke out laughing. Later, she'd tell her Admiral that Corry was spouting technobabble from one of the science fiction novels he'd lent her on the cruise. She *liked* this Captain!

"Well, we might be able to arrange something. After all, the Samas stole it from the Arlets," Ministrator Hakan decided. "Let me put it this way: There's probably a tech manual on it in the Samas vehicle. Why don't you just remove it before you give the ship back to us? That way, I don't have to say that I gave it to you."

"I've already got the manual," Terri Ellison revealed. "I can't read it."

"So? It's like any tech manual I've ever seen: totally unreadable by the user," the CO of the *Abiel* said, stating what appeared to be a universal truth. The *Torli* had a sense of humor, and the stuffy Ministrator didn't appreciate it. It told the Navy people that the Dimuzis had a sense of perspective.

"So my experts will get to work on it, and we'll learn the Samas language in the process," McCarthy said. She was wrong about that, of course. If she'd read any Navy tech manuals, she would have known that they appeared to be in English but weren't.

"But we want the Sama ship and its occupants back, dead or alive," the Ministrator insisted.

"Please tell us why. Is it so we can't learn the technology?" Kane wanted to know.

"Not at all. We're not worried about that. The technology is too advanced for you to figure out. Most of it will seem impossible in light of your present knowledge of the universe," Ministrator Hakan explained. "We intend to bring charges against the Samas for what they've done on your world, which may disrupt trade in the whole sector. When we stopped to help you, we lost the chance to get their mother ship and their Dagdas as evidence. They got away, and we can't extradite them from their home world. We want the Samas and their ship because it's evidence we'll use in metacourt. Our case against the Samas will be very difficult if we don't have it."

She turned to Apel and Kerr and, through Carew, asked, "You both understand the rules of evidence, don't you?"

This put a new spin on what the Navy contingent had already decided could be given away. So Soucek announced, "All right, you can have the ship we captured in the Solomon Sea. And we'll transfer three dead Samas and a live one to you. That's the easy part. What we want is an iron-clad agreement with you about Majestic Corporation. It's going to be a contractor to the United States Navy and it will be your contact with us. Commander Apel, are you familiar with contracts?"

She nodded and took her computer out of her shoulder bag. "I think I have some boilerplate here in memory."

Kane pulled back from the table and engaged in a private conversation with McCarthy. Then he turned to the group and said, "Soucek, Admiral McCarthy and I want you to work with Smith, Apel, and Kerr. Put together a written legal deal with the Dimuzis. Both sides have agreed in principle; get it down in writing. I'm not a legal eagle, and I have work to do with Captain Corry regarding the repair of the *Shenandoah*. If it's all right with the Dimuzis, the rest of us will be back at thirteen hundred hours to look over the agreement. Tell the Dimuzis we'll bring lunch."

"We'll also have some of our food sent over from the *Abiel*," Resik promised.

"Good! We can both get sick on each other's food!" Kane wanted to show Resik that he, too, had a sense of humor.

Corry had a nit to pick, and he wanted it picked now. "Soucek, where does *Torli* Resik want us to put the Corona?"

The reply came through Carew. "Captain, put it topside on your ship. We'll lift it from there."

Corry shook his head. "I've had enough of alien force beams playing with my ship. If it's acceptable, we'll fly it over to the end of the airstrip here. Then the *Torli* can do what he wants."

"It's in flyable condition?" Resik asked.

"Yes."

"And you can fly it?"

"One of my pilots can," Corry replied. He decided he'd let Terri Ellison prove she could. And seeing that a human pilot could fly an alien ship would certainly have some impact on the Dimuzis.

"We'll bring the remains of the Samas as well as the live one, if she's still alive," he went on. Looking at Laura Raye, he told her, "Doctor, we have work to do."

"Yes, sir, we do."

Corry turned to Kane. "We'll accompany you back to the *Shenandoah*, sir."

Thus far, the negotiations had been successful.

27

"I can?" CDR Terri Ellison responded like a little girl who's been told she can have a horse.

"Yes, but please make a tethered hover test first, JIC," Corry told her.

"I'd planned to do that anyway," Terri admitted. "I didn't want to activate the 'up' control and suddenly find myself in orbit! And without an ejection seat or a pressure suit."

"And do it with the Corona One on the flight deck where the Dimuzis can see it," Kane added. "And if you break it, you don't get another chance today with Number Two, Commander."

"Break it? In front of the Dimuzis? Sir, I'll turn in my wings if I make that mistake!" Terri promised.

Kane believed her. So did Corry, who had seen the gold wings framed on the bulkhead of her cabin. Her remote ancestor had probably taken a bigger chance flying wood-and-canvas aeroplanes from North Island. Naval aviation was in her genes.

Kane started for his cabin to change his sweat-soaked whites. Like Corry, Kane was a stickler about appearance, especially in a diplomatic meeting such as the one going on at the airstrip. But as he started to go, he turned to Corry and said, "Bill, I need to chat with you, but let's wait until these negotiations are finished. One thing at a time."

Corry hadn't the slightest idea what Kane wanted to discuss or why the Admiral wanted it to wait. It didn't bother the Commanding Officer of the U.S.S. *Shenandoah,* who had plenty to do in the few hours before returning to the airstrip at 1300.

And one of the first things he wanted to do was something he hadn't had time for until then.

He found Doctor Evelyn Lulalilo in the temporary sick

bay with Merhad, the surviving Mantid/Sama. She was chatting with the alien, who had been restrained on a gurney. And she didn't look happy. He couldn't tell if Merhad was happy or not, but he was pleased that the alien would soon be leaving the boat.

Eve didn't make eye contract with him as he stood alongside her next to the gurney. "Laura Raye just told Merhad she would be transferred to the Dimuzi ship," Eve said quietly. "Merhad isn't happy about that."

Merhad had apparently picked up a little American English and understood what Eve had said. "Want to go with Samas, not Dimuzis!" Merhad hissed.

"Tell her that her Sama companions ran away and left her," Corry said. "They took off in their mother ship when the Dimuzis were busy rescuing us."

"Samas come back for mifala."

"No, the Dimuzis won't let them. Iufala have disobeyed the Canons of Metalaw," Corry told the alien. He, too, had recalled a little of the Pidgin he'd once heard on Hawaii as a child.

Merhad merely replied, "Iumi laekem, iumi taek. Dimuzi nogud. Sapos Dimuzi kam long Merhad, mi kilim finis sapos mi duim."

Eve put her face in her hands. "I've tried so hard!" she complained in a small voice. "I've established communication with an alien. They're no better than we are! Merhad would kill me as quickly as she could if she weren't restrained. And the Dimuzis aren't much better, even though Carew said they don't kill unnecessarily."

"Sometimes it's necessary to kill," Corry told her. "We went through this exercise once, remember?"

"Yes, but I don't have to like it. And I don't have to take part in it!" She finally looked up at him. "I came to the meeting yesterday only because you asked the Chaplain to come and get me. I didn't think you cared any longer."

Corry remembered what Laura Raye Moore had told him to do. "I do, Eve. We're friends, and I don't neglect friends. I care about you. I care about my friends."

"You don't show it! They come second to your duties. Always your duties! Always your job! Always your responsibilities! But never someone who loves you!"

Corry thought about his wife. He suddenly realized why Cynthia had become more and more possessive as his naval career progressed and why she had substituted alcohol for love. But it took someone who was as selfishly possessive as Evelyn Lulalilo to make him understand his wife, who was not as intense in expressing it.

He felt very bad about Eve. He would never be able to abide her self-indulgence and refusal to face the real world. The best he could ever be was a friend, if she'd have him as such. As for Cynthia, he now believed he might be able to repair years of misunderstanding if he tried.

"Eve, you must understand that I place duty and responsibility as very high priorities," he told her sincerely, pausing occasionally to get his words in order and breathe properly to eliminate his speech defect. "In fact, duty and responsibility toward others is a form of love and caring. Think about that if you can, and you might see that I love you very much. And that we'll always be friends, even if you never join my reality." He turned to leave. Terri would be doing her hover test in a few minutes.

"I needed you! You neglected me! You ignored me!" she whispered but didn't look at him.

He turned back to face her. "I didn't n-n-n-neglect you! If I hadn't done what I did, neither of us would be alive now to t-t-t-talk of love and friendship! And realize, please, that duty and responsibility preclude me from ever being more than a f-f-f-friend to you, Eve!"

Corry stopped by his cabin to wash his face before he went up to PRIFLY.

LT Duke Peyton was there, along with SCPO Rex Caliborn. Corry remarked to the Chief Aircraft Maintenance Petty Officer, "Glad to see you up and around, Chief. How do you feel?"

"Washed out, Captain," the man replied. "But I wasn't about to lie around in my rack and miss seeing Commander Ellison fly that saucer! Uh, we got the landing legs down, sir. We had to pump some of the Corona's fuel back into it. Then Commander Bellinger figured out how to start its APU. Real strange system, but once we realized that it was really high-current-electrical in nature, it wasn't that hard. The whole ship is electromechanical, and it uses some weird room-temperature superconductors."

"I thought that might be the case, but I'm glad to have my guess confirmed by a real expert," Corry remarked. He looked down at the Corona One positioned over the for-

ward flight deck. It was covered by a loose cargo net that
was fastened to dogs on the deck. "Who's aboard, Mister
Peyton?"

"Alley Cat and Bells," the Flight Deck Officer replied,
then realized what he'd said. "Uh, I mean, Commander
Ellison and Commander Bellinger, sir!"

"Relax, Duke. I wear gold wings, too," Corry reminded
him.

"They've got a hand-held in there. I hope it's got enough
power to punch through the EM field that came up around
it when Alley Cat put idle power to the lift drive."

"What the hell drives it, Duke?"

"I don't know, sir," Peyton answered honestly.

"Chief?"

"I don't know, sir. But give me enough time and I'll figure it out."

He discovered Admiral Kane standing beside him.
CINCPAC remarked easily, "I wouldn't miss seeing this
for anything. CNO can wait." He paused, then went on to
explain, "Bill, I was bringing George Street up to speed.
Got an 'all ahead flank' from him. But he wants us to hold
communications with Pearl and Washington to a minimum.
Aerospace Force is up to something."

"What about the Chinese?"

"They know something's going on, but they don't know
what or where," Kane replied. "McCarthy's sources tell her
the Chinese are now in wait mode. They've halted their
troop movements and put their navy on hold. They think
we may be testing a new weapon around Johnston Island
because of Aerospace Force activity at Hickam and
Johnston. We'll just let them continue to think that. We've
got enough aerospace defense and ASW here to stop them
cold if they try a preemptive attack on Palmyra. And they
know it."

"Is the White House ready to use the hot line to
Beijing?" Corry wanted to know.

Kane looked askance at him and said in a quiet voice,
"This hasn't gone beyond CNO. This is a Navy scientific
and intel operation. No national security threat is involved
at this time."

Corry realized that some *very*-high-level officers had
their careers on the line because they didn't want this to
end up in the Wright-Pat archives for the next hundred

years. He could see that it was part of the Navy's roles and missions, but in his mind he hadn't yet extended them far enough in spite of all the science fiction he'd read.

"Admiral Kane and Captain Corry, please come up on Channel Tango on your N-fones so I don't have to delay the air-ground through a converter," Peyton told them. Neurophonic communication was five times faster than verbal.

Corry switched his N-fone and replaced it behind his right ear.

Starship, this is Alley Cat. We're ready to commence hover test.

The Flight Deck Officer replied, *Alley Cat, this is Starship. You're cleared to climb unrestricted to three meters and trap at your discretion.*

Thanks a whale, Starship! Power coming up from idle! The transmission from the Corona One was encountering interference. The signal level dropped and the noise level increased.

Alley Cat, Starship! You're becoming unreadable. Did you install the external antenna?

Couldn't get it to stick to the surface. This last message was almost unreadable.

The landing legs of the Corona seemed to grow longer. Then they were clear of the deck and the craft was hovering. It made no sound and showed no smoke or downwash.

But Corry had to grab his cap to keep it from flying off. His dark hair was standing straight up on his head. So was that of every other person in PRIFLY.

A corona discharge, "Saint Elmo's fire," was playing silently from every sharp point and edge on or around PRIFLY.

His N-fone screeched and quit.

"Sonofabitch!" was Caliborn's comment.

"It flies!" Kane shouted.

"Yes. We saw it do that before," Corry told him. "This time, my best pilot is flying it!"

The Corona One came up against the restraints of the cargo net dogged to the deck. Then it settled slowly back onto its landing legs.

Corry's hair settled back to his head, and the coronal discharge from the PRIFLY surfaces stopped.

"Gentlemen," Corry told everyone, "I think we've just

witnessed something akin to Kitty Hawk or the DC-X bunny hop."

"Except we didn't build it," Peyton remarked.

"Oh, we'll build one," Kane promised.

Terri's voice came through the PRIFLY speaker, "Starship, this is Alley Cat. Piece of cake!"

"Alley Cat, this is Starship," Peyton replied. "We lost comm with you. The overload circuits in our N-fones popped."

"So get some new N-fones, Duke. The accelerated speech coming out of your translator into this hand-held sounds ducky as hell!"

"How did it handle?"

"A hell of a lot better than that stupid UH-101 helicopter I once tried to fly years ago," Terry replied. "The Sama reaction times are slower than ours. I had no trouble staying with this thing. I didn't even overcontrol it."

"Yeah, but we're going to have to do something about that electromagnetic disturbance," Caliborn muttered. "I wonder if we launched it from a retracted lift and put a shielding screen mesh all around the well . . ."

Corry smiled. His practicing technologists were already at work on the problem.

"And, Captain, just to make you happy, when we take it to the airstrip, we will indeed fly low and slow," Terri reassured her Commanding Officer.

At 1300, Tikki Geiger flew them back to the airstrip in a Sea Dragon. Merhad was still strapped to the gurney and was accompanied by Laura Raye Moore. Eve Lulalilo didn't come. Chief Post had the remains of three of the Samas in strangely shaped plastic coffins nailed up by some of Chief Thomas's carpenter's mates.

Before the exchange was officially made, Kane talked with McCarthy and Soucek. A two-page document had been prepared.

"Ministrator Hakan can't read our writing," Carew remarked, "And we have no facilities here to translate it and print it out in Dimuzi hard copy format. But I translated aloud while we were putting it together, and I've read it in Dimuzi language to *Torli* Resik and *Lurel* Zalulcas."

"Is it acceptable to them?" McCarthy asked, trying to read her hard copy.

"Yes. They say it has holes in it, but . . ."

"But every agreement does, Mister Carew," McCarthy added. "Can they live with it?"

"Yes. Can you?"

"I don't see any problems. You've just put into writing what we verbally agreed this morning." Through Carew, McCarthy asked the Dimuzis, "Will this be binding?"

"I'll sign it as Ministrator," Hakan told her. "It will be reviewed by Sector Inspector Bisanabi. It's no different from most commercial contracts. Is it binding on you?"

"My contracts officer will check it," McCarthy remarked. "And the Judge Advocate General may want to see it if any problems develop. But I'm authorized to conclude contracts for Naval Intelligence." She sat down at the table and scrawled her signature at the bottom of the last page of her copy. "I'll sign your copy, and you sign both of these. And it's a done deal."

Ministrator Hakan did so. Her writing instrument was strangely shaped but fit her long hand better than the cylindrical pen nestled into McCarthy's shorter and stubbier fingers.

"Where's the Sama craft?" Carew asked. "It's now ours, you know."

Corry had already sent the signal back to the *Shenandoah.*

They saw it lift from the *Shenandoah* in the lagoon, fly slowly over the palmettos, and slowly descend to a gentle landing on the southwest end of the airstrip.

Corry noted that the flight had taken six minutes. He'd promised Terri that he would endorse her Form One as witness when she logged one-tenth of an hour in a flying saucer, no S/N, U.S.S. *Shenandoah* to Palmyra, local flight, visual flight rules, one takeoff and landing.

"We'll pick up the Sama vehicle and depart now," Carew told the humans. "I've enjoyed my stay on this world. It's too cold, but you humans are all right. A little rough around the edges, but no more so than some of the other seventy-odd outworld species. I look forward to seeing some of you again. And, Mister Soucek, you've been an outstanding colleague. Good luck with Majestic Corporation."

It was obvious that RADM Dolores McCarthy didn't like Carew's patronizing attitude. But she'd gotten what she wanted, so she didn't launch one of her famous cat attacks, fangs and claws bared, intent upon verbally destroying the adversary.

McCarthy knew that in due course of time, the Dimuzis would have to deal with human beings as true equals. She'd already set the wheels in motion, but they didn't know that.

"I need a way to contact you if problems arise," Allan Soucek said.

Carew smiled. "You insisted on being left alone to do it your way. That's a commendable attitude. We'll honor your request. In fact, we'll extend your zone of sensitivity out to the Oort Cloud. You can obviously handle the Samas if they become brave enough to try this again. If you have other problems, we'll find out about them eventually. So don't call us; we'll call you."

28

"Please sit down, Admiral McCarthy. You, too, Admiral Kane," Corry told his guests formally. His cabin office had plenty of room for the three of them. "Coffee?"

"I'd rather have bug juice, Bill," Kane replied. "I must have sweated a couple of liters of water today on the island."

"I'll have a steward bring some," Corry offered.

"Later," Kane told him.

"Are your quarters comfortable?" Corry asked. He wondered why Kane had asked to meet in the Captain's cabin.

"I didn't realize how cramped a submarine is," McCarthy observed. "But, yes, quarters are excellent. I'm not used to being on a ship."

"I'll sleep anywhere I can throw the body," Kane remarked. "But there hasn't been too much time to sleep since we got here." The planning meeting preceding the Palmyra conference had gone until quite late last night. "Quarters are fine. You run a tight boat here, Bill."

"Thank you, sir."

"And the reason I asked for the meeting here is this." He extracted a memory cube from his pocket and broke the seal. Then he handed it to Corry. "You have the data processor to decode and print this. And you'll want to put it in the boat records in any event."

Corry took the cube, opened a cabinet behind him, removed his processor, inserted the cube, and entered his password.

When the message came up on his screen, he immediately requested a hard copy printout. It slid out of the slot and he requested duplicates.

He had trouble believing what it said.

In reply
refer to:
DCNO/PERS 45-3-7658

CHIEF OF NAVAL OPERATIONS
The Pentagon
Washington DC 20301

25 August 2045

From: Deputy Chief of Naval Operations/Personnel
To: Captain William M. Corry, 523368453, USN
Via: Commander-in-Chief, Pacific Fleet
Subj: Relinquishment of command and reassignment

1. No later than 1 September 2045, you will relinquish command of the U.S.S. SHENANDOAH (SSCV-26) to Commander Arthur E. Braxton.
2. You will report to Commanding Officer, U.S. Naval Facility, Norfolk, Virginia, no later than 1 November 2045 to assume command of the U.S.S. SAGINAW SSCV-31, now building.
3. Thirty-one days accumulated leave is hereby authorized.
4. Thirty days change-of-station leave is hereby authorized.
5. Travel at government expense, including dependents, from Pearl Harbor, Hawaii, to Norfolk, Virginia, is hereby authorized.
6. Relocation expenses for household goods commensurate to rank are hereby authorized.

JOSEPH P. DOLE, VADM USN

Copies to:
CNO/OPS
CINCAIR
CINCSUB
CINCPAC
CO/NORFOLK

1st endorsement

Headquarters, Pacific Fleet
Pearl Harbor, Hawaii

25 August 2045

From: Commander-in-Chief, Pacific Fleet

To: Captain William M. Corry, 523368453, USN
1. Forwarded.

RICHARD H. KANE, VADM USN

"Well, orders are orders," Corry said with a sigh. "I don't understand why these came through. But I can work with Mister Braxton tonight and schedule a change-of-command ceremony for tomorrow morning. Then perhaps I can hitch a ride back to Pearl with you." He was sorry to be leaving the boat on such short notice, but he wanted very much to see Cynthia again.

"We'll be happy to have you, Bill," Kane told him. He saw the dismay and disappointment on his subordinate's face. "But here's a supplement. Perhaps it will clarify the reassignment. If not, Dolores and I can amplify and explain a few things."

The Commander-in-Chief of Pacific naval forces handed Corry yet another cube. This one had two seals on it. Kane broke one and handed the cube to the Commanding Officer of the U.S.S. *Shenandoah*.

This time, Corry discovered he had to go through a decoding and deciphering procedure. As a result, he didn't run a hard copy.

TOP SECRET
INTEL ORCON
SCI

In reply
refer to:
CNO/OP-32 45-32-0748
CHIEF OF NAVAL OPERATIONS
The Pentagon
Washington DC 20301
25 August 2045

From: Chief of Naval Operations
To: Captain William M. Corry, 523368453, USN
Via: Commander-in-Chief, Pacific Fleet
Subj: Detached duty assignment
Ref: DCNO/PERS 45-3-7658

1. Subsequent to reporting to Commanding Officer, U.S. Naval Facility, Norfolk, Virginia, on 1 November 2045,

you are assigned to temporary detached duty, Washington Navy Yard, Washington, D.C., to assume command of U.S.S. TUSCARORA AVR-02 and Project Corona.

2. You will report and be responsible to Deputy Chief of Naval Operations, Operations, OP-03. Administrative and financial control will be handled by the Commanding Officer, U.S. Naval Facility, Norfolk, Virginia.

                    GEORGE L. STREET, ADM USN
Eyes only copies to:
CNO/OPS
CNO/PERS
CINCPAC
CO/NORFOLK

                    TOP SECRET
                    INTEL ORCON

1st endorsement

                            Headquarters, Pacific Fleet
                            Pearl Harbor, Hawaii
25 August 2045

From: Commander-in-Chief, Pacific Fleet
To: Captain William M. Corry, 523368453, USN

1. Forwarded.

                    RICHARD H. KANE, VADM USN

"As the old saying goes, 'What the hell, sir? Over.' " Corry was baffled by these two documents.

"You ought to see *my* orders, Bill! Tell him, Dolores. You do a better job."

"Dick tells me you're a bit of a philosopher and strategic thinker. So I'm going to go into some of the deep background," the Chief of Naval Intelligence began. "Until you and your people opened this can of worms off Makasar, Captain Corry, practically every story of extraterrestrial contact or every documented contact attributed some sort of militaristic activity to it. UFOs were first perceived as a threat to national security. When no perceived threat evolved, the Air Force dropped it from high priority to 'file-and-forget' and went back to its classical roles and missions."

"Allan Soucek explained all of that, Admiral. I didn't believe him at the time," Corry admitted.

"Good, that makes my job easier," McCarthy went on. "By the way, Dick, let's bring Allan and Smitty in shortly. They need to be brought up to speed on this."

"Agreed," Kane replied. "This is an outstanding time and place to begin forming the team. It's certainly a secure environment."

Corry caught that and decided he'd better listen very closely. He was obviously being dealt into the game, and he wanted to find out what the game was.

"We're really dealing with a bunch of traders and pirates out there, not ravening hordes of jello men out to conquer Earth and enslave mankind," McCarthy went on. "The United States Navy exists because of Yankee traders and Barbary pirates. Occasionally, our roles and missions become muddied. However, the real reason the United States has a naval establishment is that Americans are traders, and the United States is a sea power. Our ultimate responsibility as a service derives from the British Royal Navy: to protect sea commerce from pirates and other predators. No air force in the world has ever had to do that. Nor could one. And the Aerospace Force hasn't the foggiest notion of how to do it beyond this planet! We do. We know it's coming. We're almost ready technically. The reason I'm here is that George Street now knows this. So do other people in the naval establishment. And the reason it's a Naval Intelligence task now is that our biggest adversary isn't China or anyone beyond our borders. It's the United States Aerospace Force; they've got the historical task, and they'll want to keep it. We can fight with them in Washington for the next twenty years until the next generation of generals and admirals are in the saddle. But we may not have twenty years. So we're going to outflank them. And you, sir, are going to be the team leader."

"I gathered as much," Corry was able to say, being somewhat overwhelmed at this point. "The U.S.S. *Saginaw* isn't even funded yet. And Congress may balk at a seventh SSCV. So, yes, I'm a little upset to be assigned command of a nonexistent boat! I presume it's a cover."

"Yes," she told him simply. She decided she'd listen to him for a moment, because it was apparent to her that CAPT William M. Corry had started to put the puzzle together for himself. "Any idea why?"

"I see the reference to Project Corona in my classified orders. I've got a Corona on the hangar deck."

"Yes. You'll transfer it to the U.S.S. *Savannah* SSCV-thirty. She'll be here tomorrow. The *Savannah* will take it to the ZI. Probably Whidbey Island to begin with, but that's going to be your call as head of the Corona Project."

"Oh. Well, Admiral, my classified orders also instruct me to assume command of the U.S.S. *Tuscarora*, which I find rather amusing, since it doesn't exist either," Corry began.

"Oh, but it will!" McCarthy insisted. "That's what Project Corona will eventually build, using what you're going to learn from the Corona and other technologies available at White Oak, for example."

"But why the AVR-zero-two? What's the AVR-zero-one?"

"It's on your hangar deck, Bill," Kane replied. "A real spaceship shouldn't be tagged like an airplane; it should carry a ship designation. And you're going to build the AVR-zero-two."

"As I started to say, since I'm the commander, do I get a choice of subordinates?" Corry wanted to know.

"Your recommendations will be most carefully considered," McCarthy said.

"I'd like Commander Terri Ellison to accompany the Corona back to the ZI. She will be my chief of flight test."

"Quite appropriate. Approved," McCarthy stated without hesitation. "Have your yeoman draft TDY orders until we can get CNO/PER to cut permanent ones like yours."

"And Major Clinch along with two Marine companies as security."

"No problem."

"What do you wish done with the Sama remains we still have aboard?" Corry asked. "Should we give them to Commander Zervas so he can take them back to Bethesda?"

"No! Zervas isn't going to get them," McCarthy stated firmly. "He's in tight with Jonathan Frip, Presidential Science Advisor, who's a Dimuzi and will shortly resign. CNO is having Zervas reassigned. Fort Stanton, New Mexico, I believe. His replacement will be Commander Moore, who obviously knows the subject matter."

"Ma'am, it rather looks like you've got everything worked out," Corry observed.

"Not everything. Only the start-up stuff and the political

bluffs. That sort of thing. What did you think we were doing at Pearl while you were cruising back across the Pacific? We have most of the structure set up, but you're going to have to build your own team, Bill," McCarthy explained.

Corry didn't miss her use of his first name. She was inviting informality. But he had yet another matter that bothered him. "I'll ask for other officers and chiefs to join the U.S.S. *Tuscarora*, but I'll do it gradually. I don't want to create any perception that this mission caused the breakup of the crew of this boat. As you know, that's an unofficial signal that the crew is no good. This is an outstanding crew, and they deserve commendations, all of them."

"Bill, you may be the de facto operational commanding officer of the Corona Project, but I'm going to be running interference for you," Kane announced. "My new orders are to report to the Pentagon as head of Development and Operational Evaluation under CNO/OP, and I'm told the next step is CNO/OP itself. I'll make sure that you get the people you want in such a way that no one will ever get the idea the crew was broken up. It is indeed being broken up, but for a damn good reason. You're building a new crew, and you're going to be commanding a starship itself if you can make it happen! It's going to take a team. Things have gotten complex, and a single person can't function alone any longer. Even Jackie Fisher had to have a team to build *Dreadnought*, and Rickover may have been the last dictatorial admiral. Today, we have to operate with a team of dedicated individuals, each doing a critical and doable task without kicking into someone else's goal. Few will get the credit, but all will be fulfilled. How many Nobel Prizes are unshared today? That's a consequence of better communication. In the *Shenandoah*, you've shown you can lead such a team, Bill."

McCarthy came back to her use of Corry's first name. "Bill, we'll be working closely together in the days and months to come. Formal protocol among us in private will waste time. You're likely to get flag rank within a year or so anyway. Please call me Dolores."

"Admiral, with all due respect, that wouldn't be proper. When and if I get my flag, I'll gladly accept your invitation," he told her respectfully.

"Do I have to give this man a direct order, Dick?"

Kane shook his head. "You're dealing with an Academy

graduate, Dolores. Live with it. After four years of that school, it's pretty difficult to get a person to throw away the protocol of Navy life."

Corry's N-fone wasn't activated, so the intercom speaker on the wall rasped, "CO, this is the OOD, Lieutenant Kilmer on duty."

"This is the CO. Go ahead, Lieutenant," Corry replied.

"Five radar targets, airborne, inbound, range six-two, angels five thousand descending, heading one-niner-seven. No communications contact yet."

Kane asked, "The *Abiel* left more than two hours ago, didn't it?"

"Yes, sir. We tracked it to escape velocity," Corry reminded him.

"This is the Aerospace Force coming for their share of the loot," McCarthy guessed.

"We can handle that," Corry assured them, then ordered his OOD, "Come to Condition Two! CAG to launch two flights of Sea Devils to intercept and escort. I'm on my way to the bridge."

Turning to the admirals, he said, "Why don't you join me on the bridge and see how we handle inbound suspected hostiles?"

Kane noticed the hint of a smile around Corry's mouth. So he said, "Be delighted to see how you handle this one, Bill."

"You're not serious, are you? Intercepting unknowns with armed aircraft?" McCarthy asked.

"When we're stuck on the surface as we are, Admiral McCarthy, every inbound target is suspect, even though these have cleared our outer aerospace defense ring of laser cruisers," Corry informed her.

Six minutes later when they were on the bridge, a radio call came in on the CTAF frequency: "Palmyra Traffic, this is Aerospace Force Blue Blazer One, fifty out, inbound for landing at Palmyra."

"Terri, let me take this one," Corry advised his CAG. "Blue Blazer One, this is the U.S.S. *Shenandoah,* call sign Starship. Identify yourself and say intentions, sir."

"This is Blue Blazer One. Flight of five. A Condor and four Caravans. Landing Palmyra airstrip. Protocol required. We have General Strasser aboard."

"Oh, good!" McCarthy chirped. Strasser was the Aerospace Force Chief of Staff. "They've certainly committed the heavies to this!"

Corry replied in the flat voice of an air controller, "Blue Blazer One, Starship. Be advised that landing will not be possible. The airstrip is occupied by Starship Air Group. Unable to accommodate you. You should have notified us that you were coming. Recommend you divert to Johnston or return to Hickam."

Another voice came on the CTAF. It was harsh and gravelly, somewhat like Major Bart Clinch's dulcet tones of command. "Starship, Blue Blazer One! General Strasser speaking! You got that? Four big stars, sailor! Get those Navy birds off the airstrip! We're coming to get the alien artifacts. Those are Aerospace Force responsibility and property!"

"Sorry, sir," Corry replied respectfully but with a smile on his face. "We did have some of those. But we gave them to the aliens about two hours ago, and they've already left. Aerospace Force Space Command may have tracked them as an outbound bogey at escape velocity straight up and ignored them because that's impossible. So I repeat, recommend that you divert to Johnston or return to Hickam. There's nothing here that belongs to the Aerospace Force, sir. This is a Navy island."

Strasser must have blown his stack all over the flight deck. "Goddammit, sailor, the first thing you can do is get those damned Sea Devils off my wingtips! What the hell do they think they're doing flying that close to me? They trying to play Blue Angels or something? And I can see they're armed! I want to talk to your commanding officer!"

"You are, General. This is Captain William Corry."

A pause, then the eruption, "Corry, get your damn airplanes off my wing! And clear that airstrip!"

"We're only providing you with an honor escort, General. And it will take about two hours to get all the pilots over to the airstrip, power up the aircraft, and move them. And I don't know where I'd put them anyway. My boat is damaged."

"And, Captain, your ass is going to be damaged after I submit my report on this! Okay, I'll return to Hickam. Hell, I have no choice. I can't land this Condor on your postage stamp of a flight deck, even if you weren't damaged. Admiral Kane will hear about this tomorrow!"

Kane leaned over Corry and spoke into the speakerphone. "General, this is Admiral Kane. Do you have a problem, sir?"

Again, momentary silence. Then, "Kane, I want you to bring that flying saucer back to Pearl and turn it over to me!"

"As Captain Corry told you, General, the aliens left about two hours ago with the flying saucer Corry captured in the Solomon Sea."

"Why the hell did you let them do that, Kane?"

"Sir, the San Andrés agreement signed by the old Air Force in 1979 said we had to give the alien artifacts back to them."

Silence. "Well, I guess we can't hit a home run every time we come to bat. But George Street will hear from me about this!"

"General, I'll be delighted to meet with you and George about this matter after I assume my new assignment with CNO in a few weeks," Kane told him.

"All right, you do that! Pilot, turn this trash hauler around and head for Hickam. Look out that you don't collide with one of those hot Navy jocks out there! Strasser out!"

"Uh, Blue Blazer One, shall we notify Hickam of your pending return so they can have protocol ready?" Corry added.

"Oh, forget it, Corry! Strasser out!"

Terri was laughing aloud. Zeke cheered. The bridge crew caught the spirit and someone yelled, "Way to go, Aerospace Farce!" over the shouts of approval for their commanding officer. Then, just as quickly, they became intense professionals again.

McCarthy had applauded. "Captain, that was the nicest piece of careful wording I've ever heard! You're going to work out well in spite of the fact that you're going to command the *Tuscarora*!"

Zeke Braxton turned suddenly from his seat next to Corry. "Sir, what's this?"

"Zeke, secure from Condition Two," Corry told him. "Set the watch. Notify the department heads that I'd like to meet with them in the wardroom in ten minutes. We have a lot of things to talk about," he told the next Commanding Officer of the U.S.S. *Shenandoah*.

APPENDIX I

SSCV-26 U.S.S. *Shenandoah*
Crew Roster

Commanding Officer: CAPT WILLIAM M. CORRY

Ship Staff
Executive Officer: CDR Arthur E. "Zeke" Braxton
Personnel & Legal Officer: LCDR Darlene H. Kerr
Quartermaster & Ship's Secretary: LTJG Frederick G. Berger
Chaplain: LT Thomas H. Chapman
Chief of the Boat: SCPO Carl G. Armstrong
Chief Staff Petty Officer: CPO Alfred K. Warren

Ship Division
Operations Department
Operations Officer: LCDR Robert A. Lovette
Communications Officer: LT Edward B. Atwater
Sonar Officer: LT Roger M. Goff
Special Sensors Officer: LT Charles B. Ames
Radar/Lidar Officer: LTJG Barbara S. Brewer
Intelligence Officer: LTJG Ralph M. Strader

Deck Department
First Lieutenant: LCDR Mark W. Walton
Gunnery Officer: CWO Joseph Z. Weaver
Cargo Officer: LTJG Olivia P. Kilmer
Steering & Damage Control Officer: LT Donald G. Morse
Underwater Special Team: LT Richard S. Brookstone
Chief Boatswain's Mate: CPO Clancy Thomas

Navigation Department
Navigator: LCDR Natalie B. Chase
Assistant Navigator: LT Bruce G. Leighton
Assistant Navigator: LT Marcella A. Zar

Engineering Department
Engineer Officer: CDR Raymond M. Stocker
Assistant Engineer Officer: LCDR Norman E. Merrill
Main Propulsion Officer: LT Paula F. Ives
Damage Control Officer: LTJG Robert P. Benedetti
Electrical Officer: LT Richard Fitzsimmons
Electronic Repair Officer: LTJG Myra A. Hofer

Supply Department
Supply Officer: LT Frances G. Allen
Disbursing Officer: LTJG Harriett B. Gordon
Stores Officer: LT Kenneth P. Keyes
Mess Officer: LTJG Calvin S. Baker

Medical Department
Medical Officer: CDR Laura Raye Moore, M.D.
Dental Officer: LT Fred S. Rue
Chief Nurse: LT William O. Molders, R.N.
Chief Pharmacist Mate: CPO Nathan C. Post, P.N.

Air Group
Commander Air Group: CDR Teresa B. Ellison (Alley Cat)
Flight Deck Officer: LT Paul J. Peyton (Duke)
Aircraft Maintenance Officer: LT Willard L. Ireland
Chief Aircraft Maintenance Petty Officer: SCPO Rex Caliborn
Squadron Commanders:
   VA-65 "Tigers" AttackRon: LCDR Patrick N. Bellinger (Bells)
   VP-35 "Black Panthers" PatrolRon: LCDR Meryl P. Delano (Flak)
   VC-50 TransportRon: LCDR Virginia S. Geiger (Tikki)

Marine Battalion

Marine Officer: Major Bartholomew C. Clinch
Battalion Sergeant Major Joseph McIvers
Marine Company A: Captain Presley N. O'Bannon
First Sergeant Solomon Wren
First Lieutenant Daniel Carmick
First Lieutenant Archibald
Henderson
Marine Company B: Captain John M. Gamble
First Sergeant Luke Quinn
First Lieutenant George H. Terrett
Second Lieutenant Anthony Gale
Marine Company C: Captain Samuel Miller
First Sergeant Jeff Mackie
First Lieutenant Alvin Edson
Second Lieutenant Chester G.
McCawley

OTHER CHARACTERS

Contact Two Team

CDR Matilda Harriet Smith, Naval Intelligence
LCDR Constantine G. Zervas, M.D., Bethesda Naval
Hospital
Dr. Evelyn Lulalilo, National Science Foundation
Dr. Barry W. Duval, National Oceanic and Atmospheric
Administration
Allan H. Soucek, Majestic Corporation

Majestic 12

Dr. Armand Grust
Dr. Jonathan Frip, Presidential Science Advisor
Dr. Bourke Renap
ADM Stephen Tyonek, USN, National Reconnaissance
Office
General Hoyt Beva, USAF Space Command
General Danforth Chesmu, AUS, Defense Mapping
Agency
Dr. Karl Songan
Dr. Enos Delsin
Newell Carew, President, Majestic Corporation

Stanfield Inteus
Lyle Muraco
Fergus Antol

Others

ADM George L. Street, USN, Chief of Naval Operations
VADM Richard H. Kane, USN, CINCPAC, Pearl Harbor, Hawaii
RADM Dolores T. McCarthy, USN, Chief of Naval Intelligence
GENERAL D. D. Martin, CO 5th Aerospace Force, Hickam AFB, Hawaii
CAPT Steven Thorne, CO CL-7 U.S.S. *Schirra*
Drek, an alien Mantid/Sama
Merhad, an alien Mantid/Sama
Torli Valrah Resik, CO Amalgamate Corvette *Abiel,* a Dimuzi
Lurel Hamon Niyen, Communications Officer, A.C. *Abiel,* a Dimuzi
Lurel Wilne Zalucas, Metalaw Officer, A.C. *Abiel,* a Dimuzi
Ministrator Adri Hakan, a Dimuzi politician/bureaucrat
CDR Roberta Apel, legal officer, CINCPAC, Pearl Harbor, Hawaii
General Carl Strasser, COS United States Aerospace Force

APPENDIX II

METALAW DEFINITIONS AND RULES CANONS

Definitions

Law: A system of rules of conduct and action governing the relationships between intelligent beings. These precepts are classified, reduced to order, put in the shape of rules, and mutually agreed upon.

Metalaw: A system of law dealing with all frames of existence and with intelligent beings of all kinds.

Intelligent being: An organized system having all of the following characteristics:

a. Self-awareness.

b. Time-binding sense—able to consider the future, conceive optional future action, and act upon the results thereof.

c. Creative—able to make bisociative syntheses of random matrices to produce new concepts.

d. Behaviorly adaptive—capable of overriding the preprogrammed behavior of instinct with behavior adapted to perceived present or imagined future circumstances.

e. Empathetic—capable of imaginative identification with another intelligent being.

f. Communicative—able to transmit information to another intelligent being in a meaningful manner.

Zone of Sensitivity: A spherical region about an intelligent being that extends out to the threshold of sensory detection, physio-bio-psycho-socio effects, or some arbitrary boundary within those limits that is announced by the being.

The Canons of Metalaw

First Canon (Haley's Rule): Do unto others as they would have you do unto them.

Second Canon: The First Canon of Metalaw must not be

applied if it might result in the destruction of an intelligent being.

Third Canon: Any intelligent being may suspend adherence to the first two Canons of Metalaw in its own self-defense to prevent other intelligent beings from restricting its freedom of choice or destroying it.

Fourth Canon: Any intelligent being must not affect the freedom of choice of the survival of another intelligent being and must not, by inaction, permit the destruction of another intelligent being.

Fifth Canon: Any intelligent being has the right of freedom of choice in lifestyle, living location, and socioeconomic cultural system consistent with the preceding Canons of Metalaw.

Sixth Canon: Sustained communication among intelligent beings must always be established and maintained with bilateral consent.

Seventh Canon: Any intelligent being may move about at will in a fashion unrestricted by other intelligent beings provided that the Zone of Sensitivity of another intelligent being is not thereby violated without permission.

Eighth Canon: In the event of canonical conflict in any relationship among intelligent beings, the involved beings shall settle said conflict by nonviolent concordance.

APPENDIX III

GLOSSARY OF TERMS AND ACRONYMS

Note: A = Air Group term
      M = Marine unit term
      S = Ship term
      G = General military/naval term

ALO: (G) Active Level of Operation readiness. Every unit has one. Usually it varies according to the whims of the high brass and how badly CNO and JCS want to assign a tough mission to an exhausted, depleted ship or outfit.

Anchor watch: (S) Personnel available for night work. When not standing watch, eating, sleeping, or recreating, naval personnel work on professional advancement, maintenance, repairs, sweepdown, and other tasks that must get done because no one else is available to do them. Some personnel standing day watches thus become available for night work.

AOG: (A) Aircraft on the ground. A grounded aircraft that is damaged or needs unavailable parts. An expensive naval aircraft is worthless unless it is either flying or flight-capable. "AOG" therefore is a super-emergency get-it-fixed-quick term applied equally to aircraft or any other air division equipment.

AP: (M) Anti-personnel. Applied to ammo, bombs, mines, or the first sergeant's latest set of work detail assignments.

APV: (M) Armored Personnel Vehicle. A small, lightly armored, fast vanlike vehicle intended to give Marines the false sense of security that they're safe from incoming while inside.

ARD: (S) A floating dry dock. Sometimes an SSCV or SSF must undergo hull repairs. The Navy maintains a few floating dry dock ships that can go to a damaged SS and repair it.

ARS: (S) A submarine salvage vessel. The sort of ship

submariners greatly dislike. They hope they never have to call for one.

Artificial Intelligence or AI: (G) Very fast computer modules with large memories which can simulate some functions of human thought and decision-making processes by bringing together many apparently disconnected pieces of data, making simple evaluations of the priority of each, and making simple decisions concerning what to do, how to do it, when to do it, and what to report to the human being in control.

ASAP: (G) As soon as possible.

ASW: (G) Anti-submarine warfare. Engaged in between submarines and sometimes between surface vessels and submarines. Often undeclared. Submariners believe in only two types of ships: submarines and targets.

AT: (M) Anti-tank. Refers to ammo, guns, missiles, or mines. Few main battle tanks are left in the twenty-first century because of the effectiveness of shoulder-launched and air-launched AT weapons.

Bag: (A) Flight suit. So named because the standard-issue full-length coverall-type flight suit is extremely baggy. Naval aviators, both male and female, have to be in outstanding physical condition and therefore arrange for smartly and tautly tailored bags. Some have opted for the tight-fitting combination flight suits and g-suits. A nonflying naval type can always be spotted on the flight deck by the baggy, untailored issue flight suit.

Bingo: (A) Minimum fuel for a comfortable and safe return. When you hit bingo fuel, you'd better either have the carrier in sight or have picked out a suitable "bingo field" to land on, because you will shortly descend.

Binnacle: (S) The stand or enclosure for a compass. Not often used in SSCVs because of sophisticated space-borne and other electronic navigational systems. A magnetic compass is still carried "just in case" the electronics suffer a nervous breakdown, something the earth's magnetic field has never been known to do.

Blue U: (G) the United States Aerospace Force Academy at Colorado Springs, Colorado. A term usually spoken with varying degrees of derision, because the Aerospace Force stole blue as a service uniform color back in the days of the "wild blue yonder." The Navy, whose uniforms have been blue for much longer, has never really forgiven the Aerospace Force for stealing the Navy's color.

Blue-water ops: (G) SSCV operations beyond the reach of land bases that can be reached by CAG aircraft or Marine unit boats. This is what the SSCVs were designed for. A submarine in a harbor or coastal waters is like a gazelle in a pen.

Bohemian Brigade: (G) War correspondents or a news media television crew. Highly disciplined military and naval personnel often dislike the sloppy appearance, sloppy dress, and sloppy discipline of news media people. The Navy assigns officers to cater to the news media in hopes that the media people will leave the rest of the real Navy types alone to do what they're paid for.

Bolter: (A) An aircraft landing attempt aboard a carrier that is aborted, forcing the pilot to take the aircraft around again, thus screwing up the whole recovery flight pattern. Once was more common when the Navy pilots landed jets on CVs and CVNs, an operation that involved crashing onto the deck under full military jet power. With VTOL aircraft on SSCVs, a bolter usually occurs because of a screwup in approach control, a damaged aircraft, an injured pilot, or bad weather.

Boomer: (G) A nuclear-powered ballistic missile submarine. Some of these are still in commission in the U.S. Navy, more in the navies of other nations. In a world where it doesn't pay to use thermonuclear area weapons, the dominant role of the SSBN diminished in favor of SSCVs and other sea control ships capable of dealing more effectively with brushfire and regional conflicts.

Braceland: (G) Naval slang referring to the United States Military Academy at West Point, New York. The Naval Academy operates with a far more sophisticated plebe disciplinary system involving more psychological pressure than physical abuse.

Briefback: (A) (M) (S) A highly detailed discussion of the intended mission in which all commanders participating take part. Some of the plan is in the computers, but not all of it, because technology has been known to fail when most urgently needed. Therefore, the operational plan is always presented, then briefed-back to ensure that it has been committed to human memory as well as computer memory.

Bug juice: (S) Fruit punch available from the galley at

any time. The Navy still runs on coffee day and night, but fruit juices contain roughage and vitamins that coffee doesn't.

Burdened vessel: (S) The vessel required to take action to avoid collision. The burden of maneuver is on the vessel that must alter its course. In twenty-first-century submarine jargon, a burdened vessel is the one that makes contact first and upon which the burden of initiating attack rests. The submarine Captain is the one who actually bears the burden of decision-making under these conditions.

CAG: (A) Commander Air Group, the SSCV's chief pilot. Or "carrier air group," the SSCV's aircraft complement.

CAP: (A) Combat Air Patrol, one of more flights of fighter or fighter-attack aircraft put aloft over a carrier submarine to protect the ship against attack from the air.

Cat's paw: (S) A puff of wind.

Channel fever: (S) A predictable behavior pattern of the crew after a long submerged patrol as the ship approaches its base or a tender.

Check minus-x: (G) Look behind you. In terms of coordinates, plus-x is ahead, minus-x is behind, plus-y is to the right, minus-y is left, plus-z is up, and minus-z is down.

CIC: (G) Combat Information Center. May be different from a command post. On an SSCV, it is usually located in the control room, which is the brainlike nerve center of the ship.

CINC: (G) Commander-in-Chief.

CJCS: (G) Chairman of the Joint Chiefs of Staff.

Class 6 supplies: (G) Beverages of high ethanol content procured through nonregulation channels; officially, only five classes of supplies exist.

CNO: (G) Chief of Naval Operations.

CO: (G) Commanding Officer.

COD: (A) Carrier Onboard Delivery aircraft used to transfer personnel and cargo to and from the SSCV.

Column of ducks: (M) A convoy proceeding through terrain where it is likely to draw fire. Has also been applied by submarine officers to the juicy torpedo target of a convoy proceeding in line astern.

Comber: (S) A deepwater wave.

Confused sea: (S) A rough sea without a pattern.

Conshelf: (S) The continental shelf.

CP: (G) Command Post.

Crabtown: The city of Annapolis, Maryland, so called by U.S. Naval Academy midshipment because of the famed seafood of the area.

CRAF: (G) Civil Reserve Air Fleet. Nonmilitary commercial aircraft of all designations and sizes that the government has paid to have militarized or navalized. All or part of the CRAF can be called up in an emergency to provide airlift support for the Department of Defense at taxpayers' expense. However. the concept of the CRAF means that the government doesn't have to buy large numbers of aircraft and maintain them for use only in emergencies.

Creamed: (G) Greased, beaten, conquered, overwhelmed.

Crush depth: (S) The depth at which the water pressure causes the pressure hull of a submarine to implode. The "never exceed" depth of a ship, numbers that are deeply engraved in the memories of the ship's officers and operating crew.

CTAF: (A) Common Traffic Advisory Frequency. A radio communications frequency set aside for use by all aircraft where ground control frequencies and facilities such as airport control towers don't exist. These are normally in the VHF frequency spectrum and can be monitored and used by any radio-equipped aircraft.

CYA: (G) Cover your ass. In polite company, "Cover your anatomy."

Dead reckoning: (S) (A) A method of navigation using direction and amount of progress from the last well-determined position to a new position. Not a widely used or desirable navigational method in the twenty-first century, but a method still taught for use in an emergency. Most officers reckon that if they have to use it, there's a high probability they'll be dead soon after. Actually, derived from the term "deduced reckoning."

Dead water: (S) A thin layer of fresher water over a deeper layer of more saline water. Dead water causes problems with sonar if you're looking for a target. On the other hand, dead water can be turned to an advantage if you're trying to avoid contact.

Deep scattering layer: (S) An ocean layer that scatters sounds of echoes vertically. Some submarines can dive deep enough to make use of this phenomenon nearly every-

294   *G. Harry Stine*

where. If you can get into a deep scattering layer, enemy sonar can be confused and even lose track of you. When the enemy uses this ploy, it becomes more than frustrating.

Degaussing: (S) Reducing the magnetic field of a ship to protect against magnetic mines. With the twenty-first-century use of titanium and composite hulls for naval vessels, degaussing has become less of a requirement. Modern SSCVs and SSFs cause practically zero magnetic anomaly.

Density layer: (S) A layer of water in which density changes sufficiently to increase buoyancy. This can raise hell with a commanding officer's planned operation by causing the ship to inadvertently change its running depth. A density layer can also cause sonar anomalies. Apparently the new masdets aren't immune to this, either.

Dodger: (S) Once a term applied to a canvas windshield on an exposed bridge. Since the topside surface bridge on an SSCV is on the retractable tower, this term has been applied to it.

Dog: (S) A metal fitting used to close ports and hatches.

Dolphin Club: (S) That portion of a naval vessel unofficially set aside exclusively for privacy between male and female crew members. Like the U.S.S. *Tuscarora,* it doesn't officially exist. However, no captain who is concerned about the physical and mental health of his mixed crew prohibits the establishment of the Dolphin Club on his ship. It is closed temporarily only during Condition Two and General Quarters. Or for longer periods of time if members of the crew abuse the privilege.

Double nuts or coconuts: (A) The CAG's aircraft usually has a ship's operational or squadron number ending in 00. This has been corrupted, in the usual bad taste of hot pilots, in the term "double nuts" if the CAG is male or "coconuts" if the CAG is female. However, the ladies who fly and otherwise occupy combat positions look upon such tasteless slang as indicating that they are "one of the boys"; they have been accepted. Some personal pilot call names are even more tasteless.

ECM: (G) Electronic countermeasures.

ELINT: (G) Electronic intelligence gathering.

FCC: (G) Federal Communications Commission.

FEBA: (M) Forward Edge of the Battle Area.

FIDO: (A) (M) Acronym for "Fuck it; drive on!" Overcome your obstacle or problem and get on with the operation.

FIG: (G) Foreign Internal Guardian mission, the sort of assignment American military units draw to protect American interests in selected locations around the world. Also known as "saving the free world for greed and lechery."

Following sea: (S) Waves moving in the same general direction as the ship. Therefore, they break over the ship with less force.

Fort Fumble: (M) Any headquarters, but especially the Pentagon when not otherwise specified. Some naval officers call the Pentagon the "Potomac Interim Training Station." More often, they use the acronym for that.

Fox One (Two, Three, or Four): (A) A radio call signifying that a specific type of attack is about to be or has been initiated. The meanings have changed over the years as new weapons have entered service. Fox One is the simplest sort of attack, usually with guns. Fox Four is an attack with complex weapons such as missiles.

Fracture zone: (S) An area of breaks in underwater rocks such as seamounts, ridges, and troughs. Nice places to hide if you're pinned down and want to become invisible to sonar.

Freshet: (S) An area of fresh water at the mouth of a stream flowing into the sea. Can change the water density, which in turn changes the buoyancy of a submarine. Something that navigators try to warn submarine commanders about well in advance.

Frogmen: (S) Underwater demolition personnel, crazy people who don scuba and flippers and then go out to play with high explosives having a high probability of going bang while they're working with them.

Furball: (G) A complex, confused fight, battle, or operation.

GA: (G) Go ahead.

Galley yarn: (G) A shipboard rumor. Much the same as "scuttlebutt." Usually clears through the nebulous Rumor Control Department.

Gig: (S) The ship's boat for the use of the Commanding Officer.

Glory hole: (G) The chief petty officers' quarters aboard ship.

Golden BB: (A) (M) A small-caliber bullet that hits

where least expected and most damaging, thus creating large problems.

Greased: (A) (M) Beaten, conquered, overwhelmed, creamed.

Hangfire: (G) The delayed detonation of an explosive charge.

Horsewhip: (S) The ship's commissioning pennant, rarely flown from a submarine. Refers to English Admiral William Blake's gesture of hoisting a horsewhip to his masthead to indicate his intention to chastise the enemy.

Hull down: (S) A ship slightly visible on the horizon.

Humper: (G) Any device whose actual name can't be recalled at the moment. Also "hummer" or "puppy."

ID or i-d: (G) Identification.

IFR: (A) Instrument flight rules, permitting relatively safe operation in conditions of limited visibility. Usually conducted through clouds that contain rocks ("cumulo granite").

Intelligence: (G) Generally considered to exist in four categories—animal, human, machine, and military.

Internal wave: (S) A wave that occurs within a fluid whose density changes with depth.

I've lost the bubble: (S) I'm confused and in trouble.

IX: (S) Designation for an unclassified miscellaneous vessel or target.

JCS: (G) Joint Chiefs of Staff.

JIC: (G) Just in Case.

KE: (G) Kinetic energy as applied to KE kill weapons. Missiles that kill or destroy by virtue of their impact energy.

Kedge: (S) To move a ship by means of a line attached to a small anchor—also called a kedge—dropped at the desired position.

Keep the bubble: (S) Maintain exactly the angle of incline or decline called for. Also maintain a level head, a cool stool, and a hot pot at General Quarters.

Klick: (G) A kilometer, a measure of distance.

Lighter: (S) A bargelike vessel used to load or unload a ship. Usually welcomed by SSCV and SSF crews who have been on long patrols and are beginning to run out of such essentials as ice cream and toilet paper.

Log bird: (A) A logistics or supply aircraft. For an SSCV, as welcome as a lighter. (See above.)

Mad minute: (G) The first intense, chaotic, wild, frenzied period of a firefight when it seems every gun in the world is being shot at you.

The Man: (G) Term used to designate the President of the United States, the Commander-in-Chief.

Masdet: (S) The highly classified mass detector sensor system used on a submarine. Has replaced passive sonar (which is nevertheless still carried). A trained masdet operator can determine bearing, depth or altitude, and (if the mass of the target is known) range of an object.

Midrats: (S) The fourth daily meal served in a submarine, usually at midnight, ship's time.

Mike-mike: (M) Marine shorthand for "millimeter."

MRE: (M) Officially, Meal Ready to Eat; Marines claim it means Meal Rarely Edible.

NCO: (M) Noncommissioned officer.

No joy: (A) (M) Failure to make visual or other contact.

Non-qual: (S) A person fresh from submarine school who is being taught firsthand how a submarine operates by on-the-job training, usually under the watchful eye of a petty officer.

NSC: (G) National Security Council.

OOD: (S) The Officer of the Deck, the officer in charge who represents the Captain.

Order of battle: (S) The disposition of ships as they ready for combat. Or the personnel roster of a Marine or Army unit.

Oscar briefing: (G) An orders briefing, a meeting where commanders give final orders to their subordinates.

Our chickens: (S) Term originating from the World War II submarine service, where it referred to friendly aircraft detailed to escort submarines engaged in rescuing downed pilots. Has been appropriated by SSCV crews to describe the aircraft based aboard their ships.

Papa briefing: (G) A planning briefing, a meeting during which operational plans are developed.

Phantom bottom: (S) A false sea bottom registered by electronic depth finders.

Playland on the Severn: (G) Derogatory term applied to the United States Naval Academy by those who never attended same. Not used in the presence of an Academy graduate without suffering the consequences.

Poopie suit: (S) Navy blue coveralls worn in a submarine.

PRIFLY: (A) The primary flight control bridge of a carrier submarine, where the CAG and others can direct air operations.

Pucker factor: (G) The detrimental effect on the human body that results from an extremely hazardous situation, such as being shot at.

Q-ship: (S) A disguised man-of-war used to decoy enemy submarines. Submariners don't give any quarter to such deception on the part of the enemy, the only good Q-ship being one that's permanently on the bottom.

Rack: (S) A submariner's bed or bunk.

Red jacket: (S) A steward in the officers' wardroom/mess.

Reg Twenty-twenty: (A) (M) (S) Slang reference to Naval Regulation 2020, which prohibits physical contact between male and female personnel when on duty except for that required in the conduct of official business.

Rigged for red: (S) The control room lighting set for night operations. Was once deep red lighting. Term remains in use meaning ready to operate under Condition Red or General Quarters.

Rip: (S) A turbulent agitation of water, generally caused by interaction of currents and winds. If this occurs deep, it can tear a submarine hull apart by simultaneously stressing it in many directions at once. A large submarine hull that will handle rips above a certain level of turbulent activity cannot be designed and built.

Rough log: (S) The original draft version of a log. The rough log is later loaded into the ship's computer memory, where it becomes the final log. The rough log can be corrected before becoming the final log.

Rules of engagement or ROE: (G) Official restrictions on the freedom of action of a commander or soldier in his confrontation with an opponent that act to increase the probability that said commander or soldier will lose the combat, all other things being equal.

SADARM: (M) Search and destroy armor, a kind of warhead. Navy types do not like this warhead because it can wreak havoc on the exposed portion of a ship on the surface.

Salinity: (S) The quantity of dissolved salts in seawater.

The degree of salinity affects the density and thus the buoyancy of the water, an important operational factor to a submarine.

Scroom!: (A) (M) Contraction of "Screw 'em!" Rarely if ever used by line naval officers; however, some CPOs and petty officers have been heard voicing it.

Scuppers: (S) Fittings on weather decks that allow water to drain overboard.

SECDEF: (G) Secretary of Defense.

Sheep screw: (G) A disorganized, embarrassing, graceless, chaotic fuckup.

Sierra Hotel: (A) What pilots say when they can't say "Shit hot!"

Simple servant: (G) A play on "civil servant," who is an employee of the "silly service."

Simulator or sim: (A) A device that can simulate the sensations perceived by a human being and the results of the human's responses. A simple toy computer or video game simulating the flight of an aircraft or the driving of a race car is an example of a primitive simulator.

Sit-guess: (M) Slang for "estimate of the situation," an educated guess about your predicament. Rarely used by submariners, who eschew such contractions for fear they could be misunderstood.

Sit-rep: (M) Short for "situation report" to notify your superior officer about the sheep screw you're in at the moment. Rarely used by submariners. (See above.)

Sked: (G) Shorthand term for "schedule."

Skimmer: (S) A submariner's term for a surface ship.

Skunk: (S) An unidentified surface ship contact.

Snivel: (A) (M) To complain about the injustice being done you.

SP: (G) Shore Patrol, the unit put ashore during liberty to maintain law and order among the ship's crew. SP works closely with local law enforcement authorities.

Spook: (G) Slang term for either a spy or a military intelligence specialist. Also used as a verb relating to reconnaissance.

Staff stooge: (G) Derogatory term referring to a staff officer. Also "staff weenie."

SS: (G) U.S. Navy designation for a submarine.

SSCV: (G) Aircraft carrier submarine.

SSF: (G) Fusion-powered fast attack submarine.

SSN: (G) Nuclear-powered fast attack submarine.

Strakes: (S) Continuous lines of fore and aft planking or a raised thin rib or fluid dynamic fence running lengthwise along the outer hull.

Submariner: (S) A person who serves or has served in a submarine and is qualified to wear the Double Dolphins. Always pronounced "submaREENer" because "subMARiner" suggests a less than qualified seaman.

SWC: (S) Scalar wave communications, a highly classified communications system that allows a submerged submarine to communicate with other submarines and shore facilities.

TAB-V: (A) Theater Air Base Vulnerability shelter. Naval aviators consider all Air Force bases to be vulnerable. Air Force pilots feel the same way about SSCVs.

TACAMO!: (G) "Take charge and move out!" Also a radio and scalar wave communications relay aircraft stationed at critical points for the purposes of communications integrity.

Tango Sierra: (G) Tough shit.

Target bearing: (S) The compass direction of a target from a firing ship.

TBS: (G) Talk Between Ships. A short-range communications system. Originally a World War II short-range radio set.

TDC: (S) Target data computer. Originally "torpedo data computer." However, the tendency of the traditionalists to hang on to acronyms resulted in this one's being held over and converted for use with any of the many weapons systems on an SSCV.

TDU: (S) Trash disposal unit. The garbage dump on a submarine. A vertical tube that ejects packaged garbage, which is weighted to sink to the bottom.

Tech-weenie: (G) The derogatory term applied by military people to the scientists, engineers, and technicians who complicate a warrior's life by insisting that the armed services have gadgetry that is the newest, fastest, most powerful, most accurate, and usually the most unreliable products of their fertile techie imaginations.

Tender: (S) A logistics support and repair ship. Like lighters and log birds, a welcome sight to SSCV crews who have been long at sea and are running short of everything.

Not much good for liberty, but a chance to go topside for sunshine and fresh air while the ship is tied up alongside.

Three-Dolphin Rating: (S) A humorous reference applied to a submariner who has paid a visit to the Dolphin Club. Refers to the fact that three dolphins are required for two of them to mate underwater. The "Two-Dolphin Rating" is the right of a person to wear the two-dolphin badge of a qualified submariner.

Tiger error: (A) What happens when an eager pilot tries too hard.

TO&E: (G) Table of Organization and Equipment.

Topsiders: (S) Rubber-soled cloth shoes worn in a submarine and when going topside on a surfaced submarine. Also known as "Jesus creepers" because someone wearing them can move with almost total silence.

TRACON: (A) A civilian Terminal Radar Control facility at an airport.

Trick: (S) A helmsman's watch at the wheel.

Umpteen hundred: (G) Some time in the distant, undertermined future.

U.S.S. Tuscarora: (S) An imaginary ship that has been in commission in the United States Navy since World War I. Somehow, it never makes port when any other ship is there and is never refitted or dry-docked. Yet it always seems to have officers and a crew. Every seagoing naval person claims either to have served aboard the ship or to have actually seen the ship in some far-off port of call. However, usually it has departed just the day before.

VLF: (G) Very Low Frequency radio wavelength. Rarely used by the Navy in its submarine service in the twenty-first century.

VTOL: (A) A vertical-takeoff-and-landing aircraft type utilizing surface blowing or Coanda Effect (surface blowing) to achieve lift at zero forward airspeed.

XO: (G) Executive Officer, the Number Two officer in a ship, air unit, or Marine unit.

Yaw: (S) The port-starboard rotation of a ship around her vertical axis.

ZI: (G) Zone of the Interior, the continental United States.

Zip gun: (S) The retractable radar-directed high-rate fully automatic 50-millimeter gun that is deployed topside by an SSCV when necessary to take care of approaching close-in unfriendlies or targets. Progeny of the twentieth-century Phoenix CWIS or the Goalkeeper system. Zip guns can also detect and handle incoming targets directly overhead, thus providing defense against space-launched anti-ship KE weapons that can go right through a submarine from deck to keel. Zip guns can't penetrate the armor of some surface ships, but can make life difficult for anyone topside on such a ship. Zip guns all have the 1775 Navy Jack painted on them, the flag with the thirteen red and white stripes, the rattlesnake, and the legend "Don't tread on me." And for good reason.

APPENDIX IV

NAVAL AND MILITARY RANKS

USN Rank	Abbrev.	USA/USAF/USMC Equiv. Rank
Fleet Admiral	FADM	General of the Army/Air Force (No USMC equiv.)
Admiral	ADM	General (No USMC equiv.)
Vice Admiral	VADM	Lieutenant General
Rear Admiral	RADM	Major General
Commodore	CMD	Brigadier General
Captain	CAPT	Colonel
Commander	CDR	Lieutenant Colonel
Lieutenant Commander	LCDR	Major
Lieutenant	LT	Captain
Lieutenant, Junior Grade	LTJG	First Lieutenant
Ensign	ENS	Second Lieutenant
Chief Warrant Officer	CWO	Chief Warrant Officer
Warrant Officer	WO	Warrant Officer
Master Chief Petty Officer	MCPO	Sergeant Major (Army & USMC) Chief Master Sergeant (USAF)
Senior Chief Petty Officer	SCPO	Master & First Sergeant (Army & USMC) Senior Master Sergeant (USAF)
Chief Petty Officer	CPO	Sergeant First Class (Army) Gunnery Sergeant (USMC) Master Sergeant (USAF)

Petty Officer 1st Class	PO1	Staff Sergeant (Army & USMC)
		Technical Sergeant (USAF)
Petty Officer 2nd Class	PO2	Sergeant (Army & USMC)
		Staff Sergeant (USAF)
Petty Officer 3rd Class	PO3	Corporal (Army & USMC)
		Sergeant (USAF)
Seaman	Seaman	Private 1st Class (Army)
		Lance Corporal (USMC)
		Airman 1st Class (USAF)
Seaman Apprentice	SA	Private (Army)
		Private 1st Class (USMC)
		Airman (USAF)
Seaman Recruit	SR	Private (Army & USMC)
		Airman Basic (USAF)